Duke Most *Wicked*

🌹 **A Wallflowers vs. Rogues Novel** 🌹

AVONBOOKS

An Imprint of HarperCollinsPublishers

DUKE MOST WICKED. Copyright © 2022 by Lenora Bell. All rights reserved. Printed in the United States of America. No part of this book may be used or reproduced in any manner whatsoever without written permission except in the case of brief quotations embodied in critical articles and reviews. For information, address HarperCollins Publishers, 195 Broadway, New York, NY 10007.

First Avon Books mass market printing: September 2022
First Avon Books hardcover printing: September 2022

Print Edition ISBN: 978-0-06-299348-9
Digital Edition ISBN: 978-0-06-299337-3

Cover design by Guido Caroti
Cover art by Paul Stinson
Cover photograph by Shirley Green Photography
Cover image © Shutterstock
Carol composed by Nancy Nash
Carol art created by Maura Lefevre

Avon, Avon & logo, and Avon Books & logo are registered trademarks of HarperCollins Publishers in the United States of America and other countries.

HarperCollins is a registered trademark of HarperCollins Publishers in the United States of America and other countries.

FIRST EDITION

22 23 24 25 26 BVGM 10 9 8 7 6 5 4 3 2 1

For my mother.
Pianist, teacher, poet, composer.
You bring music, love, and laughter to so many.

Duke Most Wicked

Prologue

❧ 🌹 ❧

BRANDAN DELAMAR HAD committed a terrible sin.

He didn't know what he'd done, only that it had been unforgivable in his father's eyes. The duke looked at him accusingly, as though Brandan should know his trespass. As though the crime had been so heinous that any love a father might have held for his only son had been irretrievably lost.

But what had he done?

Young Brandan sifted through his memories, searching for the reason his father hated him. He'd had a privileged upbringing; coddled by nurses, educated by private tutors, his every wish instantly fulfilled by a regiment of well-trained household staff.

He saw the manor staff more than he saw his own parents, though that wasn't unusual for the children of high-ranking peers. His parents were the beautiful people he caught a glimpse of when Nurse presented him for inspection in the evening, before the duke and duchess left the house for social engagements.

His father was as tall and majestic as the Alpine mountains Brandan read about in his geography primer, and equally as cold and distant. His mother had cheerful blue eyes and she smelled like the roses in the garden she loved more than anything else in life. Her hair was soft sunshine falling against his cheek as she bent to give him a kiss before bed.

Brandan hadn't asked to be born into this starring role in life's pageant. The importance of his station as heir to the Duke of Westbury had been impressed upon him since birth. One day he'd be the duke and when that happened, *he'd* be the tall and distant mountain. He'd wear a long velvet cloak and a gold sash with gold medals pinned to his breast, have important audiences with the king, and take his seat in the House of Lords to help decide the fate of the empire.

He tried so hard to please his father, excelling at his lessons and besting the other boys in sports. Nothing was good enough. Nothing ever met with any sign of approval.

The message he received from everyone else about his importance, his privilege, and his great responsibility was never the message he received from his father.

What he saw in the duke's eyes was disgust. He saw that he was flawed, stained, and unlovable. The duke beat the message into him with a cane. With his fists.

With stony, reproachful silence.

"Why does Father hate me?" Brandan mustered the courage to ask his mother when he was twelve years old and considered himself to be a man.

His mother was in the garden at Westbury Abbey, their estate in Hertfordshire, pruning the beloved roses she refused to entrust to the gardener's care. She lowered her sharp silver secateurs. "Why would you ask something like that?"

"Nothing I do is ever good enough."

"He expects much from you. You must do better. Be better."

"What did I do to displease him?"

"You've done nothing wrong." She turned away, her bonnet hiding her face. "Hand me the watering pot, will you, darling?"

She poured water onto the base of a rosebush. When she turned back to him it looked as though the water she'd used to douse the roses had reappeared on her cheeks.

"Are you crying, Mama?" he asked in a whisper.

"Of course not. Don't be silly." She pushed back the brim of her bonnet and turned her face to the sky. "Do you think it looks like rain, darling? I do so hope it will rain. My roses will be stunted if it continues so hot."

He studied the sky, which was bright blue, with not a wisp of cloud in sight. "It will rain soon. Don't worry." He knelt beside her on the wool blanket and helped her water the roses.

He ached with the awareness that he'd made her cry. He wanted to hold her hand but surely he was too old for that now.

Her smile was as unfalteringly bright as the sky, but Brandan saw that he'd made her sad by asking the question. He loved his mother with all his heart. He would never ask her the question again. He couldn't bear it if she hated him, as well.

"You'll have another sister soon," she said, glancing down at her rounded belly. "Your father wants a son, but I know it will be another girl." Her shoulders drooped like a wilting rose in desperate need of rain.

His cheeks heated. Childbearing wasn't a fit topic for men, or so his Latin tutor told him when Brandan mused aloud about whether he didn't have more than enough sisters and his mother might stop producing them.

It wasn't that he didn't like his younger sisters. He loved their dear sweet smiles and their delighted laughter when he visited them in the nursery to read to them from storybooks. Blanche was a jolly, pretty little thing with expressive blue eyes, just like their mother. Bernadette was quiet and solitary, preferring to play by herself. And the twins, Belinda and Betsy, were still crawling across the nursery floor, little more than babes.

He knew there'd been other male children born in the house. He'd heard the servants whispering about stillbirths. He'd attended the funerals, seen the tiny coffins lowered into the ground. Heard his father bellowing his rage. Covered his ears to block out his mother's heartbreaking sobs, late at night, feeling small and helpless.

"I should like another sister," he said gamely, smiling at his mother so she knew that she had his approval, at least.

"Thank you, darling." She placed a gloved

hand on his cheek and Brandan's heart filled with warmth and tenderness.

He'd make her so very proud of him.

He was the only male child of the Duke of Westbury. He'd study harder, push himself to excel in all things, be the best duke's heir in the world.

He must be stern and strong to win his father's respect.

Two MONTHS LATER, the babe arrived. But it wasn't another sister. It was a healthy baby boy, with all his fingers and toes, and a great lusty wail that no nursery wall could contain.

The duke's elation reverberated throughout Westbury Abbey. He provided a sumptuous feast for the staff in celebration. Everyone was smiling and singing and congratulating each other on the birth of the second son; the spare heir.

When Brandan received the summons to attend his father in his study that evening, he dared to hope that perhaps some of the general mood of expansive goodwill might extend to him.

A visit to his father's study was usually a terrifying occurrence. Brandan would stand in silence in front of the desk, which seemed as wide and uncrossable as an ocean, and listen to his father lecture him on all his faults and failings. He tried to bear it manfully, but when the inevitable beating came, the blow of a hand, lash of the switch, or cut from a cane made his knees knock together and his teeth chatter.

"Stop that shivering, boy," his father always

said with contempt. "The punishment is for your own good. You must learn that life is no bed of roses. Especially for one as wicked as you."

But today, in celebration of the birth of another son, his father might smile upon Brandan, as he'd smiled upon even the scullery maid, or so she'd told the cook incredulously when Brandan had snuck an apple tart from the kitchens.

Down the long corridor, heart thumping with every step. Back straight, shoulders back. Stride with purpose, as father walked. Meet him man-to-man. Whatever happened, show no sign of weakness.

The door to the study was ajar. A fire crackled in the grate, doing little to dispel the gloom of dark wood paneling and oil portraits of dour-faced ancestors.

His dour-faced father sat behind his desk, staring out the window. For one moment it seemed to Brandan that his father was already a painting, hung by a hook on the wall, immobile and all-seeing.

"Good day, Father," Brandan said.

The portrait creaked to life. The dark blue, hooded gaze found him. His upper lip curled. "It is a good day. A very propitious day, indeed. I finally have the child I've wanted for so long."

Brandan's spirits elevated and his knees stayed sturdy and strong. "What is my brother's name, please?"

"His name is Bertram."

"That's your name, Father."

"It is." Another curl of his lips. Not to be mistaken for a smile. This was the cruel and disdainful expression Brandan knew so well.

His hopes and his heart plummeted. "It's an excellent name."

"It is. And now it's time we had a little talk, you and I."

The way he said those words, the glacial grimace on his face, started Brandan's heart hammering. "Have I done anything wrong, Father?"

The answer to his innocent question was lengthy and it was delivered in the somber tones of a bishop presiding over a funeral service.

In a way it *was* a funeral, Brandan would think, years later.

That day in his father's study was the death of young Brandan Delamar, a youth who sought his father's approval, and pined for his love. And the birth of something new. Something twisted. Stunted. Something to be buried deep in the frozen ground.

When it was over, and Brandan had done all the things he'd resolved not to do—when his knees knocked together, his teeth chattered, his voice broke, and he cowered as his father beat him—the last of Brandan's youthful optimism burnt to ash.

He walked into his father's study with a tender and open heart.

He left with that heart shattered into shards that would stay lodged in his chest forever, causing pain with every breath.

Now he knew the reason his father hated him.

And he could never tell another soul for as long as he lived.

He was sent off to boarding school the next morning. During the carriage ride he had ample time to contemplate what his father had told him. He knew now that no matter how hard he tried, no matter how much he longed for his father's admiration and respect, he'd never have it. It had been a waste of time to attempt to be the best son, the worthiest heir.

He could never please his father.

So he vowed to disappoint him instead.

And he'd do it properly, with the same force of will and determination he'd employed in his doomed bid for affection.

No more seeking to please. No more abiding by scriptures or strictures.

His grave, stony-hearted, and iron-fisted father had pronounced Brandan to be wicked. Tainted. A child of sin.

And that's exactly what he'd become.

He vowed to become wild and wicked. He'd break every one of society's rules. He'd be depraved and dangerous to know.

He'd become the very best . . . at being the absolute worst duke's heir in the world.

Chapter One

❧ 🌹 ❧

EVERYONE SAID THAT Brandan Delamar, Duke of Westbury, lived life as though there would be no tomorrow. No consequences. No piper to pay. But there was always a tomorrow. A morning after. And this particular morning after was hell on earth.

"This is the worst morning of my entire life," West announced, without opening his eyes. "And I've had some truly awful ones."

His head felt like a billiard ball that had been slammed against wood and sent careening into a dark, musty cave. The inside of his mouth had the texture of fuzzy felted fabric and the taste of billiard cue chalk.

He was lying in a strange bed, fully clothed, which meant he hadn't had a very good night at all. Most mornings after of this caliber he at least woke with a curvaceous female, or two, draped across him in lieu of clothing.

"Ah . . . sleeping beauty finally awakes," a voice said from somewhere nearby. A gravelly, *male* voice.

West considered himself to be a hedonist, and a true hedonist would try any manner of pleasure at least once in a lifetime. Though West couldn't remember anything about last night, pleasurable or otherwise.

He managed to pry one eyelid open. The man sitting in a chair near the fireplace was also fully clothed. West knew that handsome face. Lord Rafe Bentley. One of the only true friends West had left in this cesspool of a town. "Rafe. What are you doing here? Where are we?"

"My club. I've been waiting to make sure you're alive. Now that I know you'll survive your injuries, I'll be leaving. You're welcome to stay as long as you like. Ring for a bath. You could use one."

"My injuries . . . ?" West tried to sit up and was stopped by a lancing pain in his ribs. Clutching his abdomen, he gritted his teeth and dragged himself to a seated position. "Who the devil kicked me? I don't remember a thing."

"I found you betting on billiards at The Devil's Staircase. You were sloshed on cheap gin and picking fights with a fellow twice your size, so I knocked you senseless and hauled you here for safekeeping. The ribs weren't me. That was the bruiser of a barkeep at the Staircase."

West touched the large, painful bump on his temple gingerly. "With friends like you, eh?"

"It was for your own good. You were being a right knob and were liable to get yourself killed."

"I can handle myself."

"You know I'm not one to judge. I've had my days of dissipation and ruin, but you're going arse over teakettle down the highway to hell. I count you as a friend and it's my duty to tell you that you should slow down on the drink, the gambling, the outrageous bets, and whatever other illegal vices you indulge in that I don't care to know about."

"Or I could accelerate the pace and hasten my entry into that early grave I hear so much about."

"The social Season begins in a few days."

"Speaking of early graves."

"You have obligations, both personal and political. You're a *duke*." Rafe stared down at him accusingly. "You're eight-and-twenty. It's time to stop wasting your life."

West collapsed back on the bed with a groan. "If I close my eyes, I can see my great-aunt Hermione standing by the bed, pointing her bony finger at me. You sound exactly like her."

He pitched his voice higher and infused it with aristocratic disdain. "Westbury, doing your best to dig your own grave while you had a younger brother was foolish and irresponsible. But since poor Bertram was taken from us too soon you must cease this depraved and immoral existence *at once*."

"She's right, you know. You had a brother and now you don't. It's all on your shoulders now."

"I didn't just have a brother. I had a shiny archetype of everything virtuous, honorable, and untainted. My father used to write me weekly letters detailing every one of Bertram's triumphs. When Bertram died in that horse riding accident my father lost the will to live." West tried to pull himself upright but the sharp pain in his ribs stopped him. "It should have been me, Rafe. I should have died young, not Bertram."

Rafe thumped his walking stick on the floor. "Enough! Don't you have a gaggle of sisters to escort to balls? You'll have to go sober long enough to fulfill your brotherly duties."

"Geese form a gaggle. Finches form a charm. I believe the collective noun for my sisters is a 'haunting.' Or perhaps, like hippopotamuses, a 'bloat.' I do love those girls." He managed to haul himself upright and swing his legs out of bed. "But the sheer number of them and the staggering grandiosity of their millinery and seamstress bills is enough to drive a duke to drink. Maybe they should be a 'banditry' of sisters. Got any tipple in this room?"

"Not a drop. Have some coffee." He waved a cup at him. "It'll wake you up."

"I don't want to be alert. I prefer a cloudy state of inebriation that gathers to a thick, impenetrable fog by nightfall."

Rafe shook his head sadly. "You've a sharp mind and a good heart buried somewhere under that tough shell of depravity."

"Lecturing me on the evils of strong spirits. Next you'll be raising your quizzing glass and telling me to do my duty and marry a girl of good birth and good upbringing. I don't need another aunt." West stumbled over to the cheval glass.

Dark stubble on his square jaw. Blood matted in his blond hair. A bluish bruise on his cheekbone that nearly matched his eyes. He tilted his head. The raised bump on his temple was a shade best described as rotting aubergine.

"My sisters aren't going to be pleased about

these scrapes and bruises." He splashed cold water from the basin on his face. "Maybe you'd agree to escort them to the first ball in my—"

"Are you seriously suggesting such a hare-brained idea? I'm not a fit escort for innocent debutantes. And if you're scheming about marrying me off to one of them, you're wasting your breath."

"God no." West flicked cold water at Rafe. "I know too much about you. All of it bad."

"Not as bad as you."

The two men were both tall and kept themselves in fine trim, though Rafe used a cane and walked with a pronounced limp after a perilous encounter with a gang of French smugglers. The two of them attracted plenty of female attention wherever they went, but both were damaged goods, in more ways than one.

"Only thought you might dance with them." West dabbed at the dried blood in his hair with a wet cloth. "Make them seem in demand. Blanche has been out for some time now. She keeps a stiff upper lip, but I can tell she's near frantic with worry."

Rafe lifted his ebony walking stick. "I'm not the most graceful of dancers these days."

"Doesn't matter. You're brother to a duke and a reformed rake. There was a time when you would have joined the drunken melee instead of shutting it down. I miss the old Rafe."

"Staring death in the face will make a man reevaluate his priorities."

"What happened on that ship?" His friend had never divulged how he received his injury.

"I don't want to talk about it."

"And I don't want to talk about the social Season. I'd rather face a ship full of unwashed and armed-to-the-teeth smugglers than a ballroom full of rose-scented, marriage-minded debutantes."

"It's not as bad as all that."

"I don't see you attending balls."

"And you never will."

"I only subject myself to such indignities for the sake of my sisters. I promised our mother before she died that I'd see all five of them safely wed, and so I will. The twins, Belinda and Betsy, make their debuts this year. I don't have to worry about the youngest, Birdie, for several years yet."

"Thankfully, I have but one sister and she's happily married. I'm the charity project my mother is scheming about. She won't rest until she finds me a respectable wife."

"No respectable young lady will have anything to do with either of us, even though you've reformed more than I ever will."

"I'm taking an extended journey to France and Switzerland with a departure date that coincides most fortuitously with the first ball of the Season."

"Lucky you."

"I have to finalize my travel arrangements. I'll tell the club to put everything on my account before I leave."

"In that case, send up some champagne and cigars. And a bottle of aged Scotch whisky."

"Seriously, West, I'm worried about you."

West waved his concern aside. "It's too late for

me to change. I've been living too long in the underworld, drowning in vice and sin. I don't know how to exist up here, on terra firma, with the sunshine seekers."

Walking through the doors of a gaming hell wasn't just about the cards, and the clink of the money on the table, the surge of excitement, and the heart-pounding risk of it all.

The cards led to the drinking. The drinking led to losing at cards. Losing at cards led to more drinking. Which led to waking up in strange beds, not remembering how he got there, with pain spiking his mind and an empty feeling in his chest.

And the emptiness led him back through the doors to hell.

He knew what he did was wrong; but he couldn't stop the cycle.

He'd more than lived up to his father's curse. He was sin incarnate. Dangerously depraved. Wicked Westbury.

He'd managed his fall from grace so thoroughly that there was nothing left of light or idealism in him. Especially since the death of his brother five years past. "My shirt smells like a gin manufactory. I'll have to borrow one from you."

"The barkeep broke a bottle of gin over your head."

"And where's my coat?"

"Ruined. Torn and bloody. Left it at the Staircase."

"I had a wallet containing several banknotes in that coat!"

"Then you shouldn't have taken it off, rolled up your shirtsleeves, and started a fight with a giant."

"At least I still have my trousers on." West grinned. Then winced. His jaw hurt like hell. "I seem to recall an infamous incident involving you sprinting bare-arsed through the streets of London being chased by a pistol-waving viscount."

Rafe shook his head. "Seems like it happened to someone else entirely."

"Makes a good story, though."

"A cautionary tale. I could have ended up with a bullet in the back, bleeding and bare-arsed on the public streets."

"I anticipate just such an ignoble end to my blighted life."

"You'd leave your sisters to fend for themselves?"

West finished his ablutions and donned a fresh shirt. "My uncle isn't the most attentive of fellows, but he'd have their best interests at heart. I can't understand why no one's offered for Blanche, at least. I was hoping her lack of dowry would be overlooked because of her beauty, propriety, and accomplishments."

"Hasn't she set her cap for Laxton? Maybe that's frightened the suitors away."

"Laxton's a conceited prig of a dandy. I keep telling her to set her sights on someone else. No matter, I'll replenish our coffers soon enough. All I require is one good night at the tables. One fateful night where Lady Luck nestles on my lap and whispers seductive things in my ear."

Rafe ground the tip of his cane against the

carpet. "That's what all wicked rogues tell themselves. Just one more drink. One more game of cards. One more meaningless liaison."

West shrugged. "I never said I was redeemable."

"I won't be here to save you next time. I'll be gone for months."

"You call punching me and dragging me to a fusty old gentleman's club saving me?"

"Just be more cautious in future, will you? I don't want to have to worry about you while I'm gone."

Rafe threw him one of the coats he kept at his club and West put it on. "I'll be all right. Let's leave. I don't like these mildewy clubs. Too many doddering old autocrats telling tales of their youthful exploits. Enough to drive a duke to drink."

"As if you require an excuse."

The two men were on their way out when West overheard his eldest sister's name. "Hold a moment." He caught Rafe by the arm. "I think they're talking about Blanche."

He moved closer to the doorway of a room where several men, just out of sight, were laughing loudly and placing wagers.

"My money's on Miss Brunhilda Shufflebottom for Wallflower of the Year. Her name alone makes me convulse with laughter. No gentleman in his right mind will ask her to dance for fear of the japes he'll endure," said a loud male voice that West didn't recognize.

"No, no, it's Lady Blanche who'll take the honors again this year."

West recognized the blasé tones of Lord Laxton, the coxcomb of a viscount whom Blanche fancied herself to be in love with.

"You've led her a merry chase, Laxton. Not going to make an honest woman of her this Season?"

"Or ever," Laxton replied, with casual cruelty. "She's not bride material. She's tainted by association with that ruinous wreck of a brother."

The floor dropped from beneath West's boots. He steadied himself with a palm against the wainscotting.

"Westbury's so wicked," Laxton continued, "that his poor sisters are clinging to respectability by a thin thread which could snap at any moment, leaving them mired in the muck of scandal. Not to mention the fact that he's gambled away most of their dowries."

"I heard he sold the ancestral jewels to settle a debt," another man said.

"That's not true," West whispered to Rafe, who gave him a sidelong glance. "I only sold the antiquities."

"I heard he contracted a wasting disease from brothels catering to gents who prefer, ahem, you know . . . flagellation and that sort of thing."

"Definitely not!" West whispered hoarsely. "I don't pay for punishment." He shuddered. "Had enough as a child. And I don't have any diseases."

"Relieved to hear it," Rafe replied with a sardonic twist to his mouth. "Now can we leave?"

"Not yet. I . . ." West gripped the carved wood. "I hadn't considered that I was causing such harm to my sisters. I want to know what they're saying about me."

The men in the billiard room continued assassinating his character, trying to outdo themselves with the outrageousness of the rumors they'd heard about him.

"I saw this one with my own eyes, gents," a man said loudly. "He picked a fight last night with the barkeep at The Devil's Staircase and had a bottle of gin broken over his head, and his ribs kicked in when he went down. Shouldn't wonder if he's lying in an alley right now, reeking of gin, with several broken ribs."

"Now that one's true as gospel," Rafe said.

West caught his friend's eye. "Rafe. Tell me truly. Have I ruined my sisters by association?"

"Well, you certainly haven't helped their reputations."

"I thought . . . I thought that they were irreproachable. They're such bright, lively, intelligent young ladies."

"Like brother, like sisters," Laxton drawled loudly. "That's all I can say on the subject, gents."

"What do you mean?" a man asked eagerly, scenting more gossip. "Do you know something salacious about the Delamar sisters?"

Laxton snorted. "The things I could tell you about Lady Blanche . . ."

"Tell us!"

"Come, Laxton, it's only us gents here. Spill your guts."

"Well, I shouldn't spread rumors," Laxton began, with a poor show of reluctance. "Lady Blanche might act proper and untouchable but when she gets you alone in a secluded alcove . . . she's as debauched and debased as her brother. I tell you I barely escaped with my trousers intact."

Several guffaws from the men.

"Are you saying she attacked you?" someone asked.

"I'm saying that her frosty facade hides a wanton. She's cut from the same wicked cloth as her brother and will make no man a respectable wife. The best she can hope for is spinster . . . or courtesan."

"The devil!" West launched toward the doorway, fists raised, only to be caught around the neck by Rafe's elbow.

"Steady on, old friend," Rafe said in a low voice.

"Did you hear what he said?" West asked hotly. "I have to kill him."

"He's obviously lying."

"Of course he's lying, trying to puff himself up, but those men don't know it." It was a shameful double standard, but it was the way of the world. Men could and indeed were expected to indulge in carnal, animalistic pursuits while a young lady must remain pure as the driven snow and unimpeachably virtuous. Even a hint of scandal could ruin his sister forever. "I'm going to make him retract it. Let me go!" He tried to twist away but Rafe applied enough pressure to his throat to make him cough. "Release me so I can murder Laxton," he croaked.

"I don't want you to do anything rash."

"He's shaming my sister."

"It won't help your sisters if you get yourself killed in a duel."

"Maybe they'd be better off without me."

"Stop saying that. Your sisters love you."

"And I care about them and that's why I'm going in there to defend their honor."

"And the younger sister," said Laxton in an insinuating tone. "Not Bernadette, the bluestocking, I'm speaking of Miss Belinda. She's as lush and libidinous as Blanche. And dreadfully indiscreet. I heard something about an amorous tryst in the park yesterday. With no dowries to speak of, and a brother who's the worst wastrel in London, those girls will be lucky to receive even one offer."

"That's it!" West broke Rafe's hold. "That miscreant is slandering my sisters. I'll make him beg for mercy!"

"Your choice." Rafe shrugged. "Just think about it. If you charge in there and challenge him to a duel think about how much worse the situation will be for your sisters. The gossip alone would ruin them. Everyone would want to know what slight or insult had been alleged. A duel would cause an even greater scandal and draw more attention to your sisters."

"Damn it, Rafe! Stop being right. I can't just stand here and do nothing." His entire body coiled tight with fury. "I have to defend them."

"There are other ways of silencing Laxton. Trust me, it will be far more satisfying to devise some method of retaliation where Laxton not only suffers, but Lady Blanche is elevated in the eyes of society."

"I can't sodding believe this," West muttered. "I can't even defend my sisters' honor without tarnishing them more than I already have. This is a damned nightmare."

"Let's leave," Rafe said gently.

"This isn't over by half. I'll have my revenge on that libelous snake."

Rafe nodded. "And I'll help."

West stomped out of the club, still seething. "I can't tell Blanche what I overheard. It would devastate her. But I can't let Laxton's words go unpunished. He's going to wish he'd never been born when I'm through with him."

"Think strategically."

"I can't think at all because someone broke a bottle over my head last night and then my best friend finished the job and put me down for the count."

"The damage to your head was done long before I planted my fist. You're poisoning yourself, West. And now that poison is spreading to your sisters. They deserve to make their own mistakes in life, not pay for yours."

"I know." West jammed his hat down lower on his head, ignoring the pain from his multiple bruises.

"Now don't bite my head off, but do you think there could be any truth to what Laxton said about Belinda having an amorous tryst? Not that it would excuse his execrable slander."

"Absolutely not. They have a strict governess, dozens of maids, and an overabundance of aunts watching over them. They're never alone. Laxton was telling tales."

He thought about the last time he'd spoken with his sisters. They'd been assembled in the conservatory with their music teacher. "Oh, come to think of it, the governess quit her post unexpectedly. I'm sure my housekeeper has advertised for another. In the meantime, the girls are very devoted to their music instructor, Miss Beaton, who's also a sort of companion for them. She's a sweet-natured, dimpled thing, though she's a member of that infernal virago club that your brother's wife patronizes."

"The Boadicea Club on the Strand."

"I warned her not to fill my sisters' heads with incendiary ideas."

Miss Beaton had already filled his mind with incendiary images. They'd collided in the hallway on one memorable occasion and the feel of her petite curves pressed against him had fueled his fantasies for months.

She certainly wasn't what he'd expected when he'd engaged a music instructor on the recommendation of his friend the Duke of Ravenwood. He hadn't been paying attention and had assumed Louis Beaton, the notorious composer, had a son.

Instead, the person who'd arrived at his home had been a curvaceous, bewitchingly green-eyed and dimpled female with a sunny smile that made everyone around her feel at ease. She wore plain gowns and hid her wavy light brown hair under a white lace cap, like a spinster, but she was young and attractive.

Far too attractive. He shouldn't be thinking about her at all. She was a member of his staff and therefore strictly off-limits.

"My sisters have sufficient supervision. Laxton wants to harm their reputations and I'm going to make him suffer for it."

"All I'm saying is that there are ways of humiliating Laxton without further humiliating your sisters. More devious, secret ways."

West had long suspected that his friend dabbled in espionage. Rafe took frequent, and very mysterious, trips abroad. And that stranglehold he'd just used hadn't been any ordinary hold. Even suffering from a disastrous morning after, West should have been able to break free from the smaller man's grip.

"Laxton aside, it's worse than I'd thought. I knew that no respectable and well-bred young lady would have me. I didn't know that my wicked ways had nearly ruined my sisters."

"It's unfortunate that they must pay the price."

"I swear on my wasted life, Rafe." West slammed his fist into his palm. "I'm going to find a way to make this right."

Chapter Two

*I*F MISS VIOLA Beaton were a character in a novel, she'd be the heroine's best friend. The one who gave trusted advice, who poured a nip of brandy into her friend's tea, offered a shoulder to cry on, and served as a staunch ally in times of adversity.

She often felt like a supporting character in her own life.

She'd been a bridesmaid three times now, and, while she was very happy for her friends, it was sometimes difficult to know that she'd always be backstage, the bridesmaid and never the bride.

Her twenty-four years of existence had revolved around the blazing sun of her father, Louis Beaton, once Britain's foremost musical composer—whose works were commissioned by kings and lauded across the globe—now disgraced, in poor health, and buried by a mountain of debt.

Their circumstances were so straitened that Viola had been forced to take employment as music instructor to the Duke of Westbury's five sisters.

Today her pupils were rehearsing the pieces they were to perform at a musical evening to be hosted here, at Westbury House, the duke's London mansion, in less than one month.

Music was what she lived for, what she loved, and she was determined that the Delamar sisters would shine brightly amidst the polished and elegant debutantes of the *ton*.

Lady Blanche, the eldest, sat at a gleaming pianoforte playing Mozart's Sonata no. 11. Not a strand of blond hair dared escape her carefully coiled coiffure, and her back remained stiff and straight as her fingers ranged methodically across the ivory keys. She was technically proficient but played with a lack of feeling that Viola found more jarring than wrong notes.

Blanche's four younger sisters were arranged before the pianoforte to simulate an audience. When Viola had begun giving them lessons, she'd had difficulty telling them apart. Their names all began with the letter *B*, and they all shared the famous Delamar brilliant blue eyes. But now that she'd been instructing them for several years, she knew them as well as if they were the sisters she'd never had.

Lady Blanche expected perfection of herself, and those around her. She took her role as eldest very seriously, scolding her younger sisters and attempting to mold them in her own polished image. She had her work cut out for her. Bernadette was a retiring, bookish young lady with not one elegant or musical bone in her body. She could butcher the simplest of tunes and render it a jangling cacophony. Viola adored her all the same.

The twins, Belinda and Betsy, shared the same brown hair and big blue eyes, but they were like night and day in all else. Belinda was high-spirited, obsessed with being fashionable, and longed to be admired by a large collection of beaus, while Betsy was a hoyden who couldn't care less about gentlemen, unless it was to best them at cricket.

Birgitta, or Birdie, who wouldn't make her debut for some years, was Viola's secret favorite, a sweet-natured girl who played the pianoforte with a sensitivity and emotion that couldn't be taught. She had shown talent for musical composition and was to perform a piece of her own authorship at the musicale.

As for their brother, the duke, his conduct was not to be held as an example for any respectable soul. He slept the day away and left the house in the evenings with the sole intent of furthering his dreadful reputation as London's Most Wicked Rogue.

Even when he was mostly absent, his formidable presence permeated the entire house. He left reminders of his decadent pursuits strewn about—playbills from bawdy entertainments, vouchers for debts at gaming hells, even the odd silk stocking or jewel-encrusted hairpin, mementos of passionate liaisons that fell, unheeded, from his coat pockets.

Blanche moved from the *andante grazioso* movement to the *menuetto* and Viola's thoughts remained with the duke. He had the same gilded hair and dark blue eyes as his sisters, but he was a colossus of a man, with broad shoulders, a chiseled jaw, and the dangerously handsome face of a fallen angel.

Her friends were always scolding her on the

subject of Wicked Westbury. They thought she was secretly in love with him. Ridiculous! She'd never be so incredibly stupid as to give her heart to such a rake. Even though he was sinfully attractive, and his commanding bass voice gave her gooseflesh.

Even though she suspected his gruff exterior hid a warm and generous heart because he doted on his sisters, and they adored him in return. She'd gleaned that whatever drove him to drink and gamble had probably originated with his father who, by all accounts, had been exceedingly cold and distant toward his firstborn son.

She wanted to know more about his past. Sometimes she led the conversation toward him, to hear his sisters' tales of their childhood. How their brother had always had a kind word for them, a smile, a new book, or toy. How all of that had changed when he was sent off to school after their brother Bertram's birth.

The family had experienced its share of tragedies. The girls' mother had passed from this earth six years ago, with Bertram following less than a year later in a horse riding accident. Their father had soon followed and the ladies whispered that he'd died of a broken heart.

When Westbury was a young man he'd gone downhill so swiftly, Blanche had told Viola with a deep sadness in her eyes. He'd lost himself in London's demimonde. Developed a compulsion to frequent gaming hells and throw his money away until he stumbled home in the wee hours of the morning.

Viola had a compulsion that wasn't as visible and didn't have such bad consequences but was, in its own way, equally as destructive. She couldn't stop thinking about Westbury.

But she was most certainly not secretly in love with him.

Even though every time she saw him, she stammered and blushed and generally made a complete ninny of herself. And even though once, when she'd stayed over at the house because Birdie had a toothache, she'd been rushing down a hallway and she and the duke had accidentally collided and his strong arms had wrapped around her, holding her close against his body.

The blue of his eyes had swallowed her whole. The heat of his body, his intimate embrace, had set her body and mind aglow. Those few seconds in his arms had inspired her to write a sonata. She'd wanted to capture the thudding beat of her heart, the music that had swelled in her mind, the way she'd swayed into him, prolonging the moment, holding the note until at last she had to breathe and—

"Miss Beaton?"

Viola crashed back into the room with a start, her heart beating wildly, her mind scrambling. "Yes, Lady Blanche?"

"Will it do?"

"You've achieved a remarkable accuracy."

"Thank you."

"But if you could infuse more emotion into the music, what you're feeling as you play has a way of coloring the music, of breathing life into it. The final movement must be played with feeling."

Blanche tilted her head. "I'm not really feeling anything. I'm concentrating on playing each note at precisely the right time."

"Try to lose yourself a little more. Let the music have its way."

Blanche gave her a blank look. "I'll try."

"Play the final movement again."

As Blanche began the final *Alla Turca* movement, Viola's heart skipped and danced in time with the famous percussive march. Try as she might to exert control over her heart, she was in an uproar thinking about the duke being here, in this very room, to watch his sisters perform.

The unmarried ladies in attendance would be watching the duke like birds of prey.

His sanctioned public appearances were so infrequent that this chance to corner him for conversation and flirtation had generated much anticipation and speculation.

Was the duke finally thinking of reforming, settling down, and taking a bride?

Viola had to confess that she'd speculated on the subject more than was prudent for the impoverished daughter of a struggling musician who had resigned herself to a spinster's life.

Perhaps he'd arrive early and catch Viola setting out the sheet music. She intended to wear her one and only presentable gown, though it was sadly out of fashion. She'd allowed herself the indulgence of purchasing a new ribbon for a sash, and one for her hair, in a deep shade of gold to set off her green eyes.

She'd think of something witty and sophisticated to say to Westbury if they had a moment alone together, as though she were one of her clever, eloquent friends. And then he'd laugh. A real laugh, from his belly, a full-blown chortle. She'd amuse him, and not because of her bumbling or blushing. She'd amuse him with her quick wit. And he'd want to know more, he'd *burn* to know more about her.

He'd say, *Miss Beaton, you're a most enigmatic creature and I must know more about you. For example, what is your favorite food? Is it gooseberry tart with clotted cream? Do you compose piano sonatas and enter them into competitions under a male pseudonym? And are you fond of reading romantic Gothic novels? I want to know everything there is to know about Viola Beaton . . .*

And that's when the duke in her mind faltered, and sort of faded around the edges, and became transparent, disappearing in a shimmer of wishful mist. Because she couldn't actually imagine him asking her any of those things.

The truth of the matter was that the Duke of Westbury barely knew she existed, even though he'd been the one to hire her on the recommendation of one of his friends.

When she'd arrived and been introduced, he'd stared at her. *I thought you would be the great composer's son,* he'd said with a perplexed look in his eyes. She'd been so afraid he might dismiss her then and there. She'd desperately needed the work. She'd lost her last position when she resisted the lecherous advances of her employer and been dismissed with no reference.

She was most grateful to the duke for hiring her. And he certainly never made any amorous advances upon her. He didn't even remember her name. On the rare occasions they spoke to one another, he invariably referred to her as Miss Bleating, or Miss Bedlam.

She meant nothing to him. He had no idea of her likes or dislikes, goals or dreams. He saw in her something of utility. A foot soldier in the army of servants and hirelings he employed to maintain this lavish London lifestyle that he couldn't afford because he'd gambled away the bulk of his fortune.

The last notes rang out and Blanche turned to Viola with a satisfied smile. "I think I'm nearly ready, wouldn't you agree, Miss Beaton?"

"Indeed. That was much better."

"Shall I play the Bach concerto now?"

Betsy groaned. "Must you? We've only heard it ten billion times. When's my turn? I'd like to get it jolly well over with."

"You have to wait your turn, Bets," said Belinda. "I'm three minutes older than you so I'm after Bernadette."

Bernadette was surreptitiously reading the book she was hiding under a lace handkerchief on her lap and didn't comment.

Betsy frowned. "You're always lording that three minutes over me."

"And you're always trying to hold me back," Belinda said.

"I jolly well will hold you back if you're thinking of doing idiotic things. Like allowing that beef-witted baron to kiss you behind a tree in the park."

Blanche gasped. "What's this?"

Belinda rounded on her twin. "You promised not to tell anyone, you beastly thing!"

"Belinda. Did you allow someone to kiss you?" Viola asked.

Birdie perched on the edge of her seat. "What was it like?"

"Birdie!" Blanche exclaimed.

"Not really," Belinda replied. "He wanted to kiss me, but I ducked away, and then Betsy interrupted and made me leave with her. Don't go telling tales, sister dear," she said haughtily, "for I could tell some about you climbing down from our bedroom window at night, dressed in trous—"

"Ah, isn't it Bernadette's turn to play?" Betsy asked. "We're all dying to hear her melodic rendition of an Irish air."

"Ha," Bernadette said, without raising her head from her novel. "Melodic and I have never met."

Viola caught Belinda's gaze. "Going behind trees with gentlemen, whether kissing occurs, or not, is perilous behavior for a young lady making her debut."

"That's putting it quite mildly!" said Blanche. "This is potentially disastrous. Did anyone see you?"

Belinda tossed her head. "Not a soul. Except my turncoat sister."

"And, Betsy," Viola continued, "if what your sister says is true, I can't lecture you for wearing trousers, because my friend the Duchess of Ravenwood frequently wears gentlemen's attire, but I can, and I will, inquire as to the destination of your nocturnal escapades and forbid you from leaving this house unattended."

Since the ladies' governess had left some months ago, Viola had filled the position as best she was able. The duke's housekeeper, Mrs. McClurg, had interviewed several candidates but pronounced them all unsuitable, sighing over what passed for education these days.

Viola had never even received a formal education. She'd been traveling across Europe with her father and benefited from sporadic lessons and the learning she'd gleaned from a voracious appetite for books.

Betsy sighed. "I only snuck into the back of a public house to watch a bantamweight prize fight. It was ever so thrilling. No one knew it was me. I swear!"

"Oh my dear sweet Lord." Blanche swayed on the piano bench, her face gone pale. "I wish Great-Aunt Hermione would return from taking the Bath waters for her rheumatism. You never would dare to do such outrageous things under her supervision. You could ruin us all! Think of poor Birdie, she's only fourteen and may never have a Season if you keep this up."

"What does a public house look like on the inside, Bets?" Birdie asked, her eyes alight with curiosity.

"Dirty, smelly, and filled with belching, cursing, fart—"

"That's quite enough, Betsy," Viola said firmly. "You and I will speak of this further. In private."

"I simply can't bear it!" wailed Blanche. "I'm a very calm person but my nerves are at the breaking point. If I don't find a match this year, then none of you will. Do you understand?"

"I don't want to find a match," Bernadette said, raising her head briefly from the book. "At least not yet. I have many more important things to do first." She turned to Viola. "I wrote a letter to your friends at The Boadicea Club for Ladies on the Strand about my studies of soil composition and insects and Lady Beatrice Wright wrote back a very encouraging missive and told me that if I wanted to consult the library, I'd be welcome to—"

"Lady Beatrice married the carpenter on her brother's estate." Blanche shuddered delicately. "You mustn't prefer books to balls or you'll marry a tradesperson, Bernadette."

"It was a love match," said Viola, defending her best friend, Beatrice. "They're blissfully happy. And Mr. Wright has built her ever so many bookshelves."

"I don't care if she's happy and has more bookshelves than Hatchards Bookshop. She's an object of ridicule," said Blanche. "I couldn't bear it if I was shunned by polite society. We must all make suitable matches."

"She's one of my heroes," said Bernadette. "She and the Duchess of Ravenwood, the intrepid archaeologist."

Viola smiled at her. "They're both wonderful women and you would do well to emulate them."

"I'm beginning to despair of you." Blanche narrowed her eyes, fixing each of her sisters with a glare in turn. "You must be on your best behavior, and behave like perfect ladies, not dreadful hoydens, isn't that right, Miss Beaton?"

"Lady Blanche is right," Viola said.

Betsy groaned.

"She's right," Viola continued, "though one may maintain an outward appearance of decorum and propriety while maintaining an inner freedom of thought."

"Is that what you do, Miss Beaton?" asked Bernadette. "I can't imagine you being a hoyden in any way. You're so sweet and accommodating at all times."

Accommodating. She was that. Like a portmanteau stuffed so full of items that the seams were stretching and beginning to fray and the whole thing was in danger of ripping apart. She was responsible for so many things. She was her father's caretaker. He was gradually going deaf for undiagnosed reasons and the worse his hearing got, the worse his tempers became.

"You two must promise to behave," Viola said sternly, speaking to the twins.

"We promise," Belinda and Betsy said in unison, too glibly for Viola's liking.

Blanche smoothed her hair and straightened her skirts. "All must be perfect for the musicale. I'll play the Bach concerto which I happen to know is a particular favorite of Lord Laxton's and will inspire him to offer for me on the spot."

"Oh, Blanche." Viola knew all about pinning

hopes and dreams on an unattainable outcome. "Isn't there anyone else you might consider? It doesn't appear that Lord Laxton . . ." How could she put this tactfully? "It doesn't appear that he's of a mind to marry at the moment."

"You can forget about Laxton," a bass voice pronounced forcefully.

Viola nearly started out of her chair. The duke was here. In the room with them. Days too early! She looked a fright, her hair mussed from playing croquet in the gardens with Betsy earlier, her gray gown stained from Bernadette's disastrous attempt at making cherry cordial to bring to a meeting of her book club.

Maybe he wasn't really here. Maybe she'd imagined him. She turned her head slightly, only to snap it back to face the pianoforte.

He was here. Every broad-shouldered, blond-haired, blue-eyed, square-jawed inch of him.

Every time she saw him, something went ping inside her heart, as though she were a pianoforte played so forcefully that one of the strings snapped.

Every time she saw him, she was lost. Over and over again.

"West! You're here!" Birdie jumped up from her chair and ran across the room to embrace him.

He laughed. "How's my little Birdie today?"

"Bored. But now you're here and you're *never* boring."

"Glad to hear it."

"West," said Blanche in measured tones. "Why do you have bruises on your face?"

"You should see the other fellow," the duke joked.

"Were you bare-knuckle boxing?" Betsy asked eagerly, leaving her seat to join her brother by the door.

"Something like that."

Viola had to acknowledge his presence. She couldn't sit here frozen forever, staring at the piano keys as if she could disappear between the cracks.

"Your Grace," she said, and turned toward him, only to knock the music off the pianoforte in a cascade of fluttering white pages. She bent to retrieve the pages and hit her head on the edge of the pianoforte as she came back up.

"Mother of . . ." she muttered, seeing red stars dancing before her eyes. The pain was intense, but nothing compared to the humiliation she would experience as she recalled this excruciating moment later.

"Are you quite all right, Miss Beetle?" the duke asked.

A new name. A small insect to be crushed under his custom-made leather boots. Appropriate.

Viola's eyes were still screwed shut to block out the pain. She had to open them sometime. The girls would be staring at her with concern and their brother . . . he would gaze at her with tender solicitation as he knelt to help her lift the sheet music and accidentally on purpose brush his hand against hers.

Miss Beaton, I feel as though I've never truly seen you before this moment.

"Miss Beetle," the duke said impatiently. "Are you quite all right? I hope you didn't hit your head too forcefully. Allow me to help you up."

Viola opened her eyes. There was a hand extended in front of her. *His* hand. She was meant to take it, to be lifted by him, lifted from the floor and into his . . .

On no account would she touch the Duke of Westbury.

She had an irrational feeling that if she touched him, her foolish, forbidden fantasies would be communicated through the contact.

She lifted herself upright and sank onto the piano bench, holding the sheet music to her chest like a shield against dukes.

Westbury gazed at her with what could only be described as fleeting concern, the same momentary pity one might feel when witnessing a stranger stumble on an uneven cobblestone.

"I'm quite well, Your Grace. We were rehearsing for the musicale."

"You can stop rehearsing. This"—he gestured toward the pianoforte—"is unnecessary now. We'll send out a notice of cancellation to the invitees."

"But the ladies have worked so very hard," Viola said with dismay.

"Why should we cancel it?" Blanche asked. "We must have the musicale. We simply must!"

"We must!" Belinda agreed. "I've a new gown to wear with the most adorable cherry blossoms embroidered around the hem."

"Bully!" Betsy raised her fist. "The musicale is canceled!"

She and Bernadette exchanged delighted grins.

"The musicale isn't necessary," the duke repeated. "You don't have to display your talents in an antiquated mating ritual. I've procured husbands for you."

"Pardon?" Blanche, who prided herself on always maintaining her composure, even when severely tried by her recalcitrant sisters, was actually seen to gape. "You've procured *what*?"

"Husbands, dear Blanche. Two for you to choose from, one likely gentleman suitor for Bernadette, that was a rather more difficult task, I must say, and several promising prospects for the fine ladies Belinda and Betsy, though you two may take your time in making a decision since you're still so young."

The room erupted into chaos, the ladies speaking over one another.

"I don't want a husband!" said Bernadette.

"We haven't even had our first Season," cried Belinda. "You can't steal my moment in the sun!"

"Ladies," Viola said. "Ladies! Allow your brother to explain. I'm sure he doesn't mean that the way it sounded." He'd better not. He couldn't simply arrange marriages for his sisters without consulting them first. That would be the height of male arrogance and presumption.

"Thank you, Miss Beetle," he said, without glancing in her direction.

"Beaton," she muttered under her breath.

"There's really no explanation required. I'm making an executive decision. You don't have to prance about at balls, dropping your fans and other such transparent maneuvers. I've taken care of everything. It's much simpler this way. And more economical."

"Brother," said Blanche, "am I to understand that you've made some marital arrangements on my behalf?"

"No contract as of yet, but two outstanding candidates." He crossed to the sofa and settled in, a footman immediately bringing him a tumbler of brandy. "When I do something, I don't do it by half, by God." He slapped his gloves upon his thigh.

Viola stared at his massive buckskin-encased thigh for a giddy moment or two, her mind reeling, before she brought herself to heel.

"And how did you manage this?" Bernadette asked. "I do hope you haven't bribed one of your friends to marry me. Or given me away in exchange for a debt."

"Nothing of the sort, Bernadette. I simply sold my title to the highest bidder. And we are now wealthy beyond belief. Your dowries have been tripled." He propped his boots up on a table and swigged his brandy. "I'm going to be wed."

Chapter Three

❧ 🌹 ❧

"You're to be married, Your Grace?" Viola blurted out. Her elbow hit several piano keys and produced a crash of bass notes. Her heart pinged in a different way, jangling and jarring her from the inside out.

"To an American heiress," was the nonchalant reply, with a shrug of one large shoulder.

"Which one, Your Grace?"

"Does it matter, Miss Beetle? The one with the wealthiest father."

"Do you mean Miss Vanessa Chandler?" Viola had memorized the list of potential heiresses Westbury might marry. She wasn't proud of that fact.

"As a matter of fact, yes. Never conversed with the lady, though I've seen her and she's a beauty. And her father is obscenely rich."

Miss Chandler was a statuesque woman known for her lustrous auburn hair, fine dark eyes, and utter lack of tact. Last Season she'd caused quite the sensation, nearly sending several matrons into apoplectic fits with her outspoken and outrageous American ways.

"The shocking Miss Chandler?" Blanche said.

"You can't be serious. She's not a suitable duchess. She'll make a mockery of the Westbury name!"

The Westbury name was already tarnished to a dull, rusty disreputableness, thanks to the duke. Blanche had a very good point.

"I may not be restoring the family name, but our fortune will be so vast that all objections to the match will be overlooked."

"Great-Aunt Hermione will not approve," Blanche said. "You know she wants you to marry Lady Winifred Woolfrey."

"I'm well aware of that. Our great-aunt has been attempting to match me with that estimable lady for years."

"What's wrong with Lady Winifred?" asked Blanche. "She's the consummate English rose. Beautiful, good-mannered, of good family, good fortune, and—"

"*Good* is the saliant word in your description for a reason. She's altogether too pious and perfect for the likes of me. She'd want me to reform. I'd make her miserable. Miss Chandler knows exactly what I am and all she requires from me is my title."

"Perhaps you should speak with the young lady before you decide to marry her," Viola suggested.

"I've spoken with her father. He made me an offer I couldn't refuse."

"Great-Aunt Hermione would *not* approve," said Bernadette.

"Great-Aunt Hermione isn't here." The duke drank his brandy. "And that's partly why I'm doing this. I'll reform just enough to wed and to see my dear sisters safely settled, without any of the pitfalls and expenses of the social Season. Blanche, you already have two offers from very eager gentlemen."

Blanche frowned. "Which gentlemen?"

"Unobjectionable ones. Honorable ones."

"I do fervently hope that Lord Laxton has offered for me."

"He's not worthy to breathe the same air as you."

"Pardon me? Lord Laxton is the gentleman I will marry. He'll propose this Season, I know he will. He simply must!"

"You can forget about Laxton," the duke growled.

"And which gentlemen have you chosen to replace him?" Viola asked. She agreed about Lord Laxton. She'd met him on several occasions and he'd always struck her as vapid and conceited.

"Flanders or Middleton." He gestured expansively. "Take your pick, Blanche."

"Lord *Flounder* and Lord *Middling*?" Blanche collapsed onto a sofa. "How could you?"

"They're both sober, steady gentlemen who aren't bad looking, have all their teeth, are solvent enough, and would be overjoyed to wed you."

"Flanders is like a brother to me—we grew up together and he can't think of me amorously, nor I of him. And Middleton. Why, he's fifty if he's a day!"

"I don't care whom you've chosen for me," Bernadette announced grandly. "I've no intention of marrying until much later in life, if ever. I'm going to be a lady scholar and join the Lady's Club on the Strand."

"Miss Beetle." Westbury turned to Viola. "Have you been filling my sisters' heads with your blue-stocking notions? I know all about your club of bloodthirsty warrior queens."

"I'd hardly describe our little club as blood-thirsty, Your Grace. We're a charitable organi-zation. We believe in greater opportunities for females in the spheres of the Arts and Sciences."

"I want to marry," Belinda chimed in, "but not until I've had my debut at court. I've been prac-ticing my presentation for months. I haven't the slightest hint of wobble." She performed an adroit curtsy, left knee locked firmly behind her right, with an impeccably smooth descent. "This is to be *my* year. I'm looking forward to at least forty balls, an equal number of parties, thirty dinners, and dozens of breakfasts. Not to mention the rid-ing in Hyde Park, morning calls, and shopping excursions. You simply can't take the Season away from me."

"Course he can," said Betsy. "He's the duke. He can order us to be married and to cloister our-selves in the countryside and we must comply." She nodded sharply. "And I heartily approve. I've no desire to mince about a dance floor, nor tor-ture the ivories in front of an audience. I suppose I'll have to marry someday, and one fellow's in-terchangeable with another. I'll manage it so he won't interfere with my life."

"Very sensible, Bets," said the duke. "At least

one of you is taking the news with equanimity. I don't know why everyone is reacting with such dismay. I've saved you all a lot of nonsense and expense. I thought you wanted a husband, Blanche. I seem to recall you saying that your life would end if you hadn't received a proposal by the end of the Season. Well, I've secured you not one, but two. I'm giving you a choice."

"A choice between two men I don't love and who have no affection for me."

"What's love got to do with it?" The duke accepted another glass of spirits from a footman and drank half the contents in one swallow. "Marriage isn't about love. It's a mutually beneficial business contract."

It wasn't Viola's place to comment on the duke's commandments, but these were her pupils, her *friends*. And she'd formed some very strong opinions on the subject of love. She'd witnessed her best friends finding, and being transformed by, true love. Her chance at finding the love of her life was gone and buried. She was resigned to life as a spinster, a caregiver to her father, and a doting aunt to her friends' offspring.

But the duke's sisters had every expectation, every right, to find their perfect matches. She couldn't stand by and watch them be forced into loveless unions by the infuriating man pronouncing his sisters' fates like some pitiless Greek god.

"Your Grace." She rose from the piano bench. "Love has *everything* to do with it. Why, a marriage without love is like . . . it's like toast without butter. Dry and unpalatable. It's like dinner with no dessert. Summer with no sunshine. An orchestra with no conductor." Her words tumbled from her, carrying her across the music room toward the duke. She lifted the roll of sheet music she held, using it to punctuate her point like a conductor's baton. "Marriage without love is a diminished chord, unresolved and lingering in our minds discordantly. Love is the note our ears long to hear, life's satisfying resolution."

The duke leaned forward, resting his elbows on his knees. "Love spoken with a capital *L* and that moony look in your eyes, Miss Beetle, is a sentiment manufactured by poets to sell books of verse. Love is neither necessary, nor advisable, for a marriage that profits both parties."

"How can you say that?" she protested.

The ladies were staring at Viola and the duke. Viola collected herself and lowered the roll of sheet music. "I only mean to say that love is essential to a harmonious union, Your Grace. And also that . . . well, just this: love makes life worth living."

There, she'd said her piece. The duke wasn't pleased by her outburst. He glowered at her with such ferocity that she retreated backward toward the relative safety of the piano bench.

"You're so right, Miss Beaton!" Blanche clasped her hands in front of her chest. "Love makes life worth living. And I love Laxton and I'll die if I can't have him. I shan't marry anyone else." She dissolved into sobs, burying her head in a velvet cushion.

"Now see what you've done?" the duke asked Viola.

"What I've done?" Viola sputtered.

The duke stood up. "If you'll excuse me, ladies, it's been a very long night and day. I sustained several injuries." He stabbed the air near the bruises around his eye. "And I signed an agreement to marry. Both activities which require a prolonged period of recuperation. We'll have ample time for further discussion after I've had a nice soak and a long sleep."

The image of Westbury rising from a soaking tub kidnapped Viola's mind for a few hot and steamy seconds.

Blanche lifted her tear-stained face. "I don't want anyone but Laxton."

The duke's expression hardened. "I don't want to hear that name spoken ever again in this house. Is that understood?"

"But why?"

"He's not worthy of you, and he never will be. You must forget about him. I've found two good options and you're going to choose one of them . . . and that's final!" He spun on his heel and strode from the room, leaving Viola and his sisters staring after him.

Birdie was wide-eyed, and the twins had the same expression of astonishment on their faces.

Blanche sniffled and clutched the velvet cushion to her breast.

Only Bernadette seemed unaffected. "That was rather odd," she said reflectively. "I wonder if he received one too many blows to the head?"

Viola had been wondering the same thing. She

placed the sheet music on the pianoforte and went to Blanche. "Hush now." She patted her shoulder.

"How can he do this to me? I don't want to marry Flanders or Middleton."

"Don't panic, ladies," Viola said. "We'll find a solution."

"*I'm* not panicking. I'm perfectly calm," said Bernadette. "If he attempts to force me to marry, I'll simply run away to find succor at your club, Miss Beaton. I shall go there and throw myself upon the lady scholars' mercy."

"No one's running away," said Viola firmly. "And you will all perform as scheduled at the musicale."

"But you heard him," Belinda said, her lower lip wobbling. "No balls, no musicale . . . no Season. Oh, it's too, too horrible to contemplate. My friends will laugh at me and pity me."

"Then they're not your true friends," Viola said.

Betsy bounced to her feet. "Since we're not practicing for the musicale, may I go out and play cricket?" She had a group of male friends who accepted her as one of their ranks, mostly because she was better at every sport than any of them.

"Stay here, ladies," said Viola. "I'm going to go and talk to your brother. I'll explain everything rationally, in language he can understand."

Her emotional proclamations about the power of love had been the absolute wrong approach. The duke cared about his sisters. His genuine affection for them was the leverage she must use to make him see that he was acting wrongly.

Blanche lifted her head and managed a wobbly smile. "Oh, would you?"

Normally, she wouldn't. Under ordinary circumstances, she would stay as far away as possible from Westbury, for fear of betraying her forbidden feelings about him in some unguarded word, or, heaven forbid, touch.

But this was too important.

"Yes." She nodded forcefully. "I'll make him understand why you must be allowed to have a Season and to have your choice of suitors."

She knew enough about him that she ought to be able to influence him. Use subtle persuasive tactics and bring him round to her way of thinking. He mustn't rob his sisters of the only freedom afforded to young ladies before marriage.

The thought of a private audience with the duke made her palms clammy and her heart jump into her throat. Hopefully he wasn't already disrobing for his bath. She must move swiftly, for she could never confront a half-robed Westbury. He must be fully clothed. And she must keep her wits about her and be on guard against any uncharacteristic clumsiness or emotional outbursts occasioned by his proximity.

She had no idea how she would accomplish it, but she must make the duke see the error of his ways.

Chapter Four

WEST STOOD IN front of his father's colossal oak desk and dared himself to falter, to tremble, to feel any of the helplessness that used to overwhelm him in this room. In every house they'd lived in, whether in London or the countryside, the study had always been the same.

A place where he was made to feel small. Made to feel sinful.

He visited the study to remind himself of who he'd been and who he was now. *Why* he was this way.

He'd been small and defenseless. Just a boy who'd been eager to please, who would have done anything for a kind word, a smile. Instead: a sneer and a malediction.

You're wicked and shameful. Stop that quaking. I tell you this for your betterment, so that you may seek to correct your course, to stamp out the taint of sin.

He'd loved his father. Right up until that love had transformed into a hatred so intense that he still felt it blazing in his blood, years after the old man was dead and buried.

His father had been right about one thing: life was no bed of roses. And neither was marriage.

Miss Beaton had stars in her eyes and romantic notions buzzing in her mind like a swarm of bees. She'd attacked him as though he were a monster who cared nothing for his sisters' happiness when he was doing this to ensure they had the respect of society and a comfortable and financially secure future.

They hadn't taken the news very well.

Blanche was distraught, Bernadette rebellious, and Belinda appalled. Only Betsy had reacted sensibly. Blanche fancied herself to be in love with Laxton because she didn't really know him. He was one of those silver-tongued dandies who flattered a girl to her face and then slandered her in private.

Blanche must never find out about the malicious rumors that Laxton had been spreading about her. When news of West's engagement and Blanche's multiple offers rippled through the *ton*, no one would pay any heed to Laxton, or his lies.

West intended to deal with him personally. Find a foolproof way to make certain he wouldn't spread more untruths about the girls. He'd try Rafe's subtle and devious methods of retribution first, but if those didn't work he'd do things his way. With his fists.

His butler, Sebastian, entered the room. "Welker is preparing your bath, Your Grace." He glanced sideways at his bruised forehead. "And I asked Cook for a cold compress for your wounds."

"And can you arrange to strike the memory of this cursed day from the annals of my mind?"

"That is beyond even my abilities, Your Grace."

"I'm to be married, Sebastian," West said glumly, sinking into a chair by the fire.

"Felicitations, Your Grace. And the fortunate young lady is . . . ?"

"Miss Vanessa Chandler. An American heiress. Mr. Chandler wishes to purchase a title for his darling daughter. And I wish to settle my debts and see my sisters' futures secured."

Even though Sebastian's impassive face displayed no hint of censure, West felt the disapproval rolling from him in waves. Even his butler disapproved of the match. Bernadette had the right of it—Great-Aunt Hermione, from his mother's side of the family, would be appalled when she learned of his choice of bride. That formidable and highly opinionated elderly lady had been attempting to marry him off to Lady Winifred, one of London's elite, polished, to-the-manor-born ladies, for years now.

You must marry the perfect duchess, Westbury. It's the only way to repair the ruin you've made of the Westbury name and fortunes.

Miss Chandler wasn't the perfect duchess. But she'd make him rich enough to buy their way back into society. And she didn't mind about his bad reputation. All she wanted was his title.

It was simpler this way. No foolishness about courtship. No expectation that he would be reformed by falling in love.

It was far too late for any meaningful reform. And falling in love was out of the question. Miss Beaton could keep her buttered toast and her musical metaphors.

Though she had looked rather magnificent brandishing that roll of music in the air, bearing down upon him with her green eyes sparking and her bosom rising and falling rapidly.

Not that he should spend any more time picturing her heaving bosom.

Marriages of convenience. The settling of debts. Those were approved subjects. "Miss Chandler and her mother will pay us a visit Tuesday next to discuss the details of the wedding."

"Very good, Your Grace. I'll inform Mrs. McClurg."

"I can see by your expression that you have something to say to me, Sebastian. Out with it."

"I, Your Grace?"

"You don't approve of me marrying an American."

"I would never presume to comment on your choices in life."

"And that's a brazen lie. You always find a way of letting me know your displeasure. This is my attempt to do the right thing, Sebastian."

"And I have every faith in you, Your Grace." His tone of voice said quite the opposite. "Will there be anything else?"

"Tell Welker I'll be up soon."

"Very good." Sebastian bowed and left the room, taking his cloud of judgment and disapproval with him.

West glared at the cheerful crackling fire in the grate. Was he making an enormous mistake?

It was done now. He'd made his decision and

signed a contract with Mr. Chandler. Some of his debts were being settled this very day.

There was no going back now.

At least Miss Chandler labored under no illusions that this was a love match. He needn't woo her or make false promises. She wanted the title. He wanted her fortune. It was a straightforward business arrangement with a minimum of fuss.

A soft knock sounded on the open door. "Your Grace?"

He knew that mellow, lilting female voice.

"Go away," he called. "I've had my quota of lectures today."

Miss Beaton walked briskly into the room.

"You're disobeying an order," he said.

"And you're being surly."

"Please leave."

"Not until I say my piece," she said calmly.

The faded gray gown she wore couldn't hide the pleasing curves of her generous bosom, a nicely indented waist, and the extravagant flare of her hips. Her nostrils were flared, as well. Her words were confrontational. but her eyes betrayed her emotions. She was terrified, poor thing.

And well she should be.

"You can save your breath if you're here to convince me that I'm wrong." He rose from his chair and stalked toward her. "I was just leaving."

"Lady Blanche is inconsolable."

"She'll come round."

"She won't. She's nursed this affection for Lord

Laxton for years now and she won't easily abandon it."

West stopped in front of his father's desk. "I said I didn't want that name spoken in this house."

"But why—can you at least give me a reason?"

"He's not a fit partner for my sister and that's an end to it. I want her to marry someone who respects her, who holds her in esteem, and will never humiliate her. Now, if you'll pardon me, Miss Beastly, I'm in no mood—"

"It's Miss Beaton! My name is Viola Beaton. My father is Louis Beaton, the famous, or some would say infamous, composer."

He knew her name. He couldn't say why he pretended not to. Something about appropriate distance between an employer and his staff.

"You hired me, Your Grace. Please endeavor to recall my name," she said primly.

"Viola suits you. You're all scrolling curves and indentations and your voice has a mellow, husky musical quality."

Confusion filled her eyes and she blushed prettily. "I, er, thank you?"

She was here to scold him. He wasn't in the mood for forbidden flirtations. He gestured toward the door. "Good day, Miss Beaton."

Resolve replaced confusion in her eyes. "Your Grace, your sisters adore you, you're all the close family they have left, and this will break their hearts. Think of their feelings before you make any hasty decisions on their behalf."

"I wasn't aware that I required your blessing

for family decisions. I'm paying you a salary to instruct my sisters in music, nothing more."

"You're not paying me at all."

He ducked his head. "I'm not?"

"Your butler told me that my salary has been delayed. It's been delayed for months now."

"A clerical error which will be remedied immediately. The point is, you're not employed to lecture me."

"I can't stand by and watch you destroy your sisters' lives. They're good girls and they deserve better. You can't just bring home a husband for Blanche and Bernadette like you would new gloves or a parasol."

"It happens all the time. I'm finally doing my duty. That's how society will see it."

"You may do your duty, marry if you choose, but selecting husbands for your sisters instead of allowing them to find their own suitors is the most arrogant, wrongheaded . . ."

She stopped speaking abruptly. By the play of emotions across her face, and the decided lack of dimples, she was probably wrestling back several more insults. She took a deep breath that plumped her breasts against her bodice in a thoroughly distracting manner and curved her lips into a smile.

A man could become lost in those dimples and never find himself again.

"It's not in their best interests, Your Grace," she said sweetly, patiently. "Your sisters have been sheltered, as all noble young ladies are, from anything other than a narrowly dictated list of acceptable occupations. They know how to stitch a Psalm on muslin. They know a smattering of French. They can play a piano sonata (some of them with more success than others). But they lack practical experience of the world. I know that you are fond of your sisters and wish the best for them."

Another bright smile. A kind, encouraging spark in her green eyes.

"Because of your obvious affection for them you must allow them to experience the modicum of freedom afforded them by the excitements and social engagements of the Season. Let them be young, Your Grace. Allow them to converse with gentlemen, fill their dance cards, observe London at the horse races, walk along a moonlit path at Vauxhall Gardens—"

"Let me just stop you there."

"But I'm not finished yet."

"It's a very pretty speech, and very winningly said, but it won't have the desired effect. My mind is made up, I'm afraid."

The smile left her eyes and lips. "So, you've been gambling and being . . . wicked for years and suddenly you simply decide to marry and force your sisters into unhappy marriages on a whim?"

"It's not a whim." The memory of Laxton's poisoned barbs reverberated through his mind, turning his thoughts dark and vengeful. "This is my duty. I should have taken responsibility for their prospects before now. I've already signed a preliminary marriage contract with Miss Chandler.

I asked her father all of the necessary questions and received satisfactory answers."

"What questions did you ask, pray tell?"

"The urgent details of any marital union. How many months out of every year she'll spend in Boston, leaving me free in London. What her spending habits are. Whether she wants a large family. That sort of thing."

Miss Beaton was not impressed. "That's the most bloodless, mercenary description of a courtship conversation I've ever heard."

"There's not going to be any courtship."

She sniffed. "Obviously."

"I was satisfied by her father's answers. She spends extravagantly but he's good for it. She only wants a small family, and she'll stay in Boston for at least six months of every year, sometimes longer."

"Leaving you to your own devices. Or vices, as it were. And you honestly think that these conditions will make a happy marriage?"

"No less harmonious than most."

"I knew you were reckless and gambled with your sisters' dowries, but I didn't take you for coldhearted and calculating."

That touched a nerve. His father had been the coldhearted one. "Miss Chandler will have as much benefit from the marriage as I'll have. She'll be a duchess, the envy of all her friends—she'll trot her title around Boston, and be the reigning queen of society there."

"She'll do nothing for your reputation in England."

"My great-aunt is always attempting to foist some well-bred young lady or another upon me on the infrequent occasions I appear in society. I took matters into my own hands and I chose a bride who may not be English, and well-connected, or born to be a duchess, but who is so wealthy that any objections will be brushed aside. Wealth is the great equalizer. Her fortune will smooth my sisters' way in society. They've had a rough time of it since our mother died. This is my way of trying to do my duty."

"They want more from you than duty. You should hear the way they talk about you. They want you to stop drinking, gambling, and to come home in the evenings and sit by the fire with them. And Miss Chandler may wish for your company, as well."

"It's a heartwarming portrait you paint of me sitting in domestic bliss by the fireside, but it's never going to happen. I gave up a conventional life long ago. It's too late for me to be truly reformed. I'll do my duty in this matter, but that only goes so far."

"Do you have any idea what Miss Chandler expects from this union? Do you know the very least little thing about her besides the size of her father's fortune?" Miss Beaton's cheeks flushed and her eyes glittered. "Her preference in literature, her favorite food, her favorite thing to do on a rainy day? I'll wager you don't even know the color of her eyes."

"They're brown. I think."

"You *think*?" She rolled her eyes. "There are

so many shades of brown. Are they a dark rich brown or a do they have streaks of amber? What does their color remind you of?"

Miss Beaton's green eyes were nothing like emeralds, more of a fern green, warm and alive.

She didn't require fashionable gowns to be pretty. Even wearing that prudish white lace cap and lecturing him like a prim schoolmistress, she floored him with her loveliness and audacity.

He smelled a faint hint of lavender, the scent that always lingered in the hallways after she left the house.

"You don't know the color of her eyes because when you look into them all you'll see is her father's gold coins," she concluded, with an accusatory sniff.

"Gold is a noble color. The wife I have chosen for myself is one who will make very few demands upon me because we are both making use of each other. She wants my title to be the envy of all her friends in Boston. And I want a very large fortune. It's a marriage of convenience and no one will question it."

"Will she be a good role model for your sisters? If Miss Chandler will live chiefly in Boston she won't be here to ease their way in society. Mightn't it be better if you found a wealthy and respectable English lady to marry? A lady who was raised to become a duchess."

"You're quite opinionated on the subject of my marital arrangements."

"Because you're not setting the right example for your sisters."

"I don't owe you any explanation for my actions or my choices. I'm the duke."

"You can't just explain everything away by saying you're the duke."

"Seems to work most of the time."

"That's your problem. You've been given free rein in life. You've never had to answer for your actions or suffer the consequences for misdeeds. And when you require a bride, why all you have to do is select the wealthiest, most beautiful one."

He raised his eyebrows. "Are you jealous, by chance?"

"Don't be ridiculous." Her answer came glibly but something flickered in her eyes. He'd hit the mark. Interesting. "I could be soaking in a hot bath with a glass of mulled wine instead of standing here being chastised by a pint-sized virago about my choices."

"I'm here to ask you to think about someone other than yourself. Think about your sisters. Their wishes. Their futures."

"You'd do well to think of your own future, Miss Beaton," he said gruffly, beginning to feel real annoyance surface.

"Is that a threat of dismissal, Your Grace? Honestly, of all the . . . you're going to stand there being the most . . ."

"Yes?"

She was fighting for control. Clenching and unclenching her small fists. Probably wished to beat them against his chest.

What would it be like when the mild-mannered Miss Beaton exploded with rage?

Or pleasure.

Now *that* would be something to see. Those green eyes sparking with desire, her cheeks rosy and her lips swollen and cherry-red from his kisses. The white lace cap would come off and waves of light brown hair would luxuriate over her shoulders, down her chest, covering the tops of her breasts but leaving her nipples exposed to his . . .

It had been a very long night and an even longer day.

She was obviously off-limits and completely forbidden given that she was his employee, and teacher and confidante to his sisters.

Here he was in the place where he was chastised and disciplined during his childhood. He'd be damned if he'd allow her to get under his skin. Or tell him what to do and how to live his life.

"If I'm a virago, Your Grace, then you're a . . . you're a . . ."

"If you're going to insult me, Miss Beaton, please make it creative. I don't want any dull, worn-out invectives. Find something that will really sting. I'm ready for it."

"You're a . . ."

"Yes?" He closed the distance between them. "What am I?"

FAR TOO NEAR. That's what he was.

He stood so close that a slight step forward would bring her directly in contact with his imposing bulk.

How could she think of cutting insults when

he was standing close enough to touch? All her mind wanted to do was invent scenarios in which kissing might occur. Even though he was arrogant and wrongheaded. And engaged to be married.

"If you're not going to insult me, Miss Beaton, then you really should leave. For if you don't leave, I may have to throw you over my shoulder like a roll of carpet and carry you out of this study."

He wanted her to insult him so that he'd have reason to dismiss her. She should do quite the opposite. She should be charming and sweet and wrap him around her finger. Oh, why couldn't she think of the disarming, witty remarks that would make him see things from her perspective?

She'd never been adept at repartee. She didn't make brilliant, sophisticated responses when gentlemen attempted to banter with her. Sometimes, she thought of the perfect response days, even weeks, later. She'd be transcribing some melody her father was humming and the clever rejoinder she should have spoken would appear in her mind, in a bubble, as though she were an illustration by a caricaturist.

The duke threw her off-balance. He turned her mind to mush.

As she stood before him, fuming, growing redder about the face, no doubt, unable to think of disarming witticisms or cutting insults alike, she reminded herself to tread carefully.

She must keep her temper even and her words diplomatic. "I've no wish to insult you, Your Grace, though, if I had, I'd think of something late at night, something very inventive and original and I'd say it then."

"A shame I wouldn't be in your bedchamber to hear you deliver the set-down, Miss Beaton."

Was he flirting with her?

He flirted with everyone, she reminded herself. He flirted with life; he conquered it with a wink and a sultry glance. Nothing was able to withstand the onslaught of him.

"Let me simply say this, Your Grace," she said in a rush, before he made good on his threat to throw her over his shoulder. "The social Season isn't only about finding a mate. It's the only time a young lady is able to experience life before she becomes a wife and a mother."

"I disagree. The Season is nothing more nor less than a mating ritual. Let them marry and then experience life afterward. The suitors I've gathered are all good men, and I'm sure their lives will be tranquil."

"But they will lack passion."

"Is it freedom, love, or passion you are advocating for?"

"They are of equal importance."

"And you're the expert on passion?" Said with a smoldering stare that actually made her take a shaky step backward.

"Of course not. I'm a wallflower on the brink of spinsterhood. I spent my childhood touring with my father in Europe and he never had the means for a proper debut for me. So, no, I'm not the expert on love or passion. But I do have many female friends who have made love matches and they would speak as I do. A marriage without love is a sad, empty fate."

"I think I've heard your opinion on the subject. Dry toast with no butter, and such. I disagree. Love is no prerequisite for a harmonious union. Love is too often blind, and too often one-sided. Love fades. It provokes people to desperate acts. It is withheld. It sets you up for failure. It's an unattainable ideal."

"You're wrong, Your Grace. Love transforms, it heals, and it transports. I've seen my friends blossom and thrive under its influence. Love takes your breath away and at the same time it gives you all the room in the world to grow."

"You've lost me, I'm afraid," the duke drawled.

I never had you. "Your sisters deserve a chance to find love."

"My sisters will be better off making sensible matches with honorable, unobjectionable men."

"And what of Miss Chandler? Is she to gain an honorable groom?"

"Have a care, Miss Beaton. My personal choices are none of your affair. I'm trying to do something right for once in my life."

"But you're going about it all wrong!"

"I'll make the decisions I feel are in the best interests of this family. I've made too many mistakes, and my bad reputation has harmed my sisters and I plan to turn it all around. The Season is no longer required. I will marry. Blanche and Bernadette will marry, and there's an end to it."

"Your sisters must have their balls and their musicale, Your Grace." She must take a stand. She couldn't allow him to disappoint those bright, trusting, hopeful young ladies.

"Must they? Because the last time I heard them play the pianoforte or attempt to sing an artful air, they weren't exactly soloist material. I'm sparing them, and the audience, an evening of misery."

"Of all the horrible things . . ." Viola sputtered. "If you ever took the time to come and listen to your sisters practicing then you would know they've worked very hard and have improved considerably and will be a credit to you."

"There will be no musicale. Which means your services are no longer required."

Viola's jaw clenched so tight she was in danger of cracking a tooth. The duke couldn't possibly dismiss her after she'd devoted so much time and attention to his sisters and hadn't even been paid for her time.

Anger and frustration boiled over in her mind. He was lucky she wasn't holding anything heavy or sharp.

"You can't sack me, Your Grace," she ground out. "Because I quit!"

Chapter Five

❧ 🌹 ❧

VIOLA TRUDGED THROUGH a drizzling gray spring rain on the walk from Westbury's stately mansion to the modest lodgings she and her father occupied. As she walked, a tempest raged in her breast. A great seething maelstrom of emotions.

Outrage. Hurt. Regret.

She never stormed out of rooms unless provoked beyond reason.

She wasn't given to erratic weather patterns of any kind. Her general outlook was blue skies and tranquil seas. She'd had to be calm and on an even keel with a mercurial genius for a father.

But the duke had towered over her, telling her that she was wrong, that she had no business interfering in the lives of his sisters, and something just snapped. Something inside her, something stretched so taut that she hadn't known it had worn thin, gave way and a dam of emotion poured forth.

She loved those young ladies as though they were her own sisters. Their fate felt like her fate. Their happiness, her own. She'd become emotionally entwined with them . . . and with their brother. She'd tried so hard to vanquish this impossible longing, this forbidden desire, but it was tenacious. It grabbed hold of her mind and infiltrated her dreams.

She'd tried to convince herself that she cared nothing about the duke. She'd been lying to herself.

Why else would the news of his engagement throw her into such a turbulent state of mind? He had to marry an heiress out of necessity. She'd known this day would come. What had she been hoping? That London's most wicked, and yet most eligible, duke would suddenly realize he was madly in love with a music teacher with no money, no pedigree, no connections, and sweep her off her feet?

He hadn't even bothered to learn her name.

A gust of wind caught her black silk umbrella and turned it inside out. As she was wrestling it back into shape, one of the metal ribs snapped in half. Useless. She tucked the broken umbrella under her arm. Perhaps she'd be able to find a way to mend it—Lord knows they had no funds to buy a new one.

The drizzle became a downpour. She wiped rain out of her eyes.

Even if the duke had fallen in love with her, marriage would have been out of the question.

Her father was distantly related to an earl, but that didn't change the fact that she was the daughter of a disgraced composer and an Italian opera singer whose marriage had lasted only one year, whereupon her mother had abandoned them to continue her career.

Viola had toured Europe with him as a child, watching as his symphonies were performed in crowded concert halls and royal reception chambers.

Music was her life. And teaching gave her great joy. And the salary she made helped keep them afloat. And now she'd thrown away her employment and the duke wouldn't give her a reference after that outburst.

She was the worst kind of fool. The kind that harbored secret hopes and dreams that she hadn't even admitted to herself until they'd been torn to bits and scattered to the winds.

She didn't want the duke to marry anyone else, but she'd learned that life didn't usually give her what she wanted. And that meant she'd had to lower her expectations. She'd learned not to want anything too far out of reach.

She couldn't blame him for seeking a financially beneficial matrimonial arrangement, though Miss Chandler was far from the bride his family would have chosen for him.

But she could, and would, blame him for upending his sisters' lives in such a callous manner.

The Season was everything they'd talked of, dreamed of, and speculated upon for the past year. Even though Bernadette had no plans to marry immediately, she still wanted to chatter with her friends, observe the social rituals, and widen her sphere of experience.

They wanted to see and be seen, flirt with gentlemen, dance and laugh. They wanted to be young and free, and to choose their own partners.

And he would take all that away from them.

At least she could have insulted him properly. Instead, she'd quit her employment without even delivering a scathing set-down that would stick in his memory and fester for years to come.

If he ever thought about their encounter in his study, it would be with mild amusement at her expense. He'd remember how she sputtered and failed to insult him.

As she entered their lodgings, shaking rain from her hair, she saw the entrance hall as if for the first time. The paint was peeling from the woodwork, the carpet was fraying at the edges, and there was a permanent odor of dirty wet woolens and lye that emanated from the laundress next door that couldn't be dispelled with the sprigs of dried lavender she tied from the ceiling beams and tucked into their linen closet.

They didn't even own their own home. She'd had to economize and make do with only one maid who came to do the washing, and Withers, her father's elderly manservant, who'd been with him since the glory days and still held the composer in great reverence.

"You're home early, Miss Viola," Withers said as he took the bent umbrella and helped her off with her sodden bonnet and cloak.

"I'm afraid I've done something rash, Withers." The full consequences of her hasty actions were only now beginning to sink in. "I ended my employment with the Duke of Westbury."

"Good. Never liked you working there. He has a dreadful reputation."

"It's not good. He won't give me a reference now. Dukes don't take kindly to having doors slammed in their faces."

"You shouldn't have to work, Miss Viola. It's not right."

"I don't mind. I genuinely enjoyed teaching the Delamar sisters." She'd justified staying on without remuneration because she truly cared for those young ladies. What would they say when they learned she was gone? At least they would mourn her absence.

"How is Father today?"

"You'll see," the manservant replied, his gray eyebrows furrowing.

"A bad day?"

"I tried to stop him, I did. But will he heed me? Oh no, heavens, no. Heed loyal old Withers, who's been with him since the beginning and seen him through thick and thin? Never."

What now? Viola followed him into the small parlor that had been converted into a music room. Her father was on his knees, sawing off the final remaining leg of their gorgeous Austrian pianoforte.

"Papa! What are you doing?"

He kept sawing, the sharp teeth gouging the expensive maple wood.

She ran across the room, knelt next to him, and threw her arms around his shoulders, stopping his forward motion.

She turned him to face her so that he could read her lips. "What are you doing?"

He maneuvered the leg off and the pianoforte

crashed to the floor. "There," he said triumphantly. He flattened onto his belly beside the butchered pianoforte, laying his ear against the wooden floor, and played the keys with his fingers.

A look of delight danced across his face.

She put her ear to the floor and heard the vibrations. Her father was using the floor as a sounding board. He was desperate to hold on to his slender connection with sound, his fierce inner music not enough to sustain him.

The pianoforte had been their most valuable possession, a gift from Lord Sprague, her father's last remaining patron and financier.

The tears she'd wanted to shed earlier, at the duke's house, sprang to her eyes as she listened to her father play. He'd been composing his Symphony no. 10 in D minor for more than five years. The four-movement symphony would be surpassingly beautiful . . . if her father ever finished it.

It had been commissioned by the Philharmonic Society for fifty pounds. She'd written to them several years ago, explaining their straitened circumstances, and they'd sent another fifty pounds. She couldn't ask for more.

Her father had been relying on Lord Sprague's patronage which made Viola very uncomfortable. The baron had been trying to make her his mistress and she was afraid that his patience was wearing thin.

The baron was the last patron left of the dozens who used to lavish money and gifts on the composer. Her father had fallen out of favor with the nobility six years ago. The money had flowed freely then, and her father had been much in demand as a composer and conductor. Until he'd pursued the wrong nobleman's wife. He'd been sued for adultery and the sordid trial had transfixed all of London. As the salacious details were written about in newspapers and scandal sheets, her father had been pilloried. Suddenly, no one would perform his works. Britain turned its back on its favorite composer.

Now the audiences clamored for soft, romantic music, not her father's darkly dynamic and sometimes sorrowful works.

He was lost inside his music today, happier than she'd seen him in months. She wiped her tears away and left him to his work.

She must find a way to pay the rent, and the servants, and settle the household accounts without troubling her father with tidings of destitution.

Now that the heat of her anger and hurt had evaporated, Viola knew she'd have to swallow her pride and ask for her back wages from the duke. She needn't speak to the man himself. Dukes were cushioned sorts of creatures, cocooned from the reality of life's pesky domestic matters.

What would her intrepid archaeologist friend India, the Duchess of Ravenwood, do? She'd corner the duke in a back alley outside of a gaming hell and threaten him with a judiciously placed knife until he paid her the back wages.

Not exactly Viola's way of doing things. Her friends were all powerful women and they'd helped her so much in the past. She didn't want to accept outright charity, but she would ask her friends if they knew of anyone who required a music instructor.

Oh, how she would miss Lady Blanche, Bernadette, the twins, and, especially, young Birdie, who showed such promise as a musician and a composer.

She'd miss the Delamar sisters, but she was absolutely determined not to miss their brother.

It was only a matter of time. One year from now she'd open a newspaper and read something about the Duke and Duchess of Westbury, and she'd feel nothing. She'd be very dispassionate about it. She'd think, *Ah yes, I used to make a fool of myself over that arrogant duke.*

Everything her friends had said about Westbury was true. He'd never had to work at anything. And what did he do with his wealth and position? He squandered it. And was rewarded for his bad behavior.

Her heart was an enigmatic organ. It beat to its own music, and try as she might to conduct a sprightlier, more suitable melody, it wanted to wallow in the minor chords of a hopeless infatuation. Hopeless not only because she could never marry him, and because he would never want, or be able, to marry her.

Hopeless because he wasn't worthy of hope.

She'd known better than to develop feelings for him.

She'd simply have to force her heart to play a new tune.

Chapter Six

❧ 🌹 ❧

"WHAT IN THE scorching fires of Hades is going on in the kitchens?" West asked urgently.

"Open warfare," replied Bernadette.

A noisy clanging of metal pots and a shattering sound like pottery hitting a wall punctuated her words. "Cook and Sebastian loathe each other. She says that he's a despot and he maintains that she's trying to poison us slowly."

"I had no idea there was such civil unrest in this house. Can you put a stop to it, please? Miss Chandler and her mother will be here any moment." West grimaced. "They're coming to discuss plans for the wedding."

"I can't stop it. It was Miss Beaton who always smoothed the ruffled feathers and eased the conflict between those two."

"Miss Beaton," West grumbled. "Everything's gone to hell since she left. My toast was burnt this morning, and Welker tried to dress me in mismatched boots. Not very comfortable."

More clattering and clanging floated up from the kitchens, this time with a muffled curse or two and then a loud female voice interjecting.

"Oh no, Mrs. McClurg is involved now," Bernadette reported. "That's not good."

"My housekeeper makes things worse?"

"Only Miss Beaton was able to keep the peace between Sebastian and Cook," Bernadette replied. "And that's not all. She had a way of easing tensions in the house. She kept Blanche from constantly swooning over Laxton, supplied me with books about insects from her club library, curbed Belinda's oversized vanity, and kept Bets mostly in line. And she and Birdie were composing songs together. Birdie was to perform an original composition at the musicale."

"Well, the saintly Miss Beaton quit her post in a flurry of rage and so you'll have to make do without her."

Bernadette narrowed her eyes. "What did you do to make her quit?"

"Nothing."

"I don't believe you."

"Don't believe him about what?" asked Birdie, looking up from the pianoforte as West and Bernadette entered the parlor.

"He says that he didn't say anything to make Miss Beaton leave."

"I don't believe that one bit," Belinda said, glancing up from the book she was reading.

They were ganging up on him. "Where's Blanche?"

"She said something about a sick headache," Belinda replied.

"And Betsy?"

"I told her to come in, she's running about on the lawn taking her exercise, but she never listens to me."

"Go and fetch her, please, Bernadette," West said.

"No time. Their carriage is here!" Belinda jumped up from the window seat. "I can't wait to see what Miss Chandler is wearing. It's bound to be daring and ever so fashionable."

"Behave yourselves, please," said West. "That means you, Bernadette. Nothing too outlandish."

"Who, me?" Bernadette gave him an angelic look and batted her eyelashes.

"Yes, you."

West caught Sebastian as he was preparing to go and greet the guests. "And you, Sebastian, you know what to do."

"I have my orders, Your Grace. If the meeting goes longer than one hour, I'm to come to the door with an urgent reason for you to leave."

With his exit strategy in place, West prepared to greet his future wife and her mother.

"Mrs. Chandler. Miss Chandler."

"Your Grace." Miss Chandler's curtsy was very American. When she dipped, she bent forward to show him her overflowing bosom, and then glanced up to see what effect the sight had on him.

Strangely, the sight did nothing much except make him think of how Miss Beaton's gowns weren't cut low enough to see anything, and what a pity that had been.

Mrs. Chandler was a tall, handsome woman with the same auburn hair and deep brown eyes as her daughter. She was rail thin with sharp cheekbones and a piercing voice. The opposite of her husband, West thought. Mr. Chandler had been a soft-spoken, corpulent man with ruddy cheeks and a ready smile.

"May I present my sisters, Miss Bernadette, Miss Belinda, and Miss Birgitta, though we all call her Birdie," said West, smiling at his sisters, who had lined up beside him.

"Mrs. Chandler, Miss Chandler, it's a pleasure," said Bernadette. "Miss Chandler, your pelisse is the exact yellow-green shade as many of the *Scarabaeidae* family of insects, more commonly known as dung beetles."

Miss Chandler sniffed. "I assure you I had no idea."

"Dung beetles are lovely, lovely creatures. So industrious. Wait a moment, I think I have one here." Bernadette pulled a square of black velvet from some hidden inner pocket and unfolded it. "Yes, a stunning example of the genus *Onthophagus*. See?" She held up the insect by its legs in front of Miss Chandler's skirts. "The very color!"

"Oh!" Miss Chandler shrank away from the beetle. "How horrid."

"Would you like to keep it, Miss Chandler?" Bernadette asked enthusiastically. "I was going to mount it on a pin for my collection, but I think it would make a fetching brooch for your shawl, or an ornament for one of your bonnets."

"No, no thank you," Miss Chandler said hastily. "You keep it, please."

"Put it away, Bernadette," West said, giving her a warning look.

Bernadette shrugged. "I've been told that fashion is all about accessorizing. I have several beetle brooches. Can't see why they're not all the rage."

"My sister is a lover of insects," Belinda explained with a grimace. "Which means that she always has something hideous tucked away about her person. I think your ensemble is the height of elegance, Miss Chandler," she said with a wide smile.

"Why, thank you," Miss Chandler replied, edging away from Bernadette toward Belinda.

"Come, sit beside me," Belinda said, taking her hand. "We're going to be fast friends, I can tell."

"I thought you had five sisters, Your Grace?" Mrs. Chandler commented as a footman helped her to a seat.

"The eldest, Lady Blanche, is indisposed today. And Belinda's twin, Betsy, is taking some exercise but will join us very soon."

Mrs. Chandler glanced toward the door, expecting to see servants bearing tea trays.

"We'll take our refreshment in a moment, Mrs. Chandler. There was a minor mishap in the kitchens this morning," West explained. They'd better be quick about it. He required fortification.

"I do hope your cook wasn't injured. It's so very difficult to find a good cook. They're worth their weight in gold. I wish we'd brought ours from Boston."

"We lost our dear Miss Beaton, and nothing's been the same since," said Birdie with an accusatory edge to her voice.

"Your Miss Beaton?" Miss Chandler inquired.

"Our music instructor. But she was our *everything*, really." Birdie drummed her fingers on her knee as though she were playing the pianoforte.

"What happened to her?" asked Miss Chandler.

"She left her post. Because *certain people* can't be civil."

"That's enough, Birdie," West said. They weren't here to discuss the lack of Miss Beaton. This was about wedding details, a subject best dispensed of as swiftly as possible. "Now then, about the wedding."

"It must be the grandest, most expensive, most impressive wedding of the Season," Mrs. Chandler said.

"To be sure," replied Miss Chandler. "It must be far more grand and more expensive than Dottie Dalrymple's wedding. She's a lady now, you see. She married the Earl of Dexter last year. She came back to Boston and put on *such* airs. We were all meant to scrape our foreheads to the floor every time she entered a room. I'm going to return as a duchess, which bests a countess, wouldn't you agree?"

"Quite right," said Belinda. "You'll be much higher ranking. She'll have to defer to you."

Miss Chandler clapped her hands. "I can't wait for that moment. She'll be the same color of green as my pelisse."

"I attended her wedding," Belinda said. "It was monstrously lavish. They had hothouse roses festooning the cathedral and her gown was embroidered all over with real gold thread."

"Then I shall have hothouse orchids, which are far more difficult to grow in England, and my gown will be encrusted with diamonds."

"And you'll have more nobility in attendance, I'm determined," said Mrs. Chandler. "A member of the royal family would be ideal. And I want as many dukes in the room as possible. I want to dazzle everyone with dukes."

"Don't worry, I'll provide the dukes," West said.

"I want the wedding to be written up in the best London papers. We have the *The Times* delivered in Boston. It's pored over most thoroughly by the hostesses there. It would be best if the announcement was as near the front page as possible. Do you have connections at *The Times*, Your Grace?"

"I'm often written about in the papers. None of it very flattering, I'm afraid."

"Do put in a word. The public notice will be good for my husband's political ambitions."

West sat up straighter. "I wasn't aware that I was marrying into a political family."

"Mr. Chandler is to become a senator."

"He didn't mention it to me in our meeting the other day."

"He's very modest."

Or, Mr. Chandler had no political ambitions, and his wife was pushing him into the public arena. West thought that far more likely.

"Will marrying a British duke increase your husband's chances?" asked Belinda. "I thought Americans sometimes held a less-than-flattering opinion of our nobility."

"They may profess to, but our society in Boston emulates yours down to the most finicky details. When my daughter is a duchess, everyone will know her name, and not only in Boston."

Perhaps West should have done more digging into the Chandler family ambitions before he agreed to marry. Too late now. They said never to look a gift horse in the mouth.

Not that his fiancée was in any way equine. She was a very attractive woman. Very artfully arranged. Her hair braided and pinned into an elaborate bow atop her head, ringlets hanging down on the sides of her face. Very vivacious and animated. Every coquettish tilt of her head, every shrug of her shoulders that lifted her breasts, every move she made was calculated to inspire adulation.

Her clothing was all shining silk, layers of lace, and little bows everywhere. The fashions for women these days seemed designed to make them appear as though they were Venus, emerging from a frothing pile of lace and silk, instead of an ocean.

Miss Beaton didn't follow the fashion. She was a young lady of reduced circumstances. Her father had squandered his money and hadn't composed anything new in years. She couldn't afford layers of lace. Somehow, he couldn't picture her wanting to wear such frills. Her adorable dimples, the natural curl to her hair (what he could see of it under those silly caps she wore), the musical way she spoke, and the rolling melody of her walk . . . those were the only ornaments she required, and he'd balk if she ever wore more than two ribbons.

What Miss Beaton wore, or didn't wear, was no business of his.

Miss Beaton not wearing anything. Now *that* was a thought to inspire a man to . . .

"Your Grace."

He reentered the room, giving himself a mental shake. "Mrs. Chandler."

"I wanted your opinion on the flavor of ices to serve at the wedding breakfast. It will be summertime and the guests will want a cooling refreshment."

Why was there all this fuss about weddings? All that was required was a chapel and a bishop. "Something sugary. Conduct the wedding however you please. Tell me where and when it will occur, and I'll be there."

"I've always been partial to lemon or Seville orange–flavored ices," Birdie said.

"I should like a rose ice," Belinda offered. "And you could use coloring to make it even more red. It would be so pretty."

"Did you know that the carmine we use for coloring foods is created from crushing up cochineal, a scale insect in the suborder *Sternorrhyncha*?" Bernadette asked.

West groaned softly. "Bernadette, please."

"How horrid!" said Miss Chandler, her eyes wide.

Birdie stifled a giggle.

"What have I said?" asked Bernadette. "It's only the truth."

Miss Chandler sniffed. "I shan't have any in-sects served at my wedding feast, nor any fas-tened upon my person."

"Of course not, dear heart." Mrs. Chandler frowned at Bernadette. "No one is suggesting such a thing."

"Every detail must be more lavish and costly than Dottie's wedding."

Belinda nodded. "I'll make a list for you. And I'm certain I saved the notice about the wedding in a book. I'm collecting ideas for my own wed-ding, you see."

What was this fixation upon weddings? West had never heard the like of it. The ladies contin-ued their planning, piling on extravagances. At least he wasn't paying for it. All he had to do was appear in the cathedral freshly shaven and shod and say *I do.*

I do take this American heiress, whom I barely know, to be my wife. Till death do us part.

A sobering thought.

Do you know the very least little thing about her? he heard Miss Beaton ask and remembered how indignant his answer had made her.

Miss Chandler's father had assured West that he could live in London and his wife would live mostly in Boston.

That was all he needed to know.

His life could go back to dimly lit rooms, aged whisky in his glass, and not a hint of frothy lace or rose-flavored ices in sight.

A blur whisked by the parlor window and then back again. A face peered through the window.

Of course it was Betsy, doing her best impression of a mischievous sprite from some country folktale. West made a surreptitious beckoning motion. Betsy shook her head. West glowered. Betsy brandished a cricket bat and ran away.

Could he blame her? West wished he could escape and go play cricket with his rebellious sister. He'd rather be smashing balls with bats than discussing . . . what were they deciding now?

". . . hand-embroidered serviettes with our initials in gold thread . . ."

Suddenly there was a loud *crack* and a cricket ball shattered the far window and sailed into the parlor, headed directly for Miss Chandler's head. West launched from his chair and dove at the ball, catching it neatly, crashing into a roll on the carpet and landing with a thud against Miss Chandler's chair. She shrieked and her chair wobbled backward, nearly spilling her to the floor.

Mrs. Chandler rushed to her daughter, grabbing her by the arms. "Are you injured? My poor baby. Speak to me!"

His sisters sat there, mouths gaping open.

"Are you all right, Miss Chandler?" West asked.

Her hand flew to her throat. "I—I'm unharmed. I think."

At least she hadn't fainted. Betsy had gone too far this time.

"If you hadn't caught that ball, Your Grace," Mrs. Chandler cried, "it would have smashed directly into my darling child's face. Oh, my Vanessa. This is . . ." Her cheeks were reddening to match her husband's. "This is too much!"

Betsy's head appeared in the center of the jagged edges of the window. "I'm terribly sorry, everyone," she called merrily. "That one got away from me."

"Betsy Grace Delamar." A more unsuitable middle name could not have been assigned. West rose and shook the cricket ball at his sister. "Come inside this instant."

"Crikey, I'm sorry. Didn't mean for it to happen."

"Well, I never!" Mrs. Chandler was not to be mollified. She was still gasping and fluttering about her daughter's near escape. West had to admit it had been a close call.

Betsy entered a few moments later, the hem of her gown covered in grass stains, fingernails dirty and ragged.

"You nearly hit Miss Chandler with that runaway ball," West said sternly.

Betsy hung her head. "I'm sorry, Miss Chandler. I didn't mean to. Moresby was teasing me and he made me lose my temper and I hit the ball hard as I could, but I was so angry that I smashed it in the wrong direction completely."

"If that ball had struck my darling girl it could have broken her nose. Or worse," Mrs. Chandler wailed, wringing her hands.

"I'm awfully sorry, Miss Chandler. I didn't mean it."

"Well!" Mrs. Chandler harrumphed. "I was led to believe, and indeed I have witnessed firsthand,

that the English nobility are restrained and refined. Not here. Such goings-on! Dried beetles and
runaway cricket balls. And not a teapot or crum-
pet to be seen."

"Here's the tea now," said West with relief, as
several footmen arrived bearing the tea things.

"No thank you, Your Grace." Mrs. Chandler
grabbed her daughter's hand. "We're leaving.
I've just remembered we have another engagement."

"Try one of these cherry tarts," pleaded Belinda. "We promise that everything will be ever
so calm and refined from this moment forth."

A footman swept up the glass from the window while another pulled the curtains over the
jagged hole.

Miss Chandler glanced at the pastry longingly,
but her mother caught her by the hand and led
her toward the door.

"I'll meet you for tea in a restaurant, shall I?"
he asked. A public outing would be a more easily
controlled situation. A date was arranged. West
made his bows and escorted them to the door.

Then he assembled his sisters in the parlor.

He marched up and down the row of mutinous
young ladies. "What the deuce was that all about?
Are you trying to drive my fiancée away just because she's American?"

"What was that crashing noise?" asked Blanche,
entering the room.

"Bets smashed her cricket ball through the
window and it almost hit Miss Chandler," Birdie
said excitedly.

"But West dove for the ball and caught it mere inches from her nose," said Bernadette.

"Oh, Bets," Blanche groaned.

"And where were you?" West asked Blanche. "You don't look ill to me."

Blanche gave him a demure look. "I'm feeling better now, thank you for inquiring."

"I'll ask again," West growled. "What in the blazes was all that?"

"It's not our fault, brother dear," said Birdie sweetly. "Now that we have no musicale to prepare for, we're all out of sorts."

"The blasted musicale. We're back to that, are we? A lot of bored gossips sitting in chairs watching you torture the pianoforte and murder the harp. The last I heard you weren't . . ." He'd been going to say that they hadn't been much good. "You weren't quite soloist material."

"Miss Beaton helped me master Mozart's Sonata no. 11," said Blanche, "and I was going to play Bach for Lord Laxton."

"Who will never set foot in this house."

"Why not? What has he done?"

"He's not an honorable gentleman and you must put him from your mind and forget all about him. Best to marry Flanders. You know exactly what you're getting there. A good, trustworthy fellow."

"I don't think of Lord Flanders that way. He's like a brother to me. I know far too much about him. He was always tugging on my plaits and sticking his tongue out at me."

"And you don't know the first thing about

Laxton. Please trust me on this. It's for your own good." West hated the words the second they left his lips. He'd sounded like his father. "I do wish I could tell you why but there are—"

"You don't know the first thing about Miss Chandler," Blanche cried.

"It's true," said Bernadette. "You heard her mother. They have political ambitions. Do you want to ally yourself with them? Their family could have dark hidden secrets."

"Most families do."

"I don't care what secrets Laxton is hiding," said Blanche, working herself up for another bout of tears. "I love him. Can't you understand? I love him madly!"

West caught her by the elbows before she could fling herself onto a sofa. "Blanche, he said some terrible things about you. I overheard him saying them."

"He wouldn't. He wouldn't say anything bad about me. You're lying. Everything has gone all wrong. You shouldn't marry Miss Chandler. I don't care how wealthy she is. You must marry Lady Winifred Woolfrey. She's a much better choice. And we must have Miss Beaton back. We simply must."

Birdie nodded vigorously. "We simply must. And we should have our musicale."

West glared at them. "So, this is mutiny, then?"

"It's not only us," said Bernadette. "Cook is threatening to quit because of Sebastian's accusations. And Fanny, one of the downstairs maids, has a dreadful wheezing condition that comes on in springtime and only Miss Beaton knows how to brew a special herbal tea that eases her difficult breathing."

"Miss Beaton, Miss Beaton," West exploded. "Bloody Miss Beaton! None of you will let me forget about her for even one second."

"She was the peacekeeper of the house," said Betsy. "She just has a way about her. We all want to be better for her."

"Shall I go and tell her that you smashed a cricket ball through the window and nearly injured my fiancée?"

"You smashed a cricket ball through the window of our lives when you rearranged everything without consulting us," said Bernadette.

"If Miss Beaton had been here," said Blanche, "everything would have gone swimmingly. She would have given me a headache powder and coaxed me downstairs, then she would have enticed Bets indoors with the promise of cherry tarts, which would have been all delectable and ready to serve because Miss Beaton would have negotiated a truce between Cook and Sebastian."

West inhaled deeply. "All right, all right!" He held up his hands in surrender. "You win. I'll send someone round to her house with her back wages and an offer to double her salary if she'll only return and keep the peace."

Birdie clicked her tongue against her teeth. "That won't do. That won't do at all. You must go in person and apologize to her."

"Apologize for what, exactly?"

"For whatever you said to her in the study to

make her shout, slam the door, and run from the house without even saying goodbye to us."

"It wasn't like her at all," Bernadette agreed. "You must have provoked her mightily."

"Dukes don't go chasing after music instructors and begging them to come back."

"I miss her dreadfully," said Blanche.

"She's not only our music teacher," Birdie said. "She's our companion, and our confidante, and she's . . . she's our friend, West. Our dear, dear friend. We want her back." Her lower lip trembled. "I—I want to perform at the musicale. I've been practicing my whole life for this moment."

Oh, Lord. West could withstand anything but tears. "Don't cry, Birdie."

"I want her back."

"Oh, very well."

"Do you mean it? You'll go and fetch her?" Bernadette asked.

"I'll go and I'll be civil."

"You have to be more than civil. Perhaps you should compose a sonnet about her eyes," Birdie suggested.

"There will be no sonnets."

"At least bring her a bouquet of red roses," Bernadette suggested.

"No sonnets. No roses. I'll offer her a queenly salary and if that doesn't work, I'll throw her over my shoulder and stuff her into my carriage and bring her back to you."

"Please try not to be too disagreeable," Blanche remonstrated. "Don't mention your opinion about her lady's club, for example."

"And don't call her Miss Bedlam," said Bernadette.

"And tell her she has pretty dimples and you should like to see them." That from Birdie. "I do miss her dimples. Her smile is so bright and cheery."

West hated to admit it, but he'd noticed that without Miss Beaton there was a decided lack of cheeriness in this house. It seemed she was the source of all sunshine. Always a smile on her lips, always a bright look in her eyes. Without her, the entire house felt colder, as though the sun had gone behind the clouds and the house was in perpetual shadow.

"I'm going to rehire Miss Beaton and then I'm going to have some peace and quiet. Away from this house."

Away from females.

He'd go and gamble with some of this hard-won new money in a dark room filled with men who had no agenda other than to shake the dice and have a good time.

"We'll be waiting," said Blanche.

"Don't worry, I'll bring her back."

He must have her back. His sanity depended upon it.

Chapter Seven

❧ 🌹 ❧

"*F*ATHER, I HAVE the most wonderful news!" Viola ran into the music room, waving the letter they'd just received. Sometimes she still forgot that he couldn't hear her clearly. His condition had worsened gradually, and no physician had been able to offer a satisfactory explanation.

She approached the table where he was bent over an ink-covered symphonic score. She placed her hand gently on his shoulder.

"Eh? Viola?" He lifted his metal ear trumpet.

"Good news, Papa," she said, speaking directly into the trumpet. She gave him the letter that could be the answer to her prayers. She'd had no luck finding another position this last week. And her appeals to the duke for her back wages had gone unanswered.

The memory of the heated words they'd exchanged still stung. And she hadn't even had a chance to say goodbye to the ladies. She'd have to find a way to see them, to explain that she'd quit her employ because the duke had insinuated that he would sack her.

The blusterous jug-bitten blunderbuss!

She'd read that in a novel by her favorite author, Daphne Villeneuve, and had decided to appropriate it for use should she ever have the occasion to speak with the duke again. It described him perfectly. He was arrogant, frequently inebriated, and insensitive in the extreme.

Her father read the invitation quickly, impatient to return to his work.

"Isn't it a stroke of good fortune?" she asked.

"I should say not."

"Why? I thought you'd be pleased."

Reaching for a fresh sheet of paper, he wrote her a note. Sometimes he preferred to communicate in writing.

I don't compose trivial tunes for yuletide galas. I'm working on the world's greatest symphony. I've no time for anything else. This is my legacy. The culmination of my life's work.

Viola sighed and wrote her reply.

This is an invitation from the Royal Society of Musicians. You can't refuse. It's only been sent to five composers in England. These Christmas carols will be published in a volume and sent to choirs across the realm. Your name will be on everyone's lips once again. This is your chance to be restored to favor with the Monarchy and with your Public.

Another vehement head shake and a frown. Her father's reply was brief: *I'm not a trained monkey. They don't have me on a lead.*

We need the money. And the future royalties, she replied. She'd tried to shield him from the worst of their financial woes. Perhaps that had been a mistake.

You set a yuletide poem to music, was his reply. *I know you've published under my name before.*

Viola dropped her pen, splattering ink across the page. She had accepted a small number of commissions in her father's name, penning an oratorio for the dedication of a new library, or setting poetry to music for chamber ensembles and vocalists. She'd had no choice. Every commission helped. She hadn't thought her father was aware of her harmless endeavors.

You knew? she wrote.

He nodded. And then he did a very strange and uncharacteristic thing. He smiled. A true, open and affectionate smile.

She returned the smile, feeling a weight lift from her heart. Her father knew and approved of the work she was doing in his name. It was so much more than she'd hoped for.

He put pen to paper again: *Compose the best Christmas carol those fools have ever heard. Better than the other four composers they've invited. Charlatans all. Only leave me to my symphony.*

She hugged him. He laughed and laid a hand on her head like a benediction.

The letter had been delayed reaching them, lost in a pile of bills she'd been avoiding. She only had one month to either compose or commission the lyrics and set them to music.

It was the perfect distraction to help her forget about the duke and to keep her from missing the Delamar sisters and her life at Westbury House.

This was an enormous opportunity. If her father became popular again, the commissions would resume. The royalties from his previous works, which had been scant of late, would flow again.

Humming happily to herself, she mounted the stairs to her room. She'd start searching for the right poem immediately in her small library, and if she couldn't find it there, she'd go to the Lady's Club on the Strand, which had an extensive library stocked with mostly female authors.

She paused halfway up when she heard Withers answer the door. Her spirits fell when she recognized the grating voice of Mr. Barker, their landlord.

"Mr. Beaton is not at home," she heard Withers say.

"I know he's here so let me pass. This is a matter of urgency."

"He's not here, I tell you."

Viola tucked a few stray curls under her cap and straightened her skirts. She must project an air of calm and solvency.

"Mr. Barker, how kind of you to pay a visit," she said as she entered the front hallway.

"Don't pretend this is a social call, Miss Beaton, you know very well why I'm here. Where is your father?"

"He's not to be disturbed, he's working on a very important symphony."

"So you've been saying for the last six months. I'm here to disturb him."

"Ah, but we will be able to pay you in full very soon, Mr. Barker." She waved the letter in the air. "This is an invitation for my father to compose an important work for a Christmastide gala to be held at the Hanover Square Rooms."

"Not good enough, Miss Beaton. I've taken your promises as payment for too long now. I sold this building and you must vacate immediately."

"You can't do that without giving us notice!"

"It's all in the rental contract your father signed. I've been more than lenient. Measures had to be taken."

"To whom did you sell the house?" Viola asked, thinking to make a plea to the new landlord for a continued occupancy.

"To me, Miss Beaton." A tall, fair-haired man walked through the doorway. For a split second Viola thought it was Westbury—until she recognized the pinched, haughty features of Lord Sprague, her father's only remaining patron.

"Here you are then, Your Lordship, here's the key and I daresay you'll find everything to your liking. Very pretty furnishings, indeed." Mr. Barker's smile was insinuating and lascivious as he took his leave.

A bell rang and Withers left to tend to his master, leaving Viola alone with Lord Sprague.

"Why didn't you write to me about your financial troubles?" the baron asked. "You know I'm always willing to help."

The baron's help came with a high price. He'd been attempting to make her his mistress since she was a girl of fifteen and they'd met in Germany. She'd managed to repel his advances since then, but it hadn't been easy.

She led him into the front parlor, buying time to think of a way out of this predicament.

"I'm afraid I can't allow you to extend such largess, Lord Sprague. We'll move immediately." But they had nowhere to go, and no money to rent a new house.

"You can't leave right now. Louis is so close to finishing the symphony. He wrote to me and told me so and I was ecstatic to hear the news. I've been waiting a long time to hear it. I think I'll stay here a few nights a week so that I may be near to hand when he finishes it. Then we'll all celebrate together."

His words and the way he stared at her made Viola's skin crawl.

"I can't live in the same house as you, surely you understand, Lord Sprague. I'm an unmarried lady. My employment as music instructor to the Duke of Westbury's five sisters requires that my conduct be unimpeachable."

"You lost that position, did you not? I believe you left without even a reference from His Grace."

He knew too much about her. It was almost as if he'd hired someone to spy on her.

"You can't live here with us," she said firmly.

"I can live wherever I want. Would you rather

be cast out onto the street? Do you think your father could finish his symphony at the poorhouse?"

"I have powerful friends. Someone will help us." Many of her friends were still at their country residences, though they would be back in London soon.

"I wish you would be slightly more accommodating after everything I've done for you. You will be mine. It's inevitable. You can just stop fighting it and let it happen."

"I'm not a form of currency."

"And I say that you are. Your father is deeply in debt to me. And now I own the very roof over your head. If he doesn't complete the symphony and deliver it to the Philharmonic Society in one month's time, my patience will be exhausted, and I'll demand back every shilling I've invested in your father for breach of contract. A woman in your position has very few choices."

A wave of revulsion, swift and bile bitter, crested over her. She'd never become his mistress. He thought of her as a helpless female. He didn't know that she had fierce friends who'd taught her to stand up for herself. Taught her to defend herself against men who sought to break her, to bring her low to make themselves feel large.

She kept her voice even while her heart hammered. "I must ask you to leave now, Lord Sprague."

He reached out and stroked her cheek. "How do you become more beautiful every time I visit? I thought you were a pretty thing all those years ago in Germany, but now you've grown into such a luscious, such a ripe, young woman. It's such a shame to waste such beauty. You're not made to be a spinster."

She'd learned how to improvise weaponry from what was at hand. Her knitting basket was nearby on a table. She backed toward it and the baron followed.

"Don't resist me, sweet Viola," he said, his gaze skimming over her lips and down her body. "This is inevitable and we both know it. The only wonder is that I haven't had you yet. A mistake I mean to remedy this very day."

Viola edged closer to the table. If she could grab one of the knitting needles, she could hold it to his throat as a weapon.

"It only makes things more exciting when you retreat," he said, panting slightly, perverse desire burning in his eyes. "I'm going to kiss you now, and there's nothing you can do about it. And then, tonight, I'll make you mine."

She backed away, he followed. She'd nearly reached the knitting basket now. She placed herself in front of it, reaching behind her back to grasp one of the needles.

He meant to attack her in broad daylight. He'd grown tired of waiting. The day of reckoning had arrived. Her fingers closed around the middle of the needle. She brought it up behind her back with the sharp point on top.

She wasn't going to maim him, only show him that she was no meek and easily conquered victim.

"I've thought about this moment for so long. You'll be my mistress at last."

"I'm no man's mistress."

"You must have more befitting garments. You would look well in green silk, I think. Green to match your eyes. And low-cut, here, to display your charms." He drew his finger along the edge of her bodice. "And these spinsterish caps will have to go." He plucked the cap from her head and threw it aside.

"Leave now or you'll regret it."

He grabbed her by the shoulders, his fingers digging into her painfully. "Not until I have my kiss."

"I won't ask you to leave again."

"Or what? What will you do, Viola?"

"Withers will be back soon."

"A servant can't stop me."

"Will the thought of my father, your friend, stop you?"

"Nothing will stop me. I've waited too long."

What if he twisted the knitting needle away from her? What if he succeeded in his attack?

With growing desperation, she sought to recall her lessons. She had no knife. No pistol. Only the hard metal needle clutched in her fist which suddenly felt too slim to inflict any real damage or strike fear into a heart twisted by violence.

He bent toward her, his breath scorching her face.

She raised the knitting needle behind her back and prepared to drive it against his jugular, not enough to pierce the skin, only to show him that she was in control, that she wasn't helpless.

"Leave or I'll make you sorry!" she said in a low, steady voice.

"The lady asked you to leave," a bass voice spoke.

Viola paused with the knitting needle half-raised.

Lord Sprague dropped his hold on her arms and whirled around. "Whoever you are, you'll be the one leaving."

"Westbury!" Viola caught her breath.

The duke glowered at Lord Sprague with blue eyes gone gray and stormy. Shoulders wide and strong and tensed for action. Fists raised.

"I'm not going anywhere," he said menacingly. "But you are, sir. You're going to a special place in hell. Put up your fists. Because you're going to need them."

Chapter Eight

VIOLA BLINKED. THE duke remained standing there. Filling her doorway.

My, but he was formidable. Blunt jaw and powerful frame. A lethal mountain of duke rising to her rescue. It did make her slightly weak at the knees.

But that was probably just the relief of it all. She hadn't really wanted to test out her improvised weapon.

"Now then, there's no call for fisticuffs," Lord Sprague said smoothly. "There's been a misunderstanding. You see, this is my house. And you're intruding."

"No misunderstanding." Westbury's voice was harsh. "Stand and fight."

"Your Grace," Viola said. "It's very good of you to come. Lord Sprague was about to leave, isn't that right?" She couldn't look at the baron, at his repulsive lips and furious eyes, but she also didn't want bloodshed in the house. The duke looked ready to kill.

"I . . ." Sprague's voice wavered. "I have the right to remain here."

The duke stalked toward him, leading with

those enormous fists. With a sudden movement he grabbed Lord Sprague by the collar and dragged him onto his toes. "You don't own Miss Beaton. You will not treat her as your property."

Lord Sprague scrabbled at the duke's fingers but couldn't free himself. "How dare you attack me in my own home!"

"I'm the Duke of Westbury. And I'll attack you wherever and whenever I feel the urge. When you least expect it, I'll be there." He pulled Lord Sprague's face to within an inch of his own. "I'll be watching you. And if you ever go near Miss Beaton again with anything other than the greatest deference and respect, there won't be anything left of you to identify you as a man. Do I make myself clear?"

Lord Sprague gulped. "Perfectly clear."

"Now I think I'll break your nose, just to make sure you understand."

"No, please! I'll leave. Don't harm me."

She touched his arm softly. "Your Grace, there's no call for violence. Let's be civilized, shall we?"

She held the duke's gaze for a moment. His stormy eyes cleared but his expression remained stern and lethal. He released Lord Sprague, who stumbled backward, straightening his cravat.

"You say that you own this house, Sprague?" he asked the baron.

"I do."

"Then Miss Beaton and her father are leaving with me."

"We are?" Viola asked.

"That's why I'm here," Westbury said. "I'm

commissioning a wedding march for my upcoming nuptials and I think it best for the great composer to have the use of my superior pianofortes and a spacious abode. The dower house next to Westbury House is vacant at the moment."

"What of my symphony?" the baron asked, his jaw working with fury. "Your father must finish the symphony first! Remember, one month, Miss Beaton. He has one month or all of his debts come due."

"I'm certain that the symphony will be finished swiftly once he's installed in his new music conservatory," Viola said brightly.

"Now then, Sprague, you're going to leave so that I can finalize the arrangements of the move with Miss Beaton."

Lord Sprague shot her a murderous glare as he departed. When he was gone, she laid a hand on the sofa to steady her legs.

"Are you injured?" The duke rushed to her side. "Here. Sit down." He helped her to a seat.

"Only shaken up. Thank you, Your Grace. Your timing was most fortuitous. I've never been so happy to see such a blusterous jug-bitten blunderbuss."

He frowned and then his lips twitched. "I really hope that isn't the scathing insult you arrived at late at night in your lonely bed."

"I read it in a novel."

"It's too tame for a wicked beast such as I. You should consult a tavern down by the docks. You'll find far more injurious insults there."

"Did you just insult my insult?"

He shrugged. "I'm only saying that if a lady wishes to deliver a set-down, she should do it properly. Make it hurt."

"I don't know whether to be angry with you or to shower you with gratitude for arriving just when you did and scaring Sprague away."

"Seriously, Miss Beaton. I don't ever want you to be in a room alone with that man again," Westbury said, glowering at her. "What if I hadn't arrived? What then?"

She threw back her shoulders. "I would have defended myself."

"With what?"

She was still holding the knitting needle. She waved it at him. "With this." She set it down on a nearby table.

The duke snorted. "You can't be serious."

"I'm very serious. I learned how to use the sharp point of a knitting needle as a weapon from Mina, Duchess of Thorndon, who is an expert in improvised and modified weaponry."

"While Thorndon's wife might be an expert in weaponry, you're not. And that man is dangerous. He could have harmed you. And then I would have had to kill him."

The raw intensity of the anger etched across his face startled her. Did he care that much for her honor?

She laughed softly. "You're making too much of it, Your Grace. He's been making insinuations and advances since I was a girl and I've always managed to evade him."

He curled his hands around hers. The heat

and strength of his fingers caught her off guard. Suddenly there wasn't enough air to breathe in the room. After the frightening experience with Lord Sprague, all she wanted to do was nestle against the duke's chest, seek a safe haven in his arms.

"Viola," he said, and his low, gruff voice speaking her name so intimately set something quivering inside her. "You're very brave, but you can't take that chance. That man is dangerous to you."

This man was dangerous to her. It was the midnight encounter in the hallway all over again. The sonata she'd begun writing that night filled her head. A simple melody that swirled and overlayed and built into a crashing, passionate crescendo.

She mustn't mistake his momentary concern for caring.

She mustn't allow the music swelling in her heart to overwhelm her, the need for comfort, the longing for his warm, strong arms to enfold her.

"I can take care of myself," she said firmly. "If a knitting needle to the jugular didn't discourage him, I would have pretended compliance and brought him to the sofa and then given him a sharp jab with my knee to the . . ." She glanced at his breeches flap. Mistake.

Never look at Westbury's tight buckskin breeches and the way they molded over his groin and thighs ever again.

"To the bollocks," he finished her sentence. He chuckled and released her hands. "I'm impressed. That's actually a very good plan. I'm glad to hear that you're aware of the only foolproof method to incapacitate a man."

"I'm no damsel in distress." She straightened her spine. "Why are you here, Your Grace? Did you really think to commission a wedding march from my father?"

"I came to give you this." He reached inside his coat and extracted a leather wallet, handing it to her. She glanced inside and her eyes widened. "That's quite a lot of banknotes, Your Grace. At least thrice what you owe me in back wages."

"Those are future wages, as well. I require you to return to your post. And having you nearby will be even more convenient. You and your father will occupy the adjacent dower house built for my late grandmother. My great-aunt Hermione lives in one wing when she's in London, but the remainder is vacant."

If she wasn't allowed to look at his breeches, she certainly wasn't allowed to live next door to him. "While I appreciate your offer I can find my own lodgings."

"Think of it as reparations for overdue wages. You may live there until you find another place of your own. And there are several handsome pianofortes for your father's use. My grandmother was a pianist."

"It's very good of you but my father can be rather difficult. He's going deaf which is the very worst thing that can happen to a musician. It's so frustrating for him that he sometimes flies into a rage." Not to mention that he might saw the legs off the duke's pianofortes.

"Do the doctors know why he's going deaf?"

"No one's been able to make a definitive diagnosis."

"Well we won't mind if he's loud. The dower house is quite separate and bordered on all sides by gardens. I won't take no for an answer. I require you to return and keep the peace between the servants and inspire my sisters to behave like ladies again. My fiancée and her mother visited today. Blanche never made an appearance, claiming a headache; Bernadette told Miss Chandler that her dress was the color of a dung beetle, and then produced said beetle from her pocket; and Betsy smashed a cricket ball through the library window, narrowly missing poor Miss Chandler's head."

Viola couldn't help but laugh. "Oh dear, that sounds dreadful."

"It was an unmitigated disaster. And I'm fairly certain the girls did everything on purpose to force me to rehire you. That's why I'm here."

"I'm expedient for your purposes. I make your life easier."

"Well . . . yes."

"You could've just sent a man round with my salary offer," she said stiffly.

"My sisters urged me to come in person and I'm glad I arrived when I did. You'd be safer staying close to me for a time. Until your father finishes his symphony and you are free from obligation to Sprague."

"And for your expedience."

"That's right. And the well-being of my sisters. Isn't the salary enough?"

"It's more than enough."

"I expect a proper return on my investment."

"I haven't accepted your offer yet."

"You will."

"You're overconfident."

"I don't think so. You have nowhere to live at the moment. This is a large salary, temporary accommodations with world-class pianofortes, and you like my sisters."

"I do like your sisters." She smiled. "They're remarkable young women."

"More importantly, they like you, they trust you, and they want to please you."

She should refuse but it was so much money and the salary came with a place to live away from Sprague. And she wanted to keep teaching the ladies. But living next door to Westbury. Seeing him nearly every day. She'd resolved to forget him. Force her heart to stop beating to his tune.

She could control her heart.

"Very well, Your Grace, I'll consult with my father, and we'll consider your offer."

"I want you moved into your new lodgings by tomorrow morning."

Viola bristled at his commanding tone. "You do enjoy ordering people about, don't you?"

"No more arguing. Inform your father of his new living arrangements and pack your things, Miss Beaton."

She lifted her chin and stared directly into his eyes, feigning a bravado she was far from feeling. "And if I refuse?"

His brows knit together over those turbulent

ocean-blue eyes. "Then I'll throw you over my shoulder, stuff you into my carriage, and convey you back to my sisters where you belong."

Grabbing the knitting needle from the table, she brandished it at him. "I should like to see you try, Your Grace!"

DAMN BUT SHE was lovely when she challenged him like that, throwing her small shoulders back, attempting to appear more substantial, and lifting that tiny knitting needle like a giant sword. She wasn't wearing a cap and her hair curled about her cheeks fetchingly.

West had noticed that she was pretty. He'd have to have been dead not to. He'd noticed that she was pretty in the same way he reflected that a blue sky was appealing, or the rich gold brandy poured into his glass was pleasing.

She'd been a harmonious arrangement of shapes and colors, pleasant to contemplate, but absolutely forbidden to taste. But when she looked at him with those luminous green eyes, filled with intelligence and determination, she was more than pleasing, more than merely pretty.

She took his breath away.

She'd looked so tiny and defenseless next to that idiot, Sprague. West's protective instincts were on high alert. He was making light of it, but he would never allow her to remain in this house.

He drew closer, bumping his chest against the point of her knitting needle. "Name your price, Miss Beaton. I will have you back."

"I want . . ." Her gaze faltered and she glanced

at his cravat. She took a deep breath and met his eyes again. "I want an apology, Your Grace. And I want your promise that your sisters will be allowed to enjoy the social Season. They should have fun, be young and lighthearted. Allow them to experience life before marriage. Give your sisters their moment in the sun and watch them bloom."

"Ha." He chuckled at her audacity. "I'm not very good at making apologies. I'll acknowledge that I could have broken the news to my sisters more gently. Let them have time to become accustomed to the idea of my marrying, and their replenished dowries and prospects."

"Then you're going forward with marrying Blanche and Bernadette to suitors of your choosing?"

"I wouldn't put it that way."

"How would you put it?"

"I'm providing them with avenues they should, and will, choose to pursue."

"You're giving them a choice?"

"Obviously I can't force them to marry and I wouldn't want to. I found them suitors and I only ask that they seriously entertain the idea. I believe they'll make the right choice."

"Here's the thing about young ladies, Your Grace, they don't much like being told that their options are limited and their futures have been decided for them."

Despite the challenging words, she was coming round. He could see it in her eyes. He pressed his advantage. "My sisters crave your good opinion,

Miss Beaton. They told me that they want to be better for you. I haven't heard them say something like that since our mother died." A smile touched his lips and nearly reached his heart. "Joie de vivre radiates from you like sunshine, casting a golden glow on everyone around you."

She shrugged off his words with a nervous laugh. "I was only doing my job."

"You don't like compliments."

"I'm not accustomed to them."

"Then accept the exorbitant salary I'm willing to pay as inducement." He pried the knitting needle from her fingers and set it aside. "My sisters need you. I need you." He brushed a stray curl away from her cheek. "Accept my offer of safe, comfortable lodgings, superior pianofortes fit for a famous composer, and, if I agree to allow my sisters to attend the Season, you'll accompany them."

"Pardon?" She tucked her chin. "I've never attended a Season in my life. I've been to balls with my friends but I've always been a wallflower. I know almost no one in the fashionable world. I'm not the right choice as chaperone."

"My sisters have plenty of female relations to chaperone them and introduce them to the right people. You'll be there as someone they trust and admire. An unofficial chaperone, companion, and confidante. You'll keep me informed if anything seems amiss. I don't want them falling prey to dishonorable, exploitive men like Sprague or Laxton."

"Ah." She gave him a knowing look. "You want me to spy on them."

"Absolutely not." A smile kept trying to creep back to his lips. What was it about this woman that disarmed him so? "Simply be their confidante and ensure that they never find themselves in a situation requiring defensive maneuvers with knitting needles . . . or knee jabs."

Her gaze softened and he detected a hint of dimple. "I haven't yet heard an apology, Your Grace. Three little words." She held up her thumb. "I." Then her forefinger. "Am." And finally her middle finger. "Sorry." She cocked her head. "Now it's your turn."

"What am I sorry for?"

Her gaze narrowed.

He laughed. "Very well, Miss Beaton. I'm sorry your salary was delayed. And I'm sorry I goaded you into an unbecoming fit of rage in the library. I promise not to provoke your passions in future."

Even though the thought of provoking her to a different sort of passion had crossed his mind at least a dozen times in the last few minutes.

"That's not much of an apology," she huffed.

"I'll send my man round to collect your things tomorrow morning. Think of it this way, Miss Beaton, when you think of a truly cutting insult, I'll be just next door."

Chapter Nine

ॐ ❀ ॐ

Westbury sent not one, but five servants to move their small household the next day. Viola could have managed it herself. They had very few possessions. Her father's manuscripts were the bulk of it, boxes and trunks filled with music. They wouldn't be taking the butchered pianoforte. Lord Sprague could keep his ruined gift.

She'd explained to her father that he had a new noble patron who wanted to commission a wedding march. Her father had been delighted with the patronage and temporary living arrangements, and curtly dismissive of the commission. He'd requested that Viola compose any "wedding marches, military marches, operettas, and all such trivial balderdash" on his behalf while he finished his symphonic masterwork.

This afternoon she was visiting The Boadicea Club on the Strand where she went as often as possible to use the music study where she played pianoforte and composed music in peace, without fear of anyone overhearing her working on her father's commissions. She must embark immediately upon the Christmas carol.

The building used to be an antiquarian bookshop and still had a vast collection of books for use by the ladies of the club. Viola always felt a rush of pride when she saw the gray stone facade and the sparkling leaded glass windows. The idea for an all-female club that she and her friend India had hatched years ago had become such a solid and welcoming reality.

Her friends Isobel Mayberry and Ardella Finchley were taking tea in the cozy front sitting room.

"Viola," Della called. "Come and join us."

Viola stuck her head in the door. "I wish I had time for tea, but I've work to do and only a few free hours."

"Well, at least come in and tell us what you're working on," Isobel urged. "I can tell by the intense light in your eyes that it's a new composition."

Viola smiled and joined her friends. "I've accepted an invitation in Papa's name to compose a new Christmas carol for a gala celebration. The music and lyrics will be distributed to choirs throughout England. This could be a way for my father to regain favor and restore our fortunes. I'm going to search through the library for a suitable poem by a female poet to set to music."

"It sounds like a spectacular opportunity," said Della enthusiastically, her blue eyes bright and lively and her gestures animated. "We'll all have to go and listen to it performed."

"And we'll know it was the daughter, not the father, who composed it," said Isobel.

Viola smiled. "That's all the recognition I require."

Isobel was one of the more daring members of their club, as she had attended a school of law and accepted a clerkship at a law firm in the guise of her invalid brother—with his permission. Her tall, thin frame and sharp-featured face made the deception easier.

"That reminds me." Della opened her reticule and searched through it, pulling out various glass vials, a magnifying glass, and several eye droppers. She assisted her father at his perfumery and was a devoted chemist. "Oh, where is that clipping? Ah! Here it is." She smoothed the wrinkles from a page of newsprint and held it to the light. "'If anyone has information as to the whereabouts of one Mr. Vincent Beam whose composition won second place in the Royal Society of Musicians' contest for new symphonic works, please contact the publishing house of Atwater and Herrick . . .' It goes on to give more details and offers a monetary reward."

"Why do they want to contact Mr. Beam?" Viola asked.

"That's the exciting part. They want to publish your work, Viola! They'll pay you for it."

Viola sat down in a chair. "But I can't reveal myself as Mr. Beam."

"And why not? There are dozens of female composers of note," said Isobel indignantly.

"I can't have people scrutinizing the work I did as Mr. Beam. Someone could discover that I've been publishing more music using my father's name. They might uncover the role I've been playing and discredit my father's compositions. I must keep it a closely guarded secret. Especially with his final symphony nearly complete."

Della placed a hand on her arm. "That's a shame. It seems that you should be able to take credit for your work."

"Winning second place in the competition was enough for me, even if I never collected my prize. I was gratified to know that they judged me fairly, and not with the bias they would have shown if they'd known it had been composed by a woman."

"But the prize money, the payment for publication, and the royalties. I know how much those would mean to you," Isobel insisted. "You earned them, Viola. You deserve to be paid for your accomplishment."

"I'm sure it would only be a small remuneration. My father's earnings have never been huge. He's had to rely on patronage to finance his art."

"And how is your father these days?" Isobel asked.

"At the moment he's hiding from the bustle and activity in our house. As am I."

"What's happening at your house?"

"We're moving." She hadn't wanted to tell her friends about her new living arrangements. Not just yet. They were bound to be very opiniated on the subject. "I should be going to the library."

"Why are you moving?" Isobel asked.

"Because I wasn't able to pay our rent and we were expelled from our home by our landlord."

"Without giving you any notice?" Isobel asked.

"It's already done. He sold the house to Lord Sprague."

"Lord Sprague?" Della frowned. "Isn't he that horrid baron who wants you for his mistress? Ugh. I'm sure this was all Sprague's doing."

"I fear the same. He arrived moments after the landlord informed me that he'd sold the building." She pushed away the sickening memory of Lord Sprague gripping her shoulders. "He said some disgusting things and tried to kiss me, but I was prepared to defend myself with a knitting needle."

"Well!" Della gulped her tea. "That must have been terrifying."

"It was. Until Westbury arrived and terrified Lord Sprague in turn."

"Wait," Isobel said. "The Duke of Westbury was at your house?"

"He rescued her." Della grinned. "It sounds very romantic."

"It wasn't romantic. He was only there because his sisters staged a mutiny and made him promise to rehire me. It was all for his convenience."

"I heard that he's to marry Miss Vanessa Chandler," Della said gently, with a worried glance at Viola. "I read the announcement in the paper. She sounds like a handful."

"It's only what Westbury deserves," said Isobel. "He's a debased, debauched—"

"Jug-bitten blunderbuss," Viola finished.

"Precisely." Isobel nodded approvingly.

"I told him so just yesterday."

"Good for you. You've finally come to your senses."

"I insulted him but then he offered me so much money that I accepted his offer of employment. Papa and I are going to live in the dower house adjacent to Westbury House."

Both ladies set down their teacups abruptly.

"Live next door to that arrogant rogue? Are you mad?" Isobel asked.

"You can't do that. Why didn't you tell us that you were so late with your rent?" Della's brow furrowed.

"You've all been so generous already. I didn't want to ask for more charity."

"My widowed aunt has a vacant cottage on her property near Watford," said Isobel. "You'd be welcome to use it anytime. She's a music enthusiast. I'm certain she'd be delighted to rent the cottage to you and your father for a pittance. I just now thought of it—why it hasn't occurred to me before I've no idea. It would be the ideal situation."

"If I'm to continue my employment as music teacher to the duke's sisters I must live in town."

"I just don't understand why you must live next door to him," Della said, the frown returning to her face.

"I understand," said Isobel. "I see it very plainly."

"Please don't raise your brows insinuatingly." Viola pushed the sugar bowl across the table, avoiding her friend's eyes. "It's only temporary. Until Papa finishes his symphony and we find new accommodations. I agreed to accompany the Delamar sisters to social occasions, to serve as their companion and confidante. I'm doing this for them, not for the duke."

"But is it advisable to live next door to him?" Della asked.

"Only be careful, my dear. I don't want you to have exchanged the wolf's fangs for the lion's jaws," Isobel said.

"Especially given your feelings about the duke," Della agreed.

"Oh that?" Viola said breezily. "That's all over and done with. I had a silly infatuation and it's completely gone now. He's engaged to be married, after all."

Della and Isobel exchanged meaningful glances.

"Will you be safe?" Della asked.

"Westbury would never importune me in any way."

"I'm not worried about that. I'm worried about your heart," said Della. "We know you to be warmhearted and giving to a fault. You always put others' needs before your own. Is this the right move for you? Not for your father, or the duke, or his sisters. For Viola."

"It's already arranged. There's no backing out now. I'm in no danger."

Isobel snorted. "You do know that you're deluding yourself, right? You're not going to be able to ignore that handsome beast of a duke."

"I can certainly control my own mind," said Viola.

"Yes, but can you control your heart?" asked Della.

"You won't have difficulty keeping your emotions under control?" prodded Isobel.

"Not one bit."

"Your heart doesn't thump like an orchestral percussion section when he's near?"

"Not one little tap on a kettle drum."

"Please take care. That's all we ask," said Della.

"Stop worrying. You sound like a bunch of mother hens. I've been hired to complete a task and complete it I shall. I won't be at all distracted by the duke's broad shoulders, buckskin-clad thighs, or smoldering blue gaze."

Wait, that had sounded . . . suspicious.

She schooled her face into her best schoolmarm expression of detached geniality. "The duke means nothing to me. It's all very tidy and manageable and straightforward."

"If you say so," Isobel said, looking unconvinced.

"I'll be perfectly safe," she reassured her friends. "The duke's not dangerous. I can manage him, just as I manage his sisters."

WEST HAD HAD enough of managing his emotions and restraining his thirst for vengeance. His encounter with that sneaking cowardly baron had primed him for bloodshed. He'd wanted so badly to break the man's nose, leave him with some permanent mark for attempting to force himself on Viola.

He saw her again, so small, so brave. Fury blazed through him until he could barely breathe. What if he hadn't arrived? He couldn't think about it. He had arrived. She was safe. And she would remain safe. He'd see to that.

He'd only held back because broken noses were gruesome, messy affairs and Viola wouldn't have liked blood sprayed across her sofa.

There were no sofas here. Only a wood plank floor sprinkled with sawdust to soak up the blood and sweat. Here he could indulge his bloodlust.

Indulge it with one target in particular: Laxton.

He didn't usually go in for these tame bare-knuckle boxing establishments where lords paid to be trained in the pugilistic arts, but he'd found out that Laxton came here every Tuesday afternoon.

It was time to take matters into his own fists.

The subtle means of retribution suggested by his friend Rafe hadn't paid any dividends yet. They'd found some questionable investments, and several unpaid debts, but no scandal big enough to use as leverage to shame him, make him flee London with his tail between his legs.

Rafe had said the investigation would take time.

West wasn't feeling patient.

He bound his fists round with white cloth. He pretended the punching bag was Laxton. He could see the gold and diamond stickpin in the shape of a rose that he always wore on his lapel. The gleaming boots and flamboyant waistcoats. Smell the sickly sweet scent of his hair pomade. See his long nose with flat nostrils pinched in aristocratic disdain.

Laxton was tall and broad-shouldered but he'd

be lily-livered under all that finery, West had no doubt.

He'd wipe that mocking smile from his face.

Thwack. He slammed his fists again and again into the punching bag.

The Season started soon. West wanted Laxton brought to heel before he spread more malicious rumors about his sisters.

He might not be able to challenge him publicly, but he could damn well put the thumbscrews to him in private.

West had explained the situation to the attendant and boxing instructor. Neither one of them had any love for Laxton. They'd agreed to take a break for a quarter hour.

Laxton entered the private boxing studio already stripped to the waist and wearing white trousers. He glanced around, puzzled. "What are you doing here, Westbury?"

"Thought you'd enjoy a challenge today."

"Er, I don't think so. I'll just go and find—"

"The attendant? Your instructor? They've gone for a pint at the tavern. Go a few rounds with me. I'll give you the first punch. Or are you afraid?"

"Course not," Laxton scoffed, approaching with a swagger in his step. "Only you're not a member of this establishment as far as I'm aware and this isn't a scheduled practice session."

"You sound like a patroness at Almack's. Let's forget about memberships and schedules and talk man-to-man."

"I wasn't aware you and I had any business to discuss."

Laxton was no lightweight. They were almost evenly matched. West opened his arms wide. "Hit me anywhere but the bollocks. Hit me like you mean it."

"I don't see why you must insist on me hitting you, but I should warn you that I've been training in pugilism for years and I'm perfectly sober whereas you appear to be three sheets to the wind."

"Don't worry about that. Just hit me."

Laxton shrugged. "Very well." The bored expression was gone. He lowered his head, assumed a fighter's stance.

The uppercut caught West in the kidneys. He grunted but didn't stagger.

"Again," he said.

Laxton went for his jaw this time. It cracked West's head sideways. He laughed, spitting blood. "Is that all you've got?"

Laxton frowned. "What's this about, then?"

"Hit me."

Laxton laughed. "You're sick, Westbury. You know that? There's something wrong with you." He pounded his fist into West's right ear.

West shook his head, his ears ringing. Rage scorched the backs of his eyes, turning his sight red, raising his fists. The humiliation. His father raising his cane.

You're bad. Wicked. I'll beat the taint out of you.

"What in God's name is wrong with you?" asked Laxton.

"I'm teaching you a lesson."

"By allowing me to beat you bloody?"

"This is what you've been doing, Laxton. Hitting defenseless people. Battering their reputations with your words."

"I haven't the faintest idea what you're speaking of."

"Don't you? 'The best she can hope for is spinster . . . or courtesan.' Ring any bells?"

Laxton's face drained of color. "You heard that?"

"I was listening and by God, if my mate hadn't been there to stop me, you'd be dead right now."

"Now, let's talk about this civilly." Laxton laughed hoarsely. "You know that was just men being men. Saying what we'll say at the club. I didn't really mean it."

"You're damn right you didn't mean it. It's not true. Blanche may be foolish enough to believe herself to be in love with a jackass like you, but she'd never debase herself in the manner you described."

"Of course not, of course not. You know how it is. Puffing myself up for the boys."

"No, I don't know how it is. I may have gambled away my sisters' dowries, and wasted my blighted life, but I have a very healthy respect for women and never make the kind of disparaging comments you make so glibly, with no thought to the harm you do to the young lady's reputation."

"Those gents won't repeat it. Westbury, I swear to you. No one will ever know."

"I'm going to make sure of that." West crouched into a fighter's stance. "Fists up, Laxton. This time I'm hitting back."

Laxton's laconic facade crumpled like paper. "Don't hurt me, Westbury."

"On your mark."

"You're mad."

"Probably. I'm also angry. And that's a dangerous combination."

Laxton landed one more punch and West was on him immediately with a crushing blow to the jaw. Laxton staggered backward.

"That was for Blanche." He followed with a right hook. "And that was for Belinda. And this . . . this is for me." The uppercut caught Laxton square in the gut. He sank to his knees, moaning.

West raised his fist, ready to smash it into his nose.

"Don't break my nose," Laxton pleaded.

He didn't even have to strike him. West stopped, his fist a half inch from Laxton's quivering body, his blubbering face. "If I ever hear of you mentioning my sisters, any of my sisters, again in conversation I'll be back to finish the job."

He saw Viola's sweet face in his mind. Her eyes were disappointed. Her dimples nowhere to be found. She wouldn't like this method of retribution.

Your Grace, there's no call for violence. Let's be civilized, shall we?

She would have advised him to think of the perfect insult. To be the better man.

He calmed his breathing. "I could beat you to oblivion and no one in this establishment would come to your aid. But I'm feeling charitable, Laxton. I'll leave if you give me your solemn promise never to speak of my sisters again and to leave London tomorrow and stay away for the Season."

"Consider it done. I'll never even look at them again. And I just recalled an urgent matter I must attend to at my country estate."

Too easy. The man was a coward, just as West had suspected.

He left Laxton in a quivering heap on the floor, satisfied that he'd made his point.

Laxton wouldn't be spreading any more malicious rumors about his sisters.

Chapter Ten

❦ ❦ ❦

*V*IOLA LAUGHED HAPPILY as the Delamar sisters clustered around her, all speaking at once.

"We know you're the one who convinced West to allow us to attend the Season," Lady Blanche said, her eyes alive with delight.

"And hold our musicale!" Birdie said.

"Thanks *very much* for that," said Betsy with an eyeroll, but she was grinning.

"And your father is here!" said Bernadette. "We're so honored that he'll compose his symphony next door."

"Oh, we did miss you terribly, Miss Beaton." Birdie took her hand. "Did you miss us?"

"Of course I did. I thought about you all the time. What's happened since I left?"

Birdie danced toward the pianoforte. "I finished the sonatina I've been working on. I'll play it for you!"

"Blanche wrote a letter to Lord Laxton and he hasn't responded yet."

"Bets," Lady Blanche exclaimed. "You tattletale. How did you know?"

"You run downstairs to ask about the post every day. It's not very secretive."

"Your brother won't be pleased," Viola said.

"I don't care," said Blanche. "I know Lord Laxton will respond. He's been called away from London unexpectedly, but he'll write to me."

"I improved my bowling line and length," Betsy said proudly.

"And I've been identifying and studying the insect specimens sent to me by Lady Philippa Bramble from your club," said Bernadette.

"My, you've all been very busy," Viola said with a laugh. She'd missed them so much.

"West told us that your father is losing his hearing," said Birdie. "It must be dreadful for a composer. West instructed us to be very sensitive to his condition. We have a real live genius living next door. It's so exciting! Do you think we might hear him play?"

"I'm quite certain you'll hear him do a great many things. He's not very quiet."

"We're so very glad you're back, Miss Beaton. And you're to be our companion as well as our music teacher. It's more than I dared hope for," said Belinda.

"I may be your companion, but I'll have my eye on you in the manner of a chaperone," Viola said sternly.

"We're very proud of West for convincing you to return." Blanche leaned in. "How did he do it? We couldn't coax anything out of him."

"He tripled my salary." She wouldn't mention that he'd rescued her from unwelcome attentions. Or how thrillingly, dangerously handsome he'd looked doing it.

Bernadette nodded approvingly. "As he should. He can afford it since he's marrying Miss Chandler. Many of his debts have already been settled. And he's been throwing money at us."

"I have a whole new wardrobe!" Belinda cried. "I modeled my gowns after Miss Chandler's. She's very fashionable and beautiful, even if she's dreadfully American."

"I heard what you lot did to her when she visited. That was very badly done of you," Viola scolded.

"I didn't mean to hit the ball through the window," Betsy protested.

"How was I to know she'd be insulted by the idea of her gown being the same color as a dung beetle?" Bernadette shrugged. "It was meant as a compliment."

Viola tried not to smile and failed. "I've missed you."

"We've missed you!" Birdie encircled Viola's waist with her arms and placed her head on her shoulder. "Never leave us again."

Viola's smile faltered. She didn't want to think about that day. She was only their hired staff, after all. They weren't her family, as much as she'd love them to be.

And the duke was marrying an heiress, as she'd always known he would someday. The thought was like accidentally touching a boiling hot kettle, causing fresh pain every time she remembered the fact. The pain would dull with time. She had no business caring one way or the other. He was only doing what dukes must do.

Marry. Miss Chandler wasn't his social equal, but she'd make him wealthy.

"Now then, we haven't a moment to lose," she said briskly, pushing thoughts of the duke away. "The first ball of the Season is tomorrow which means the musicale is close at hand!"

WEST HAD NEVER had a fiancée before. He was beginning to heartily regret the acquisition.

Fiancées of the very pampered and very American variety expected to be courted in grand and public fashion, something which West wasn't prepared to do.

He and Miss Chandler had been placed at the most visible table in Gunter's Tea Shop, Berkley Square. Every passerby stopped to gawk at them.

Small wonder. Miss Chandler was wearing a vibrant crimson-and-green-striped gown with voluminous puffed sleeves ornamented by an unfortunate combination of crimson bows dotted with emeralds.

Miss Chandler pursed her carmine lips. "You must present me with fifty red roses tomorrow before the ball."

"*Fifty?*"

"Not enough? You're right. Not nearly enough. I must have . . ." She raised her finger. "I must have *one hundred* red roses."

"Don't think I can carry that many," he muttered.

"Bring footmen. Make a parade of it. I want to be showered in roses."

"You'll be smothered by roses. Buried by 'em.

No one will be able to see it's you under all those petals."

"They will see, and they will know."

"What will they know?"

"That I have achieved the unachievable, landed the unlandable, tamed the untamable. That I've brought the mightily wicked Duke of Westbury to his knees."

"To the altar, you mean."

"To his knees," she insisted. "You'll present me with the roses on bended knee."

"I'm not going to act the besotted suitor, Miss Chandler. Everyone knows this is a business arrangement."

"I know . . ." She twirled a lock of her shiny hair around her finger. "But if you play your part well enough, and make me the biggest triumph of the Season, I'll depart London soon after the wedding and you won't see me for two years, at least."

"Deal," West said, holding out his hand.

She shook it with a smile. "I knew we could come to an agreement."

"But within limits. It's out of character for me to shower you with roses. No one will believe it."

"Seeing is believing, they say. Whatever Dottie Dalrymple received during her courtship by the Earl of Dexter, I want you to give me the same thing, only ten times more grand."

"In that case, why stop at one hundred roses? You should have a new variety of roses developed and have it named The Vanessa and instead of an arrangement that will wither and wilt, your name will be immortalized in British gardens forever."

"Brilliant." She clapped her hands. "Dottie will be wild with jealousy."

"I was joking, Miss Chandler."

"It's a splendid idea." She waved her hand imperiously. "Make it so."

"You're very accustomed to having your own way."

"In every little thing. I don't expect you'll be any different. Daddy dear is paying for your devotion, after all."

"Daddy dear is paying for my title—there was nothing in the contract about devotion. And why are you so bent on besting the Countess of Dexter?"

"We've been friends since childhood, but she turned against me and stole my friends and then she stole my thunder when she came back to Boston a countess. Everyone chose her over me and treated her like the queen of England."

"I'm sure you'll be a great success."

"Play your part, Westbury, and you'll have more money than you can shake a stick at. You can open your own gambling house if you want to for all I care."

"I hate to say it, Miss Chandler, but everyone in London knows why this marriage is taking place. They won't believe I'm courting you in earnest."

"Then you'll have to sell it in a big way. I'm not asking for much. All I want is for you to make me the envy of every woman in London."

Miss Chandler pouted, which should have been a winsome sight, except that all West could see when he looked at her was a woman who had something to prove—and he was her means to prove it. Fair enough. They were using each other.

Why that gave him a qualm of conscience he didn't want to analyze. Something to do with the speech Miss Beaton had given him in the study.

A marriage without love is a sad, empty fate.

At least he could learn a little more about Miss Chandler before she became his wife. Her eyes were a rich dark shade of brown with no flecks of amber, he noticed.

"What's your preference in literature, Miss Chandler?"

"I don't have much time for reading. This coiffure alone took two hours." She patted the hair sculpted atop her head in an ornate arrangement of braids and curls.

"Your favorite food?"

"I'm partial to beefsteak with butter sauce, but my mother won't allow me to so much as glance at butter until after our wedding."

"Your favorite thing to do on a rainy day?"

She tilted her head quizzically. "Stay indoors and play a card game."

He catalogued her responses to report to Miss Beaton, to prove to her that he'd done his homework and knew the woman he was to marry.

She stared at him. "You're not going to do anything foolish, like fall in love with me, are you, dear Duke? Because I want to keep this a strictly business arrangement."

A startled laugh escaped his lips. "You're remarkably forthright."

"I'm American."

"Your mother said something about political ambitions."

"Daddy is going to be a senator. He'll be the next president of the United States if Mama has anything to do with it. And she's grooming my brother to become a politician as well."

"You have one brother and no sisters?"

"That's right. Why all the questions?"

"I'm only trying to know you a little better."

"I know what I want, and I go out and get it. Here's what I want from you. I want you to court me. But it will only be playacting. You won't fall in love with me, and I certainly won't fall in love with you."

West placed a hand over his heart. "I'm wounded."

"No, you're not. You're just like all men. You collect broken hearts to mount on your wall. Trophies of the beasts you hunted and killed."

"Spoken like a woman who's had her heart broken. What was his name?"

"It doesn't matter."

"Who was he?"

"A nobody." She tossed her head. "His father owned a timber mill near Boston. I could never have married him without disgracing myself and my family." He saw real emotion in her eyes for the first time. "Please don't tell Mama I told you anything about it. It's supposed to be a secret. I don't know why I told you."

"It's all right. Your secret's safe with me," he said gently. "I'll play my role to perfection,

Miss Chandler. I'll make you London's reigning belle."

Her face lit up. "I think we shall suit, Your Grace."

"Perfectly, Miss Chandler."

They shook hands on a deal that was mutually beneficial to all parties.

Even though it all felt empty, somehow.

WHEN WEST RETURNED home, he was greeted by the sound of laughter and excited voices. He followed the merriment to the music room. His sisters were clustered around Miss Beaton as she sat at the pianoforte, playing a sprightly air. Her eyes glowed and her hair had come loose from her cap, sending tendrils of soft brown curls around her shoulders.

"Lady Blanche, may I have this dance?" Betsy asked in a low voice, making a deep bow.

Blanche giggled and accepted her arm. The two of them twirled onto the carpet, pretending to be dancing at a ball.

West smiled and nearly walked into the room. He stopped himself just in time. His presence would only put a damper on the warmth and intimacy of the moment. He never spent time with his sisters of an evening. He was always out at the gaming hells indulging in fleeting pleasures. Burying himself under layer upon layer of iniquity until he couldn't even stand to look at his face in the mirror.

He wasn't carefree. He wasn't happy.

He'd known that for a long time. Contentment was something that only belonged to other people. He didn't know what true happiness felt like.

He knew the taste of pleasure, the compulsion to gamble, the blessed oblivion of gin and whisky.

Miss Beaton—Viola—knew happiness. She glowed with it. That ready smile of hers, the dimples she bestowed upon the world so effortlessly, the charming way she had of humming under her breath as she walked.

She was joyful by nature, and happiness found her because she had a sweet and giving disposition. That was it, wasn't it?

He'd suppressed that warm, open side of himself when he was still a young man. He'd vowed to become bad and wicked and he'd accomplished his goal so thoroughly that he'd become everything his father said he was.

It didn't matter if he wanted to enter the music room and receive his share of Viola's attention. Make her smile and then bask in the warm glow.

A memory, faint and hazy, entered his mind. His mother at the door of the nursery, watching him read to Belinda and Betsy from a picture book, her eyes lit with pride.

Brandan, she'd said later that day, *you have a warm and a giving heart. Always remember that small acts of kindness multiply and yield richer dividends than all the gold and diamonds in this world.* She'd ruffled his hair. *You'll be a good man someday. You'll make some lucky woman a wonderful husband.*

He'd wanted her approval and love with the same powerful longing that swamped his senses now. The craving for companionship, the lure of easy laughter and warm smiles, was only a memory from his past. He'd buried his weakness, his need for love, drowned it in gin, smothered it with hedonistic pursuits.

You're wicked and shameful. Tainted by sin. Life is no bed of roses for one such as you.

It was too late for him to change. He'd do what he always did.

Walk away from his sisters, from their innocent laughter, from Viola's wide-open smile. From the soft light in her green eyes.

Turn your back and walk away, into the dark night.

And head straight for hell.

Chapter Eleven

❧ 🌹 ❧

WEST FINALLY STUMBLED home at well-past-inebriated o'clock. There was a lamp lit in the music room of the dower house. Viola hadn't struck him as a late-night sort of person.

As he approached the house he heard the sound of piano music. But this was a far cry from the elegant air he'd heard Viola play earlier. This was something entirely different. Strident, almost bombastic chords, crashing into the air like waves battering a cliff during a squall.

This must be the father, composing his fabled Symphony no. 10. West could have a brief listen outside the music room door, a preview of the great composer's masterwork.

The sleepy servant who answered West's knock evinced no surprise at seeing him there. It was his house, after all.

West sent him back to bed and made his way to the music conservatory, lured by the music and the promise of hearing the genius at work.

The playing stopped at intervals and was replaced by the scratching of a pen across paper.

West reached the conservatory and paused outside. The door was ajar, the room striped with shadows. The figure sitting at the piano was slight and . . . shapely.

Viola wore a shadow-colored gown. The light in the room danced in the flickering candelabras mounted on either side of the pianoforte and the flames in the fireplace.

Her back was to him, she'd never even know he'd been here.

She stopped making notations and resumed playing.

How could such a small person create such an overwhelming wave of sound? Her fingers flew across the keys and her whole body swayed in time with the music.

She gave herself to the music, letting it possess her, move her, as she would give herself to a lover.

You're drunk. Go to bed.

He had to stop having these thoughts about her. She was his employee and the woman he'd hired as companion to his sisters. And he was engaged.

And she was living under his roof.

After a difficult passage which she repeated three times, she finally mastered it and laughed aloud. Her voice had a husky richness to it that made him shiver.

Would she laugh with delight like that after he made her come?

All right. You're really *drunk. Off to bed, you bounder.*

He backed away, heading for safety. His boot caught on the carpet and he nearly fell, righting himself with a hand against the wall.

Viola started, her fingers playing a disharmonious chord. "Who's there?"

He cleared his throat.

She whirled around. "Your Grace? I didn't know I had an audience."

"I was just leaving."

"Please come in for a moment. I want to ask you something about Lady Blanche."

A conversation about his sisters. No harm in that. He entered the room, hat in hand. "That was an astounding piece of music you were just playing. Unlike anything I've heard you play before."

"It's the instrument." She ran her hand over the scrolling wood. "I've never played an Erard pianoforte before. It's remarkably sonorous. The action is smooth as silk." She played a shimmering scale. "Such beauty and power."

Just like you, he wanted to say, stopping himself just in time.

She gazed at the piano, enraptured, and then turned that smile on him, as though he'd given her the instrument as a gift.

He suddenly wished with all his heart that he had given it to her, that he had been the author of that smile.

"What were you playing just now?"

"Oh that?" She shrugged one shoulder. "That was one of my father's compositions that I was embellishing upon, creating variations on his theme."

"Do you compose your own music?"

"I dabble."

"It was intoxicating."

"Did you think so?"

"Absolutely." He took a seat next to her on the piano bench. Should have sat in a chair instead. But he was here now. And she hadn't jumped up and run away. "When did you learn to play?"

"I've known since earliest childhood that my role in life was to be a muse for my father's art. I practiced and practiced until my fingers cramped and my shoulders ached and my head throbbed. I had to play his music flawlessly or suffer the consequences."

"He didn't beat you, did he?"

"Nothing like that. He made his disappointment known if I played even one wrong note, he'd shake his head sadly and tell me that the angels were weeping in heaven to hear his music thus mistreated."

"No pressure to achieve there," he said drily. "And your mother?" He realized that he had no idea who her mother was, or what her childhood had been like. He wanted to know more about her. What had given her that inner light of peace and happiness?

"An Italian opera singer, a lyric soprano, with a voice direct from heaven. She was so dedicated to her art that after they were married, and she gave birth to me, she immediately left us to continue her career. She never sought to see me again."

"What was her name—is she famous?"

"Mirella Bartoli. I don't think she achieved the fame she sought. My father calls her The Songbird. He says that she was too young to be tied down, that she was a bird in flight, and we were only meant to hear her song on the wind as she passed overhead. He wrote his Symphony no. 5 about her."

"You haven't attempted to contact her?"

"What good would that do? She didn't want me. That's an end to it."

West tilted his head and searched her face. The words were sad but her smile never faltered. "What was your childhood like? Where were you educated?"

Her smile wavered. "I wasn't given a formal education. My girlhood was spent touring with my father across the continent of Europe, performing for royalty and crowded concert halls. It was a dazzling education, in its way. I learned by observation, a silent witness to the parties and musical salons. I soaked in the wit and wisdom of some of Europe's greatest minds. I visited dozens of countries before I was sixteen."

"You said that you never made your debut in England."

"Never. I wanted to . . . desperately. I didn't want to keep moving from city to city, never settling anywhere. We finally did move to London but then my father was disgraced."

"I remember the scandal. It must have been difficult."

"His sun burned so brightly in those days, so hot, that it consumed everything and everyone around him. It was almost as if he absorbed the energy of everyone around him and he relied on me to feed his creativity, to care for him.

I'm mostly happy to be the torch bearer, his amanuensis, his muse, and his nurse. But some days . . ."

"You want more."

"I've propped him up for so long now that I'm not sure if I have my own limbs to stand upon, or if their only purpose is to support him."

"You could be onstage, you know. The kind of talent you have is rare."

"I never perform in public. I haven't since I was a young girl."

"Why did you stop performing?"

"The devastating realization that my father was losing his hearing. When his hearing loss became inescapable, when it began rapidly escalating, I became his caregiver."

"Leaving no time for yourself."

"I still have my music, even though I don't perform. And I love teaching your sisters. It's so rewarding to see them awakening to the power of music, to see it change them. Music makes us feel. It makes us weep and laugh. I wouldn't want to live without it. It carries us away from the humdrum and places us amongst the stars, with light shining all around and shimmering in our ears. Music will always be there for me, even when I'm old and my hair has turned gray."

The light shining in her eyes, the brightness of her smile, her graceful hands caressing the piano keys had a similar effect on West. She was dazzling. He had to look away. He should leave now. And yet he wanted to linger. To stay close to this vividly alive woman.

"That's all well and good," he said gruffly, "but don't you want to have a family of your own?"

"I always wished that I was born into a large family like yours. I wanted siblings rushing around. A mother and father. My chance for a large family of my own is long past. I'm perfectly content to be an aunt to my friends' children. And I hope to perform the same role for your sisters after they marry. I do dote on children. And I can't imagine a mother abandoning her child. Mine must not have loved me at all." She played a soft melody with her right hand. "What was your mother like?"

"She was like . . ." West closed his eyes. "Like summer roses, so beautiful it almost makes your eyes hurt to look at them. She was sweet-tempered and tried so hard to please my flint-hearted father, but she never could. And that turned her sweet nature to sadness. She was ill for many years before she died. In a way, I'm glad she went before Bertram, my younger brother. At least she was spared the pain of his loss."

Her fingers never stopped teasing a soothing melody from the keys. "Your sisters speak of Bertram often. They miss him every day."

"As do I. I always expected that he would be the one to continue the line since I'd set myself on a collision course with an early death."

They sat side by side. The lamplight made the ivory of the keys warm and soft and she was warm and soft beside him.

"It should have been me that died, not him. He had everything to live for. He was the apple of our father's eye. He would have made a wonderful duke." Now why had he said that? Must be the aftereffects of the gin.

"Don't say that."

"It's true. I've wasted my life. Squandered it. Wastrel, that's what they call me and that's what I am. It doesn't matter how much I practice gambling, I'll never get any better because I'm cursed. Lady Luck heard my vow to be the worst duke's heir in the world, to play fast and loose with my father's cursed money. She heard it and she never lets me forget it. I'll never turn my vice into a virtue. I've never mastered anything in my life except being a disappointment."

"Do you truly feel that way?"

"It's the truth. I was taught that my only purpose in life was to be the duke's heir. That's all I learned. And then all I rejected. Just as you learned to perform and gave it up. You could have the world at your feet."

"I don't like being the center of attention. I'll never perform again in public."

"But why?"

She evaded his question by asking one of her own. "What are your reasons for forbidding Blanche to think of Lord Laxton as a suitor? I asked her why she fell in love with him and she chattered for an hour about how he quotes romantic poets to her and compares her eyes to sapphires and how he's the only person in the world who truly sees her. She fancies herself in love with him."

"I know." He played a bass chord that clashed with Viola's melody. "I have my reasons."

"If I am to be their confidante, I should know the potential dangers that they face. I've inferred that Laxton did something unforgivable?"

"I overheard Laxton and his friends slandering Blanche and Belinda. Laxton said that Blanche . . . well, he implied that she cornered him in a dark alcove and attacked him with amorous intent."

"Lady Blanche would never do anything improper. I'm sure of it. I've never met a lady more concerned with doing things note perfect and by the book."

"And he said that Belinda was caught in an amorous liaison behind a tree in Hyde Park."

She stopped playing. "About that . . ."

He leaned toward her. "Do you know something I don't?"

"I did hear Betsy accuse Belinda of going behind a tree with a baron. But she didn't allow him to kiss her. I talked to her about what was right and proper and she promised never to put herself in such a perilous position again."

West let out the breath he'd been holding. "That's all right, then. She didn't actually kiss anyone. Laxton made it sound far more scandalous."

"What right does he have to slander your sisters?"

"Believe me, he won't be spreading any more rumors. I took care of him."

"He'd better not or when I see him I'll employ the stealthy maneuver I described to you that I was planning to visit upon Lord Sprague."

He snorted. "I should very much like to witness

that, but you won't be seeing Laxton. He's decided to stay in the countryside. One of his estates is in dire need of repairs."

"What did you do?" She regarded him suspiciously.

"I only had a little chat with him."

"I thought you had some fresh bruises."

"Violence was justified in this instance. You should have heard him talking about Belinda. It made my stomach turn."

"Belinda is an impulsive young lady, and very infatuated with the idea of . . . well, the idea of the male sex in general. I do fear for her sometimes because she's so very fond of flattery and the right man with a silver tongue could lead her astray."

"Then you and their chaperones will have to be vigilant."

"Belinda should be allowed to be carefree and to make mistakes and she should also know that she has someone to talk to, someone to confide in, and she shouldn't be blinded, or blinkered, to the realities of this world. The innocent are led astray when they're so ignorant they don't even know what is happening. I would have your sisters make educated choices."

"I agree."

"Laxton's not worthy of Blanche. I'll do what I can to convince her of that."

"I chose Lord Flanders as a suitor for her because of their childhood friendship."

"I'm afraid she sees him more as an annoying little brother who used to plague her and call her names."

"He's only one year younger than she is. And I do believe that he has genuine affection for her. He's a decent, sober fellow."

"I'll see if I can influence her. Though she'll be very popular with her new dowry and her beauty. I don't fear for her chances. I only hope her heart can relinquish its attachment to the unworthy Lord Laxton. I'll try to hint, to make her see. If Lord Flanders wants Blanche to transfer her affections, he'll have to work at it. He can't just reach an agreement with you, her brother. He ought to court her."

"Are you of the same mind as my fiancée? He should bring her one hundred red roses, compose sonnets, sing under her window—all flashy and showy methods of proclaiming he's smitten. It's a lot of bollocks, pardon me. But it is."

"Courtship doesn't have to be all about roses and sonnets. My dear friends have been courted in unconventional ways, to very effective ends. Mr. Ford Wright built my friend Lady Beatrice bookshelves and taught her how to use a sledge-hammer to knock down walls."

"Very enterprising of him."

"Bookshelves are a surefire method to a bookish lady's heart. And Mina, the Duchess of Thorndon, was shot at by smugglers but Thorndon risked his life to protect her.

"I know about that. My friend Rafe, Thorndon's brother, was there as well. He took a bullet."

"I've observed the unconventional courtships of my friends. And I've read every one of Miss Daphne Villeneuve's Gothic romances. She's ever so inventive when it comes to courtship and marriage proposals."

"Ah-ha! Now we arrive at the truth of it. You've been reading romantic novels which we all know bear no relation to the real world. Those are fictional heroes doing preposterous things no real man would ever do. They give unrealistic expectations. Marriage is a contract between two people with mutual goals."

"And here I thought you were a hedonist."

"What's that got to do with anything?"

"Where's the passion? Where's the emotion in a contract of that sort?"

"So you're saying that you want my sisters to be shot at in the name of love and adventure?"

"That's not what I'm saying at all. I'm only saying that courtship doesn't have to be done in the usual ways. It can be a grand, romantic gesture, or it can be something more subtle. A small gesture that shows you're thinking of someone. That you listened to what they said, and you took the time to learn their preferences."

"It's nothing but moonbeams and fairy tales. Your ideals are unrealistic at best, potentially even harmful."

"Harmful? I don't see how insisting on a fulfilling life and finding true love could be harmful."

"It creates unrealistic expectations. It sets my sisters up for disappointment. My union with Miss Chandler will be based on realistic goals and expectations. We had a frank conversation today. Oh, and by the way, she doesn't read novels, her favorite food is beefsteak with butter sauce, and she likes to play card games on a rainy day. See? I followed your instructions and learned more about her. I confirmed that neither of us is in danger of losing our heads or our hearts. It's strictly business. And that's the way it should be."

"Do you really believe that?"

"It doesn't matter, does it? I'm marrying her, and that's final."

THE WAY HE was looking at her. As though he wanted to wrap his arms around her.

As though she could save him.

The catch in his voice. He was lying. Viola knew it with certainty. He thought he wanted a marriage of convenience, an absentee wife, but he didn't. Not really. There was too much pain in his voice when he spoke of his past. And too much warmth when he spoke of his sisters.

He wasn't unfeeling or heartless. He'd only lost the path. He needed love to find his way home again.

A dangerous line of thinking. He was probably gazing at her so intently because he was drunk.

Don't marry Miss Chandler. She's not right for you. You must learn to love and accept love in return if you'll ever have a chance for happiness.

She could taste the words. Hear them spoken aloud.

And what alternative would she offer? A certain music teacher with an opera singer for a mother and a disgraced father?

Don't be stupid.

Blanche had objected to Miss Chandler because

she wasn't a suitable duchess. But the marriage was all arranged and it would be financially beneficial. He had sisters, servants, tenants, relations, all relying on him to provide for them.

He must marry for money.

And she must stop this pointless meandering of mind.

It had been easier when he'd called her Miss Bedlam and treated her with careless disregard.

This sitting next to him on the piano bench, talking of their pasts, and their families, was perilous. And pleasurable.

Life's pleasures had been so simple before. A hot cup of tea pressed to her cheek to ease the aching tension in her jaw. A simple melody that suggested endless variations. Her father's praise when she played his music. The satisfaction of seeing her pupils progress, of awakening a love of music in a young mind.

And those pleasures had been enough. Should be enough.

Not everyone was made for love. For coupling.

Not everyone was lucky enough to find their soul mate.

But oh! When he looked at her like that.

She rumbled and vibrated, plucked and humming and filled with sound, overflowing with music, and she wanted him.

It wasn't pleasure in general she wanted to experience. It was *him*. She knew herself well enough to know that. She wasn't curious about lovemaking as an abstract principle. She'd rather go through her whole life alone than give herself to the wrong person. And he was the wrong person. He was someone who by his own avowal would never give his heart. He was engaged to be married to another woman.

And even if he weren't, there were oceans separating them. She was a penniless music teacher who'd never even made her debut.

He was a duke with a wicked reputation.

The wife he chose must be either extraordinarily wealthy, or extraordinarily perfect, polished, and well-connected.

But when he looked at her like that . . . she wanted him. She wanted to touch him. To feel his hands on her.

She pressed her fingers to the piano keys instead, knowing exactly how much pressure to exert to make a staccato note or a bare whisper of a grace note.

"It's late, Your Grace," she whispered.

He cleared his throat. "Yes."

"And we're alone."

"Yes." His voice a caress now. His gaze soft and seductive.

She could touch him if she wanted to. Feel him, warm and solid. His thigh nearly touching hers. She could kiss him.

His gaze smoldered, heating her skin. He wanted to kiss her, too. She knew it in the same way she'd known that he was lying about being satisfied with a loveless marriage of convenience.

He wanted to kiss her.

But he was promised to another.

She dropped her eyes to the piano keys. He shifted away from her.

"Oh, I nearly forgot to give you this." He pulled a small package from an inner pocket. "This is for your father. A special shell-type auricle hearing device made of thin metal and ivory by F.C. Rein and Sons. I was told it could aid his hearing."

"Thank you, Your Grace, that's very kind." And wholly unexpected.

"Good night, Viola." He left swiftly, there one moment, and gone the next, leaving her cold. Confused.

No confusion. Nothing unclear about the situation.

He was promised to another.

And she had promised her friends that she was in control of her heart.

She would attend the ball tomorrow and ensure that the Delamar sisters had a wonderful, safe, and carefree evening.

She'd ignore Westbury as best she could.

Though if she caught a glimpse of him dancing with Miss Chandler, it would only serve to drive the final nail into the coffin of this doomed, delusional desire.

Chapter Twelve

❧ 🌹 ❧

Westbury was impossible to ignore.

Everywhere Viola looked in Lady Pickering's elegant ballroom, there he was, the stern, understated black-and-white evening attire he wore serving to emphasize the impressive width of his shoulders and the long, lean lines of his body.

He was a fallen angel on the prowl, halo of golden hair and the devil glinting in his eyes.

He was wicked, he was trouble, and he was beautiful.

And betrothed.

Miss Vanessa Chandler was a bewitching creature. Always in graceful motion, set to bold music, her hair a deep auburn shade and her lips vermillion, brown eyes bright and gaze vivacious. Garbed in a gown of white satin with a silver net overlay that sparkled like starlight with every sinuous movement, she captured and held every gaze in the room.

Next to Miss Chandler's shimmering, silvery flute of a presence, Viola felt like an inelegant French horn that had been left out in the rain and had rusted until the only sound it produced was a waterlogged croak.

She fingered the worn ecru muslin of her gown which had seen its best days five years ago. She'd been so pleased with the new gold satin sash she'd purchased to tie around her waist, and the matching gold ribbon she'd threaded through her upswept ringlets. Now they seemed drab and pointless compared with the real silver netting adorning Miss Chandler's statuesque figure, and the astoundingly large diamonds glittering around her swan's neck.

Viola's neck was short, just like the rest of her, and circled by a simple strand of pearls, the only jewelry she possessed. Her stature was too small, and her curves too full, for the current fashion.

Miss Chandler laughed at something Westbury said and swatted his arm playfully with a carved ivory and silver fan.

Viola heard the murmurs of the crowd.

She's a beauty but so excessively American.

Westbury should have chosen a more suitable duchess . . . although I suppose his wickedness frightened most respectable ladies away and Miss Chandler's fortune was the deciding factor.

They were something out of a fairy tale, the most arrestingly attractive couple London had ever beheld, both shocking and scandalous in their own ways.

She forced herself to stare at them even though it was like rubbing salt into a wound.

Stare at them, burn the image into your mind, like looking at the sun. They are beautiful. Made for each other. He fair, she dark. He titled, she wealthy beyond belief. They are two halves of a whole.

Her jealousy was irrational and pitiful and must be stamped out ruthlessly like a fire in a dry forest on a hot summer's day. She wasn't here to moon over Westbury, she was here for his sisters.

Their official chaperone tonight was one of their elderly spinster aunts, Miss Miriam Delamar, a soft-edged woman who fluttered her bejeweled fingers nervously when she spoke—which was constantly. She'd kept up a steady stream of commentary since they'd arrived, barely pausing to breathe. At least she'd accepted Viola's presence as companion to the Delamar sisters with approval.

"I'm happy to have the help, Miss Beaton," she confided as she and Viola stood against the wall, watching the young ladies dance. "Miss Belinda has such high spirits. I fear she's less than proper at times. Just look at her playing the coquette. Has she slipped the bodice of her gown lower when I wasn't looking? Good gracious! She's in danger of showing more than she ought. And isn't her partner enjoying the sight. If his neck cranes any lower, he'll topple over and take them both to the floor! At last, the dance is ending. I must go and take Belinda to the retiring room and adjust her costume."

Aunt Miriam bustled off and Bernadette joined Viola at the wall.

"Have you enjoyed the dancing?" Viola asked her.

"Not particularly. Mr. Lawson, whom West thinks I ought to marry, is a dullard. He doesn't even know the difference between the species in the order of *Hymenoptera*."

"Er, I'm not sure that's common knowledge."

"The major differences between bees and wasps are obvious to anyone. I'm sure you would be able to tell them apart after I made an explanation, but he was incapable of such discernment. We have no interests in common. His conversation consisted of musings about the outcome of horse races and whether his new boots would be ready from the bootmaker before a planned outing to the countryside. He actually described his boots for a full five minutes. He was as bad as Belinda on the topic of footgear. Perhaps *she* should marry him and they could discuss the details of their apparel for hours on end."

Viola smiled. "Have I told you that you look lovely this evening? I like your beetle brooch." Only Bernadette would wear a lacquered metallic-green beetle as a brooch.

"Thank you. I tried to give this one to Miss Chandler but she didn't want it. I can't think why."

"Miss Chandler looks to be having a marvelous time tonight, and your sisters appear to be enjoying themselves. Belinda's not lacking for suitors. And neither is Blanche." Lady Blanche was serene and elegant in a white silk gown and a delicate diamond tiara. Now that word of her replenished dowry was out, and Laxton was nowhere to be found, the suitors were flocking.

"Which one of Lady Blanche's suitors is Lord Flanders?" Viola asked, eyeing the group of gentlemen surrounding Blanche.

"The one hanging back wearing spectacles and casting lovelorn looks at her."

Lord Flanders wasn't conventionally handsome. He had the awkward hunching posture of a man who was overtall and overlarge, but there was something kindly and humble in his address. He was gazing at Blanche with such awestruck devotion that Viola knew instantly that the poor fellow was hopelessly in love with her.

Viola recognized the look of doomed devotion. Despite his towering height and substantial presence, he'd been edged aside by the dandies flirting with Blanche.

"Does Blanche know that he's in love with her?" Viola asked Bernadette.

"She hasn't an inkling. She thinks he's supremely annoying because he was always teasing her, and playing silly pranks, but it was only because he was so smitten by her. I can't think why she doesn't marry him. He's a very sensible fellow. Interested in the sciences. We had a delightful conversation once about advancements in the study of electricity."

"Has he a fortune?"

"Nothing out of the ordinary."

"She'll have her pick of gentlemen now. Poor Flanders has been pushed aside." Another set was forming, and Blanche took the arm of a tall, good-looking young buck with dark hair and a mischievous grin.

Bernadette edged behind Viola.

"You know it won't do to hide behind me," Viola said with a laugh. "I'm much shorter than you are."

Bernadette sighed heavily. "I know. I'm promised to Lord Darby for this dance. I was rather hoping he'd developed a sudden case of dysentery."

"Bernadette," Viola said sternly. "You didn't slip anything into Lord Darby's punch, did you?"

"While I certainly could list multiple ways of incapacitating potential dance partners, I promised you that I'd be on my best behavior and therefore," she sighed tragically, "I will dance."

"Here's Lord Darby now, I presume."

Viola smiled at the look of misery on Bernadette's face as she was led away by the eager Lord Darby. Bernadette wasn't ready for romance. Perhaps she never would be. Several members of Viola's club for ladies had chosen solitary lives of scholarship.

Miss Chandler had a cluster of gentlemen about her who didn't seem in the least bit deterred by her engagement to Westbury. They swarmed like bees around her honeyed smiles, perhaps wanting her all the more now that she was off the market.

She wasn't off the market yet. Not until the wedding happened. And weddings were sometimes canceled. Although this one must go on, because Westbury had already been spending the marriage settlement and the young ladies must have their dowries.

Miss Chandler thrived on being the center of attention. She pouted if any of the gentlemen ceased their attentions for even one moment. She didn't seem to mind that Westbury was nowhere in sight.

Where was he?

"You're not dancing, Miss Beaton?" a low voice asked at her elbow.

Viola whirled around to find the duke had snuck up on her while her attention was trained on Miss Chandler. She hoped he hadn't noticed how intently she was observing his fiancée. "Of course I'm not dancing, Your Grace. You didn't hire me to dance. You hired me to watch over your sisters."

"You want to dance, though," he observed, ducking his head a little to meet her gaze.

"I don't."

"You lie. Your foot is tapping in time to the music."

She glanced down. "Involuntarily. I'm a musician. I keep time with music."

"I think you want to be on the dance floor joining in the fun. Wallflower doesn't suit you. You're far too merry and bright."

"You make me sound like the description of a yuletide celebration."

"Precisely. You're a flickering, dancing flame. A hot mug of spiced cider with brandy." His gaze intensified. "A kiss under the mistletoe."

A heated flush crept up her neck. Did he think about kissing when he looked at her? Because that's really all she ever thought about when she stood this close to him.

Close enough to see the faint shadowing of whiskers along his strong jawline. Smell the scent of his musky cologne. Feel the charged atmosphere that crackled around him, pulling her in, making her long to touch him.

Did he feel it, too?

"And you're . . ." she whispered, searching her duke-addled mind for a way to put a swift end to this inappropriate intimacy. "You're soused on brandy. You must have mistaken me for your fiancée. The woman who should be receiving your compliments."

"Ah." He cleared his throat. "I think she's receiving enough compliments at the moment."

They watched as Miss Chandler flirted simultaneously with five different gentlemen who hung on her every word, devouring her with their eyes.

"And I have a feeling that you haven't received nearly enough in your lifetime," he added.

"I don't want compliments. Or dance partners."

"Why not? You have strong opinions about love and courtship and living a fulfilled life and yet here you are, watching from the wings. It's natural to want more for yourself, Viola. You *should* want more."

"I'm perfectly content with my lot in life, Your Grace," she said, a little stiffly. "I won't let spinsterhood relegate me to an empty life. I find fulfilment in caring for my father, nurturing his career, and those of my friends. Imparting the joy of music to others through my teaching."

"You're about to be engaged for a dance."

"Pardon?"

"There's a young gentleman with ginger-colored hair approaching. He's not bad looking, either. He's been staring at you for the last hour and has finally gathered the courage to make his move."

Viola searched the room, finding the gentleman in question who did appear to be heading her way. He looked familiar for some reason, though she couldn't quite place him. "He must have me confused with someone else."

"I don't think so."

"Oh dear."

"Now then," the duke said. "After you dance with him, you'll dance with me. That should set tongues wagging enough to ensure you're in demand the rest of the evening. Where's your dance card?"

"I don't have a dance card and I'm not stepping out with anyone. I must keep an eye on your sisters."

"They have Aunt Miriam to watch over them. They're all dancing now. Even Betsy."

Betsy wasn't a very graceful dancer but every time she stumbled or stepped on her partner's toes she broke out into an impish grin, which made Viola wonder if perhaps she was feigning ineptitude on purpose to give her partners grief.

"Acknowledge that you could have dance partners if you wanted them," Westbury said.

"I won't. Because it's not true."

"Look around us, it's not only Ginger Hair who's noticed you. You've received more than your share of admiring glances because you're bonny, Viola."

"And poor, with a disgraced father, and well past my youth. They're all staring at you. The wild, wicked Duke of Westbury become quite domesticated and conventional."

"I told you I would reform only enough to see

my sisters settled. I'll never be domesticated or conventional. And I maintain they're staring at you." His gaze swept her face and moved down her body. "And I don't blame them one bit. I've never seen you in anything but gray serviceable gowns with your hair scraped back and hidden under those damnable caps. You should always have soft curls framing your face and a gown that shows your figure to advantage."

And there he went again, making her heart-strings quiver and ping. "What advantage, Your Grace?" she asked shakily. "I'm far too short and too round for current fashion."

"One of these days you're going to accept a compliment, Viola. You don't like to be the center of attention. Whereas my fiancée thrives upon it."

Miss Chandler glanced their way, narrowing her eyes and making a beckoning gesture with her chin.

"It appears I'm being summoned."

"Then off you go, Your Grace."

The duke left and the ginger-haired gentleman approached. He made a bow. "Are you, by chance, Miss Viola Beaton?"

"I am."

"Pardon my rudeness in introducing myself, but I'm Miss Ardella Finchley's brother and she's described you to me so many times that I feel as though I know you. I'm John. John Finchley."

"How lovely to meet you. Della speaks of you often. You were studying abroad?"

"Indeed. I've only recently returned. I was studying painting. I'm a great disappointment to my father, having no aptitude for chemistry whatsoever. Would you care to dance with me, Miss Beaton?"

Even though she'd said she wouldn't dance, her encounter with the duke had melted her resolve to remain hidden this evening, watching the revelry instead of joining in. Perhaps she could permit herself one dance with a friend's brother.

And then what . . . a waltz with Westbury? Oh no you don't!

"I'd be delighted," she said with a smile. "You can tell me about your travels. Della is always so proud of your accomplishments. She says you'll be a famous painter."

They lined up with the other couples for the quadrille. They would only meet at intervals, skipping around one another, joining hands for a moment, or briefly promenading.

Viola would be able to observe the young ladies as she danced.

She and the duke met for a promenade. He took her left hand and clasped his right around her waist.

"You see?" he whispered with a grin. "You're in demand."

"Mr. Finchley is the brother of a dear friend of mine. He only asked me out of courtesy."

"Then why is he blushing the same color as his hair whenever you speak to you?"

"You like to think that you're right about everything but you're not. He's only being kind."

The steps of the dance led her away from the

duke and back to John Finchley. He wasn't un-
attractive, and he did have a very ready smile,
but when their hands touched she felt none of
the sparks and confusion she felt when the duke
merely glanced her way.

"I haven't seen you at a ball before, Miss Beaton."

"I'm here as companion to the Duke of Westbury's sisters."

"I tried to convince Della to come tonight but
she was too busy with her chemical experiments.
I do hope the house is still standing when I return
home."

Viola laughed. "I remember the time she came
to one of our book club meetings with singed eyebrows."

Mr. Finchley chuckled and Viola moved on to
another partner.

Her gaze kept finding the duke. And every
time she looked at him, he was staring at her.

Why, oh why, couldn't she stop herself from
having these inappropriate feelings?

Dancing was a mating ritual, as the duke had
observed. And mating was on her mind.

She had a bodily reaction when she saw him
that she couldn't control. He was so wholly bad
and dangerous. So virile. She imagined that the
way she felt about him was similar to the way
he felt about gambling. A dangerous occupation,
fraught with an illicit thrill, the possibility of last-
ing harm, a compulsion.

It wasn't love; it was compulsion.

She craved him like a gambler craved the rattle
of dice. Like a drunkard craved strong spirits.

This craving was bad for her heart, her mind. It was bad. Simply bad. And every time she resolved never to think about him again it never worked.

"Are you having fun?" Westbury asked when they were paired again.

"I'll admit that you were right. I do like dancing," she said, a little breathlessly, as they met and his hands clasped hers.

"You see?" He grinned. "It's not so difficult to admit that I'm right."

His smile was dazzlingly intimate. She couldn't remember ever seeing him smile at her before. "You should smile more often, Your Grace."

"I don't make a habit of it, Miss Beaton. But perhaps you bring it out in me. You're always smiling. It takes a concerted effort not to join in."

"What is life without joy?"

"Dry toast with no butter?"

Another intimate exchange of smiles. This could begin to be a habit. Giving smiles and having them returned by handsome dukes.

Handsome dukes who were engaged to other ladies.

The dance separated them and brought her back to Mr. Finchley. The set ended and he made his bows and sought his next partner.

Would Westbury claim the next dance, as he'd promised? What if it were a waltz—she'd be held in his arms, just the two of them . . . floating on the music of violins, exchanging smiles and—

"Miss Beaton, is it?"

It was Miss Chandler standing before her,

looking Viola up and down with an unsubtle appraisal.

"Yes. Are you having a good time, Miss Chandler?"

"I do love balls." She flicked her skirts away from silver slippers that sparkled with diamonds. "My, I'm fatigued from dancing so much." She fanned herself, glancing over as Westbury brought Blanche a glass of punch. "Westbury's monstrously handsome, isn't he?"

"He's pleasing enough," Viola said cautiously.

"It's convenient that the highest title in the room goes with the most handsome face in the room. And he's all mine. See how Lady Dexter is glaring. She hates my triumph. He's doing a wonderful job of pretending to be in love with me. I have to remember to reciprocate." She caught Westbury's eye and wriggled her fingers at him.

"You're only pretending to be in love with him?"

"I'm not going to fall in love with my husband. Don't be silly." She laughed. "You're so quaint. I heard that you're living in the dower house." All laughter left her eyes. "Should I be jealous?"

Viola nearly took a step back. The intensity of her stare caught her off guard.

"Er, of course not."

Miss Chandler giggled. "Oh, I know, I know. I'm only joking." She tapped Viola on the shoulder with her fan. "You're penniless. Though you are pretty. Or you could be, if you had a new gown and tried a different way of dressing your hair."

"There's no need for that. I'm not here to find a match."

"Oh, aren't you? I could have sworn I saw you dancing. Well, never mind. I'm sure you'll do your duty and restrict yourself to watching the girls from now on."

Viola gave her a tight smile. "Of course."

"Well, I'm off then. The next dance is the waltz and I'm promised to Westbury. I'm glad we had this little chat, my dear." She floated away in a cloud of silver spangles and expensive floral perfume that lingered after she left.

Putting me in my place, thought Viola.

Probably only what she deserved. Her mind had run away from her again, imagining impossible and forbidden things.

Best to stay against the wall for the rest of the evening.

HIS FIANCÉE DANCED well but with the same self-awareness she applied to every movement, doing it not for the pleasure of it, but to be admired. She posed and smiled up at him, and then darted glances around to see who was watching, who was envious. She couldn't simply be there in his arms; she was too aware of how dancing with him made her the belle of the ball. He was a player in the pantomime she was performing for the benefit of her rival, Lady Dexter.

"Say something scandalous and improper loud enough for everyone to hear," she whispered in his ear.

He obliged, telling her about a few of the things she'd learn on their wedding night.

She tossed her head, projecting her tinkling

laugh to the far corners of the room. "You wicked duke. You say the most outrageous things."

Lady Dexter watched them with ill-disguised envy, tossing her chestnut curls and whispering something to a friend behind her fan.

"Honestly, if she stares any harder her eyes will go crossed. Oh, I'm enjoying this. You're performing your role splendidly."

"It's not difficult to pretend I'm a rake and a rogue."

"Ah, but if you act scandalous with your fiancée, everyone will applaud us for it. They'll say we're in love and isn't it delightful."

He wouldn't call this evening delightful. He hated society affairs. Too many snobbish noblemen and ladies passing judgment on him, waiting for him to do something wicked and scandalous.

Sorry, ladies and gents. You'll have to look elsewhere for your scandal tonight. I'm on a tight leash.

Only until after the wedding.

His sisters seemed to be enjoying themselves, however, and that was the whole point. Blanche had danced every dance, and Belinda was much in demand. Bernadette had grimaced through the bare minimum of dances and was now happily huddled with her wallflower friends by the wall.

Betsy danced with her male friends if one could call it dancing. It was something far less graceful than that. She galloped, and galumphed, but judging by the smile on her face and her bright eyes she was having a grand time stomping on her friends' toes and watching them manfully pretend it didn't hurt.

Guilt twinged at his heart. He shouldn't have tried to take this away from them. Viola had been right about allowing them to be young and light-hearted.

And she should do the same.

She'd danced once with the ginger-haired man and was back with his aunt on the edge of the dance floor.

Miss Chandler followed the drift of his gaze. "I saw you chatting with your music teacher, or governess, or whatever she is. Very kind of you."

He made a noncommittal noise.

"I spoke to her just now. I'm not sure if she understands her place."

"What do you mean?"

"She was dancing, when she should be observing your sisters."

"I encouraged her to dance. She should be allowed to have some pleasure in the evening."

"She's quite old, of course, but still pretty. I suppose she could have suitors if she had a more modish gown and styled her hair differently."

West liked Viola's simple gown and gold sash. She made the other women look overdone. And she was only a few years older than Blanche. He liked the small laugh lines around her eyes. She was always smiling, always ready to laugh.

"I think I'll make her one of my charity projects after the wedding," Miss Chandler announced. "I'll take her shopping and teach her how to dress to attract male attention."

West liked Viola exactly the way she was. "She said she didn't want courtship or marriage."

"She's lying. Spinsters will say that until a suitor comes along and then they light up like fireworks."

"If she marries then she can't be my music instructor anymore." And the house would be colder without her.

"You'll find another."

Miss Chandler's mother gave them a proud smile and turned back to the group of ladies she stood with, discussing wedding details, no doubt. Mr. Chandler was nowhere to be seen.

"Where's your father gone off to?" West asked.

"He hates balls. He'll be in the billiards room smoking cigars and making new business associates."

West wished to hell he could join him.

The dance was halfway through when a disturbance at the entrance to the ballroom caught West's eye.

A towering giant of a man wearing oddly mismatched evening attire strode into the room trailed by two gesticulating footmen who were obviously attempting to escort him back out. He swatted them off like flies.

"I'm here to speak with Miss Vanessa Chandler and I won't leave until I do," the man called loudly in a harsh American accent.

West spun Miss Chandler around to face the man. "I do believe one of your countrymen is here to see you. Perhaps it's your brother, or—?"

The roses drained from her cheeks. "Ian. But it can't be! He's in Canada milling lumber."

"Ah. I gather this is the man who broke your heart. He's very much here. And he's headed our way."

The footmen were no match for the determined American. He easily evaded their entreaties and attempts to steer him back to the entrance, and stomped across the floor, spreading scandalized matrons, fluttering young misses, and outraged gentlemen as he made his way to West and Miss Chandler.

"Ian," Miss Chandler said urgently. "What are you doing here? You can't be here."

"It's you who don't belong here, Vanessa. I came as soon as I heard you'd gone to London. And what do I hear when my ship docks? You're marrying some priggish English duke? You can't marry him! You're promised to me."

"The devil?" West said. "Is this true?"

Ian was even taller and broader about the shoulders than West, and he had arms as thick as tree trunks and a thick black beard. He was a big, handsome brute of a man, even West could see that.

"We were promised, but then you left me," Miss Chandler said. "You ran off with that woman. I didn't hear from you for months."

"That woman was my aunt. I didn't have time to explain everything. I wrote you letters but you must have already left Boston. I've been fighting a forest fire that raged for weeks. We lost so many lives. My father included."

"Oh, Ian. I'm so sorry."

The entire ballroom was transfixed. Mrs. Chandler finally unfroze and surged toward them. "Mr. Murphy, you must leave at once!"

"I said I'm not leaving without Vanessa. She can't marry this fop of a duke."

"My title is Your Grace," said West, giving him a dangerous look.

"Oh, you're all dainty and graceful, are you? All golden-haired and la-di-da I'm as blue-blooded as they come."

Americans.

There were outraged gasps around them.

"I'm your one true love, Vanessa, and you know it," Mr. Murphy said wildly.

"Pummel him, Westbury," came a shout from the onlookers.

"Demand satisfaction!"

"Call him out, Westbury!" A grumbling groundswell of malcontent.

West laughed mirthlessly. "Take her and be gone, man."

Mr. Murphy raised his fists. "Damn you, Duke. I'll take her but I'll fight you first."

West assumed a boxer's stance. If the man wanted a fight, he'd get one.

"Please, Ian," pleaded Miss Chandler. "May we speak later in private? You're causing a dreadful scandal."

Which Lady Dexter was watching with obvious delight.

Mrs. Chandler searched the crowd frantically for her husband, who was presumably still enjoying his port and cigars.

"You're going to have my sons, Vanessa," Mr. Murphy said loudly. "And we're going to build the biggest house in Boston. I inherited everything. I have enough money now to marry you. That's what I was waiting for."

The footmen closed in, five of them. "All right, all right. I'm leaving." He turned his anguished face to Vanessa. "Come with me." He held out his hand.

West saw the emotions warring on Miss Chandler's lovely face. One mocking word from Lady Dexter and she'd toss her former love out the door. But Mr. Murphy just kept talking softly to her, telling her about the house they'd have, the children they'd raise, and she melted into his arms. "Yes, Ian, oh yes. I'm yours. I've always been yours."

The American let out a loud whoop, grabbed Miss Chandler's hand, and rushed her out of the room.

Matrons gaped. Gentlemen shouted.

Mrs. Chandler swooned into the arms of a footman who half carried her toward the door, following her wayward daughter.

True love had won the day. Miss Beaton would be so pleased. West found her in the crowd. She was standing stock-still, her face rigid with shock.

All he'd wanted was to make things right. Make his sisters so wealthy that they would have their choice of eager suitors.

And he'd managed to cause an even bigger scandal.

He should have just stayed at The Devil's

Staircase. He didn't belong in ballrooms. Trouble found him because he was wicked. Even with good intentions he'd found a way to ruin everything. He could almost hear his father's voice in his head, gloating over this latest transgression.

"Go after them, Westbury! This isn't to be borne!" Lord Pickering, their host, was at his elbow. "I'll be your second."

West held up his hands. "Ladies and gentlemen, there will be no duel this evening. I don't fancy risking my neck over an American. That lumberman is welcome to her. And now, if you'll excuse me, I have an urgent assignation with a bottle of gin."

He stalked from the room, turning his back on good intentions, and sympathetic green eyes. Wanting only to be gone.

Chapter Thirteen

*E*VERYONE STOOD IN stunned silence. Had something like that really happened in Lady Pickering's ballroom? With three hundred candles glowing in shimmering crystal chandeliers, an entire army of liveried footmen in attendance, and a lavish arrangement of pink confectionary sweets arranged in the shape of a heart?

Yes. It had happened. And it had happened to Westbury.

Strange bells began pealing in Viola's mind.

He's no longer engaged! her heart sang along with the bells.

Silence, foolish heart. This was no cause for celebration. Think of Blanche and her sisters.

She must collect them and leave at once. People were beginning to stir from their shocked trances, and the whispers were growing to a roar.

How could Westbury be engaged to such a common American creature? Shameful!

Wicked Westbury will always cause a scandal.

He should have demanded satisfaction, if not for himself, for King and Country!

The first grand occasion of the Season is ruined. Utterly ruined!

"We must collect the ladies," she whispered urgently to Aunt Miriam, who still stood with her mouth hanging open.

"Oh yes, of course we must. Oh good gracious. I can't believe this is happening. What a to-do, what a to-do."

"Collect yourself, Miss Miriam." She used her schoolmarm voice; the calm, efficient tones she employed when her father was being difficult. "Follow me."

She made a beeline for Blanche, looking neither to the right, nor to the left, attempting to ignore the whispers. This could only harm the ladies' prospects. She gathered the still-stunned Blanche and Belinda, and beckoned to Bernadette, who came running, followed closely by Betsy, who galloped more than ran.

"Now *that* gave them something to gawk at," Betsy whispered. "Wish I'd hit that Miss Vanessa Chandler with my cricket ball when I had the chance. How dare she jilt our brother?"

"Hush, Betsy. Now's not the time." Viola took Blanche's arm. "Ladies, we leave at once."

The ladies, to their credit, held their heads high and walked with elegance and grace through the crowd, which parted before them. Well, Betsy wasn't particularly elegant or graceful, but the tilt of her chin and the dauntless look in her eye said she didn't give one fig what anyone thought of her, or her brother.

When they were safely out of the house, down the marble stairs, and back to the carriage, Viola breathed a small sigh of relief.

"Oh dear," Aunt Miriam said, fluttering her hands. "What's to be done? What can we do? Such a scandal. And at the very first ball of the Season. And your dowries. This is a disaster."

Viola placed her hands on her shoulders. "Miss Miriam, please escort the young ladies back to the house."

"Oh yes. That's what I must do."

"West's carriage is still here," Betsy pointed out. They'd been too large of a party and had split themselves into several conveyances.

"He'll be off on foot to a tavern, or gaming hell, by now," said Bernadette glumly. "Sometimes I do believe I might take up strong drink myself."

"I don't think so," Belinda said. "I watched him through the windows as he left and I think he turned down the garden path. Shouldn't wonder if he's out there having a good cry. I certainly would be weeping if I'd been jilted in such a public manner by an *American*. She may have exquisite taste in clothing, but her judgment in men is deplorable."

Blanche was silent, which worried Viola more than if she'd been wailing. "Are you all right, Lady Blanche?"

"Nothing will ever be right again." Her face was pale and anguished in the moonlight. "We've been publicly humiliated. Lord Laxton will surely have nothing to do with me when he hears the story."

Viola had tried to reason with her earlier, telling her as much as she could about Laxton's slanderous comments but apparently Blanche hadn't been dissuaded.

"Are we going to be ostracized?" Belinda asked. "Is our Season over before it even began?" Tears gathered in her eyes.

A large man rushed down the steps and approached them. Viola immediately recognized the ungainly Lord Flanders.

"Lady Blanche, might I be of assistance in any way?" he asked, twisting his large hands together.

Blanche stared at a point to the left of his face. "It's good of you, Lord Flanders, but we're just leaving."

"Mightn't I see you safely home now that the duke has . . . left precipitously?"

Viola gave him a warm smile. "We're not certain where His Grace has gone. Perhaps you might search for him and see that he arrives safely home this evening?"

Lord Flanders made a bow. "It would be my great honor to be of any assistance. Do you have a suggestion for where I might begin my search?"

"He may be in Lady Pickering's garden," said Bernadette. "But if you don't find him there he's likely gone to number 20 Ryder Street, colloquially known as The Devil's Staircase, and if he's there, I'm afraid you won't have an easy time extracting him."

"You'd better hope he hasn't been into the gin," said Betsy. "He might pick a fight with you then."

"Heavens," said Lord Flanders, his eyes widening. "I'm afraid I'm not much of a fighter."

"Oh, this is pointless," said Blanche impatiently. "Miss Beaton, you must go and fetch our brother. You're the only one he listens to these days. You have a great deal of influence over him. Take West's carriage and his footmen if he's not in the gardens. Lord Flanders, Bernadette and I will travel home in your equipage while the twins return with Aunt Miriam."

Lord Flanders beamed. "It would be my great honor and pleasure."

"I, er," said Viola. "I'm not certain that I have as much influence as you think I—"

"It's all settled, Miss Beaton," said Blanche, her face calm and resigned. "You must convince our brother to come home and cause no further scandal tonight. I simply couldn't bear it."

"Yes, please do find my nephew and make him come home," urged Aunt Miriam. "My nerves can't stand any more bad news this evening."

Blanche took Lord Flanders's proffered arm and the ladies set off, leaving Viola to face the daunting prospect of finding a jilted duke and convincing him to steer clear of further scandal.

She'd try the garden first.

It was a warm midspring evening with a soft yellow moon hanging gently in the sky. The air was scented with roses. Candles hung in globes from the trees, illuminating the white stone footpath that took her deeper into the garden.

The ball had resumed and she could see couples dancing and laughing through the windows.

If this were a setting in a novel it would be quite romantic, she reflected. The wallflower walking down the garden path for a moonlit assignation

with a handsome duke, her heart beating a staccato rhythm.

This had nothing to do with romance. She had
a duty to perform. That was all.

"Your Grace," she called softly. "Westbury."

A gruff, groaning sound turned her head. She
would recognize those broad shoulders anywhere. He was seated on a white marble bench,
golden head bent, and shoulders shaking.

Perhaps Belinda had been right. He might feel
the shame of the jilting, or the loss of the marriage settlement and the reinstatement of financial ruin, so keenly that he was weeping.

He wouldn't want her to see him crying. She
hovered nearby, trying to decide the best course
of action. She must comfort him. It really wasn't
his fault, after all.

"Your Grace." She touched his shoulder. "It's
me, Miss Beaton."

His shoulders heaved and he emitted a stran-
gled noise somewhere in between a snort and a
grunt.

Poor duke. He was overcome by emotion.
Should she . . . hug him? If he were one of her
friends she would gather him into her embrace
and offer her bosom for comfort.

Absolutely not.

No offering of bosoms. If promenading with
him during a quadrille had filled her head with
impossible longings, she most certainly couldn't
throw her arms around him.

"Your Grace." She patted his shoulder. "I'm
here to fetch you home."

He raised his head, but instead of tears shining in the moonlight, he broke into a mischievous grin. "D-did you see that?" he asked, chortling loudly. He slapped his knee. "'Oh, you're all dainty and graceful are you?'" He laughed even harder, wiping at his eyes with his sleeve.

"Are you *laughing*, Your Grace?"

"I'm experiencing euphoric relief. I'm so very happy that I don't have to marry that woman or spend any more time with her ambitious mama."

"Well! This is no laughing matter," Viola said in her clipped schoolmarm tones. "Let's get you home. Your sisters have already left with Aunt Miriam and Lord Flanders as escort."

"You simply can't invent a moment like that. It was something out of a French farce."

"You're clearly hysterical."

"I'm free again." He jumped up from the bench, blue eyes glittering in the moonlight. "Didn't I engage you for a dance, Miss Beaton?" He held out his hand. "Please do me the honor."

"What, now? Your mind's addled. I'm not going to dance with you out here in the garden while the assembled arbiters of propriety are dissecting the scandal of the Season. A Season which had only just begun, let me remind you."

"If you won't dance with me, come with me to The Devil's Staircase. I don't feel like going home. Let's live a little. We're young, beautiful, and free as birds."

Those seriously inappropriate bells began ringing in her mind again. *He thinks I'm beautiful*, they rang out.

"You've gone mad," she said testily. "I most certainly will not accompany you to that den of iniquity. I've been there briefly, with a friend, and it was decadent and depraved, stuffed with red velvet chaises, men with insolent eyes, and buxom barmaids."

He chuckled. "That's a first-rate description. Although the clientele has become very nearly respectable since my friend Jax Smith assumed ownership and renovated the place."

"I'm not going to watch you throw away more of your fortune."

He grasped her hand. "Maybe you're my good luck charm."

She pulled her hand away. "I'm not going with you because I'm going home to see how your sisters are faring. This was quite a blow to their prospects, as you know. Please endeavor to think of them."

The grin fell from his lips. "You're right. Forgive me. It was all just so unbelievable, and I was so very relieved to be free of any obligation to Miss Chandler. We should go home and be with my sisters."

He tucked her gloved hand into the crook of his arm and led her back through the scented gardens.

Strolling through moonlit gardens with him wasn't romantic in the slightest. Not given the circumstances. And climbing into a dark carriage with him, alone, was all part of her employment . . . hold just a moment. She was climbing into a dark carriage with him.

They would be *alone*.

Oh no. She hadn't thought this all the way through. She squared her shoulders. No matter. She was only doing her duty. Being alone with Westbury as his sisters' companion, and emissary, was all very respectable and aboveboard.

It was just as she'd said to her friends. It was all tidy and manageable. She needn't even look at him. She'd open the curtains and stare out the window at the passing streets.

It was a brief journey.

The coach loomed ahead. A footman opened the door. Viola was about to use the step when the duke gripped her by the waist. "Up you go." He hoisted her into the carriage and she landed with a startled thump on the cushions.

She was still recovering from the shock of his large hands around her waist when he climbed in and sat beside her.

"You're light as a feather," he remarked. "Are you eating enough? We'll have to raid Cook's larder tonight. You should eat more pastry."

"I eat enough for sustenance." And they hadn't exactly had the money for rich repasts.

"Always so cautious. Do you ever loosen up and say something unguarded?"

"Only when provoked beyond reason."

"Ah, like that day in the study. When you quit your employment in a fit of rage. But you never did manage to insult me properly."

"I'm certain that the crowd in that ballroom has come up with a few new epithets."

"I don't care about them. I want to hear Miss

Viola Beaton's litany of libel. Go on then. You found me laughing in the gardens when my poor sisters lost their dowries yet again. I'm the most insensitive, arrogant, downright dastardly duke in the world. There." He settled back in his seat and flung his legs out, crossing them at the ankle. "I've begun your list for you. It's your turn."

Her mind went blank, as it always did when she was in close proximity with him. All she could think was that his hands had been so very large and strong when he lifted her into the carriage. And his legs were so long, filling the length of the carriage.

He tugged at his cravat, loosening it and exposing his throat. Instead of looking out the window, she couldn't stop staring at that small triangle of exposed duke. Her fingers wanted to explore. Did he have hair upon his chest? She couldn't quite tell. She'd have to open his shirt more to find out.

He sprawled on the seat beside her, one hand casually placed next to her thigh. His other hand was braced against the carriage door. "Go on then. Let me have it. I'm ready."

Let him have *what* exactly? Her hands exploring . . . their lips meeting . . .

Oh, Viola. You stupid, stupid thing. He's talking about insults, not kisses.

"I shan't insult you, Your Grace," she said primly, "because I know that you've suffered a grave financial loss this evening. Which is a loss for your sisters, as well."

"I'll say. A truly staggering settlement all gone in the blink of an eye. Not all of it. The marriage contract was very clear. If she begged off, I kept every penny spent thus far, even the debts her father already settled. Mr. Chandler saw me as the one at risk for flight, not his daughter."

"That's something, then."

"Yes, but I'll still have to find another heiress. And they don't grow on trees."

"And not just any heiress. This time you'll have to reform enough to find the perfect respectable duchess."

He groaned. "You sound like Great-Aunt Hermione. Next you'll be telling me to propose to Lady Winifred Woolfrey."

"If you truly object to that lady, I'll ask your sisters to make up a list of other candidates."

"You'd do that for me?"

"For your sisters."

"Right. Of course. For my sisters. What were their reactions, pray tell?"

"Blanche and Belinda were devastated, of course. Their suitors melted away like winter frost in spring. All except for Lord Flanders."

"Good old Flanders. He hasn't a large fortune but I don't think he'd mind if Blanche were poor as a church mouse. I think he genuinely cares for her."

"I think so, too. It's such a pity that she doesn't return his affection."

"And the other girls?"

"Bernadette said that she might consider taking up strong drink. And Betsy wished she'd hit Miss Chandler with her cricket ball when she had a chance."

Westbury snorted. "They're such dear, clever things. I hope society won't vent any of its displeasure on them. This is all on my shoulders. I should have researched the Chandler family more carefully before entering into a business arrangement with them."

"It's not your fault that Miss Chandler had a secret prior attachment."

"Actually, she told me during our afternoon tea that she'd had her heart broken. It made me feel sympathetic toward her. I don't think she had any idea that Mr. Murphy still meant to seek her hand in marriage. Theirs was not a sanctioned match because of the difference in their social positions." He shrugged. "I'm happy for her, in a way."

"That's magnanimous of you."

"It's a victory for true love, with a capital *L*. Aren't you thrilled, Miss Beaton?"

She remembered her first reaction. The bells chiming in her mind. "I'm sorry that it came at your expense. And that of your sisters. I'm no stranger to disappointed dreams, Your Grace. I know how much they sting."

"Have you been disappointed in love?" he asked, his gaze intent on her face in the low light of the carriage lamps.

"Not in love . . . in life."

She'd never meant to be sidelined, to feel like a supporting character instead of the star of her own life. It had just happened.

"You want more than being your father's caretaker, and music instructor to a duke's sisters."

"As I've said before, there was a time when I wanted a family of my own, yes." She spoke carefully, unwilling to betray the very real pain and longing behind her simple words. "But I resolved never to marry without love. And my chance for that is past now," she said brightly. "I'm quite content with my life. I'm happy to be of assistance."

"With your talent you could be playing the pianoforte onstage. Why not perform at the musicale I'm hosting? It may inspire a clamoring throng of suitors to beg for your hand."

"I told you that I don't perform in public."

"Why not?"

"I wouldn't want to outshine your sisters. It's their moment, not mine. Look, we're already home. Why don't I have a chat with Blanche and Belinda, while you speak with Bernadette and Betsy."

"That sounds sensible. You'll know what to say to Blanche better than I would. When you're finished come and give me a report. And bring me that list of duchess candidates."

"Very well."

"We'll come through this together."

"I'm sure you will."

"We, Viola. You and me, and the girls. We'll weather this storm together."

He helped her alight from the carriage and this time, when he placed her feet on the ground, he held on to her waist for another fraction of a second. Enough to make her breathless.

He couldn't know that his touch and those words utterly destroyed her resolve to remain dispassionate. He was paying her a princely salary to be his sisters' companion and teacher. It didn't make her part of the family.

And she'd do well to remember it.

Chapter Fourteen

❧ 🌹 ❧

VIOLA HAD AGREED to a midnight rendezvous with a depraved duke, but she hadn't bothered to find out where said rendezvous would occur. Surely not in his bedchamber. It had better not be there. He must be waiting for her in his study.

It was her duty to his sisters to keep him inside this evening and out of trouble. She'd promised Blanche she would do so.

He wasn't in the study. He'd been there recently, though. The fire had died down and she could smell the clove spice of his cologne. Perhaps he'd gone to bed early and she wouldn't have to meet with him tonight at all.

Small chance of that. He never went to bed early. His days began at midnight.

She tiptoed up the stairs and down the hallway, her heart thumping with every step. She'd never seen the inside of his bedchamber, though she'd visited it many times in her dreams.

This was no dream. She was really here. Outside his bedroom door. Preparing to knock for entry.

The house was quiet. The servants were all abed.

She should be safe in her bed, not knocking on dukes' doors.

Maybe all she had to do was knock. She could ascertain that he was still here and not out carousing, tell him through the door that she was feeling tired and they could speak further in the morning.

This would be a very brief, very proper and businesslike conversation.

Through the unopened door.

Gathering her courage, she knocked. She pressed her ear against the door to listen for the response. Unfortunately, at the very moment she leaned forward, he flung open the door, as though he'd been waiting behind it for her knock.

She tumbled off balance and fell into his arms.

Stunned into silence, she rested her head against his chest, trying to catch her breath. His arms supported her elbows. Her mouth opened but no sound emerged.

"Miss Beaton, good, you're here."

Forming a reply was beyond her. She was directly at eye level with his chest. He wore a dark blue velvet dressing gown over trousers.

With no shirt underneath.

There was a light dusting of blond hair on his exposed chest. Her hand had fallen upon the knotted sash of his robe, as if it had a mind of its own, and had decided to unwrap him.

"Miss Beaton?" He glanced down at her questioningly.

She finally raised her eyes from his chest to

his face. The knowing glint in his eyes, which matched his velvet robe perfectly, she observed, informed her that he was well aware of her sensual response to their embrace.

She righted herself and broke the embrace. "Your Grace. I'm here."

"I see that." He was amused.

Keep yourself tightly knotted up. Don't let him see the naked longing in your heart. The longing for naked ...

This was a very bad idea.

"Your Grace, I'm sure you're tired after your ordeal. We can discuss things tomorrow."

"I'm not tired in the slightest."

"I'm usually in bed by half eleven of an evening."

"The ball would have lasted until three or four this morning."

"The ball was cut very short."

"You can make an exception. I want to hear how Blanche is doing."

"She's resting peacefully. She agrees that it wasn't your fault. And of course she's worried about being entangled in the scandal."

"I'll make this right, I swear it. Did she give you more names of heiresses?"

"She did."

"I've prepared you a writing desk with all the necessary accoutrements for you to make a list of candidates." He guided her to an escritoire and settled her in the chair.

She took a deep breath. "Very well." She'd simply concentrate on the task at hand. She arranged the inkpot, pen, and paper into a tidy formation.

"I require fortification for lists of heiresses," he said, opening a bottle of whisky. "Join me in a nip?"

She was here to be a good influence and whisky was not that. "Remember what I said about reforming, Your Grace? I think it would be better for you to enjoy a calming cup of chamomile tea instead."

"I don't drink tea."

"That's not very English of you."

"I drink whisky. Or gin. Occasionally brandy."

"It may surprise you to know that I also drink brandy from time to time," she said primly. "We always put a few drops in our tea at the meetings of my lady's club."

"Bluestockings on the bottle, eh?"

"Nothing like that. Only a little brandy in our tea. It makes the conversation flow. I'll bring you up a cup of tea and we'll add a few drops."

"How about we skip the tea and just drink the brandy. I have an excellent French Cognac here." He held up an amber-colored bottle.

He didn't wish to be alone tonight. He may have been laughing when she found him, and treating this all as a lark, but the events of the evening had shaken him.

She read it plain as day on his face.

Here was a man who'd thought he was doing the right thing and had had everything planned out and it all went to hell. He could be out gambling, drinking, taking a new lover. Drowning his sorrows in vice.

He was here at home because he cared about his sisters' future. He wanted to do the right thing.

She could encourage that.

"Your sister is fixated on Lady Winifred Woolfrey, I'm afraid."

"Lady Winifred is terrified of me."

"She's terrified of you because she's a virtuous lady and you've a dreadful reputation."

"True."

"Once you reform, she'll warm to the prospect."

"Who said I was reforming?"

"Do be serious, Your Grace."

"At least give me several options."

"I'll just see if there are any suitably wealthy and eligible young ladies on the guest list for the musicale." She pulled the list out of an inner pocket and ran her finger down the names. "Ah, here's one . . . Lady Elizabeth Gorham."

She wrote it down on the paper he'd provided.

The duke swallowed more brandy. "No."

"What are your objections?"

"Too numerous to name."

"Name one."

"Lady Elizabeth, while she does have delightful freckles, has only one topic of conversation: hunting. She breeds greyhounds. She regaled me with stories of every one of their births and gave a very bloodthirsty account of her last hunt. I think she wanted to tear apart the fox with her own teeth."

"Can you please be serious?" This wasn't easy

for her and he was making a big joke out of it, as usual.

"Give me more." He settled back into the chair, crossing his long legs at the ankle.

"Miss Eugenie Comstock and Miss Brunhilda Shufflebottom."

"Shufflebottom?"

"She's a very lovely young lady," said Viola. "A bit retiring and shy but kind and gentle to a fault. She can't help her name."

"No and . . . no."

Viola clenched her jaw. She rolled up the list, replacing the ribbon around it until such time as he could treat it with more respect. She shook the roll at him. "The least you can do is treat my considerable efforts on behalf of your matrimonial prospects with the gravity they deserve."

"I do love it when you threaten me with paper batons," he drawled.

"If it was a brass paperweight, I'd throw it at you."

"Oh dear. Have I provoked you beyond reason?"

"I'm nearly there," she fumed. "I honestly don't know why you must be so coy. Just choose a lady and have done with it!"

"What happened to prolonged courtship? Learning the exact color of her eyes and finding out what books she likes to read?"

"I mean choose one and then go about courting her. After you've shown her that you're willing to reform."

"Does this look like the bedchamber of a man who's willing to reform?"

"I'm ignoring your bedchamber. I'm only here to make you a list of respectable and well-connected heiresses." She'd been avoiding looking at his bed. She could feel it over there, sprawling and huge and curtained with purple velvet. The room was half bed, it seemed.

"I demand an impertinent and insulting reaction." He rose and came to stand nearby, sipping brandy and staring down at her with that same glint of amusement in his eyes.

She glanced around the room, avoiding the bed area. "Everything is as I pictured it to be, Your Grace. Thick silk carpets and heavy mahogany furnishings. Very manly. The oil paintings which, upon closer inspection, will turn out to be mostly female nudes reclining on settees or cavorting in the woods with fawns." She peered into the dark corners of the room. "Yes. All very much as expected."

His lip quirked. "You sound as though you've seen dozens of such chambers."

"Oh no," she hastened to clarify. "Just the one. You're only living up to your scandalous reputation. You can't help yourself. You must hang voluptuous nudes on your walls and have a huge bed with purple velvet curtains. Now, if you had a sparsely furnished, tasteful, and light-filled chamber I would have been very much surprised."

"Ha. That is exactly the kind of set-down I was hoping for. Do go on."

"Your rooms are well stocked with strong spirits, snuff boxes, and cigars. You keep the curtains closed to block out the light after nights spent carousing . . . and you have a great marble slab of . . ." She stopped because her gaze had found something she couldn't identify. A huge slab of marble with a carved angel on top. "What on earth is that? It looks rather like a . . . tombstone?"

"*My* tombstone."

"How morbid." She shuddered. "Why would you have something like that in your bedchamber?"

"I was drunk one night, several years ago, and I told my friend Rafe what I wanted inscribed on my tombstone and damned if he didn't go out immediately and commission it for me. Rafe used to be quite wild. We did have some devilish good fun."

She rose and traced the inscription with one finger. "'Here lies Brandan Delamar, Wicked Duke of Westbury, who lived Fast and died Young.' I'll admit, the prank tombstone is a surprise."

"It's not a prank. It's my actual tombstone. The one I'll be interred beneath for all eternity. I've earned it. I've dug my own grave."

"Don't joke about such a thing. Your sisters would be heartbroken if you left this world early."

"Sometimes I think they'd be better off without me. My uncle Marcus would inherit then. He's childless but at least he's not a gambler."

"You say these reckless things but I don't think you truly mean them. Not anymore. You've decided to do the right thing, to be a part of your sisters' lives. You have something to live for now. Don't you want to be an uncle to their children, Your Grace?"

"Call me West, please. I don't go in for formalities between friends."

"You're my employer."

"Is that all I am to you?"

No. You're also my secret fantasy. And you've done the most deliciously sinful things to me in my imagination.

And I won't think about that right now.

She pursed her lips, returned to the desk, smoothed out another sheet of paper, and dipped her pen in ink. "Please endeavor to concentrate on the task at hand. Now then, the list is only the first step. What follows is on your shoulders. You've already made one poor choice. I think you're going to have to try something completely different this time. You'll have to court your intended. Become acquainted with her first."

He leaned against the mantelpiece. "Seems to me I don't have to do anything but choose the lady with the most blameless reputation and the largest fortune and convince her to marry me, even though I have a terrible reputation."

"You'll have to find whether you suit each other before proposing. You've seen how an engagement can go wrong in the blink of an eye. You must become acquainted with the prospects before proposing to one of them. Have conversations with them. Learn about their childhoods, and their goals, and interests. Ensure that they're compatible with your own, and your family's goals."

"Once I make a show of reforming, the ladies will be courting me . . . you'll see. I'll be able to sit back and take my pick."

"You should find a good woman to marry, instead of negotiating for the one with the heaviest purse. And that requires courtship. You can't skip the conversations . . . or the small gestures that show you've truly listened to her. Heard her."

"One kiss and any lady will swoon into my arms."

"That's the most ridiculous thing I've ever heard."

"It's true."

"Because your kisses are some manner of magic elixir, I suppose?"

"I know my way around a kiss. When properly applied, a kiss is so much more than a kiss. It's a promise, a prelude, and a tantalizing taste of fuller pleasures to come."

"That's seduction, not courtship."

"Pretty poems, custom-made bookshelves, acts of chivalry . . . do you honestly think any of those actions were taken in the absence of kisses? They weren't. The kissing came first, then the bookshelves. I'll guarantee it."

Viola's cheeks flushed. She'd heard her friends describe their kisses for years now. Truth be told, she'd been more than a little envious of their amorous explorations. "You may be right."

"If there's one thing I know, it's kissing. A man who sets out to be the most wicked duke's heir in the world must excel at the art."

"It wouldn't be right to simply grab a lady and kiss her."

"I never grab unless grabbing is explicitly desired."

"A lady would never desire to be handled so."

He quirked one eyebrow. "I think you'd be surprised. Even the most decorous of women, when her passions are aroused, can be quite ferocious in her needs."

"You're so convinced of your charms. You think any woman would be lucky to have you."

"I'm a duke. I'm handsome. I have all my teeth. I have a good head of hair. All my best parts are in excellent working order. If I wasn't so wicked, I'd be every heiress's dream. My kisses inspire devotion. No courtship necessary."

"I'm quite certain there are plenty of ladies who could resist your kisses and remain impassive and undevoted."

"I always start with a kiss on the hand. Like this."

He demonstrated, lifting Viola's hand. His touch was firm, commanding. His skin warm.

He pulled gently until she stood before him, hardly daring to breathe.

He lifted her hand and brushed his lips over her knuckles.

"A kiss on the hand is an act of obeisance. It says that I want to touch you, to test the softness of your skin, inhale the fragrance you applied to your wrist. I want my lips to brush your hand while my fingers hold you." He turned her hand palm up and kissed the inside of her wrist.

She shivered from the contact of his lips against her skin. A little rough against that soft, sensitive place.

"It's a gesture that can be more seductive than

a kiss on the lips. It says, I'll hold your small wrist in my big hand. I could overwhelm you, and yet I'd never do such a thing, because when I hold your wrist in my fingers, when I feel that faint pulse beat against my thumb . . ." He dragged his thumb across her wrist. "You're the one in control. You hold the power. One word from you, one small little word, would send me away, or bring me closer . . . to your lips. It's all up to you."

Her knees quivered slightly so she corrected her posture, standing sturdy in the face of so much seductive duke. She must stand firm. She had a point to prove.

"I'm sure a lady would pull her hand away and scold you for taking such liberties in public."

"We're not in public. We're in a bedchamber."

"Then she would leave straightaway. Or call loudly for her chaperone."

"You *are* the chaperone."

"Then I should leave."

"Yes, you probably should. Because you don't want to know what I'd do next . . ."

"I don't want to know. That is . . . what do you do next?"

His smile was wolfish. "Then I look into her eyes . . . like this." His eyes burned, smoldered; they were temptation itself. "My eyes speak of the things I'll do to her, the ways we'll experience pleasure. The things she'll learn . . . the things she'll teach me."

"And then . . . ?" she whispered. She couldn't help herself. It was as though someone else possessed her body.

"And then I kiss her. Really kiss her. Deeply. Passionately. And she swoons into my arms."

Viola snatched her hand from his grasp. "If you were to kiss me I would remain impassive and undevoted."

"Is that a challenge?" His hooded gaze seared her skin.

Something changed, heated, became more charged with possibility . . . and danger.

"Yes," she whispered bravely.

Foolishly.

Chapter Fifteen

"Let's up the stakes," said Westbury, his voice a low, seductive growl. "If I kiss you, and you ask for another kiss, you'll perform at the musicale."

"Pardon? Absolutely not. I told you I'd never perform onstage again."

"It's not a stage, not really. Just velvet curtains they hang in the music room. And only a small gathering for an audience. Perhaps extremely small after the scandal tonight."

"I won't perform."

"Are you afraid you'll beg me for another kiss?"

"Don't be ridiculous! I can certainly control myself."

"Then what's the danger?"

"No danger. A kiss is just a kiss. I've had kisses before."

"You have?"

"In books. My favorite author, Miss Villeneuve, always includes plenty of kisses."

"This will be different. You won't be able to shut the book and go about your business. This kiss, my kiss, will be an awakening."

"You truly are the most maddeningly arrogant rogue in London. I have to kiss you now, don't I, if only to prove to you that not every woman succumbs to your charm."

"It's your moral imperative. For womankind."

He was goading her on, possibly even laughing at her. But what they were talking about was a kiss. And she'd thought about kissing him so many times before. This was her opportunity to put her wild imaginings to the test. Surely his kiss couldn't possibly live up to her dreams.

She closed her eyes. "Kiss me, Your Grace. And be swift about it."

A low laugh. Heat from his body as he drew closer. His enormous hands cupping her face. Fingers against her throat. A finger sliding over her lower lip.

"You have such lush lips," he murmured. "I've thought about kissing them. Tasting them."

"You have?"

"Many, many times."

A soft sigh of contentment. Hers. An admission that she'd thought about the same thing and she wished he'd get on with making it a reality. But he prolonged the moment, driving her nearly mad with anticipation.

With both of his hands wrapped around the back of her neck, he used his thumbs to tilt her chin up. She felt so small inside his grip. The light pressure of his fingers against her throat, the way he positioned her to his liking . . . it was all thrilling and new.

Her nipples hardened into peaks against the thin muslin of her gown. If she moved slightly forward they would brush against his chest . . .

ah, there, that felt good. She wanted to press against him, but stopped herself.

Just a kiss. *One* kiss, she reminded herself.

Finally, he kissed her. It wasn't a mere peck upon the lips. This was something entirely different. A slow, sensuous exploration that demanded a passionate response.

A kiss was rather like a sonata. There was an exposition, wherein the duke stated his purpose: namely, to drive her insane with desire. And then there was a development, wherein she responded passionately, opening her lips to his exploration, moaning softly as his tongue stroked inside her mouth, awakening the most delightful sensations. An interlude of gathering tension, increasing tempo . . . followed by a recapitulation, wherein the duke repeated the elements of the exposition, kissing her with soft, lingering strokes, until it was as though she'd been looking at separate elements of a landscape, a hill, a tree, a sky, and now . . . now she'd reached the summit and could see the entirety and grandeur of the scene.

His hands migrated to her waist, clasping her tightly, triggering a melting sensation, a lovely ache of awareness inside her body, and inside her heart.

He slid the yellow cashmere shawl she wore down from her shoulders and it pooled on the carpet.

One of his hands moved higher, his thumb brushing over her nipple.

He set the tempo, teaching her the way of it,

the melody of it, the lilt and sway, lips teasing, nibbling, and then tongue sliding inside, smooth and legato.

Her body reacted with a trill of grace notes up her spine, her heart beating the percussion, accompanied by a rush of heat inside her belly, and a pulse between her thighs.

She was actually kissing Westbury. Not some fictional duke she'd conjured in her mind. West. The one in her arms, the one she was learning, firm lips and questing hands.

She wasn't submitting to him, she was studying his hedonistic language, the language of tongues, sighs, and moans . . . taking the simple, ageless theme he taught her and embellishing it into endless variations.

He moved his lips away from hers, kissing the hollow of her neck, his touch like the brush of fingers on piano keys.

"Viola," he whispered against her neck, his low voice vibrating in her ear. "You taste so sweet."

Her mind wanted to impose some kind of order on this moment but there was only delicious sensation like the first bite of a profiterole, piercing the thin skin of the dough to uncover the sweet cream beneath and sinking your teeth through it and the sweetness melting on your tongue.

Or the ringing of a bell quavering in the air and you wanted to hold on to it but it faded away.

She would savor this moment, store the memory for later, when she was old and gray.

She mustn't think that she was special, or that the kiss meant anything to him. He kissed her because he was Wicked Westbury and that's what he did with willing partners.

And she kissed him because it was what she'd wanted to do since the very first moment she'd laid eyes on him.

She'd kissed him before many times in her dreams. He'd come to her room at night, professed his love, and she'd allowed him a few liberties, a few measured favors, a kiss, a touch. Nothing like this wildfire of sensation, his hands roaming to her breasts, shaping her nipples.

Her imaginings had been truncated by inexperience. She'd touched herself, the secret wellspring of pleasure she'd discovered, and brought herself to crisis imagining him kissing her.

She'd imagined so many impossible things.

In her dreams she'd been the perfect duchess candidate: high-born, elegant, a society darling, with an enormous fortune. And why stop there? She'd dreamed of a society wedding.

A trousseau of silky undergarments.

A wedding night.

She'd seen love shining in his eyes. He'd whispered promises to adore her forever.

The real West made no promises. He didn't speak at all. He kissed her and he explored her with a breathtaking mastery.

It was only a kiss. It meant nothing to him, her mind argued, and so therefore it should mean nothing to her—it should be a passing fancy, a natural urge, a primal quest for union.

But it did mean something. It meant . . . *everything*.

She'd forever be changed by this moment.

She'd been never-been-kissed Viola and now she was Viola, a bell awakened, ringing a clarion call.

There was some line that mustn't be crossed. What was it?

All of it. All of it was forbidden.

She was far from the perfect duchess candidate. And she certainly wouldn't become his mistress.

She'd have her heart broken if she allowed herself to be seduced by him. To love him.

Just one more kiss, she promised herself. *Then I'll end this.*

SHE WAS MELTING sugar in his arms. She kissed the way she played the piano—those afternoons he'd snuck downstairs to listen outside the music room door—with a light, sure, nimble touch that teased artistry into blossom.

He'd known she'd make those soft little moans of pleasure in the back of her throat. She couldn't help herself. She always accompanied everything with music. She hummed and tapped her fingers on her thighs . . . even the way she walked was musical, a rolling melody of womanly hips swaying.

Her body was made for sin, so tiny and small-boned but with those generous curves that he wanted so badly to explore. Her lips felt like satin against his lips, and when he delved inside her mouth with his tongue she tasted like boiled sweets and brandy.

The innocent scent of lavender clung to her hair and her neck. She still wore her ball gown, which was modest, but far lower cut than her usual garb.

The tops of her breasts plumped against his chest as he held her tightly, kissing her deeply.

His arousal was instant and impressively eager, twitching against his trousers, seeking a way to feel all that warm, sensual woman in a more intimate way.

He'd been thinking about doing this for days, weeks . . . possibly his whole life.

This woman in his arms, opening for him, winding her hands around his neck. It all felt so familiar . . . and yet completely different. Somehow *more*.

More desirable. More seductive.

More forbidden.

His mind reasserted itself. She was forbidden.

Employee. Teacher to his sisters. Living under his roof. Penniless.

He broke free, reluctantly ending the kiss. His breathing heavy, he took a moment before saying the words he knew he must say.

"I can't. We can't." He wasn't making sense. "What I mean is that we have to stop, Viola. It's not right. I'm your employer. You're companion to my sisters. You have moonbeams and fairy tales in your mind and I'm bad. I'm bad, tainted, and wicked. We shouldn't be kissing."

"Kiss me again," she said, pulling his face down to her. "Kiss me until I can't breathe."

He very nearly did. He was so close to wrapping his arms around her and giving her exactly what she asked for, exactly what he craved so very badly. He could have her warmth, her brightness, her dimpled smile.

No, he couldn't.

"Ha," he said with a casualness he was far from feeling. "Did you just ask me for another kiss?" He crossed his arms over his chest to keep them from pulling her close. "I win. You have to perform at the musicale."

The haze of desire left her green eyes and her cheeks turned bright pink. "Insufferable jackass!"

He raised his eyebrows. "Now that was slightly better. Keeping insults simple and straightforward is sometimes best."

"This is all just a joke to you, isn't it? Everything is a wager at the gaming table. You're never serious about anything." She straightened her bodice and smoothed stray tendrils of hair back into place. "It was only a challenge."

He watched the emotions playing across her face. Anger, hurt, and desire. And then she schooled herself back to the placid, pleasant expression she customarily wore. "At least I accomplished my goal tonight, Your Grace."

"Which was?"

"I promised Lady Blanche I'd keep you out of the gaming hells this evening so you wouldn't heap further disgrace upon this family. And here you are, safe at home where you belong. See? You've already begun your campaign of reform."

She spun around and left his room without a backward glance.

She was right, damn it. He never stayed home of an evening. And yet he hadn't even visited The Devil's Staircase in weeks.

He'd meant to go to the gaming hell tonight and instead he was having conversations about courtship and musicales with a music instructor. And kissing an innocent young lady who was in his employ.

Badly done, West. You really are an insufferable jackass.

Chapter Sixteen

❧ 🌹 ❧

"*T*HAT KISS NEVER happened," Viola told her reflection in the glass the next morning.

It couldn't have, she shouldn't have, and therefore, she hadn't.

One could simply refuse to believe one's own memory.

Didn't it, though? Her reflection begged to differ. Her lips were still red and tender from his kisses. She brushed her thumb over her lower lip, as he had done, and a flush crept over her cheekbones and a dreamy light filled her eyes.

She picked up her hairbrush and began vigorously brushing out her hair, yanking the bristles through the tangled curls until tears sprang to her eyes.

Better to pretend that the kiss hadn't happened . . . kisses plural . . . so many of them. She could remember each one. She'd learned more with each kiss. How he tasted, how large his hands were, how his fingers around her wrist had felt like an iron band and she'd liked that feeling of being small and delicate. She was petite but she'd always felt that her petite size belied her sturdy, steadfast personality. Yet he'd made her feel so powerful, so filled with passionate desire.

It had happened.

She'd gone to his room to make him a list of new duchess candidates, and to keep him out of trouble, and they'd ended up kissing. And why, pray tell, was that shocking? What had she expected to happen? She'd walked right into it, willingly, and she'd only gotten what she deserved.

And she wanted more.

No, *no*! She didn't want more kissing. Not when it meant nothing to Westbury. It had all just been a lark. He'd won the wager. She'd succumbed too easily.

She'd asked him for another kiss, confirming his inflated opinion of himself. How very embarrassing. He wasn't anything like the duke she'd invented in her mind. That gallant and attentive gentleman would never have kissed her and then turned it into a victory for rogues.

Hold on to this indignation and anger. Nurse it. Feed the flames. It was easier to be angry at him than to face the other forbidden emotions crowding her mind and heart.

He was arrogant and heartless and she could have nothing more to do with him than the dictates of their professional relationship prescribed. No more calling him West and going to his rooms at night.

And absolutely, positively never again would she kiss that man!

With her hair knotted tightly at the nape of her neck, and a collar that buttoned all the way up her throat, she was restored to order. The final touch was a white lace cap pulled down over her ears. Now she was a never-to-be-kissed-again spinster.

She greeted her father at the breakfast table and buttered a roll to eat with her tea.

"How was the ball last night?" her father asked, placing the shell-shaped metal sound collectors of the auricle hearing device the duke had given him on either side of his head and fitting the ivory earpieces into his ears.

"Disastrous. The duke was publicly jilted by the American heiress."

"Ha." Her father took another helping of eggs. "Plenty of fish in the sea for a duke."

True. But not all the fish had money and social connections enough to save Wicked Westbury.

Her father glanced at her slyly. "He's a handsome fellow, the duke."

"Undoubtably." Viola spread more butter on her roll, determined to remain unperturbed and buttoned-up.

"And you've been spending quite a lot of time with him."

"With his sisters, you mean."

"You're blushing."

"Am not."

"That's more butter than roll now," her father pointed out.

Viola glanced down. She'd spread a good inch of butter on the bread. "I like it that way." She choked down a bite, the rich butter leaving a film inside her mouth like the aftertaste of her lies.

"Viola," her father said warningly. "You're hiding something from me."

"Of course not." Time to deflect this conversation away from her. "How is the symphony coming along?"

"The finale is giving me no end of misery." He set down his fork and clutched at his shock of white hair, which was always standing on end. "It's a cantata, a choral fantasy, and I want it to be on a much grander scale than anything I've done before. I can hear the choir singing, Viola. I can hear them but when I try to capture it . . . it's a symphony within a symphony and it plays hide-and-seek with me, it runs away, just out of reach. I must get it right!"

He was becoming agitated, his hands grasping at the air as if he held a baton, his face clouding over, the muscles of his jaw working.

She went to him, clasping his hand. "You'll get it right, Papa. I have faith in you."

He calmed beneath her soft touch, his shoulders stopped trembling, and the wild look left his eyes.

"My Viola." He squeezed her hand. "What would I do without you?"

"Come," she said. "Let's go into the music room and you can show me the beginning of the finale and we'll see if we can chase it down."

She wasn't due to teach a music lesson until later that morning. She was worried about the young ladies. Blanche had been so quiet last evening, and Belinda so distraught.

She had time to help her father. Though when she'd find the time to work on the Christmas carol commission she didn't know.

She was mostly happy to be the amanuensis who transcribed his music, who made him hot tea, and kept him fed and clothed when he worked on his music day and night, consumed by the creative process. Most days she was happy to be the one who helped facilitate the birth of his creative brilliance.

And then there were the days when her own music called to her, asking to be written, begging to be born. She'd try to find time this evening to work on the carol. She hadn't found a poem to use and had decided to attempt to write lyrics of her own.

She shoved those thoughts to the back of her mind and helped her father for several hours, before going next door to help the ladies practice for the musicale.

"Oh, Miss Beaton," Belinda wailed when she saw her. "We're the scandal of the Season and it's only just begun."

"I'd say Miss Chandler is the scandal of the Season," Viola replied.

"Society doesn't think that way."

"I suppose they are herd animals," Bernadette agreed. "Our brother, who was already seen as a man of no moral fiber whatsoever, inadvertently caused the scandal and therefore we, as his sisters, are also to blame. We mustn't take it personally, Belinda, it's in their nature. They're too small-minded to go against the herd."

"They're like lemmings," said Betsy, "and we're the cliff."

"Is that supposed to make me feel better?" Belinda asked.

"That's a myth, Betsy," Bernadette said. "Lemmings have such a large population that sometimes a smaller herd will break off and migrate to a new home and if they encounter an obstacle, such as a river, they will all jump in together to swim across. Some of them don't make it, but that doesn't mean they committed suicide."

"And why anyone should know something like that, especially a lady, is beyond me." Blanche sniffed, entering the music room. "Miss Beaton, thank you for keeping our brother out of the gaming hells last evening."

Do not *blush*. "Of course."

"We must do our best to impress upon him the need for a complete and total reform," Blanche continued. "No more gambling, drinking, or profligacy."

"What's profligacy?" Birdie asked, joining them with a sheaf of staff paper rolled under her arm.

"Never you mind," said Blanche. "The day after a ball we are supposed to have suitors ringing our bell, bringing us flowers. And not one suitor has arrived."

"Lord Flanders paid you a call this morning," Bernadette pointed out.

"He doesn't count."

"He does seem rather taken with you," Viola said.

"As a boy he was always plaguing me. I can't imagine why he's courting me now."

"Have you thought that perhaps he did that to be noticed by you?"

"We're not talking about Flanders. We want West to find a new duchess. Despite her fortune, Miss Chandler was the most unsuitable candidate imaginable. He must choose someone better this time. She must be of excellent family and prospects."

"If Great-Aunt Hermione were here, she would champion Lady Winifred Woolfrey," Bernadette said. "She loves her. She's always comparing us to her and finding us sorely lacking. And she's so amiable and good that I can't even hate her. She's really the loveliest person. Even if her conversation is rather conventional and boring."

"Conventional and boring is precisely what our brother requires," Blanche said.

"There's no hint of scandal in her family?" Viola asked.

"None whatsoever."

"I don't think West likes her very much," Betsy said. "And how are we supposed to make him reform?"

All five young ladies considered that for a moment, their faces grave.

"It won't be easy," Bernadette said. "We'll have to keep him with us at all times."

Betsy nodded. "And hide his spirits."

"We'll make him come to the opera with us tonight," said Blanche.

"He's still asleep," Birdie said. "I checked. I asked Sebastian to wake him but he flatly refused for fear of bodily injury."

"Someone ought to wake him."

"Not I," Betsy said.

"Not I," said Bernadette.

"Oh for heaven's sake," Viola said. "Just go pound on his door and tell him you wish to have a conference with him."

"That's a wonderful idea, Miss Beaton. You should do that."

"I?" Viola shook her head in the negative. "I couldn't possibly . . ." She'd knocked upon his door last night, and look where that had landed her.

A memory of his kiss overwhelmed her mind, bringing swift heat to her face. He'd removed her shawl, sliding it down her shoulders, and then kissed her so thoroughly that . . .

Wait. Her yellow shawl. She hadn't seen it in her room this morning. Had she left it in his chamber? She had to go retrieve it before any of the girls saw it there!

"Very well," she said. "I'll go and pound on his door and inform him that his sisters wish to speak with him on a matter of urgency."

She left swiftly, desperate to retrieve her shawl.

All was quiet as she retraced her steps from last night to the ducal bedchamber. She pounded on the door.

No response.

"Your Grace," she called. "Wake up!"

Still no response. He must slumber deeply. Or had he snuck out last night, after all?

She tried the door handle. It was unlocked. She swung the door open, careful and quiet as any thief. She couldn't tell if the duke was there. His bed curtains were closed so one would assume he was in his bed. He kept his rooms too dark for her to see anything. She bumped into a chair and nearly swore aloud.

First, open the curtains to wake him and let in some light. Then, find her shawl, give the duke a talking-to about reforming and escorting his sisters to the opera, and make a hasty exit before anyone saw her here.

The window curtains were heavy green velvet affairs so thick they let not one sliver of sunlight inside the room. She must have some light for her search.

She opened one of the curtains until she could see what she was doing. Her yellow shawl was nowhere to be seen.

The only other place to search was the bed.

She peeled aside one of his bed curtains . . . and then swiftly dropped it.

Good Lord. He slept in the nude. Sprawled on his stomach, one arm bent beneath his head. The covers had slipped down until they covered only his sculpted buttocks, leaving the powerful, bunched muscles of his back and shoulders bared to her gaze.

She opened the curtain again, just enough to search for a yellow shawl, not to stare at his bare flesh. At the well-defined hillocks and valleys of his back. At the taut mounds of his buttocks.

She lost sight of why she'd come to the room.

Think, Viola. You're angry with this man. You have to wake him up and make him promise to reform. And you have to find that yellow shawl, the evidence that you were in this very room last night, kissing him like a wanton.

And yet . . . he was the most gorgeous thing she'd ever seen. She desperately wanted to pull that sheet a little lower in order to see *all* of him.

"Your Grace," she said.

"Mmmm," he murmured, and shifted onto his side, away from her.

And there it was. Yellow fringe peeking out from beneath his torso.

He was sleeping on top of her shawl.

She drew back his bed curtain fully. "Your Grace," she said loudly.

He slumbered on.

She placed her hand on his shoulder, blushing at the feel of his warm skin and hard muscle. She shook his shoulder gently.

He opened one eye groggily. "Eh? Oh, there you are. Come back to bed, you saucy minx." He caught her by the wrist and attempted to draw her into bed.

She pulled back indignantly. "I'm not a saucy minx," she said in an outraged whisper. "I'm Viola, here to retrieve my shawl, which you are lying upon. I don't want anyone to see it here and draw unsavory conclusions."

"Wassat you say?" He turned his head and squinted at her. "Too much light. Close those curtains. It's too early. If you're not here to warm my bed, then go close those window curtains."

"I most certainly will not." She placed her hands on her hips. "Wake up and give me my shawl."

"Come and get it," he drawled sleepily.

"Don't think I won't!"

Here he was sleeping while his sisters fretted downstairs.

Would she? Did she dare?

She took a deep breath and reached for the fringe, attempting to tug the silk free from his colossal weight. She shifted her hand lower, trying to get a better grip on the fabric. Too late, she realized that the movement had put her hand in very perilous proximity to certain unmentionable areas of his anatomy.

She tugged on the shawl.

He rolled over, half freeing the shawl, and sending her staggering backward with an ungraceful grunting noise.

She held out her hand. "Give me my shawl if you please."

"Only if you agree to close the curtains first."

She went straight to his bedchamber windows and began bustling about, opening them wider.

"Stop that, you she-devil! That's way too much light. It's too early for this."

A shaft of sunlight pierced the dimness of the room. He winced, shading his eyes with his elbow. "It's too early," he grumbled. "I need more sleep."

"You have to wake up now. You're supposed to escort your sisters to the opera tonight."

"Plenty of time before then," he grumbled. "I can sleep half the day if I choose."

"No, you can't." She opened another curtain.

"If you don't stop letting light into this room I'll—"

"Throw me over your shoulder like a roll of carpet. Yes, I've heard that before. But you won't. Not this time."

"Oh, won't I?"

"You won't. Because even you have the decency not to rise absolutely naked from a bed with a lady in the room."

"I wouldn't bet on it," he growled.

"I CAN GO around and open the curtains and there's nothing you can do about it." She followed her cheeky words with misdeeds, circling the room, opening curtains. Her pert bum swaying as she bustled about his chambers.

"If you don't stop that," he roared, "I'll have to commission a tombstone for you. 'Here lies Miss Viola Beaton, who opened a duke's curtains against his will.'"

"Give me my shawl." She held out her hand.

"Hand me a dressing gown."

She threw him a dressing gown. "You have a full schedule today, Your Grace. First you must speak with your sisters and then accompany them to the opera."

"I was rather hoping to sleep all day and carouse all night."

"None of that. Up. Out of that bed."

"I'm a hedonist. I gamble, I drink, I—"

"Yes, yes. We know all about your wicked pursuits," Viola said. "You only go out at night to drown in decadence and Scotch whisky. But your sisters expect you to accompany them to the opera this evening. You must be shaved, dressed, and ready to pretend to be scandal-free for a few brief hours."

"Any other orders, General Bonaparte?"

"No more public announcements about assignations with gin bottles. No drinking, no gambling, enlist the help of your less disreputable friends as escorts for your sisters, be seen in daylight."

"What about kissing?"

"Forbidden. Until you're courting that one special lady."

"Are we going to talk about that kiss?" he asked.

"It never happened."

"If you say so." He remembered it all too vividly. And he'd better not think about it for too much longer.

"Turn around, Viola."

"Pardon?"

"Turn around while I put on this dressing gown. Or don't. Your choice."

She turned her back on him swiftly.

He swung out of bed, put on the robe, and knotted the sash. "You can look now. Or did you already have a peek while I was sleeping?"

"I would never!" was the outraged response. She was blushing a bright pink color.

"I'm only teasing, Viola." He handed her the shawl. "And I promise you, and my sisters, that I'll begin my campaign of reform this very day."

She nodded curtly. "See that you do, Your Grace."

When she was gone, he sat on the edge of the bed and slid his feet into his slippers, chuckling at the memory of the way she'd opened his curtains.

She really was the most extraordinary woman. He liked the way she wasn't too intimidated by him and delighted in putting him in his place.

He was still chuckling as Sebastian gave him a shave. He didn't trust his new valet, Welker, to the task.

"If you don't stop laughing, Your Grace, I'm liable to nick your cheek," Sebastian said, holding the razor and frowning at him.

"I'll stop. I'm sorry." One last guffaw escaped his lips and then he schooled his features into placidity.

"What's so very funny if I might ask? Your heiress has eloped and we're in a financial quagmire once again."

"I'm just remembering something funny someone said to me."

"Might that someone be Miss Beaton, by chance?"

"How did you know?"

"Because she inspires mirth and joy."

She did that. Among other more lusty, earthy emotions.

"Miss Beaton is made of strong moral fiber," said Sebastian, lathering soap across West's throat. "She's not put off by your general air of degeneracy and depravity. Though you'd do well to be careful around her. I don't want you giving her false expectations. She could never become your duchess and I won't have you ruin the girl. I like her too much."

"I'm not going to compromise her. I know she's off-limits. You don't have to remind me."

"Good, because if you did . . . I could slip, you know. I'm getting old. My hands might tremble. If you do anything to make Miss Beaton sad, I might have a sudden bout of trembling."

"Point taken, Sebastian."

"Very good, Your Grace. Are you looking forward to the opera this evening?"

West gave him an incredulous look. "Did you just ask me that?"

Sebastian smirked.

"They want me to reform so the proper young ladies will have me."

"A little reform will do you good, Your Grace."

"I doubt it. Oh, Sebastian. I'd like you to ask Bowditch to pay me a call in my study this morning." Bowditch was his humorless man of business, responsible for managing his affairs.

The razor stopped moving. "You can't just say things like that while I'm shaving you, Your Grace. You really will cause an accident. The last time I attempted to arrange an interview at Mr. Bowditch's request, you threw a boot at me and threatened to have me deported to one of the penal colonies."

"Since I'm unusually sober this morning, I may as well extend my misery and hear the full extent of my financial woes from the horse's mouth."

"It will only drive you to drink. And you must stay sober for your sisters' sake this evening."

"Must I? I was thinking a glass or two might improve the opera immeasurably."

"Miss Beaton won't like it."

She really did have every member of his household staff wrapped around her little finger.

"Just send for Bowditch. I'm man enough to take the truth."

THE TRUTH HAD been difficult to swallow. He might require a drink to wash it down.

West descended the stone steps leading to No. 20 Ryder Street. Here was a world where he knew the rules. Dark, masculine, steeped in strong spirits. It wasn't warm and comforting but it was the home away from home that he'd chosen for the last several years of his life.

The proprietor, Jacques "Jax" Smith, greeted him with a friendly nod. "Been some time, Westbury."

"I had family matters to attend to." He settled into a familiar seat at the bar.

"Your Grace," the barkeep, Gus, said, a little warily, eyeing him. The last time they'd met, West had been unruly and itching for a fight.

"No hard feelings, Gus. I know I'm the one who started the fight. And I heartily regret it. You've got a fist like the mighty hammer of a Norse god."

"Heard you've been engaged and jilted since we saw you last. You'll be wanting some of this." Gus held up a bottle of Jax's proprietary gin, infused with his own blend of botanicals.

West's mouth watered and his hands shook. He slid his hands onto the bar, palms down, to stop the slight trembling. He'd made a promise. And when he decided to do something, he didn't do it by half. "Only watered ale for me."

"Now that's something I never thought I'd hear from your lips, Westbury," said Jax.

"I promised my sisters I'd reform."

"Hate to lose my best customer," Jax joked.

"You've taken too much of my fortune already."

Jax made a bow. "Thank you for choosing our fine establishment, Your Grace."

"Oh, don't Your Grace me, you bastard. We're well past that. My life's taken a few unexpected twists since I saw you last. Found an American heiress to marry and then she tossed me over for one of her countrymen."

"You don't sound too broken up about it," Jax commented. "You'll be after another heiress then?"

"Regrettably."

Jax took the seat next to him and gave Gus a look that sent the barkeep to the far side of the bar. "Look, Westbury, I'm glad to hear that you're reforming. I've been worried about you lately."

West groaned. "Not you, too. Can't a man enjoy his watered ale in peace?"

"The last time you were here you seemed different. You had this empty look in your eyes and you started that fight with Gus. It wasn't like you. It was like . . . well, I've seen it before in the eyes of the orphans I worked with in the factory during my boyhood. A hopelessness. Almost a wish for death."

West sipped his ale, wishing it was something stronger. "I had a bad night, that's all. It won't happen again."

"If I can rise from the streets to make a good

living for myself and become the owner of a fashionable establishment, then you, who were born with a silver spoon in your mouth, can turn things around and make something of your life."

"I've made a mess of my life, just as my father, may he rot in hell, predicted."

"At least you know your parentage. The matrons at the orphanage knew nothing of my father and could only tell me that my mother wasn't from England. My guess is that she hailed from some place with a tropical climate. I hate the cold and damp here as though it was an aversion I learned in the womb. I'd like to think that my mother, whoever she was, wherever she was from, would be proud of me now. The orphaned street urchin is now the elegant, powerful, handsome devil you see before you."

"I'm sure she would be. You've done well for yourself, Jax." West clapped him on the back. "The Devil's Staircase is nearly reputable now."

"I serve sparkling wine and cater to duchesses from time to time."

"Hope you still have a barstool for reprobates like me."

"Always."

"My mother, may she rest in more peace than she had in this world, would not be proud of me."

"Then make her proud. Change your life."

"Easier said than done."

"It's never too late to turn things around. Take my friend, Ash Prince, for example. I've never seen a man more besotted by his bride. Once they decided they loved each other instead of hated each other, all bets were off. I never thought I'd say this, but that kind of wedded bliss looks rather delightful."

West nearly spilled his ale. "You believe in that true love nonsense? You sound like my sisters' music teacher, Miss Beaton."

"I didn't until I witnessed it with my own eyes. Ash is a different man now. A better one. This Miss Beaton, I think I've met her," Jax remarked. "Petite little thing? Friends with Lady Henrietta Prince, Ash's wife?"

"She may be pint-sized, but she's got an indomitable will, that one. She marched into my bedchamber at an ungodly hour this morning, ripped open my curtains, and ordered me about in no uncertain terms."

"Sure you didn't like it?"

"She did look rather devastating in the morning light. All flushed cheeks, dancing green eyes, and adorable dimples."

"Did you just say 'adorable dimples'?" Jax scoffed. "Maybe there's another reason you're not sad about losing that wealthy American fiancée."

"I can't afford a love match, Jax." Not that he was in love. Or would ever fall in love.

West pulled a crumpled handful of the bills that Bowditch had presented him with out of his coat pocket and piled them on the scarred wooden bar top. "My financial state is more desperate than I'd imagined."

"How bad is it?"

"Dismally bad."

"Sell off some more antiquities and stave off ruination bad?"

"Worse than that." The news Bowditch had given him had staggered him. He'd been allowing himself to think that maybe, just maybe, he wouldn't have to commit to a marriage of convenience.

He'd been thinking about laughing green eyes and lush lips since the moment he awoke.

But now . . . "My man of business informed me that Westbury Abbey, the family estate near Watford, is literally crumbling into the earth. The estate is in such disrepair that most of the tenants have been forced to relocate. I thought that my father's brother, my uncle, was living there and seeing to the repairs, but he's been traveling abroad for years and I never even knew about it. I've been a terrible landlord, Jax. I have to do something about it. I have to sell myself to another heiress forthwith. And that's easier said than done. No respectable lady wants anything to do with me."

"Ah." Jax sipped some gin. "Hence the reform campaign."

West nodded. "Hey ho, lads. Here's a new drinking game for you," he called out. The men sitting at the bar who drank most days away perked up their grizzled faces. "Every time I say 'past due,' you drink."

The men lifted their mugs and glasses.

"Bill for a new roof on Westbury Abbey. Past due!" He drank half his ale in one swallow and the men around him joined in.

"Bills for bonnets for five sisters. Past due." Another slug of ale. He held up another one. "Bill for"—he squinted at the piece of paper—"sundry saddlery items including six best hogskin seated footmen's saddles and—"

"Past due! Past due!" the men shouted.

"Best of luck finding a new heiress that's willing to marry the likes of you," Jax said with a smirk.

"Thanks," West replied. "I can use all the luck I can get." He gathered the bills. "Have to go now, mates."

The men at the bar raised their glasses to him.

"Off so soon?"

"I'm escorting my sisters to the opera tonight. And I have to go round up some of my less disreputable friends and recruit them for various social outings. Viola's orders."

"Viola?" Jax raised his eyebrows.

"Er, Miss Beaton."

Jax chuckled. "Are you certain you're not smitten with her?"

"Absolutely not." West hurried away before he had to endure more scrutiny from his friend's all-seeing gaze.

Chapter Seventeen

❦ 🌹 ❦

THE NEXT FEW weeks passed in a blur of parties, dances, and outings to art galleries and operas. Viola attended some and stayed home for others, receiving a detailed report from Blanche the next day.

West had been true to his word.

He'd stopped drinking, was early to bed and early to rise, and escorted his sisters everywhere. He was attentive, sober, and outwardly respectable. Society was beginning to thaw, the invitations poured in, and proper young ladies were no longer frightened to be seen talking to him.

The duke might chafe against the curtailment of his hedonistic vices, but Viola was beginning to thoroughly enjoy herself. It was fun to be out in the world, to be caught up in the social whirlwind and dissect the latest gossip with the girls afterward. And West wasn't only attentive to his sisters. Several times over the past weeks she'd caught him staring at her, sometimes with a bemused smile on his face, other times with unmistakable longing, and sometimes she swore he looked at her with something like . . . tenderness.

She told herself that she was imagining things.

Today, he and Viola were accompanying Blanche and Belinda to a fabric warehouse to choose fabric for new ball gowns.

"A whole day for shopping. It's heaven!" Belinda enthused. "We'll visit several linen drapers, then the haberdashers for trimmings, and then we'll select our designs at our modiste's establishment. Won't it be blissful?"

Viola nearly burst out laughing at the pained look on West's face.

"You know I wouldn't have been caught dead anywhere near these places a few weeks ago, right?" he whispered to her through gritted teeth.

"I'm well aware of that fact, Your Grace. It's only what you deserve."

"And then Vauxhall Gardens," Belinda said. "I'm so excited!"

"Hush, Belinda," said Blanche as they entered the silk warehouse. "People are staring."

"They're staring at West." Belinda linked her arm through his. "The question on everyone's lips is which heiress you'll propose to. You must select a bride without delay, dear brother. I should like to continue in such finery."

"Your wickedness has been forgiven and forgotten, brother," Blanche said. "And the jilting has now become a mark in your favor. The papers are painting you as a duke wronged. It's practically a matter of patriotism. Your jilting has elicited sympathy and warm sentiments in the breasts of beautiful ladies across the kingdom."

"Miss Beaton, can you account for the vagaries of haute society? They think I'm wicked no longer."

"I'm sure they couldn't be more wrong," she replied.

"Oh no, West has turned over a new leaf. He's a new man." Belinda led him toward the rows of silk and velvet fabrics. "Tell me, which heiress do you favor? Lady Winifred? Lady Gorham?"

"I shan't know until I see what gifts they bring me today," he said jokingly. "They're courting me. One of the Miss Comstocks told me that my eyes were the color of delphiniums yesterday evening."

Viola rolled her eyes. "As if you're not conceited enough already," she mumbled under her breath.

"What was that, Miss Beaton?" he asked, his voice rumbling with laughter.

"Ladies don't court gentlemen, Your Grace."

"Oh, but they do."

"My goodness," said Blanche. "Half the *ton* is here."

"They must have seen Mr. Sutter's advertisement in *La Belle Assemblée* the same as we did—they're here to purchase his fine silk velvets before the price goes up. Hurry, we must see if he has the pale peach hue I require." Belinda dragged West toward the shimmering rows of fabrics.

Viola lingered on the edge of the room. She wasn't shopping. Her serviceable gray gowns were all she required.

She watched as several lovely young ladies clustered around West, asking his opinion about the fabrics. They were openly courting him, just as he'd said. Of course, they were going about it all wrong. Viola knew how to court a scandalous duke.

It started with secret midnight kisses . . . and ended in . . . it didn't end in anything. She wasn't courting him. He wasn't gazing tenderly at her.

Shop assistants unfurled bolts of shiny silk and lustrous silk velvet, splashing waves of color over the tables. The mélange of colors and textures was as disordered as her mind when she thought about West.

She smiled as his sisters piled his strong arms high with bales of fabric even though there were footmen nearby to carry the load. They did love teasing him. And he bore it all with admirable stoicism. Viola had to give him credit, he was behaving like an honorable gentleman.

She stiffened as Lady Winifred entered the shop, looking like an expensive confectionary in a cream-colored pelisse and pink-trimmed bonnet. Blanche immediately brought West to her and then left them alone, none too subtly.

Viola threaded her way behind the piles of fabric, moving closer to hear their conversation.

"Do you think I ought to purchase this dove-gray silk velvet?" Lady Winifred asked, running her gloved hand over a length of fabric.

"It would match your eyes."

"It would, wouldn't it?"

A male shop attendant approached Viola, looking dubiously at her simple pelisse and the worn hem of her gown. "May I help you, miss?"

"No thank you, I'm here in attendance on some ladies."

"In that case, might I demonstrate some fabrics for you to show to them? This is the best silk velvet and won't be sold at this price for very much longer. See how it drapes softly?" He lifted a length of scarlet silk velvet. "It will make an elegant silhouette."

"Thank you. I'll be sure to point it out to my charges."

He bowed and moved away, sensing that she wasn't really the decision-maker of the party.

Drat. She'd missed the rest of West's conversation with Lady Winifred. Now he was talking to twin sisters Eunice and Eugenie Comstock, nearly identical brunettes wearing matching yellow gowns.

"Your Grace," one of them said. Viola couldn't tell them apart. "We're so very sorry about that awful Miss Chandler."

"Yes, it was most shameful of her," said the other. "What could restore your spirits?"

They both fluttered their eyelashes at him, clearly implying that one of them could restore his spirits if only he'd make her the next Duchess of Westbury.

"A nice cozy cup of chamomile tea," West replied with a straight face. "It's wonderfully restorative, wouldn't you say?"

"Oh we would, wouldn't we, Eunice?"

"Most definitively, Eugenie. We always drink chamomile tea of an evening."

"I also like to read novels," West said, leaning in conspiratorially.

"Do you?" the twins breathed in unison. "Who is your favorite author?"

"Authoress, you should say. I'm partial to the

works of Miss Daphne Villeneuve. Have you read any of her romances?"

The twins regarded him with astonishment.

"She's our favorite," said Eugenie.

"I've never heard of a gentleman liking her novels," Eunice said.

"Ah, but you see I am a duke reformed, ladies. I drink chamomile tea and I read Gothic romances."

How he could keep a straight face while spewing such tripe was a great mystery.

"My. That's . . . well, it's unprecedented, Your Grace."

"Thank you." He made a little bow. "Now, if you'll excuse me, ladies. My sisters require my attention." He turned away from them and caught Viola's eye.

She ducked behind a silk bale.

He knew she'd been listening, of course. Why else would he confess to doing the very things she'd told him that she liked to do?

"Spying on me, Miss Beaton?" he asked, appearing around the side of the stack of silks.

"That's laying it on a bit thick, don't you think, Your Grace?"

He chuckled. "Now the whole of society will know I've switched from gin to chamomile and from keeping mistresses to reading romances."

"You should stop."

"Stop what?"

"Stop playacting. No one will believe you've reformed if you say unbelievable things like that."

"On the contrary, it's those vivid details that will lend my reformation an air of authenticity."

"It's all a game you're playing, though, isn't it? You're still Wicked Westbury underneath."

He moved closer. "Very much so. Don't go thinking you've tamed me. I'm playing your reform game, just as you asked me to. You could probably convince me to take a long walk off a short pier if you showed me those dimples while you did it."

The heat of his gaze pressed her back against the silk. He reached out his hand and she held her breath, thinking he was going to touch her, but he touched the scarlet silk velvet instead.

"This fabric would suit you, Viola. You should have a gown made from it."

"I'm a spinster. I don't wear scarlet gowns."

"You're no more a spinster than I'm truly reformed. I picture you wearing red. Tight around here." His gaze dropped to her bosom. "With a low neckline."

"You picture me?"

"Often. Sometimes in red silk. Sometimes in . . . considerably less."

"Oh." She pictured him whenever they weren't together. Wearing his bedsheets and nothing more. Pulling her down into his rumpled bed.

Having his way with her.

Her body hummed with longing.

"It's a shame you can't have the gown made up before the musicale. It would be the perfect performance garb."

"I'm not performing. That was only a silly wager. You won't hold me to it."

"A wager is a wager. I'll have my payment. Or you'll pay a forfeit."

The way he gazed hungrily at her lips told her exactly what he meant by that.

"West?" Blanche stuck her head around the silks. "There you are. We're ready to leave now."

"Miss Beaton has agreed to have a gown made from this red silk velvet," West said, lifting the roll of cloth.

Viola struggled to calm her wildly beating heart and wipe the guilty look from her face. Blanche didn't seem to notice.

"How lovely! It will suit you, Miss Beaton."

After the silk warehouse they visited the haberdashers, and then made their way to a modiste's shop.

"I'll leave you ladies to your fittings," West said, lifting his hat. "I see one of my friends across the street."

He walked away and Viola was finally able to breathe again.

"I'm going to help choose a pattern for your gown, Miss Beaton," Belinda said.

"A simple pattern, please. I'm not a grand or a fanciful person."

"It must have a square neckline," said Belinda. "It will make your neck look longer. And short-capped sleeves will have the same effect for your arms."

Viola barely paid attention as Belinda discussed the details of her gown with the modiste, and Viola was measured and a pattern was cut and pinned.

Did West truly picture her, think about her, the way she thought about him?

She was still mulling his revelation over in her mind as she moved back to the changing rooms to don her old gown.

A shop assistant pulled the curtain closed.

"Who is that woman with the Delamar sisters?" she heard a female voice ask from the next changing room over.

"Miss Viola Beaton, I believe."

"Is she a relation? A governess?"

"Their music teacher."

"Then why is she accompanying them shopping? And did you see? The duke bought her a length of red silk velvet. And she's to have a new gown made up at his expense."

"I know! She must be his mistress. There's no other explanation."

Viola stiffened. She didn't recognize the voices.

"How shocking! Keeping his mistress next door to his sisters. Do you think she's angling for a scandalously inappropriate match?"

"Of course. Why else has she wormed her way inside the family? She's not a proper lady, anyone can tell. Her father is that disgraced composer. And who knows who her mother may be?"

Tears stung Viola's eyes. She hastily donned her gown and replaced her gloves and bonnet.

If she were bold and impetuous like some of her friends, she'd march over and challenge the gossiping ladies, confront them.

But what good would that do? It would only call further derogatory attention to herself and then Blanche and Belinda would know the lies they'd been saying.

They thought she was West's mistress and was scheming to trap him into marriage.

She may have indulged in some very foolish and naive daydreams but going so far as to imagine herself as a duchess, and mistress of Westbury Abbey? She'd never strayed so far into such laughably implausible territory. At least not with serious intent.

She hurried out of the changing room before the gossips revealed themselves.

"Lady Blanche, I feel a little faint. I'm going home," she said.

"Let our coachman drive you."

"I'll walk. It will clear my head."

Viola hastened outside, keeping her head low, and set off toward her temporary home. She'd been living in a fantasy world. She'd had no legitimate cause to accompany the ladies on this shopping excursion. She'd only wanted to be close to West.

When she should have been at home, helping her father finish the symphony and composing the Christmas carol. The due date for both was nearly at hand. She should be focusing on her own work, preparing for a future independent of the duke.

Instead, here she was gallivanting about London, ordering fancy gowns which she'd never have an occasion to wear.

Dreaming impossible dreams.

Chapter Eighteen

❦ 🌹 ❧

"W HY DID YOU run away without saying good-bye yesterday?" West asked Viola in a low voice as they waited for his sisters to arrive for the musicale. "And you didn't come to Vauxhall. We missed you."

He wanted to say that *he'd* missed her. The night at the pleasure gardens had seemed empty and cold without a smile that glowed brighter than lanterns strung in trees. And when the famous fireworks had splashed the night sky they'd been colorless without green eyes to reflect them.

Viola avoided his eyes. "I wasn't feeling very well. I'm better now."

He searched her face. "Did something happen at the modiste's shop? You went to bed early. I came by after Vauxhall but you were already asleep."

"I was nervous about today's performance. I want your sisters to shine."

They stood behind the blue velvet curtains that had been hung in the music conservatory at West-bury House. His sisters would arrive soon wearing fine silks and jewels in their hair.

Viola wore the same simple off-white gown

she'd worn to the ball, this time with a green sash about her waist and a single white rose tucked into her hair. She was as lovely as ever, but something was wrong. Her smile was nowhere in evidence and there were faint mauve shadows under her eyes.

"And shine they will," West replied, "if only with vigor and pluck. I don't expect you to have achieved a miracle with Bernadette, Bets, or Belinda, but I know this performance means much to Blanche and Birdie. The last time Blanche performed for a crowd of this size she forgot her place in the music and was mortified. That's why I hired you."

"Really? She never told me that."

"I don't think it's something she wants to remember. Today is her way of reclaiming her confidence. She puts on a very convincing show of unflappable composure and serene elegance, but she's very sensitive and feels things deeply."

His sisters filed into the backstage area wearing expressions ranging from glum (Betsy) to gleeful (Birdie).

"That horrid Moresby is here." Betsy kicked the carpet. "I didn't invite him. Why's he here? To laugh at me, no doubt. He'll make fun the whole time I'm playing the blasted harp. I think I've come down with the dreaded lurgy. I can't play. Don't make me play, brother," she pleaded.

"What's this?" West placed the back of his hand on her forehead. "You don't have a fever. It's only an attack of nerves, Bets. You'll be brilliant. And if not, it'll all be over soon enough."

"Easy for you to say," Betsy muttered.

"Right then," he said, surveying his beautiful, vibrant sisters. "I can't wait to hear you play. And Miss Beaton, of course."

"You're playing, Miss Beaton?" asked Birdie, her face lighting up with a wide smile.

"But you said that you never perform in public." Blanche gave her a puzzled glance. "What changed your mind?"

"She lost a wager," West said, keeping his expression bland.

"What sort of wager?" Birdie's bright gaze darted between West and Viola.

"Never you mind," Viola said. "I'll only play a brief selection. This is your evening, ladies. And I'm very proud of you, no matter what happens."

"I'm very, very proud of all of you." West cleared his throat around a sudden lump. "And I know that our mother would have been so delighted to see her daughters perform. She'll be looking down at you tonight and smiling."

"She'll be laughing at me," said Betsy. "Better get it over with. Off to Madame Guillotine."

West made his greeting to the overflowing crowd of guests, which included at least a dozen hopeful would-be duchesses, and introduced Betsy.

Betsy's harp playing was best described as unangelic. She plunked away forcefully in the same forthright manner that she would wield a cricket bat. West smiled encouragingly at her but she turned her gaze to the floor and plunked faster, wanting to be done with it.

Poor Belinda, accompanying her on the pianoforte, was forced to speed up as well, which flustered her into losing her place in the music, and the result was such an infernal mess that it was all West could do to keep a straight face.

Viola was turning pages for Belinda, and casting frantic glances at Betsy, but there was really nothing she could do.

The guests shifted uneasily in their chairs, several of them glancing toward the doors as if they wished to beat a hasty retreat.

Betsy finished with a plodding flourish of high notes and Belinda crashed a final chord.

West began clapping enthusiastically, in a show of brotherly support, and the audience followed suit, but with less enthusiasm.

Betsy heaved a sigh of relief, rose from her stool, and made a bow, practically galloping back behind the velvet curtain.

It was Belinda's turn next. She played a simple melody, with a minimum of errors, but seemed to think that her performance was more about displaying the sartorial splendor of her new gown than it was about excelling at the pianoforte.

After Belinda, Bernadette butchered an Irish air on the violin with insouciance, smiling as though she knew she was terrible, and she was going to lean into it, make her performance almost comically bad. At one point, she dropped her bow. And when she bent to pick it up, several very large dried scarabs fell from her pockets and skittered across the floor, frightening the ladies in the first row.

West stifled a guffaw.

When Blanche appeared, the audience breathed a collective sigh of relief, most of them having heard her perform before and knowing that she was at least a competent pianist.

More than competent, West realized, as the Bach concerto flew from her fingers. Viola had worked wonders with her. Each note was played with precision and elegance. The audience sat up straighter and listened with real enjoyment. Blanche looked so pretty and serene, her back straight, shoulders poised. So much like their mother that West felt tears gather behind his eyes.

Blanche had grown into such an accomplished young woman. Where had the years gone? Passed in a drunken stupor, a wasteland of vice and sin. He should have been here more, spent more time with his sisters. He'd enjoyed these past weeks with them more than he'd thought possible. Even though he was only playing the role of respectable gentleman, he took genuine pleasure in getting to know his sisters better.

It's never too late to turn things around. He heard Jax's voice in his mind.

Viola turned pages for Blanche, her glowing smile firmly back in place, dimples appearing at regular intervals as her pupil exceeded all expectations.

West wanted to make her smile like that, perform so well that she bestowed more than smiles, more than kisses . . .

He was so wrapped up in his thoughts that he

missed the moment when Blanche stopped playing and the audience began a round of heartfelt applause. Blanche curtsied prettily and blushed.

Lord Flanders clapped so enthusiastically that he knocked the bonnet worn by the lady sitting next to him askew.

Birdie practically flew from behind the curtain, eagerly taking her seat at the pianoforte.

"Miss Birgitta will be playing a sonatina of her own composition," West announced.

West could tell immediately that Birdie had talent. Blanche had played each note perfectly, but Birdie played with feeling, swaying to the music in the same way that Viola had when she played.

The piece was simple and brief, but it had a pleasing quality and a cheerful melody that was just like Birdie—always chattering, always bright and inquisitive.

Viola beamed at her pupil in a way that made West's breathing hitch. She truly did love his sisters. They were so lucky to have benefited from her tutelage and her friendship.

Every morning when West awoke he thought about Viola and how to make her smile that day.

Are you certain you're not smitten with her? There was Jax's voice again.

Was he?

The audience thought the musicale had reached its conclusion. Some had even begun to stand. West quickly took the stage, lifting his arms to quiet the guests. "Thank you for attending our musicale. There's one last performer that I think you'll very much enjoy. We have in this room the daughter of the celebrated composer Mr. Louis Beaton. Please stand, Miss Viola Beaton."

Viola rose gracefully. He avoided looking at her for fear the audience might see his admiration.

"If you'll give her a warm welcome, perhaps she'll be induced to honor us with a performance."

The applause was thunderous. Everyone took their seats again, anticipation coursing through the room. Viola's name on everyone's lips.

West felt quite pleased with himself. Viola wasn't meant to be hiding in the wings, turning pages for other musicians.

She was a shining, brilliant star. Anyone could see that.

As West listened to her play he stopped thinking and his body relaxed. This must be one of her father's works. It was strident and at the same time subtle. It made you *feel*. You couldn't remain impassive.

The way she played piano, rapt and swaying with the music, her fingers so assured and the sound of it, heartbreakingly beautiful, was just so sensual and superb. The music entered him, inhabited his mind, took control, and he was hers. There was nowhere else he'd rather be than here. Listening to her play.

She seemed to have forgotten that anyone was watching her.

It was her ability to lose herself in the music, to become an instrument herself. To give this stunning gift to the onlookers. Every person in the room rapt, captive, some openly in tears, dabbing at their eyes with handkerchiefs.

Some with smiles lighting their faces. Others in a trance, watching her, swaying with her; when she moved, when her hands crashed down upon the bass keys, they moved as well, as though she were their puppet master, and the music had entered them as well, and she was controlling their bodies.

She'd find pleasure in the same way that she played. Giving herself to it.

She'd sing and sigh in his ear, holding him while he stroked her smooth skin and found the hidden places, the whorl of her navel, the heat and honey between her thighs.

He wanted to taste her, tease her, until she sang a whole symphony for his ears alone.

She might be his music instructor, but he'd be the one teaching her the art of love. How two bodies came together. Bodies that walked around all day wearing so many layers of clothing, eyes and faces hidden by bonnets, toes hidden by boots, fingers by gloves.

So many layers of propriety to peel away until they were there, in his bed, with nothing between them. Then they could properly explore, learn the lay of the land.

How had she been coming and going from his home for so many years without him noticing her? He'd been so blind. He'd been sunk inside his mind. His mind that trapped him, like he was an old sea chest, wrapped round with chains and flung into the ocean. Happiness couldn't escape from such a prison. But Viola had found a way to reach him.

She played the final notes, drawing them out with consummate musicianship.

The audience burst into applause, and an audible murmur of approbation swelled around him. One gentleman even leaped to his feet shouting "Bravo, bravo, Miss Beaton!" as though he wanted to throw roses at her feet.

In that moment, it hit West with blinding clarity. It wasn't right for this woman to be relegated to the role of caretaker, amanuensis, or music instructor . . . she belonged on the stage.

She couldn't hide away behind those plain gowns and that severe hairstyle. Everyone knew the truth now.

She could be playing for kings and emperors. She could have the world at her feet.

She could have him at her feet.

Scattering rose petals over her body and tracing their path with his lips. Loving her body and paying tribute to her power.

His sisters gathered round her, smiling and congratulating her. They all joined hands and took a bow. Footmen drew the curtains closed.

West started toward the curtains, wanting to congratulate Viola, to tell her some of the thoughts crowding his mind, when Countess Chittenden, in a yellow turban ornamented by two red feathers, pushed her daughter, Lady Winifred, forward.

"Your Grace. I enjoyed the musicale immensely." He could never tell what Lady Winifred was thinking. Her utterances were all made in the same even, placid tone of voice.

"Wasn't Miss Beaton astonishing?" he asked.

The countess gave him a sharp look. "She played well, but my Winifred is also an accomplished pianist. And, I daresay, more measured and modest in her method of playing. We are hosting a small dinner party next week and I do hope we'll have the pleasure of your company?"

"I wouldn't miss it." He searched the room for Viola. He found her standing next to the punch bowl in conversation with an elderly gentleman who was standing a little too close to her, in West's opinion.

"If you'll excuse me, Lady Chittenden, Lady Winifred."

"Will you be promenading in Hyde Park tomorrow, Your Grace?" asked Lady Chittenden.

"Of course, of course. I wouldn't miss it. I do hope I will see you there, Lady Winifred." He bowed over her hand.

She smiled serenely and nodded.

West made good his exit and turned his steps toward Viola. He was nearly to her when he was waylaid by Lady Elizabeth Gorham, a blazingly beautiful woman with dark hair and appealing freckles sprinkled over her nose.

"Your Grace, you must say you'll attend the ball at my house next week," said Lady Elizabeth. "You can meet my five greyhounds."

"I shall endeavor to be there."

Lady Elizabeth began telling him the names of her greyhounds, their favorite foods, and other details that he didn't catch because he was straining to hear what Viola and the older gentleman were talking about.

The man gesticulated vehemently. Viola shook her head in the negative. She seemed to be in some distress.

Lady Elizabeth chattered on about greyhounds, balls, and who knew what else. West edged closer to try to hear what the man was saying to Viola.

He couldn't hear the words but he saw Viola's reaction. She shrank into herself, becoming smaller, a look of discomfort on her pretty face.

At the first opportunity, West interrupted Lady Elizabeth's monologue. "I, er, would you pardon me, Lady Elizabeth?"

"Will I see you in Hyde Park tomorrow?" she asked with a flirtatious look.

"I'll be there," he promised. He'd promise anything if it meant he could make his escape. He had to go to Viola and make sure she wasn't in any kind of trouble.

"Brilliant."

"Good evening, Lady Elizabeth."

"Good evening, Your Grace."

He bowed perfunctorily and set off for Viola and the unknown gentleman. He neared them just in time to hear Viola exclaim, "You're mistaken, sir. I don't know the first thing about it. Pardon me, I must tend to my music pupils." And she rushed away.

West followed but she escaped out the door and he was cornered by three of his sisters.

"Wasn't it a success?" Blanche asked.

"You were wonderful, Blanche. I confess I didn't think you had it in you."

"Wasn't she stunning?" Lord Flanders asked,

trailing after Blanche with a besotted look on his face.

"But where's Miss Beaton?" Birdie asked.

"I saw her run from the room," West said.

"Oh dear. What's wrong, do you know? Perhaps you shouldn't have invited her to perform."

"I was only trying to bring her out of her shell."

"But she doesn't like to be the center of attention. It was badly done of you, West. She didn't wish to play. You'll have to go and apologize."

"Yes, go and apologize this instant," Blanche said. "Bring back our smiling Miss Beaton. We want to celebrate with her."

"I'll find her. We'll all celebrate later. I brought home a bottle of Rosehill Park sparkling wine to cheer you with."

He rushed away. He hadn't liked the man's insistence on speaking with Viola when she clearly didn't wish to have anything to do with him. And what had he been mistaken about?

West rushed from the room, catching the faint scent of lavender in the air and following it.

Chapter Nineteen

❧ 🌹 ❧

THIS WAS THE price to pay when she overstepped her bounds, when she took center stage, Viola thought as she rushed through the garden toward the dower house.

She never should have played. Blast West for insisting that she play.

She could have refused. Why hadn't she?

A hidden streak of vanity had made her take the stage. When her fingers touched the keys she'd forgotten about the audience and played directly for West. Instead of the Bach she'd selected, she'd played the sonata she'd written about him years ago. The one about moonlight and kisses. She'd poured her doomed love and misplaced longing into the performance, saying with music the words she could never say to him.

Love me. As I love you.

She'd exposed herself. Exposed her heart. And it was just as she'd feared. Someone in the audience had guessed her secret. She'd put him off, pretended ignorance, but he'd seen right through her, insisting that it must be she who'd composed Mr. Beam's symphony.

"Viola!" West's low voice calling for her.

He'd followed her into the garden and easily caught up with her short gait.

"There you are," he said. "You ran off before everyone could congratulate you."

He looked delicious enough to eat in a cutaway black coat and white cravat, his jaw freshly shaved and his eyes filled with concern.

"This is the second time you've run out of a room without saying goodbye in as many days. What's the matter?"

She blinked away sudden tears. "Nothing. I—I have to go back. My father's nearly finished with the symphony and I must be there to help."

In reality her father had told her in no uncertain terms that he wanted to be alone. The frenzy of creation had him by the throat and all he needed right now was to be given the perfect creative conditions—which he had in the dower house—and to be left alone.

"He'll be all right for a few more minutes," West said. "My sisters are asking for you. They want to celebrate the success of the musicale."

"Have the guests departed?"

"It's only family left. And I have a bottle of sparkling wine made by your friend, Lady Henrietta Prince."

She smiled, though she felt more like crying. "Very well. I'll have a sip." She turned back toward the house.

"Wait, I want to know why you ran away. Who was that man?"

"Mr. Jonathan Atwater, of Atwater and Herrick,

a publishing house. Mr. Atwater is also a member of the Royal Society of Musicians."

"He didn't threaten you in any way?"

"No, no, nothing like that. He was a very kind gentleman. He was quizzing me about similarities between the sonata I played tonight and a movement of a symphonic work entered into a competition hosted by the Royal Society under the name of Mr. Vincent Beam."

"What's that got to do with anything?"

The secret was probably out now. She couldn't hide it anymore. "I'm Mr. Beam."

"Pardon?"

"I'm Mr. Vincent Beam. I entered the competition under a male pseudonym. And I won second place."

"Didn't Mr. Atwater know it was you?"

"I never claimed my prize and I never revealed my identity."

"Whyever not?"

"It's . . . complicated."

"Why did you enter the contest under a male pseudonym?"

"I shouldn't have done. I was inspired by my bold, fearless friends. India, Duchess of Ravenwood, has dedicated her life to uncovering the stories of women throughout history who have been overlooked, forgotten, and whose accomplishments have sometimes been erroneously attributed to men. She had just infiltrated the Society of Antiquaries in male clothing, and I thought to follow her example, on a much smaller and less risky scale, by submitting the symphonic work to the competition. I honestly never thought it would win. But when it came time to collect the prize, to reveal myself, I couldn't bring myself to do it. I'm not as intrepid as my friends."

He guided her into a secluded bower and gently pulled her onto an ironwork bench next to a burbling fountain. "Viola." He clasped both of her hands and gazed at her earnestly. "I think that you should take credit for your work. And that you should allow it to be published. It would be a great gift to the world."

With the soft scent of flowers around them, the soothing liquid accompaniment of the fountain, and his hands warm and strong, cradling hers, she allowed herself to imagine, just for one moment, what that would be like. A world where she was more fearless, and more focused on herself, on her accomplishments, instead of always nurturing those of others.

She broke the clasp of his hands and turned away from his penetrating gaze, staring at the fountain instead. "I've made my choices. It's too late to change the entire course of my life now." She laughed softly. "And have you read any reviews from the critics about female composers? The reviews of Mr. Beam's work have been glowing. Everyone wants to know who he is and whether he'll reveal his identity. The conversation would change drastically if they knew it was composed by a female. The reviews would read something like this: 'How rare it is for a woman to compose a symphony of real talent,' or they would conjecture that since I'm the daughter of a famous composer,

I must be merely copying my father. I couldn't be a talent in my own right."

And she couldn't risk the possibility of someone discovering that she'd been publishing under her father's name.

"Critics be damned!" West crooked his thumb under her chin and turned her to face him. "Don't allow a review that hasn't even been written yet to silence you. If you composed one symphonic work, there must be more inside that brilliant mind of yours."

There were those bells again. Ringing softly, just a tinkling in the night air . . . but they were ready to peal loudly, to claim joy.

"I have an entire trunk filled with my musical compositions," she admitted. "But I'm content with the life I've carved out for myself. It's only rarely that I feel that being my father's caretaker is a yawning abyss that swallows everything, consumes everything, leaving no room for me. For my creativity. My voice."

"Do you want the works you've composed to be discovered after your death and published posthumously? Everyone will say what a shame it was that the musical genius, Miss Viola Beaton, kept her opus locked away in a trunk."

"I'm the great composer's daughter. I'll be a side note in the history books if I'm mentioned at all. And that's perfectly amenable to me."

"Is it, though?" He cupped her face with his hand, stroking her cheek with his thumb. "Is that really enough? You should want more."

"I wouldn't call my works genius. I would say

they're an itch that must be scratched. I could no more stop composing music than I could stop breathing."

"And you shouldn't have to. You've been holding yourself back from truly living. I saw you perform tonight. You were amazing. You shouldn't hide that talent from the world."

"I never should have performed."

"You don't perform. You don't dance. You don't publish under your name. You believe in love with a capital *L* but you've given up on suitors and having a family of your own. The buttoned-up wallflower is only a shell you've developed to move through the world overlooked and unnoticed. The real you emerges when you play. Passionately alive, ablaze with talent. Don't squander your life like I have. Don't hide your brilliant light from the world. Be adored. Be worshipped."

"That's just it. I don't want to be adored, placed on a pedestal, by the public. I've seen what that did to my father. What fame wrought on him. The toll it's taken. It nearly killed him. Mine was a childhood filled with the requirement for survival in the eye of a storm. My father was always unpredictable, but fame made him a dictator, ruling the lives of all around him by his whims. I learned to navigate carefully. To expose myself as Mr. Beam would be to expose myself to the possibility of a new storm. The publicity that would occur around the daughter of a famous composer attempting to establish her own opus."

"It's still a shame. Judging by what I heard you

play the other evening and what I heard tonight, your works are worthy of standing on their own."

"The critics wouldn't make that distinction. I would become famous only by association with my father. Fame is dangerous. The power to move audiences, to make people weep openly, to bring them joy . . . sometimes it comes with a heavy price. I witnessed how this power changed my father, how it warped him. He thought he was above the rules of society. Until he was sued in a court of law and lost everything, including his so-called friends."

"I understand about the fear of becoming one's parent. You think that fame might change you in the same ways it changed your father. But you're not your father. You are sensible, strong, and manage those around you with sensitivity and caring."

She placed her hand over his and tilted her neck, leaning into him. "I gather from your sisters that you've lived your entire life in opposition to your father. But you can learn to forgive him. What did he do to you, West?"

His face closed, eyes dark in the shadows. "That's a long story. We should be joining my sisters."

"Humph. So you can ask me questions about my past and give me advice about my future but the moment I ask you something about yourself you change the subject and try to leave?"

"I don't talk about my father."

"You should. It might loosen some of the hold he still has over you."

"Here's something about my father. He wrote to me for years before his death. One letter per week. I have them all in a box in my room. Most of them unopened."

"You never read his letters?"

"I read the first month's worth. They were all the same. A long list of my brother Bertram's accomplishments, how perfect he was, how much my father loved him. Each one of those letters was a dagger delivered straight to my heart."

"How did your father die?"

"His heart gave out after Bertram's horse riding accident. He didn't want to go on living without his beloved, golden son. The last letter came one week before his death."

"He didn't love you as well as Bertram?"

"He hated me from birth."

"But why?"

"As you said, it's complicated. He hated me and told me that I was wicked . . . and so I became what he branded me. And after Bertram died I did nothing to take up the yoke of familial responsibilities. I've recently met with my man of business and learned that Westbury Abbey has fallen into terrible disrepair and the tenants are being displaced. My actions, my sins, have had far-reaching consequences for my sisters, my tenants, for those people who relied on me as head of this family. I've begun to take responsibility, but I have so much more to do."

Part of his responsibility to the family was to marry the perfect duchess.

Lady Winifred Woolfrey would restore his

fortune and she'd been prepared from birth for the vast duties and responsibilities of a duchess.

Unlike Viola who had received no formal education, never made her debut, and had resigned herself to becoming a spinster.

They were on opposite ends of a wide societal gulf.

So why were they sitting together in this secluded bower like lovers?

She had to be stronger and more sensible than this. She backed away from him.

"My father and I will be leaving as soon as he finishes the symphony," she said stiffly.

"Where will you go?"

"My friend Isobel has found another house for us. It's not right in London but I think the healthful air of the countryside will do my father good. The musicale is over and your sisters have shown themselves to be sensible and trustworthy. They don't need me as teacher, or companion."

"Don't you like it here? Is it because I forced you to perform?"

"My work here is finished. The girls are doing wonderfully. And you've reformed so thoroughly that you have duchess hopefuls lining up. There's only one item left on your reform campaign."

"I'm not truly reformed." His eyes darkened. "Don't delude yourself." His gaze brushed her lips, and then his thumb followed. "You make me want to be wicked, Viola."

She longed to be wicked. She wanted to throw herself into his arms instead of leaving. But if she did, the carefully constructed reasons for why they could never be together would burn in the blaze of this attraction between them.

She had to keep her head in order to protect her heart. "I think you should read the letters your father wrote."

The seductive light in his eyes faded. "Why would I do that? I know exactly what they say."

"It might help you relinquish your hatred. Your father is dead. He has no power over you. And you believing that you're doomed to be bad until you die an early death only gives him power from beyond the grave. You don't know what he wrote. Maybe he had a change of heart. Maybe he was begging you for forgiveness."

"That's impossible."

"Read the letters," she urged gently. "Make a ritual out of it. Maybe burn them after reading."

"Even thinking about those letters sends ice water through my veins."

"I think it would help release you from this hurt and resentment."

"I think it would make me even more angry. Why are you even trying to help me, Viola? I told you that I was a lost cause from the beginning. Though I'll make you a bargain. I'll read the letters if you reveal your identity as Mr. Beam." He watched her face. "Ah, not so eager to ask me to change my life now, are you?"

"Oh, West. There are other factors at play. I've been accepting minor musical commissions on my father's behalf and submitting them under his name. With his blessing, of late, but I can't risk people finding out that they weren't composed by him. Right now I'm working on a commission for an original Christmas carol to be debuted at the Hanover Square Rooms and sung by choirs all over England."

"That does change things. But not entirely. I think there's still a way for you to—"

"West? Viola?" a voice called. Birdie came into view.

They jumped apart guiltily.

"We were just coming," said West.

"Hurry or the sparkling wine will grow warm," Birdie called.

The ladies gathered round when they returned, chattering and laughing about the musicale.

"Wasn't it a wonderful evening?" Blanche asked. Viola noticed that she didn't mention Lord Laxton's absence. She had several other suitors now and had begun to forget him.

"Yes," West said, clearing his throat. The tenderness in his eyes hit Viola with an almost physical force. "It was a wonderful evening and it was all because of Miss Viola Beaton," he said, raising his glass of sparkling wine. The bubbles sparkled in the candlelight. And his smile was nearly as bright. "Who brings music, laughter, and sunshine into our home."

"To Viola!" The ladies and West raised their glasses. Even Birdie had been allowed a half glass.

Viola blinked, fighting back the urge to cry. "To music, laughter, and sunshine," she said, and they all drank.

Viola's mind was still churning through the

conversation with West. She'd opened up to him, told him more about her past than she'd told nearly anyone.

She watched him joking with his sisters, teasing them and giving them praise about their performances. She saw right through his careless, hedonistic facade to the kind, warm heart that beat beneath. He was lonely, and weary of empty pleasures. He loved his family and craved their companionship.

He'd settle down with Lady Winifred and they'd all be one big happy family.

And she had no role to play in their future.

She moved away from them, going to sit on the pianoforte bench in the next room.

"Viola? Is anything the matter?" asked Birdie, always so quick to notice other people's emotions. She sat beside her on the bench.

"I'm only a little tired."

"Is your father finished with the symphony yet?"

"Nearly. Only a few more days now."

Birdie clasped her arms around Viola's waist and laid her head on her shoulder. "That's wonderful. I can't wait to hear the grand symphony that was finished in our house."

Viola ruffled her hair. "And your composition was very much admired this evening."

Birdie smiled. "We're very lucky to have you."

"I'm afraid that after my father finishes his symphony we'll be leaving the dower house and going to live in the countryside."

"You can't leave us!"

Viola sighed. "Your brother will marry soon and it's time for me to leave."

Birdie clenched her hands into fists. "I wish you were an heiress. Then West could marry you and we'd all live happily ever after."

Viola smiled sadly. "Even if I were an heiress, I'm not highborn and have no social standing."

"Don't you want to marry West?"

"It doesn't matter what I want. It's the way of the world. Lady Winifred will make an excellent duchess."

"Who cares about Lady Winifred. She's gracious enough but you're . . . you're Viola. You're my friend. I want you with me always."

"Life doesn't always give us what we want."

"Perhaps you're a secret heiress?" Birdie asked eagerly. "Your mother was a secret princess. And she has a hoard of jewels stashed away in a cave and she'll send you a letter in code and we'll have to discover the location! The cave will be underwater and we'll all have to learn how to swim to dive down into it and retrieve the jewels. There will be tiaras, and crowns, and parures of the purest diamonds. You'll give me a set and I'll look like a princess wearing it."

Viola laughed. "Oh, Birdie." She hugged her sweet friend. "I wish it was all true. But it's not. Those kinds of things only happen in fairy tales." Viola pasted a smile on her face. "Come, let's go and join the others."

The ladies were discussing an outing to Hyde Park tomorrow.

"You'll come with us for a promenade tomorrow, won't you, Viola?" asked Belinda.

"I don't think so."

"I don't want to promenade in Hyde Park," West barked. "If you don't go, I won't."

"West," Blanche remonstrated. "You have to go. Viola, please say you'll come."

"Oh very well," Viola said. She knew better than to argue with a roomful of Delamars.

"Splendid!" Belinda clapped her hands. "I'm to wear my new promenade dress. It's a robe of dove-colored gros de Naples, and the border is finished with three rows of pointed blond lace netting . . ."

Belinda waxed eloquent about her new costume. Birdie ran to the pianoforte and began accompanying her sister with a lively tune while Betsy and West danced a galloping reel.

Order had been restored. Tender, intimate moments in rose bowers with West were forbidden. She and her father would leave soon.

Life didn't always give you what you wanted.

And that was that.

Chapter Twenty

$\mathcal{A}$ MONTH AGO, West would never have been caught dead doing something so prosaic and dull as promenade in Hyde Park of a Sunday afternoon with the fashionable set who owned splendid equipages and hailed from ancient and honorable families.

Yet here he was, ambling down the wide gravel path surrounded by a surfeit of sisters, followed by liveried footmen resplendent in Delamar blue and gold, with powdered hair and crisp white gloves.

"Everyone's saying that you're going to propose to Lady Winifred today," Belinda reported. "I think it's her mother spreading the rumor."

West shrugged. "We'll see."

The problem was that he didn't want to propose to Lady Winifred. She was a lovely young lady but she didn't have alluring green eyes and a smile that he'd do anything to see.

Viola hadn't smiled yet this morning. She hung back, walking behind the group.

Blanche walked a little ways ahead of them, flanked by Lord Middleton and Lord Flanders. From the snippets of conversation that West overheard, Middleton was boring her with talk of stable bloodlines, and Flanders wasn't doing much better, having decided to explain his scientific experimentation with electricity.

"It's a perfect day for seeing and being seen," said Belinda. "I'm in love with my new promenade dress. Isn't it simply exquisite?"

"I think we've heard enough about that blasted promenade dress," grumbled Betsy. "I say, is that a cricket match going on over there? Wish I could join."

"The chemisette is fine cambric and these gold buttons are glowing in the sunshine, and I do allow that this full ruche of blond net around the throat is the height of elegance," Belinda continued, ignoring her twin.

"Er . . . it's very becoming." West thought that the layers of netting around her throat made her look rather like those old portraits of Queen Elizabeth with her head atop a platter of stiff white lace ruff.

"And these blue forget-me-nots on my bonnet, and my gray half boots. It's like I stepped out of the pages of the *Ladies Pocket Magazine*!"

"Pride goeth before a fall," said Betsy.

"Don't you dare trip me, Betsy Grace Delamar," Belinda said, knowing her sister hated her middle name. "If I get mud on my lace netting, so help me I'll never forgive you."

"You look like a dress shop exploded and you were in the middle of it all. You can only see your cheeks and your eyes. How's a gentleman supposed to find you in all that netting?"

"Ladies," said Viola, stepping in between them. "Isn't it a splendid day? The sun is shining, and the birds are singing a song about building their nests and lining them with feathers."

"They're probably eyeing Belinda's netting," Betsy said. "Shouldn't wonder if one of them swoops down and tears off a yard or so."

West had to laugh at that. "Belinda looks very well. And, Bets, you may run over and watch the cricket match, but only until we're finished walking. And I said *watch*, mind you."

"Jolly good of you!" Betsy ran off with no hesitation, her race across the pathways generating scandalized glances and whispers.

Viola smiled at him gratefully and his heart skipped a beat. That's what he'd been waiting for this entire morning, to see those dimples.

He had the sudden and nearly uncontrollable urge to take her hand.

Wanting to kiss a pretty woman was ordinary. He would have been alarmed if he didn't want to kiss her.

Wanting to take her hand in his and stroll through a park . . . that was . . . unprecedented.

You could hold her hand. Make her smile. Give her your heart.

No, he couldn't. He was supposed to be courting Lady Winifred. It was his duty to the family. The problem was . . . his heart was torn between duty and desire.

He desired Viola, and he wanted to be with her and maybe he was even smitten with her, as Jax had accused, but he couldn't be with her for so many reasons, not the least of which was that he'd given up his right to such simple pleasures.

The smell of fresh crisp air with the hint of impending rain. The sound of robins twittering.

An alluring woman's smile of approbation that made the day feel complete in a new way.

He was saved from this dangerous line of thought by his friend Daniel, Duke of Ravenwood, and his strikingly beautiful wife meeting up with them at a crossroads. Ravenwood held the hand of a sturdy redheaded lad of about four.

"Westbury," Ravenwood said. "Been searching for you. Couldn't believe my ears when your man told me you were out promenading in Hyde Park. Thought you spontaneously combusted in direct sunlight."

"Ha-ha, Ravenwood. Thought you were in Paris."

"We're back for a time."

The duchess strode over to Viola and the two of them launched into an animated conversation.

"Who's this little fellow?" West bent down and patted the boy's cap.

"This is Ambrose, one of my brother-in-law's brood."

"What's Banksford about these days? Haven't seen him in quite some time." The Duke of Banksford was an old friend of West's.

"He's still building steam engines, financing railways, and filling the nursery with redheaded children."

The boy tugged on West's coattails. "Hullo, are you a duke?"

"Unfortunately, yes."

"My father is a duke. And I'll be a duke some-day."

"Shall you make a good duke?"

"Of course I shall. My mother says that I'm practically perfect in every way."

"Does she now."

"Oh yes, and then she kisses me and reads me stories about rabbits. You're very tall and strong. I shall be tall and strong someday. Will you lift me up on your shoulders so I can watch the cricket match?"

Westbury lifted him onto his shoulder and his chubby little legs dangled down.

"I'm so high!" Ambrose shouted gleefully. "I can see the entire park."

"I spoke with Rafe before I left Paris," Raven-wood said. "He asked me to check up on you while I was in London. I'll send him a shocking report of your conventionality. I did some re-search about you and you haven't done anything scandalous in weeks. You haven't gambled away any more of your fortune, picked any fights with prize fighters, accepted any reckless bets, not even a hint of dalliances with courtesans. What gives?"

"I find myself with duties now. I'm making up for past bad behavior by being trotted around Hyde Park, allowing heiresses to ogle me and matchmaking mamas to smack their lips and make wedding plans. All for my sisters' sake. I'll reform just enough to see them all settled."

"You know, we all warned our wives, before they were our wives, about you. We told them

'Stay away from Westbury. He's dangerously depraved.' If our past selves could see you now, we'd remove the warning label."

"I'm still the same old Westbury," West growled. "Dangerous as ever."

"You can pretend this is only temporary respectability until your sisters are settled, but this looks like domesticity to me. Look at you with that child on your shoulder. Female hearts are melting across the park."

He caught Viola gazing at him. She blushed a pink shade to match the gown she wore.

"Miss Beaton is blushing," observed Ravenwood. "She's such a charming young lady, I've always thought. One of my wife's best friends."

West didn't reply. Best to remain silent. Ravenwood would see right through him if he opened his mouth.

"Banksford married his children's governess," Ravenwood remarked.

"Banksford could afford to marry a governess. I can't."

"It's truly that bad?"

"Maybe I should try inventing steam engines."

"Or you could turn to a life of crime. Art thievery, jewel heists, and the like. Course then I'd have to hunt you down and bring you to justice."

"Banksford wanted to run one of his railways through Westbury Abbey at one point but I turned him down. I've made a lot of bad decisions in my life, Ravenwood."

His friend searched his face. "I do believe you've changed, Westbury. There's something decidedly different about you. Might it have anything to do with sweet, pretty music instructors?"

Don't answer that. Just keep walking.

VIOLA KEPT STRIDE with her dear friend India, known as Indy, with difficulty, as her friend strode instead of walking at a normal pace.

"Damn these skirts." Indy lifted her hem. "I have trousers underneath. Just waiting until we're back at the house and I can peel off this hampering gown. How have you been since I've been away?"

"Father is nearly finished with his symphony, the ladies acquitted themselves admirably at a musicale yesterday evening, and I'm hard at work on a new commission."

"I meant how are you feeling. You seem not quite your usual smiling self."

"I'm grand." Viola repeated the lie. She'd repeat it as many times as she had to in order to make it true. She couldn't shake a sense of impending doom.

"You forget that I know you well. And I know when you're lying to me. Is it about Westbury? I see the way you look at him."

"Westbury is proposing to Lady Winifred Woolfrey today," Viola said stiffly. "It will be an excellent match. Everyone approves." Her brave facade crumpled and she clutched Indy's hand. "And it's all wrong," she whispered. "I'm devastated. It's tearing me apart."

"Oh, Viola." Indy stopped walking and gave her a hug. "I didn't know you were in such pain."

"It's nothing. I'll get over it."

"You're obviously in love with him. Doesn't he love you back?"

"He's too afraid of allowing himself to love. And I'm not duchess material."

Indy shook her shoulders gently. "Don't be silly. There are many kinds of duchesses. Take me for example."

"Yes, but Westbury only requires one kind. And because of my birth and lack of education and prospects, I can't be her."

"Oh, Viola. You poor thing. I wish I'd returned earlier. Have you spoken with the rest of the club?"

"Not recently."

"Come to the book club meeting tomorrow. We'll talk it all through. You could use some wise counsel."

"Tomorrow will be too late."

Before Indy could respond, Bernadette caught up with them, leaving Belinda behind with some of her fashionable girlfriends. "Is that a knife at your hip, Your Grace?" she asked Indy, her eyes wide.

"I always carry a knife in a holster at my hip. One never knows what nefarious character one might encounter in Hyde Park."

"I've heard the thrilling tales of your adventures in archaeology. I want to be an archaeologist. Or an entomologist. I haven't decided which I like better, dirt or insects."

The duchess laughed heartily. "Most young ladies of the *ton* would be deciding between ribbons and lace. I like you, Miss Bernadette Delamar."

"You're one of my heroes, Your Grace. I should like to visit The Boadicea Club on the Strand someday and meet my other heroes."

"I'm sure that can be arranged, right, Viola?"

"Of course."

They drew closer to Westbury and Ravenwood, who had stopped to watch the cricket match. West still had a chubby toddler perched on his shoulder, pointing things out and keeping up a steady stream of chatter.

"That child is one of your brother's, isn't he?" Viola asked. "He has the same red hair as his mother, Mari."

"He's an adorable little thing, but so exhausting, even for an afternoon. I'm very glad that Raven and I decided not to have any children."

Bernadette gawked at her. "You can do that?"

"Of course you can do that. It's as valid a choice as any. I'm a very good aunt when I'm in London. I bring them the best presents from my travels."

"Is that Lord Laxton?" Bernadette asked, pointing to the stream of carriages passing one another in a slowly moving mass.

West handed the child to Ravenwood and dropped back. "Where?" he asked Bernadette.

She pointed to a gleaming coach-and-four.

"It does look like him," Viola said. "Blast. Just when Blanche was beginning to forget about him and enjoy the company of her new suitors. This could be disastrous."

Indy frowned. "What has Laxton done?"

"It damn well better not be him," West said with a glower. "I'm going over to investigate."

Viola placed a hand on his arm. "Don't do anything rash."

"I've heard that one before."

"I mean it, West," Viola urged, forgetting to call him Your Grace.

Bernadette gave her a sharp glance. "What shall I tell Lady Winifred?" she asked.

"Tell her I have something important to attend to." West pulled Viola aside. "I'll give you a full report when I return. And don't worry, I'll be civilized."

He strode away, a tall, imposing silhouette against the sun.

Viola was worried about the threat to Blanche, of course, but all she could think, all her foolish heart was saying was . . . he's not going to propose to anyone today.

Chapter Twenty-One

❧ 🌹 ❧

WEST STILL WASN'T back. Viola knew because every ten minutes she left the pianoforte to look out the window for his carriage.

It was growing dark. He'd said he would report back to her when he found anything certain about Lord Laxton's whereabouts, and whether he posed a further threat to Blanche. But he could have forgotten. He might be out carousing with his friends on the town. And why not? She and West had been spending so much time together, but it was all for his sisters' sake.

She mustn't confuse his attentiveness and the conversation they'd had last night with anything other than a developing friendship based on proximity and mutual goals.

They could go no further than friendship. And yet . . . seeing him holding that adorable toddler on his shoulder had given her a strange pang in the chest. Despite his protestations to the contrary, she was convinced that he would make a wonderful father.

Parenthood had changed her friends and their husbands. The pride and pure, joyful love she saw shining in their eyes when they were with their children sometimes made her feel like a ragged street urchin with her nose pressed against the display window of a confectioner's shop.

Longing for impossible things.

She stopped pressing her nose to the music room's window and returned to the pianoforte bench. She was supposed to be working on lyrics and music for the Christmas carol commission, not mooning over West.

The way his large hand had cradled her neck, positioning her for his masterful kiss.

That kiss.

Her body responding, vibrating and ringing with a new song.

A lyric came to her: *In the darkness comes a chime . . .*

Not a bad line for a Yuletide carol. Her left hand shaped low, minor notes, dark and somber, while her right hand found a shimmering, hopeful treble counterpoint.

In the darkness comes a chime.

Wild bells, unseen but real . . .

The two melodies called her ears in different directions and tugged at her heart. She heard a cello begin to play along with her left hand, solemn and sonorous, painting a dark, starless night with sweeping strokes.

Then orchestral bells rang out, spiraling into the night, calling for starshine, awakening hope.

The two melodies circled round and round until finally they met and merged in joyful unison.

The music spoke what she wanted to say to West.

I love you, and I think you can learn to love me, too.

It was all just a fantasy. Moonbeams and fairy tales, as West called it. Even if they loved each other, they could never be together. They were separate notes strung together by circumstance. They were an arpeggio; the notes of a chord played individually, never as a single unit.

"That's so beautiful but it's also sad," spoke a deep voice behind her.

Viola's fingers froze on the keys.

"What are you working on, the Christmas carol you told me about?"

"Yes." Although the carol had somehow transformed into a song about her and West. She closed the cover over the keys. "I was finished for the evening. Did you find Laxton?"

"It's a long story. Don't suppose you have any whisky about?"

"You're reformed, remember?"

"Just a small nip."

"There's brandy in my rooms."

"Miss Beaton, I'm shocked."

"I told you that I enjoy a few drops in my tea sometimes," she said defensively.

"And you know what I say to that." He grinned. "Lose the tea."

She led him to her sitting room. Purposefully leaving the door to her chambers open, she joined him by the small fire lit in the grate. She poured brandy into a rose-patterned teacup and handed it to him. Then she poured a little for herself.

"Thank you." He took a sip.

She settled into a chair and he followed suit. "Tell me what you found out. Is Laxton back?"

"I didn't reach the carriage we saw in Hyde Park in time to see if it was Laxton. I've been all over London searching for him. Some people thought they'd seen him, others swore he was still at his country estate. I didn't receive positive confirmation until I visited his club and persuaded one of his mates to admit that he was back."

"And how did you persuade him?" she asked, eyeing him for fresh bruises.

"No violence was necessary. All I had to do was buy him a whisky and he was happy to tell me everything he knew. Laxton is back and plotting something. He didn't know quite what, but it had something to do with a proper young lady."

"Blanche. Oh no! What will he do? I'm so afraid that she still loves him and might do something foolish."

"We must be extremely vigilant. I made certain she was safe in her room when I arrived home just now, and I arranged for a guard at the door to the house, with a view of Blanche's window, throughout the night."

"I'll talk to her tomorrow. I do think perhaps we should tell her the full extent of what he said about her. I only hinted at the depths of his disparagement, but she should know the truth."

"I agree."

"Blanche is such an intelligent woman. I honestly don't think she would do anything foolish like run away with Laxton. She's too controlled and pragmatic for that. She said she'd had enough scandal for a lifetime and wanted your family to be free from public embarrassment in future. That's why she's advocating for Lady Winifred."

"And we're back on the subject of brides. Hand me that brandy bottle if you please."

"West, you're not taking this seriously."

He placed his teacup on a table and rose to stand before the fire, so she couldn't see his face.

She could, however, see his backside. And that was a very enjoyable view, indeed. When had he removed his coat?

She gulped the remainder of the brandy in her teacup.

She'd always felt that the fashion for men's breeches was too tight, and not flattering to the average gentleman.

West was no average gentleman.

He was made for skintight breeches. They displayed his sculpted, well-defined buttocks, muscular thighs, and long legs to perfection.

Oh, Viola, she thought sadly. *When will you learn to ignore the view?*

"Do you want to know the real reason I object to Lady Winifred?" His voice held a challenge. He almost sounded angry, or some other strong emotion colored his words.

"I do. Because she's the most unobjectionable woman in London. She'll make the ideal duchess."

"I'll tell you what's wrong with her." He turned toward her, and the anguished look on his face nearly startled her into dropping her teacup. She set it down and folded her hands primly in her lap.

He advanced, his eyes dark and stormy, his blond hair aglow with firelight.

"She's not you, Viola." His gaze captured her, fixing her to the carpet. "She's not you."

"Don't be ridiculous . . . I'm not right for—"

The rest of her protestation was swallowed by a kiss.

Chapter Twenty-Two

ℰ 🌹 ℰ

ALL WEST KNEW was that he had to kiss Viola so well that she'd stop trying to make him propose to other women. A kiss to make her see how much he wanted her.

Viola. And no one else.

The best kiss he'd ever given. A searing, unmistakably passionate and possessive statement that he was claiming her for his own.

She was his. The only woman he wanted to kiss.

She twined her arms around his neck, pulling him closer, offering her lips trustingly, sweetly.

Walking through the park side by side was all well and good, and she'd looked so gorgeous by sunlight, but this was what his body had been screaming for.

He didn't know whether it was right or wrong. He barely knew his own name. He only knew that he had to taste her lips. Make her his.

He slammed the door shut with his boot and lifted her into his arms, carrying her from the sitting room into the bedchamber.

There was evidence of Viola all over her room.

Parchment paper filled with scrawled musical notation. A novel open beside the bed. The yellow shawl she'd come to his bedchamber to retrieve.

He smiled against her cheek, remembering that morning. How all he'd wanted to do was pull her down into bed with him and have his way with her.

She was making these little encouraging noises, urging him on, and all he cared about in that moment was pleasing her. Giving her pleasure.

He deposited her on the bed and pulled the white lace cap from her head, running his fingers through her hair until it hung in silken waves around her shoulders. He made quick work of her slippers and outer garments until she was only wearing a thin muslin chemise and stockings with pink ribbons at the top.

"You're so delicious, Viola. I want to eat you whole." He lay beside her, holding himself in check. Just a little taste. He eased the chemise down, feasting his gaze on her generous curves. He cupped her full, round breasts, loving the way they overflowed his palms.

As HIS LARGE hands slid over her sensitive skin a ripple of awareness resonated through her body. He kissed her lips as he caressed her breasts, teasing the nipples to aching hardness.

This. This is what I want. What I've always wanted. Kiss me harder. Take more.

She arched against him and her hands, which had been clasped behind his back, broke free and explored him, finding the rich texture of the hair at the nape of his neck, the corded muscles of his throat, the marble-hard muscles of his biceps.

She tugged at his shirt and it came free of his trousers and she slipped her hand up, over his taut abdomen, through the hair on his chest, over his heart.

All the while he kissed her, she kissed him, and they moved together, back and forth.

His hand squeezing her breast, his other hand wrapped around the back of her neck.

He moaned softly when she brushed her thumb over his nipple, mimicking what he was doing to her. Well, it seemed the right thing to do.

He lifted her on top of him, cradling her against him, drinking deeper, taking more, his arousal pressing against her belly.

He trailed kisses down her clavicle, making a melody of it, teasing her.

She bent backward, wanting his lips on her flesh. The points of her breasts.

Still he teased, kissing around her nipples, until she wanted to scream.

And then. Oh, and then . . .

His lips closed around her nipple, wet and hot, giving her what she desired.

It was perfect. It was . . . she had no words left. Only feelings.

He kissed first one nipple, then the other, sucking with his lips, and tugging so softly with his teeth, only the slightest pressure but it brought every nerve in her body alive with a new song, a new melody.

She shifted her weight, instinctively opening her thighs and rubbing against his arousal.

He moaned and closed his eyes. She tried it again, shifting her weight up his body and back down again, still with the barrier of his trousers between them. It felt so delicious to slide against him like this, to feel the power she held over him.

"Enough," he said through gritted teeth, stilling her hips with his hands. He flipped her over onto her back. His hands roamed, finding the hem of her chemise, and going higher.

She shifted her thighs apart to give him better access to the place that was waiting impatiently for his touch.

His fingers played her, stroked her, parted her thighs.

This was life, lusty life. And she was living it. Not watching from the wings. Not hearing about it secondhand.

This was life. Her life. She wanted it all. More. Give her more.

"Give me more," she said, her words tumbling out. "I want more."

He moved down her body and his head went underneath her chemise. "You want this?" His lips and tongue moved over her core, drawing music from her as a cellist created warm, sonorous tones with a bow.

"Mmm." She bit her lip. It was strange. It was so, so beautiful. "Yes."

His tongue flicked over her lightly, and then he dipped inside her with his fingers—two of them, she judged—sliding inside her, using her body's wetness to ease their passage.

His tongue stroked her core while his fingers moved inside her, stretching her, exploring and claiming.

She heard music, the beginning of the melody she'd been writing about him.

She heard how it grew, how it changed and how it became more passionate.

It was building to a crescendo, becoming more frenzied. She began moving with him, her body finding a rhythm that pleased her.

Her head fell back against the pillows. She turned away from him, not wanting him to see her face because she must be grimacing now. There was some effort involved here, some work she was doing.

It was a race, and she was about to win.

The sensations swelled and she clenched her inner muscles around his fingers and then the race was won. She shuddered, pleasure breaking, timpani crashing, with violins playing a lilting finale.

She collapsed back onto the bed feeling boneless, wrung out, and oh so happy.

But not finished yet. Not nearly finished.

She wrapped her arms around his neck and whispered in his ear the words that came from her heart. "I want more. I want everything."

She touched his arousal, shaping it with her palm.

"Damnation, Viola." He shuddered, his body

tense. "You don't know how much I want to give you more."

"Then do it."

"If we . . . do it . . . I'll be forced to . . ."

He didn't finish the rest of the sentence so she finished it for him in her mind.

I'll be forced to propose to you and that would be the worst possible thing in the world for me, my family, and my fortune.

"I understand." Viola gathered herself together. Of course they couldn't do what she'd been wanting to do. They shouldn't have done what they'd just done.

The spell was broken.

The music receded.

She came back to her senses. She was nearly naked.

She'd betrayed her feelings. She'd let him see how much she cared. How much she was willing to give him. How much control he had over her.

"Viola, speak to me." He held both of her hands. "Do you want this?"

He meant: did she want to become his mistress. Because he couldn't propose to her. She'd known it all along and ignored it.

"I think it's best if you leave, Your Grace." She twisted away from him, blindly searching for her clothing. She jumped off the bed, clutching her gown to her body.

"Wait, Viola. Let's talk about this," West said. She was upset and rightfully so.

"Just go, West." She nodded at the door.

"I don't want to hurt you. You're too beautiful and filled with life. I want to see you blossom. Take your place on center stage. You should claim the musical prize you won. Steal the show as you did at the musicale."

As she was in danger of stealing his heart.

"Are you saying that you'd like to see me marry someone else?"

"Isn't that what you've been telling me to do this entire time?"

"Yes, because it's the right and the prudent thing to do. Oh this is all such a tangle."

He came to her, placing his arms around her.

"Viola." He drew a ragged breath, resting his forehead against hers. He didn't know what to say to her. He cared deeply for her but he was all wrong for her. She was a romantic who believed in love. He was broken, tainted, and lost. "What you said in the garden. You were right. I should read my father's letters and let go of this anger and shame. But I can't. Not yet. I'm not ready."

"I know you can face this, West." Even when she was angry at him she still cared enough to urge him to face his past.

A knock on her door sent them flying to opposite corners of the room. "Just a moment," Viola called.

"Your father is asking for you, Miss Beaton," the elderly manservant named Withers called.

"I'll be down shortly."

West helped her dress and stood for a moment,

clasping her hands. "I wish circumstances were different."

"It's all right, West. I have no expectations. I want nothing from you." She shoved her hair back into a knot and replaced her white cap.

"You should want something from me. And I wish to God I could give it to you."

"Go home, West," she said. "This can never happen again."

She left the room.

He wished he was a different person, a better man. And that he was free to marry whom he chose instead of needing to marry for money, for his sisters' honor and their position in society.

If he were free . . . but he wasn't. And he couldn't act like he was.

Chapter Twenty-Three

❧ 🌹 ❧

"THIS BOOK FEELS different to me, almost as if it was written by a different person," mused Isobel the next afternoon.

Viola and her friends were gathered at their clubhouse to discuss Daphne Villeneuve's *The Dastardly Duke's Secrets*, the final book in a Gothic romance trilogy which they'd all been waiting impatiently for.

Viola was glad to leave the house for a few hours to sort through the complicated emotions crowding her mind. There was no safer and more welcoming place to be than a book club meeting with her friends.

"*The Mad Marquess's Secret* and *The Wicked Earl's Wishes* were excellent, of course, but this one . . . it's almost as if the author knows me," Della gushed. "Oh, Daphne, I do wish you would reveal your identity to the world so that we could invite you here to give a lecture."

"I want to ask her why Vespera was so stupid as to barter herself to that dastardly duke," Isobel said. "I don't find it plausible. She's otherwise sensible, but when he appears, she turns into a blithering ninny."

Viola could tell her friend a thing or two about that.

"This one was rather more . . . sensual than the other two," said their shy and bookish friend Lady Philippa Bramble. "Like a kettle boiling over and filling a room with steam. I had to fan myself as I was reading."

"And my spectacles fogged up because I was breathing rather rapidly," said Lady Beatrice Wright. "Ford asked me if I was feeling quite well. I'll give it to him to read next. That scene with the candle wax . . . I had no idea."

"I know. And that scene where the duke was taking a swim in the lake and then he emerged wearing that soaking white shirt that didn't hide *anything*," breathed Della.

Viola tried to follow the conversation, but her mind kept wandering back to her own recent steamy encounter. Which was probably far steamier than anything that had occurred in the book.

The things West had done. Her wanton response. And then the sensual spell had been broken and she'd crashed back into the real world where they could never truly be together.

"You're very quiet, Viola," Beatrice remarked. "It's not like you."

"I've been so preoccupied of late with my pupils, my father, and the Christmas carol I'm composing."

"And with a certain duke?" teased Della.

"And how is that going? Is he as easy to manage and control as you anticipated?" Isobel asked.

"Not really."

"I do hope you haven't been kissing him," scolded Isobel. "You know he's an unrepentant rogue."

"Ladies, why should we read about dastardly fictional dukes when Viola can tell us about real ones?" asked Philippa.

"Sometimes rogues give the best kisses," Beatrice said. "I should know. Viola is no blushing young miss and if there happen to have been kisses—"

"I kissed him!" Viola blurted. She'd never been very good at keeping secrets. "I kissed him . . . and more."

Several of the ladies moved their chairs closer.

"What do you mean *and more*?" asked Della.

"Do be specific," urged Philippa.

"I was only trying to do the right thing. I asked him why he hadn't proposed marriage to the perfect, respectable, and unobjectionable Lady Winifred Woolfrey yet and do you know what he said?"

"Never mind what he said . . . I want to know what he did," said Philippa.

"His whole demeanor changed and he stared into my eyes and he said, 'Viola, the reason I haven't proposed to Lady Winifred is that she's not you.'"

"Oh my." Della placed a hand over her heart. "That's dreadfully romantic."

"I don't think it's romantic at all," said Isobel. "It might be if he were a respectable, honorable man."

"Oh but it was romantic, Isobel. It was. And I'm afraid I felt its effects most devastatingly and I tried to mount some manner of objection, but he swallowed my words with kisses and then I may have . . . I may have wrapped my arms around him and pulled him tightly into my embrace."

The ladies stared at her.

"At least I think I did, or maybe he swept me into his arms, either way, I ended up being carried across the room in his powerful arms and then . . ." Viola paused. Perhaps she shouldn't divulge the true details. But these were her best friends, after all. "He laid me down upon the bed."

"You were in a bedchamber alone with him?" asked Philippa, eyes widening.

"I'm afraid so."

"Miss Viola Beaton, did I not warn you about just such an occurrence?" Isobel scolded.

"You did—you certainly did. All of you did. I've no excuse. I don't know what comes over me every time I see him. I can't seem to control myself. He's been so different lately. Almost as if he's transforming into the duke I'd invented in my mind. The honorable, thoughtful one. He even purchased a special auditory aid for my father."

"But then what happened? You were on the bed . . ." prompted Philippa.

"While there was no candle wax involved, it was quite steamy. He was intent solely on my pleasure and he gave most freely."

"Perhaps he's a romantic disguised as a rogue?" Della asked hopefully.

"Even if he were, we can never be together, for he's lost his fortune at the gaming hells and must marry for money. And swiftly."

"You can't trust that man, Viola," Isobel said sternly. "Are you willing to become his mistress?"

"I overheard some ladies speculating that I was his mistress and it made me feel horrid. I could never do that, especially because I care so much for his sisters and it would harm them if such a scandal came to light."

"Erm, do you think we might go back to a previous point?" Philippa tapped her finger on the table. "You were in the bed, he gave you pleasure . . . what I want to know is, precisely what manner of pleasure did he give?"

Viola's face heated. "It's not a proper topic. Let's return to the book, shall we? I shouldn't have said anything."

"We all know that whatever Westbury did to you in that bed was being done to Vespera by her dastardly duke. It just happened off the page. And so . . . why don't you fill in the blank pages for us?" asked Philippa.

Viola lowered her voice. "I'm not sure . . . that is I don't even know what to call it, really. You see, his head was under my chemise, and he was, he was . . ."

"Gamahuching," Beatrice whispered. "I knew it. Good on him. All the best rogues excel at it."

"Is that what it's called?" Viola asked in a whisper.

"According to a book I once read, yes. The word *gamahuche* is of unknown etymology, which is always a delightful challenge." Beatrice was a lover of word origins and had completed an etymological dictionary. "One bawdy book in Ford's collection calls it 'dipping into her honeypot,' which made me giggle."

"Why are we all whispering?" asked Della.

"Because it's not a proper topic," Viola replied.

"When have we ever been proper inside these walls?" Philippa asked. "That's what we have the club for—to break all the rules."

"Gamahuching!" Beatrice cried loudly.

"Hush," Della said, giggling so hard she began hiccuping. "Mrs. Kettle might hear you."

"I can't believe we're discussing such things," said Isobel.

"Tell us more!" Philippa urged.

"There's nothing more to tell. And it can never happen again. We both agreed so."

"But shouldn't he propose to you now?" Philippa asked.

"Of course not! He's going to marry Lady Winifred. He was supposed to propose to her on our outing in Hyde Park but he was delayed. He requires a respectable duchess, someone to repair the family reputation. I possess none of the requirements. I'm poor, of low parentage, and I have no social connections."

"You have us," Beatrice said.

"I know, my dears, I have you but we're rather on the fringes of society, are we not?"

"I think you ought to have expectations," said Isobel.

"Everything's in a tangle and the only thing to

be done is to leave before I hurt myself . . . or anyone else. I told West that we're leaving after Papa finishes his symphony, which is due in two days. Isobel, I was hoping that your aunt's cottage in Watford is still available?"

"It is. And I've already told her about you and your father and she'd be delighted for you to live there."

"Is that really what you want, Viola?" asked Philippa.

"It's just better if I leave. Go back to my old life. I'm not as bold and fearless as all of you. I've always been the quiet one, the supporter, the shoulder to lean on."

"I, for one, know someone who will be very happy if Viola doesn't marry the duke," Della said. "My brother, John. After your dance at Lady Pickering's ball he was quite taken with you. He keeps asking me about you."

He'd been very kind and handsome, but she'd felt nothing for him. She'd only had eyes for West.

"Do you think that the duke prefers Lady Winifred?" Isobel asked.

"Why would he want a milksop like her when he could have a firebrand like Viola?" Beatrice asked.

"You think I'm a firebrand?" Viola asked, taken aback.

"Absolutely. You stood up for me when I didn't believe in myself," Beatrice replied.

"You've always been there for us—a fierce advocate and loyal friend," agreed Isobel.

"You deserve a starring role in your own life,"

said Beatrice. "You're so much stronger than you know. I wish you could see yourself the way we see you."

"It takes great strength to constantly prop everyone else up," Isobel agreed. "And now we want to repay the favor." She caught Viola's gaze and held it, standing up from her chair and squaring her shoulders. "Miss Viola Beaton, you should leave this book club meeting and march right over to that musical publisher, reveal yourself as Mr. Vincent Beam, and claim compensation for your work."

Viola took a deep breath, ready to mount her objections, but before she could speak, Beatrice rose from the table and stood shoulder to shoulder with Isobel. "And I believe that after you reveal your true identity to the world, you should reveal your true feelings to the duke. No matter the outcome."

She stared at her friends. "Do you really think I'm that brave?"

They nodded. "We do."

"I think you're the most brave, bold, and intrepid woman in this room," said Philippa, joining Isobel and Beatrice.

"And I agree," said Della, standing up. "Even though my brother John will be crushed, I think you would make a first-rate duchess, and damn anyone who has the gall to say otherwise!"

"You've all gone mad," Viola said, not knowing whether to laugh or cry.

Her friends surged toward her and Della grabbed her hands and pulled her out of the chair. "You can do this, Viola," she said. "We believe in you."

Could she do this? Once she revealed her identity as Mr. Beam there'd be no going back.

West had told her to reveal herself. Her best friends were united in their belief that it was the right thing to do.

The breath she drew was shaky, and a little tentative, but it filled her lungs with fresh life, fresh resolve.

"Do you know what?" She lifted her head and squared her shoulders. "I believe you're right. At least about Mr. Beam—I'm going to march over to that publishing house and claim my prize!"

"That's my girl!"

"You'll show them!"

The encouragement of her friends rang in her ears as she left the club.

When she reached the publishing house of Atwater and Herrick she very nearly lost her nerve. The building looked dark inside. No one was there.

This had been a bad idea, anyway. She'd knock upon the door but if no one answered she'd leave immediately.

She lifted her hand to the door knocker and the door opened.

"Good evening, miss. I was just leaving but I'd be happy to answer your inquiry," said Mr. Atwater, the white-haired gentleman she'd spoken with at the musicale. "Wait . . ." He peered at her through round spectacles. "Miss Beaton? I'm so glad you decided to come. Do come in, my dear. Mr. Herrick," he called. "I say, Mr. Herrick, Miss Beaton has come!"

Another white-haired and bespectacled gentleman bustled out from some inner office. "Miss Beaton. What an honor." He pumped her hand up and down. "Do sit down, please." He swept a pile of papers from a chair and gestured for her to take a seat.

Viola's heart was beating so violently she thought they must be able to hear it.

Mr. Atwater beamed at her. "Now, will you reveal the mystery of Mr. Vincent Beam?"

"Are you going to tell us that Mr. Beam is actually your father?" asked Mr. Herrick. "Dipping his toes back into the waters of publishing, as it were. It's been long enough since his scandal. We'd be delighted to publish his new works."

"Most delighted," Mr. Atwater agreed. "But, Mr. Herrick, I contend that Mr. Vincent Beam is actually . . . Miss Viola Beaton. Am I correct?"

Viola nodded. "You are correct, sir." There. She'd done it. "I composed the symphony and submitted it under a pseudonym so that it would be judged fairly, without the bias attached to works by females."

Mr. Herrick adjusted his spectacles. "How very daring of you."

"I know you probably won't wish to publish it now. I only wanted to tell you to solve the mystery. I never collected my prize and I don't expect, or even desire, the work to be published."

"That would be a terrible shame." Mr. Atwater hooked his thumbs into his waistcoat pockets. "It should be published. And performed."

"We do publish the works of several female composers, Miss Beaton," Mr. Herrick assured her.

"I don't wish to come forward publicly as Mr. Beam. I only want to claim my prize."

"Are you certain?" Mr. Atwater asked. "For it seems to me that it takes rather a bold lady to come forward and claim that she entered a contest under a male pseudonym."

"Perhaps it was bold of me to come. But that's all I wanted, Mr. Atwater. To explain the confusion."

"Allow us a moment, Miss Beaton. Please, don't leave."

The gentlemen adjourned to another room. Viola wondered what there was to discuss. She'd revealed her identity, and the news would probably circulate throughout the Royal Society of Musicians, but she'd decided not to have the work published.

The gentlemen returned wearing identical beaming smiles.

"We really do want to publish your symphony, Miss Beaton. And we want to publish it under your name," Mr. Atwater said. "As a mark of our seriousness, we're prepared to offer you two hundred pounds in advance." He held out an envelope. "You'll find it's all here."

Viola made a startled sound. "Two hundred pounds. Are you both insane?"

Two hundred pounds was a dizzying sum. It didn't make her heiress enough for West, but it was a great deal of money.

"We're very shrewd investors, Miss Beaton, I assure you," said Mr. Herrick.

"I suppose . . ." Viola's mind whirled. "I suppose I might see my way to considering your offer."

"What changed your mind about coming forward?" Mr. Atwater asked. "When we spoke at the Duke of Westbury's musicale you were most adamant in your denial of any knowledge of the work."

"A gentleman of my acquaintance urged me not to hide my musical compositions away in a trunk to be discovered only after my death."

"You have other compositions, Miss Beaton?" Mr. Atwater asked eagerly.

"An entire trunk's worth."

"This is very good news indeed," said Mr. Herrick.

"Your gentleman friend is quite right, Miss Beaton. Quite right, indeed. A talent such as yours shouldn't be hidden away. My grandfather founded this publishing company, but it was my grandmother Kitty who was the musician who inspired him. She was a composer in her own right, her works mostly attributed to her brother, or swept aside by male critics."

"Your grandmother was Kitty Atwater? I didn't make the connection. She's one of my inspirations."

"Then it's kismet, Miss Beaton." He held out

the envelope. "Take this. And give us your hand-shake that we will be your exclusive London publisher."

"I hardly know what to say."

"Say you'll be ours," Mr. Herrick said with a wide smile.

She laughed. "Very well, Mr. Atwater and Mr. Herrick. I'll be yours. And blast the critics!"

"Hear, hear!" Mr. Atwater cried.

She shook their hands. She couldn't tell them about accepting commissions in her father's name and the risk she was taking of discovery. But the thought had struck her that perhaps her fears were baseless. People might be more inclined to think that she had copied her father's ideas for her own compositions, rather than completing his works in secret.

"I've never had such a sum of money, gentlemen." She tucked the envelope into her reticule. She felt rich. And she felt a little bit reckless.

Publishing the symphony under her own name had been a bold step to take. A very big leap into an unknown future.

Maybe it was time to be even more bold.

"What will you do with your earnings?" Mr. Atwater asked.

"Settle some debts."

"I do hope you'll indulge yourself a little, my dear." Mr. Herrick patted her arm. "You should celebrate."

Perhaps she should.

She was sick of being backstage. Her friends were right. She was tired of telling West to choose another woman. And she was weary of always putting the needs of others before her own.

She was always making these impassioned speeches about love and how it made life worth living but it was always about other people.

In this one crystallized moment in time she wasn't going to think about everyone else. This was for her. Her needs. Her desires.

She wanted West and she didn't know what that meant for the future. Or whether they even had a future together. But right now she had money in her reticule and her new red gown had been delivered this morning.

She'd claimed her publishing prize.

Now it was time to claim her duke.

Chapter Twenty-Four

❧ 🌹 ❧

WEST WAS BACK at The Devil's Staircase, but he wasn't there to drink or gamble. He wanted to talk to a friend.

"Westbury. You look terrible," Jax said. "Haven't seen you here for ages."

"I'm reformed."

"So I hear. Didn't believe it until Ravenwood came in and confirmed that it was true. Said he saw you strolling through Hyde Park surrounded by elegant ladies."

"My sisters."

"And their music instructor. What was her name?"

"Viola Beaton."

"Ah yes . . . Viola. Ravenwood seems to think you're quite taken with her."

West propped his elbows on the bar. "Doesn't matter one way or the other. I'm supposed to propose to Lady Winifred Woolfrey."

"Don't do it, man. You'll regret marrying someone you don't love."

"I always thought that marriage should be a business contract and that if too many feelings were involved it would end badly. But now that I'm facing the prospect of life with Lady Winifred . . . she's kind, gentle, gracious, elegant and . . . boring. She'd bore me to tears. She doesn't challenge me, there's no fire in her."

"She's not Viola."

"Yes. That's the problem. But I'm torn in half, Jax. I'm torn between duty and desire."

"Do you love her?"

"I don't know how to love. I turned my back on love years ago."

"Nobody ever knows how to love. It just happens, or so I've been told. Ash said it was like falling off the edge of a cliff and hanging on to a rock for dear life, knowing that if you let go, if you stop clinging to that rock, you'd be dashed to your death. Perhaps loving Viola is your only chance at life, and not loving her, denying your love for her, would be flinging yourself into a waking death."

West cocked his head. "I don't feel like I'm falling. I'd already fallen as low as I could go. I was trapped beneath the ice, watching everyone else live their lives above me. Viola's up there in the sunshine and there's a frozen layer of ice between us. I can't break through it. It's too thick. I've been frozen too long. Not even the blaze of her smile can thaw my heart."

Jax clapped a large hand onto his shoulder. "That's a load of asinine nonsense and you know it. Go and talk to her instead of me. Tell her how you feel. See if her kisses might melt that frozen heart of yours."

"She told me to read the letters my father wrote to me every week for months before his death."

"You never read them?"

"I read the first few but they were all the same. Praise for my younger brother and disgust for me."

"Sounds harsh."

"Viola thinks that if I read the letters, one by one, as a kind of ritual, burning them afterward, it might help me forgive my father and relinquish my hatred for him."

"Then do it. Read the letters. Life's too short for regrets."

"But it's too late for me to change my wicked ways."

"It's never too late, Westbury. Don't spend your life looking backward. What do you truly want in life?"

"All I want is to make her smile."

"You might just get your chance sooner, rather than later," said Jax, chuckling.

"What do you mean?"

"I met her once, you know. She came here with Ash's wife, Henrietta. Miss Beaton was a shy little thing, glancing around warily. She was very adamant in her disavowal of gambling and all those who practiced the dark art."

West smiled. "She's very proper and buttoned-up. Wears these high-necked gray gowns with lace caps over her hair like she's already a spinster but she's young and pretty and talented. If you ever have the privilege of hearing her play the pianoforte . . . my God, you'd fall at her feet."

"She'd never willingly visit here again?"

"Never. She called it a den of iniquity."

"I see. And she'd never go anywhere alone, wearing a low-cut red gown . . . ?"

"I told you, she's very buttoned-up. What are you going on about?"

"Turn around."

"Pardon?" West turned around. And nearly fell out of his chair. A woman stood near the doorway. The most beautiful woman he'd ever seen, in a glowing scarlet gown with a square neckline that dipped very low in front, and exposed so much of her lush charms, that every man in the room was staring at her bosom.

The woman saw him and her face broke into a seductive smile bracketed by the most adorable dimples.

"Viola?" West said, his head spinning as his two worlds collided.

He jumped off his barstool and closed the distance between them. "What on earth are you doing here?"

"I have money to wager." She waved several banknotes at him.

"Don't wave your money around, there are rough characters about." West guided her into a secluded alcove. "And where did you get those banknotes?"

She stuffed them back into her reticule. "I followed your advice. I went to the publishing house, met with Mr. Atwater and Mr. Herrick, and revealed myself as Mr. Beam. They offered to publish my symphony, and I made a handshake contract to deliver several more compositions. This is my first advance. Two hundred pounds," she said proudly.

"You'll take it directly to a bank tomorrow morning and deposit it for safekeeping."

"Ha!" She wrinkled her pert nose. "You sound like a parson. Your sisters are having a night in with Aunt Miriam. My father is happily finishing his symphony. And I want to gamble some of this money away. Who knows? I might even win."

"I'm very proud of you for revealing your identity and claiming your winnings. But this is no place for you. And money is always safer in a bank than at the hazard table."

"You do enjoy dispensing advice that you never keep yourself, I've noticed."

"Do you even know how to play hazard?"

"No, but you do."

"Please, Viola. Let's go home."

"I don't want to go home. We're young and beautiful and free as birds."

He couldn't disagree. She was the most ravishing sight he'd ever beheld. "That gown is stunning. I knew the color would suit you."

"Do you like it, Your Grace?" She ran her hand down her waist. "The velvet silk is as soft as rose petals."

Dear God he wanted to grab her and pull her onto his lap, kiss the rose petal softness of her lips. "Viola, what's gotten into you?"

"This is the new me. I'm a wallflower gone slightly wicked. I'm bold and free."

"I don't think it's a good idea."

"Why, are you going to lose my money?"

"Probably. I haven't had any luck at the tables for years. When I started gambling I was doing it to spite my father. He hated me and so I gambled to wound him, as he wounded me. Then I started wanting to win, and I did, for a time, until I started drinking and that made me reckless and careless. I lost the last of my conscience, that voice in my head that used to curb my wild and self-destructive impulses."

"If you could stay sober and if you knew when to quit, you could win again."

He crossed his arms. "We're not gambling. We're leaving."

"Why can't I be here? You invited me to The Devil's Staircase after the ball."

"My mind was addled by the jilting."

"First reactions are often very telling."

"You shouldn't throw your money away. We'll find a nice, safe investment for you, perhaps in my friend Banksford's steam engines."

"I'm finished with playing it safe. I don't want to be meek and mild Miss Beaton anymore. I'm through being a supporting character in my own life. This gown makes me feel powerful. And this money, this is mine to do whatever I want with. And I want to chance it at the hazard table. I want to feel the thrill that kept you coming back here, night after night."

"This is a very bad idea," he muttered.

"This is an excellent idea. Show me your world, West. We can quit when we're ahead. I'll be your conscience, I'll help you curb your wild and self-destructive impulses."

"For the love of . . ." He took a shuddering breath. "One hour. You have one hour and then I'm throwing you over my shoulder if I have to."

She tossed her head and slanted a look at him from under her long dark lashes. "I've heard that one before."

West led her to the hazard table and gave her a quick, whispered lesson. "The man to your left is the caster. He shakes the dice and spills them across the table. There's the groom porter sitting on his stool, raking the dice after they're thrown. Hazard is a game of chance, the dice falling where they may, with plenty of opportunity for the house to cheat by distracting the players. You can tell the gaming hell's employees immediately. That gentleman in the brown beaver hat is a crowpee, hired to watch the play. That one, with the slouched shoulders, a decoy, who's paid to win big and encourage others to play. I know the owner, Jax Smith, so none of them will bother us."

"Goodness, I had no idea the house might employ such methods."

"The house usually wins, Viola. That's why I lost my fortune. That and the drinking."

All of it was familiar. The table inlaid with white holly wood, the rattle of the dice, the rise and fall of conversation.

What wasn't familiar was Viola. Gone was the pragmatic wallflower with the schoolmarm tones. In her place stood this magnificently seductive woman wearing silky red velvet that clung like a second skin to her ripe curves.

Her hair was twisted atop her head with ringlets falling over her neck.

Gamble on me, her eyes challenged. *Take your winnings. I'm yours, for one night, or forever.*

In that moment all West wanted to do was ravish her on the table. But they were in public and there would be no ravishing.

He placed a wager for her, watching her, mesmerized by her beauty, instead of the caster as he shook the dice and then spilled them across the table.

The evening passed in a blur of scarlet and delighted smiles. Every man in the room was enthralled by Viola. Every time she won, she threw her head back and laughed.

And she kept winning . . . and winning.

Jax came over and congratulated her, offering her a glass of sparkling wine. "This is made by your friend and mine, Lady Henrietta."

"Hetty makes the best wine in England." She drank deeply, giggling as the bubbles tickled her nose. "Have some, West."

"You told me I had to stop drinking."

"A little sparkling wine can only improve your surly mood. I've tripled my money, West," she whispered excitedly.

"Which is the perfect time to quit. While you're ahead."

"I want to play more. Luck is on my side."

"I know that shimmering, can't-lose feeling but it's only a mirage. If you keep playing now, eventually you'll lose. Possibly everything. You'll walk out of here with nothing."

"I can't believe you're lecturing me like a school-marm about knowing when to quit. I thought you were a hedonist. One more wager, just one more."

"I'm doing this because I care about you, Viola."

"If you cared about me you'd allow me to have this night, to be free, to be reckless!"

"Reckless isn't you, Viola. You're careful and you'll regret this tomorrow. I'm doing this for your own good."

"What are you doing, West? You haven't done anything but—oof. Put me down!"

She beat on his back with her fists. "Put me down."

He fixed her over his shoulder with an arm around her shapely buttocks.

Loud shouting and laughter erupted in the crowded room.

"Send the winnings to Westbury House," West shouted to Jax, and carried a squirming Viola outside.

"Oof," Viola said as West deposited her, none too gently, on the carriage seat. His coachman had evinced no surprise at seeing him carry a woman out of The Devil's Staircase.

It may have happened before, come to think it.

But this was Viola. Not just any woman. And he had to convey her home before she lost all her money.

"I can't believe you just did that," she huffed.

He climbed in beside her and thumped his fist

on the carriage ceiling to signal they were ready to leave. "Said I would, didn't I?"

Viola fluffed her skirts around her. "It was most undignified and wholly unnecessary."

"I did it to save you from your wild, self-destructive impulses."

"And you're the expert on curbing your cravings for pleasure?"

"I didn't want you to fall victim to my failings."

"Such a reversal of our roles. You're acting the chaperone." She tossed her head, sending pins tumbling. "I don't require chaperoning."

"You're going to thank me for this tomorrow."

"I'm not drunk, you know," she said frostily.

"Not on spirits. You're drunk on gambling."

"It is quite thrilling. You ruined my fun."

"You were going to place one wager too many and lose it all, and then some."

"Or maybe I would have kept winning and become wealthy."

"The odds of that happening are so small as to be nearly nonexistent. We're making a brief stop and then I'm taking you home. To your father."

"Where are we?" she asked as the carriage drew to a halt.

"Lord Rafe Bentley's house. Ravenwood delivered a letter from Rafe asking me to find something in his house and mail it to him."

"Why you?"

"Because I have the key to the location where it's hidden."

"This is all very mysterious."

"Rafe's a mysterious fellow."

"I'm coming inside with you."

"Stay in the carriage."

"I've wanted to see the infamous pleasure chambers of the notorious Lord Rafe ever since my friend Mina, who, as you know, married his brother, the Duke of Thorndon, told me about a most impolite chair she saw once."

"A what?"

"You'll see . . ." She grabbed the key from his hand, let herself down from the carriage, and sashayed up the front steps.

West swore under his breath and followed after her.

Lord, save him from wallflowers gone wicked.

Or at least grant him the strength to resist her.

Chapter Twenty-Five

❧ 🌹 ❧

"*I* WONDER WHERE the impolite chair is?" Viola asked, searching through the rooms. She found the door that led to Rafe's naughty sitting room.

"Don't go in there!"

She opened the door. "I can't credit it."

"What?" West came to stand beside her.

"There's red silk on the walls, just as Mina described, but no impolite chair with levers, no low velvet-cushioned stool for administering punishment. Ah! There's the lacquered cabinet of curiosities." She flung the doors wide, only to make a disappointed noise. "It's only filled with books."

"What did you expect it to be filled with?"

"Mina told me she'd seen a collection of naughty . . . statuettes that were shaped like . . ." She glanced at his breeches flap.

"Phalluses?" he supplied.

"Exactly. Now there's just books. How disappointing."

"Rafe is reformed."

"Well, that's no fun now, is it?"

"I thought you were a champion of reform."

"I was . . . I am. Only not for tonight," she said, flouncing away from him. "Tonight I'm wicked.

At least there's still a bed," she called from the next room.

And that was his cue to leave.

Just leave her here and instruct the coachman to take her home when she emerged. Walk away and never look back. If he followed her into that bedroom all would be lost.

He unlocked the hidden drawer inside the cabinet and located the small leather-bound notebook that Rafe had asked him to post to Geneva. He'd said he needed it to solve a mystery. "I found what I came for," he called to Viola. "It's time to leave."

She didn't answer.

"Viola?"

Still no answer.

"Damn it, Viola. It's time to leave."

What was she doing in there? He stalked to the bedchamber door and flung it open. He nearly slammed it shut again.

Viola was seated in the center of the bed, knees off to one side, red silk swirling around her bare toes. "Are you coming to bed?"

"Viola," West groaned, clenching his hands into fists to stop from spreading his hands all over her tempting body. "Do you know what you're doing to me?"

"I know exactly what I'm doing." She lifted her arms and began removing hairpins from her coiffure.

"Stop that. Don't remove any more pins."

"Why not?"

"Because all I want most in the world is to see

your hair falling around your shoulders, touch it, run my fingers through it, use it to pull your neck back to take my kiss."

"Then do it," she whispered.

"I can't."

"We're alone." She pulled more pins out of her hair and shook it free. "There."

"You are so incredibly beautiful. Look at you. Glowing like flame in that gown, your lips lush and begging to be kissed. Your eyes daring me to break all the rules. I never meant to drag you down into my world. You're not meant for fleeting pleasures. You're a forever kind of girl. You're sunshine and buttered toast. I don't want to hurt you."

"I'm not fragile, West. I won't break easily. I know exactly what I'm doing to you. I'm seducing you." She pulled her gown down one shoulder so slowly that his heart nearly stopped beating. "We're not at Westbury House. I'm not companion to your sisters after tonight. And I'm not your employee anymore. You're not even a duke here, with the weight of all that anger and regret attached to the title. Here we can be West and Viola."

"I want you so badly." The words were wrested from his throat on a growl. He fought desperately for the control he required to walk away.

"You told me to want things for myself, and to take what I want. You said I lived only in service to others and claimed nothing for myself."

"You know why this is a terrible idea."

"Maybe so, but it doesn't change how I feel. I want you, West. For me. Now come to bed," she said, lowering the other sleeve of her gown until her breasts bounced free.

There was no chance in hell that he could resist.

He'd give her whatever she desired. He'd lay his heart at her feet.

That was a good place to start. Kneel down on the carpet and pull her forward on the bed until she was in the right position.

Pull up her skirts, nuzzle beneath them . . .

"West . . ." Such exquisite music. His name on her lips.

He worked his tongue over her, inside her, teasing and licking.

She made him think impossible things.

She was his new addiction. His new compulsion.

He moved over her on the bed, lavishing attention on her breasts, the soft skin of her neck, and her full lips.

When her dimples appeared his heart burst into song. And when she touched him, it was like a bolt of the finest cobweb-thin silk rolled out and poured over him, enveloping his senses: scent of warm, sweet woman, sound of her lilting sighs.

The sheen of sweat on her brow, between her breasts. Tasting her skin slowly, drawing out this perfect pleasure.

He undid her gown and slid it off her body. Her corset, chemise, and stockings came next, until she was naked underneath him.

Take her waist between his palms, lift her hips, lift her soft belly to his questing tongue.

Fingers supporting her back, thumbs lightly brushing the sides of her belly. Kiss her navel, tongue pressing. Slide his hands under her back, down the ridges of her spine, until he cupped her bottom with his hands. Part her thighs with his tongue.

She knows the way of pleasure now. She's not so shy, not so hesitant. She opens for him while he angles her hips upward. Lick the outer edges softly, building her anticipation, don't just get right to it, don't be too greedy, too abrupt.

Taste her. Salt sweet. Silk smooth and delicious.

Her body so different than his, requiring more finesse, requiring him to listen, to respond, make small adjustments.

There was nothing else to do, nowhere else to be, but between her thighs. Loving her with his tongue, his lips and, now, one of his fingers because he had to feel her heat, had to feel her clench around some part of him.

Two fingers now, moving back and upward in a fluttering motion, searching for the place that made her sighs more urgent.

His tongue stroking in concert with the little rolling movements she made with her hips, urging him on. Her fingers clutched his hair, digging into his scalp, none too gently, and he knew she was close. Her stomach muscles tightened, she tensed, she was so silent . . . holding her breath.

He focused entirely on her pleasure, he would never stop, not until she came.

He stroked with his tongue, moving his fingers inside her, and finally . . . finally she shuddered, tensed, and came undone. Her hips bucked beneath him and she cried his name.

"West! My goodness. That's . . . oh. My."

The most beautiful music in the world, her little moans and the stuttered rhythm of her breathing.

He withdrew his fingers and licked them, watching her, watching him. "You taste so good."

She lowered her head but continued to watch.

"Was that enough, my wicked wallflower?"

"Mmm." She stretched like a cat, her eyes closed, hair tumbling in waves around her shoulders, over her breasts. "Not nearly enough."

Her eyes opened and the new-fern green pierced his heart.

Life begins with a woman with green eyes that see into my soul and a smile that makes me want to be a better man.

She tugged at his shirt and attempted, inexpertly, to open his trousers.

He helped her along, removing everything until he was uncovered for her.

Her gaze flicked to his cock and he sucked in a ragged breath. He gripped himself with his fist. Offering himself to her. "Is this what you want?"

"Y-yes." Her voice faltered slightly.

"If you're scared, if you don't want this, we can stop. All you have to do is say the word."

"I know. And I want this. I want to feel you deep inside me. I want to know what it's like to join with you, our bodies, our minds." She placed a hand on his chest. "Our hearts."

He was in so much trouble. "I want to know that, too." He'd never felt this way about anyone before and her hand over his heart felt like a benediction. He was forgiven.

He could reinvent himself. Become something better. Something worthy of this beautiful woman and her sweet, gentle smile.

"Kiss me." She held out her arms and he nestled home, into her embrace. Their kiss was an urgent coupling, a tangling of tongues, and it told him everything he needed to know. She was here with him in this moment. Unafraid. Magnificently uninhibited.

She wrapped her soft thighs around his hips, and urged him against her core. He didn't want to hurt her. Instead of stabbing ahead, he reached between their bodies and dipped his fingers inside her until they were well coated with her spending and spread the moisture over the head of his cock.

Using his fingers to stretch her open, he slid into position, his body shuddering with the strain of holding himself in check.

Go slow now. This is her first time. Take her gently. Give her time to adjust, to relax.

His breathing came in gasps. He was well seated now, halfway inside her. He rose up on his hands and looked down.

The sight of her stretched around him gave him a surge of lust and pride.

Her eyes flew open. "You stopped."

"I'm going slowly. I don't want to hurt you."

A soft growl, deep in her throat. "I want you. All of you. Now." Her hips surged up and her hands moved to his shoulders, driving him down.

"Viola," he moaned as he sheathed himself fully inside her. "It's so good."

She crossed her ankles against his buttocks, pulling him tight against her, telling him she wanted him deeper.

They rocked together, back and forth, bodies slippery with sweat, his heart pounding a primal beat of possessiveness.

Mine. You're mine. I'll never let you go.

He lifted her up, still inside her, and carried her to the wall, holding her against it with his body.

She wrapped her legs around his hips, her arms around his neck, their bodies lashed together, riding this storm of passion.

He wanted to lose himself inside her forever. Stay like this with her encompassing him, the warm, soft curves of her body, the sensual motion of her hips.

His hands squeezing her plump bottom. Groaning with every thrust. Wanting to last forever but knowing his orgasm would overtake him soon, flood his mind and body with a rush of pure pleasure.

Viola was his new addiction. In her he was made new.

For her he was a new man.

This would change him. He'd never had that thought during the act of sex before.

Sex wasn't something that changed him, it was something that he mastered, that he performed, and performed well. It had never been transformative. Never gripped both his body and his heart with equal urgency.

This was wholly new. And he wanted it to last.

He gripped her hips, stilling her movements, and carried her back to the bed, lowered her down, and reseated himself. He moved slower this time, with measured, silken strokes. He reached between them and brushed his thumb over just the right place.

"Oh . . . ohhhh," she sang, her head falling back and eyes closing.

He chased the sound of her sighs, the stuttered rhythm of her breathing, and he held himself back until she came again, her inner muscles squeezing him tightly. Only then did he allow himself to lose control, burying his cock to the hilt as he came hard, moaning her name.

"Viola. Christ."

He collapsed onto her, bliss still rocking his body and tenderness surging through his heart. He clasped her tightly, unwilling to leave the heat of her. Wanting to stay inside her forever.

He kissed her throat and she arched her neck.

"Are you . . . humming?" he asked, lifting his head.

"I didn't realize I was. But it's . . . oh, West, it felt so good, and strange, and right and I heard music as you moved inside me. As I moved with you. I want to write it down."

"You'll just have to remember it. I'm not letting you out of my grasp." He held her closer, inhaling her sweet, womanly fragrance. Listening to her humming softly, composing a new melody.

Chapter Twenty-Six

❧ 🌹 ❧

"*I* WISH WE could stay like this forever," Viola said, basking in the feeling of being held in his arms, cherished and safe.

"I know. It feels so right."

"Doesn't it?"

She lay in his arms for a few more golden, pleasure-soaked moments. And then the call of nature interrupted.

"West?"

"Mmmm."

"I need to relieve myself."

He unclasped his arms. "Go through that door," he said sleepily, motioning to the door with his head.

"You've done this before."

"What have I done?"

"Taken a woman here while Rafe was gone. You said that you were both wild rakes."

"I may have."

It only confirmed what she knew to be true— but the thought of him being her very first, and her just being one in a long line of lovers troubled her.

She performed her ablutions, washing herself

carefully, her body feeling tender and swollen, and her mind feeling a little bruised, as well.

She joined him back in the bed and he hugged her close, fitting her against him. "Does that bother you, Viola? I've never hidden my wicked past from you."

"A little," she said. "I suppose I'm nothing special."

He stilled. "That's not true. I've never felt like this before. I feel completely new. You've remade me, Viola. I'm wholly yours."

"Mine until the morning light, which is fast approaching." She didn't want to speak of his wicked past. This night was her chance to own her power.

To take center stage.

"We still have an hour or so left before dawn. We can . . . talk." She nestled closer to him. "I want to know more about your past. You never did tell me why your father hated you."

He settled his chin against the top of her head. His voice was thick and sleepy. "When I was twelve, my brother Bertram was born. My father rejoiced to have a healthy baby boy . . . a spare heir. He called me to his study and I thought he meant for me to share in the celebration. Instead, he told me what I'd sensed my whole life, but hadn't had confirmed. He hated me because he saw me as a symbol of my mother's sin."

"I thought it might be something like that."

"My mother was a good woman. Absolutely faithful to my father in marriage. The sin my father could never forgive her for happened before they were married. She conceived a child with the village blacksmith. That child was me. Her parents forced her to marry my father to cover the scandal, and because she was an heiress, and he was a duke. The match was socially acceptable."

"And the village blacksmith . . . ?"

"Owen Blake. Her parents paid him a fortune to stay silent. He's dead now. I visited his grave once. He never married, true to my mother's memory to the last. I'm the only child he sired."

"How did your father learn of the deception?"

"She gave birth to me too soon after the wedding. I had blue eyes, and my mother's blond hair, but the timing was too suspicious. He became convinced that I wasn't his son. It ate away at him, like a cancerous tumor. He beat my mother. And he beat me. He finally forced her to confess that she'd been with child when they married, but she never told him who my father was, no matter how hard he beat her. She was afraid that he'd kill her former lover. She only told me my true father's name the night she died."

Viola stroked his jaw, her heart breaking. "West, I'm so very sorry."

"I was born into a loveless marriage. He vented his hatred and his anger on me and my mother. She was so sad all the time. I was always trying to make her more cheerful. And when Bertram was born, my father smiled upon her for the first time. But not upon me. He hated me, but he couldn't disinherit me because I'd been born within wedlock. The only revenge he could take was to will away the settlement my mother had come to the marriage with—her lands, her fortune—and give it all to Bertram, instead of me."

"But Bertram died. Didn't it revert to you?"

"My father was too vindictive for that. His will stated that in the event of Bertram's death, my uncle would inherit his fortune. The estate, Westbury Abbey, renamed after it came to my father through marriage, became a symbol to me of his hatred. It's owned by my uncle, who's not a bad fellow, but extremely negligent. While I was busy gambling and being a right bastard, my uncle was traveling abroad for years and has allowed the estate to go to hell. And I've done nothing to save it. I was too busy being wicked."

"What did your father say to you that day after Bertram was born, when he called you into his study?"

"He told me the shameful story of my birth. Informed me that he was going to will everything of my mother's to Bertram. And reiterated the refrain I'd heard my whole life: I was bad and stained. A symbol of sin. And the punishment he administered so liberally was for my own good. To stamp out the wickedness of my origins."

"And so you began to hate yourself, punish yourself for a crime you never committed. Your birth wasn't your fault. You can't take the blame for the break it caused between your father and mother."

"Everything that happened after that day is my fault. The depraved path I chose to tread."

"It's never too late to choose a new path."

"Jax Smith told me that. But I've been down

here in the darkness too long, Viola. I don't know any other way to live."

He brushed her hair away from her cheek. "I've been broken ever since that day in the study with my father. I have no idea how to become whole again. My soul is heavy with the weight of my misdeeds. I have anger wrapped like a lead weight around my neck, bowing my head toward the earth until I can't see the sky."

"You're not broken." She raised her head and looked him in the eye. "You only think you are. You champion your sisters, you love them dearly. And they love you in return. They want your affection, your pride, and your encouragement. All of which I've seen you give them over the last weeks."

"I want to believe that I can be a better man, a better brother. But I've been bad so long."

"Your father beat that message into you, over and over again. Hearing that you were sinful made you believe it was so. But it's just a story you've told yourself so many times that it became your reality. You walk down the same shadowy path in your mind every single day and you end up in a big deep hole. Maybe if you read those letters your father wrote to you, you'd be able to find your way back into the light."

"I don't think so. I'm still down here, sunk in a deep, dark hole, and you're up there, in the light, living life with a smile and a song. Worlds away from me."

"You know that I've faced difficulties. That my life hasn't been moonbeams and fairy tales. You know that my smile is hard-won. Be patient with yourself. Be kind to yourself. We don't have to be our thoughts. That voice in your head telling you that you're bad and tainted. You can hear it, acknowledge it, but you don't have to live it, or live up to it. Forgive your father and then forgive yourself. We all fail, we all fall."

"I fell harder than most. I chose to fall."

"And you can choose to forgive yourself. You'll never be able to love yourself, or anyone else, until you forgive your father. I can't make you believe in love but I do know this . . . I love you, West. I've fought very hard against it but I can't help myself."

"You can't love me. I've been honest with you about my feelings on the subject."

"You don't have a choice in the matter. I love you, West. And I loved what you did to me, what we did together in this bed. And against the wall."

"Did you now?" His voice dropped to a low growl. "I loved it, too."

"There, you see? You do love something . . . fornication!"

He snorted.

"And you're rather skilled at it, I must say." Keep things playful. Keep him smiling. Don't allow him to dwell too much in the darkness. Keep him here with her.

"I'm the best," he said immodestly.

"And are you ready for more?"

"Pardon?" His voice was almost a squeak.

"Because I am," she purred. "I want more. I want you inside me again. Stretching me to my limits. Your heavy body pinning me against the bed." The wanton words poured forth from her mouth as though she truly were wicked. Maybe she was and she'd only just discovered it.

She kissed his neck. "I want to feel my breasts crushed beneath your chest as you take me again."

He laughed, his breathing ragged. "I don't know if I can, sweetheart. Give me a moment."

She shifted her hips, rubbing against him. She felt him swell and harden against her thigh and cooed her approval. "There, I knew you had it in you."

His laughter rumbled, filling her heart with happiness. "Greedy girl."

"I am greedy. I want more."

"You want this?" He flipped her onto her back, then teased the tips of her breasts with his tongue until her mind swirled with desire.

"Yes," she moaned.

"And this?"

He moved lower, his tongue exploring her navel, her hip bones, and moving between her thighs.

"Oh, West. Yes. That's what I want."

"Where do you want me?"

"Between my thighs."

"That can be arranged."

He set to work, teasing her already sensitive flesh. She reached her peak swiftly this time, the pleasure rippling out from his tongue and lifting her hips off the bed.

She lay, languid and spent, wrung out by pleasure, as he moved up her body and notched his hard, heavy erection between her thighs.

There was no gentle nudge this time. He entered her in one smooth, glorious motion. He was so in control of his body.

And yet, she controlled him, didn't she? He'd been drifting off to sleep and a few small movements of her hips had made him hard for her again.

The two Wests, the one she'd invented in her mind and the one who'd wasted his life, began to merge and mingle, as their bodies were mingling.

He wasn't wholly wicked. Nor wholly good.

And neither was she. They could be both at the same time.

"Viola," he moaned. He moved with more urgency. She wound her legs more tightly around him, holding on as he pressed her deeper into the bed.

He reached around and broke the clasp of her legs, using his palms to hold her thighs against the bed. A few more long, hot strokes and he shuddered . . . then stilled, collapsing against her, covering her completely.

He gathered her into his arms. She moved closer, seeking his warmth, feeling a little awkward and shy about what they'd just done. The earthiness of it. Twice in one night. Who knew?

There was a new closeness, a new intimacy in his embrace. Their bodies had been joined and now it seemed to her that their hearts had learned to beat in time.

Light crept in through the curtains. They only had a few more stolen moments before they must go back. They'd have to arrive separately. No one could know what had happened here tonight. Not even her best friends. If anyone had seen her in the gaming hell . . . but she hadn't recognized anyone.

Tonight she'd staked her claim on West's body . . . and on his heart. She didn't expect him to change overnight. She didn't expect the reasons they couldn't be together to suddenly disappear.

She didn't know what this meant. All she knew was that she'd done this for herself.

Because she felt powerful. And free.

And more than slightly wicked.

Chapter Twenty-Seven

WHEN VIOLA CAME downstairs the next morning after a few fitful hours of sleep in her bed at the dower house, she went directly to the music conservatory. It looked as though a cyclone had hit. Staff paper was strewn across the carpets, fixed to the walls with nails, and covered every other surface. Her father sat at the pianoforte, working out a melody.

His hair stood on end and his face was ashen, but he looked happy.

"Oh, Miss Viola." Withers wiped a tear from his eye, meeting her at the door. "It's truly miraculous. It's something about this house, I think. I haven't seen him like this since the old days, in Paris, when the music flowed from him in waves. He's so close now. Only a few more hours. He's played some parts of it for me and I can imagine the rest. It's going to be magnificent."

"Has he been eating?"

"Voraciously."

"He hasn't been asking for me? I've been so preoccupied."

"Don't worry about a thing. He said something funny the other day, about how you were off courting the duke, or cavorting with the duke, or something like that. I'm sure I misunderstood him." Withers glanced at her sharply. "Correct?"

"Of course. I've been preparing the young ladies for the musicale."

And cavorting with the duke.

"History is being made here in this house, Miss Beaton. And I will be here to witness it."

A knock sounded on the door and West appeared, looking just as disheveled and sleep deprived as she felt. "Viola, I must speak with you."

"You honor us, Your Grace." Withers bowed. "Should I order some refreshment?"

"What is it, Your Grace?" Viola remembered to use his title at the last moment.

His eyes were shadowed and his face grim. "It wasn't Blanche we should have been worrying about," he said urgently. "It was Belinda."

"What do you mean?"

"Please, just come with me. I'll explain everything on the way. You'll want a warm cloak and gloves. We're taking my curricle. I have a coach following behind."

Viola collected her things and rushed out of the house. West helped her into the curricle and spurred his matched set of bay horses to motion.

"What's all this about?" Viola asked. "Where are we going? West, you're scaring me."

He urged the horses onward, swerving to avoid a collision. "Damn these farm carts. We must go faster!"

"West." Viola tugged at his sleeve. "The poor

horses are going as fast as they can in this crush. Slow down a little and tell me what's happened."

"Laxton's abducted Belinda. Only she thinks she's eloped with him and they're to be married."

"No," Viola gasped. "It can't be true."

"I'll say this for Belinda, she's a good actress. She was quite her normal self this morning, eating more than one helping of toast, expounding upon the new trimmings she wished to purchase for a new bonnet. No one had any idea what she was planning. She left a note behind. It's only luck that we found it so soon after she left. She said she was going shopping, and she took a maid with her, and I thought nothing of it. She goes shopping as often as possible. Betsy found the note a mere half hour after she'd left."

"What did it say?"

"She thinks Laxton is in love with her. She went with him willingly thinking they were eloping. Poor deluded Belinda. My money's on Laxton conveying her to the nearest coaching inn outside London and no farther than that."

"He won't marry her. She'll be ruined." Viola's heart lurched. "They'll all be ruined. Oh my God, West. This is terrible." If the young ladies were ruined there was nothing Viola could do to save their reputations. "We must go faster!"

"I know. If only we can reach them in time. I'm so frightened for Belinda. If Laxton has shown her his true colors she must be feeling so scared and alone."

"Why would he do this? Why prey upon Belinda in such a heartless manner?"

"It's all my fault. Laxton's doing this because I thrashed him. He's after revenge. And he's found the best way to hurt me by hurting those I love. I should have listened to Rafe and to you. I shouldn't have taken matters into my fists."

"Don't blame yourself. Belinda went willingly. He must have filled her head with trickery and lies. She's only eighteen and a complete innocent who lives for attention and admiration. Oh! I just remembered something that I noticed when we were walking in Hyde Park. She and her friends were giggling about something and when I approached, it looked as though Belinda was stuffing a letter into her reticule. West . . . I should have demanded to see the letter but I was distracted by Ravenwood and Indy's arrival."

"There's no sense blaming yourself, either. This is all my doing. I brought you with me because I want someone Belinda trusts and admires to be there to comfort her, no matter what has happened."

"West," she said gently. "Belinda trusts and admires *you*."

"I'll be dealing with Laxton." His jaw clenched in rigid lines. "This will mean a duel. There's no other option. I'll have to call him out this time. Unless he's already done the deed, in which case, as loathsome as it may sound, I'll have to attempt to force them to marry."

"Belinda can't marry Laxton! She would be miserable. Blanche would be miserable. This is such a hideous tangle. We should have been with the girls last night instead of . . . I don't know what came over me."

"Please don't, Viola. There were two of us there. I never should have taken you to Rafe's house with me."

"I seduced you, remember?"

"You seduced me the very moment I laid eyes on you. I've been resisting my desire ever since. Last night I lost all control. This entire debacle is on my shoulders."

"I'm not going to be ashamed of what we did last night. It wasn't wicked, it was wondrous."

"I'm not ashamed. It's only this business with Laxton and Belinda. I might have to force him to marry her." He flicked the reins. "Viola. You and I must marry."

Her heart stopped beating for a brief, stunned second. "West, this isn't the time to make hasty decisions."

"It's what has to happen. I just hope that you don't . . . that you don't mind marrying a scoundrel like me. Or perhaps you won't have to. I may fight a duel and die by Laxton's bullet."

She stared at the passing scenery as they left London behind, the trees and houses only a blur now, glimpsed through tears. How had the glowing tenderness of last night become this dreadful mess?

"I should think I have something to say about whether I marry you or not, Your Grace," she said finally, when she trusted her voice not to wobble.

"I'll be a good husband to you, Viola. I swear it. If I live to see tomorrow."

He swore he'd be a good husband, but he couldn't tell her that he loved her. And he was only proposing out of a sense of obligation. Because his sister had been abducted and he was drawing some twisted parallel between the two circumstances.

"We both know that I'm not the right choice for your duchess. If your sisters are ruined, they'll require someone polished and unassailable to champion them in society."

"If my sisters are ruined, Lady Winifred may not wish to marry me. Anyway," he said with an impatient twitch of the reins, "that's all beside the point now. We're marrying by special license and that's final. For better or for worse."

Viola's chest tightened. She knew he was worried about Belinda, knew that fear was making his tone curt and words harsh, but that knowledge didn't make this hurt any less.

"I refuse your proposal, Your Grace," she said primly, in her schoolmarm voice.

"You can't refuse."

"I most certainly can! I won't accept the perfunctory and unromantic proposal of a man who is only seeking my hand in marriage out of a sense of obligation."

He turned his head for a moment, searching her face, before staring ahead again. "You said that you loved me."

"And sometimes love isn't enough. You were right all along, Your Grace. There's more to marriage than love. And love doesn't conquer all difficulties. I do have moonbeams in my eyes and fairy tales in my head. I've never been a part of your privileged world. I'm not a suitable duchess."

"And I'm not suited to the role of duke. But I'm learning. I'm making up for past mistakes. We'll learn together. We'll support each other."

"You were born to the role. It's in your blood. You turned away from it and now you've returned and society welcomed you back with open arms."

"Society might welcome you, as well, Viola. I've seen the way you make everyone around you want to please you, to be better for you."

"It's not that I don't think I'm good enough, or that you're better than me because you have a title. We live in two different worlds. You're talking about taking your rightful place in society. Restoring Westbury Abbey to its former splendor. You speak of rehabilitating the Westbury family name. And all of these things should be done."

"Then we're in agreement."

"They should be done, but I won't help your cause. I'm not the perfect duchess. I could never even have made your list. I'm being rational and making plans with my head, and not my heart. Marriage is a business arrangement. You've found your business partner in Lady Winifred. But please endeavor to ask for her hand in a more romantic manner than you just employed," she said severely.

"But what about last night?"

"What about it? It's as you said, I was drunk

on gambling, on the thrill and excitement of it. I had a little money in my reticule, and a fancy new gown, and I became a different person for one night. And one night only."

WEST TOOK HIS eyes off the road for a moment to soak in a quick view of her lovely profile. "I'm fairly sure that was the real you last night, Viola. You were magnificent."

"I'm a spinster."

"Hardly."

"And I'll remain a spinster. Once again, I don't accept your proposal."

"You will." He would make her accept him, just as soon as he dealt with Laxton. He had too much to live for now. He wouldn't allow that miscreant to sink a bullet in him.

"I won't. But let's not beleaguer this argument, Your Grace. We must present a united front, for Belinda's sake."

"Back to Your Grace?"

"I'm attempting to keep my head clear, my heart armored, and my spirits high. Our goal is to rescue Belinda and return her, unharmed, to your family."

"Poor Belinda. It hit her especially hard when our mother died," West said, some ways down the road. "Belinda was her favorite. Betsy has always been stoic, but Belinda was inconsolable for years."

"It must have been so difficult for you and your sisters."

"I should have told Blanche and Belinda what

Laxton said about them. What if we're too late? I'll never forgive myself."

"You haven't forgiven yourself for too many things."

"And now I may have to commit murder."

Viola turned, her bonnet ribbons fluttering in the breeze. "Murdering, or being murdered, won't solve anything. It will only make things worse. Violence is never the answer."

"And yet sometimes it's unavoidable."

Even though they couldn't see eye to eye on anything today except rescuing Belinda, West was very glad Viola sat beside him. Facing this alone would have been unbearable. He simply wanted to be with her. All of the time. When he wasn't with her he thought about her constantly.

And now that she sat beside him, this horrendous situation seemed more bearable.

"We don't know that he's already ruined her," she said. "We'll deal with the situation when we know it. And we'll take measured action. We'll think about Belinda's feelings first and foremost. She'll be very frightened and very sorry right now."

"Thank you for coming, Viola."

"Of course. You know that I care for those girls like my own family."

The road grew rougher and West had to concentrate on driving. A sudden wind whipped up and Viola clutched her bonnet to her head.

"Are we nearly there?" she asked sometime later, when the horses were beginning to flag and the wind had picked up even more.

He gestured into the distance. "The Coach and Horses is up ahead. We'll try there first. If they're not there we can ask if they stopped through."

West threw the lead to a groom upon arrival and they entered the coaching inn. They followed a narrow passageway that opened into a large taproom. The first thing West saw was Belinda sitting at a table, her head cradled in her arms, sobbing as if her heart were broken.

Chapter Twenty-Eight

❧ 🌹 ❧

Viola's heart leaped into her throat. "We're too late."

"Where's Laxton?" West roared. "I'll murder him."

Belinda lifted her tearstained face. "H-he's not here."

"Which way did he go?"

"West, calm down. Let Belinda explain."

"Did he harm you?" West demanded.

"Not here," said Viola, glancing around at the other patrons who were staring with open curiosity.

"A private sitting room," West called to the innkeeper, as he helped Belinda to her feet. "And quickly."

"My ankle is twisted," Belinda said piteously. West lifted her into his arms where she sniffled and hiccupped as they followed the innkeeper to a private room with a view of a small garden and a small fire in the grate to take the chill away.

Viola settled Belinda in a chair by the fire, wrapping her shawl around Belinda's knees. "Now then, Belinda. Tell us exactly what happened."

West paced up and down the room. "I should

go after him. I don't want him to have too much of a head start."

"I j-jumped from the carriage. He left me on the side of the road in a heap. I walked here. Look." She held up her uninjured ankle. "My gray Italian leather half boots are absolutely ruined."

"But you're not," said Viola, her face wreathed in smiles. "You're not, my brave girl. Did you really jump from the carriage?"

"I had no other choice. That horrid Laxton said that he loved me but no man who loved me would so mishandle the white Valenciennes lace of my fichu. He tore it, the dreadful beast."

"He attempted to unclothe you?" West asked in a low growl.

"He attempted to kiss me and I told him only after the wedding and he pawed at me and tore my lace. He said not to fight him, that it was all inevitable and we were meant to be together and other such villainous things. And I knew then and there that he'd lied. He'd never loved me. He meant me harm. He ripped my Valenciennes lace and so I . . . I smacked him over the head with my reticule in which I keep my tin of face powder and jumped out of the carriage and rolled down a hill. And look. My clothing is all r-ruined." She burst into tears.

Viola hugged her to her breast. "My darling, a little mud and muck and torn lace is a very small price to pay."

"And I t-twisted my ankle. And the men in the dining room have been looking at me insinuatingly and I was frightened. But I know it's all my fault. West, I'm so sorry. Can you forgive me? Will Blanche forgive me?"

West knelt beside her. "Of course. It was a foolish thing to do, but I know you didn't do it to hurt anyone. And I'm so very glad that you're unharmed. Are you quite certain that he never importuned you?"

"He never even had a chance to kiss me, the lace murderer," she huffed.

"I believe Laxton was seeking revenge on me and wanted to hurt me through you. You're a very brave girl, do you know that?"

"I don't feel very brave. I feel like the worst kind of fool. What will Blanche say? She loves Laxton and I . . . I ran away with him. He told me he'd never loved Blanche, that it had been me all along. He's been writing to me for weeks in secret."

"Never mind," Viola said. "We'll sort it all out later. The most important thing is to get you home and into bed so that a doctor can attend to your ankle."

"Thank you," said Belinda, grabbing Viola's hand and kissing it.

"You can't go after Laxton, West. You don't even know where he went."

"I'll find him. And he'll wish he'd never been born."

"I don't want you to fight a d-duel," said Belinda, almost ready to begin crying again.

"There won't be any duels," Viola said briskly. "Now then, can you stand if we help you?"

"I think so."

"Then let's go home."

"Yes, let's."

"The coach I asked to follow us will be here soon. We will travel back in style. It will be better for your ankle, Belinda. I'll have a groom drive my curricle back to London."

"Oh, West," Belinda sobbed. "I'm truly so very sorry."

He patted her shoulder awkwardly. "I know you are, sweetheart. I know you are."

Viola gave him an encouraging smile. "I'll go and order some tea while we wait."

She needed a moment to collect herself. She was so relieved that Belinda was safe from ruin. And that meant the other sisters had escaped damage to their reputations, as well.

Which didn't change her response to West's hasty and unromantic proposal. She could never marry a man who didn't love her.

She stood by her words. She'd go back to the dower house and fetch her father. They would deliver the symphony on time and move into their new cottage.

Chapter Twenty-Nine

SEBASTIAN MET THEM at the door upon their return. "Your Grace, your great-aunt Hermione has arrived and she is with Lady Blanche, Miss Betsy, and Miss Birgitta in the Blue Parlor."

"I thought she wasn't due back for months yet."

"She's here and in fine fettle."

"Sebastian, send for the doctor. Miss Belinda has sprained her ankle."

"Right away, Your Grace."

"I don't want to see Great-Aunt Hermione right now," Belinda said. "And I can't face Blanche. Not yet."

"You must elevate your ankle. I'll take you upstairs, shall I?" Viola asked.

"Thank you," West said gratefully. "My great-aunt can be something of a battle-ax."

"I've heard a lot about her. Good luck."

Sebastian helped Viola support Belinda up the stairs while West mentally girded his loins for a meeting with his formidable great-aunt.

Upon entering the parlor, she immediately attacked.

"What's this, Westbury? I leave for six months and all hell breaks loose?"

"And good day to you, too, Great-Aunt," he said evenly, pecking her on the cheek. "We replaced you with Aunt Miriam."

"Miriam! That fool woman couldn't chaperone a baby in a crib. Better to have no chaperone than that flibbertigibbet fluttering about. I can't believe the state in which I find this household. You've let my apartments out. Belinda is missing. Blanche has become a spinster. Betsy is acting the most dreadful hoyden, and Birdie . . . well she's a little angel, now aren't you, my love?"

"You do know the girls are sitting right here, Great-Aunt?" West asked.

She sniffed. "They should hear it from someone. Did you bring Belinda back? Foolish, foolish child. Where did she run off to?"

"Yes, is Belinda all right?" Blanche asked, her eyes filled with worry.

"I'm very happy to report that Miss Beaton and I retrieved Belinda from a public coaching inn and she's unharmed, except for a lightly sprained ankle. The doctor will be here any moment. She's resting in bed."

"I wouldn't call a sprained ankle unharmed," Blanche said. "Poor thing. I don't understand any of this. Betsy won't tell me anything. Which is completely unlike you, Bets, you love tattling on Belinda."

"Not this time," Betsy said, ducking her head down. "I'll let someone else break the news to you."

"What news?"

"Yes, what news, Westbury?" Great-Aunt Hermione asked.

West sat down in the chair opposite Blanche and cleared his throat. "There's been an . . . unfortunate happening. Your sister was abducted by Lord Laxton."

"What?" Blanche exclaimed. "How can this be! I don't understand."

"She wasn't abducted, she left with him because she thought he loved her, stupid goose," Betsy said. "I could have told her that it was all a load of lies, but she didn't confide in me, now did she?"

Her words were tough, though West could tell that she was extremely worried about her twin sister.

"Why did she think he was in love with her?" Blanche asked.

"He'd been writing letters to her. Filled with lies, I'm afraid," West explained.

"Is she . . ." Blanche clutched a hand to the lace at her throat. "Is she ruined?"

"She is not."

"Oh, thank heavens." The ladies let out sighs of relief.

"Your sister is very brave. When she discovered his nefarious plan, she beat him over the head with her reticule and jumped from the carriage."

"She *did*?" Betsy gazed at him incredulously. "That doesn't sound like Belinda. I didn't think she had it in her."

"Laxton tore her special lace fichu and that was, apparently, the final straw. We're very lucky that she had the fortitude to escape him. Laxton seeks revenge on me. I didn't tell you this,

Blanche, and I should have. I overheard Laxton slandering you most grievously and I took matters into my own fists and gave him a good thrashing."

"Miss Beaton told me that he'd slandered me but I didn't believe it."

"He's a bad man," said Birdie.

"Yes, very bad," West agreed.

"This is all most unfortunate," said Great-Aunt Hermione with an aggrieved sniff. "I always knew there was something off about that man. Do you remember, Blanche, years ago when you set your cap for him and I told you to wait for Banksford? Well, he's taken. But you can still make a better match than Laxton."

"Not if I have no dowry."

"Piffle. You have your pretty face, though you do look very peaked today, I must say, with those dark circles under your eyes."

"I just found out that my sister ran off with the man I thought I was in love with. I can't believe he would do it . . . he's . . . he's a villain."

"Does anyone know about this, Westbury?" Great-Aunt Hermione asked.

"Some of Belinda's friends may know what she was planning. And Laxton may have told some friends, as well. But as far as I know, no one can confirm that it actually took place except for me, Miss Beaton, Laxton's servants, and the patrons at the inn. I spread some coin at the inn in exchange for promises of silence."

"I hope this can be contained," said his great-aunt. "The scandal would sink this family even deeper into the mire of ruin than it has already sunk."

"I'm going to deal with Laxton as soon as I find him." West had sent word to Jax before they left to keep an eye out for Laxton.

"I do hope you won't fight a duel," Birdie said, running to him and throwing her arms around his shoulders.

"Not if I can help it."

"Now, girls," said Great-Aunt Hermione, "I would speak with your brother in private."

His sisters dutifully left the room.

"Now then, my boy. Do you know why I cut short my restorative sojourn in Bath and raced back to London even though my rheumatism is far from cured?"

"I feel certain that you're going to tell me."

"A most scurrilous rumor has reached my ears that you are planning to propose marriage to the girls' music instructor. Please tell me it's not true. What's this? A sheepish expression on your face. Good gracious, Westbury, it won't do. It won't do at all!"

VIOLA CLOSED THE door to Belinda's room, leaving her resting peacefully.

"How is she?" Betsy asked anxiously, pacing up and down the hallway outside her sister's door. "Does she want to see me yet?"

"The doctor gave her a sedative for her nerves. Her ankle isn't badly turned. He advised bed rest.

I'm sure she'll talk to you all tomorrow. She's had an ordeal."

"Everyone knows all about it now. West told everyone, including Great-Aunt Hermione. She was nearly apoplectic. She's lecturing West right now. I was happy to make my escape."

"Why don't you look in on Belinda? She may still be awake."

Betsy smiled and opened the door gently.

Viola made her way downstairs, stopping when she heard raised voices coming from the parlor. She tiptoed to the closed door and placed her ear against it.

"It's not to be borne, Westbury! You must send that woman away. I'm warning you, my boy, don't fall for a pretty face with no fortune and no connections. She may be a very good girl, very sweet and accommodating, but you must do your duty and marry Lady Winifred, like I've been telling you all along."

"You're right," West replied.

"Of course I'm right."

Viola's heart sank.

"I know that Viola—"

"Miss Beaton."

"I know she's not the right choice, she's the first one to admit it."

"Very good. That's the first sensible thing I've heard about her."

"She's made it very clear that she doesn't want to marry me."

"That's excellent news, my boy. I'm very glad to hear it."

"And I know that I shouldn't marry her if I'm to do my duty."

Viola didn't tarry to hear more. This was far too painful. West was only repeating her own words which she knew to be true . . . but to hear them from his lips . . .

It stung most desperately.

She escaped back to the dower house to see whether her father had completed the symphony. Today was the day Lord Sprague had demanded its completion. It was time to make plans for a future that didn't include West.

Past time.

WEST KEPT HIS temper in check with difficulty. "You're right, Great-Aunt, but it doesn't change anything. I'm going to find Laxton and make him pay for what he did, and ensure his silence on the subject, but after that I'm going to marry Miss Viola Beaton. And duty be damned!"

"Think of what you're saying, my boy. Think of your sisters."

"I am thinking of them. They adore her."

"As their music teacher. How will they feel when they go out in society and everyone's whispering about your lowborn bride? And what of her lack of fortune?"

"I swear that I'll find a way to restore our fortunes. I'll make this right. I'm turning my life around."

"Your sisters have no dowries *now*. And Blanche isn't getting any younger. She can't wait much longer. Think of her. Think long and think hard."

"That's all I've been thinking of for months. I've tried to do the right thing by them, but I've come to the conclusion that marrying Viola is the right thing. If she'll have me. I haven't convinced her yet."

"Of all the preposterous notions—a music teacher refusing a duke. She's addled in the head. She's playing games with you."

"I was the one playing games. But no more. I'm marrying Viola because I . . . because I love her." In that moment he knew it to be true. "And I'm not worthy of her."

"Pardon me? Not worthy of a music teacher?"

"Your Grace." Sebastian entered the room. "An urgent note has been delivered for you from a Mr. Jacques Smith." Sebastian handed him the letter on a silver tray.

West ripped it open. "They've found Laxton. Mr. Smith is keeping him occupied until I arrive. I have to go now."

Great-Aunt Hermione sniffed. "Do be careful, my boy. While I don't approve of any of these goings-on, I would hate to attend your funeral. And don't think this conversation is over. I have much more to say on the subject."

Chapter Thirty

WEST WAS SEQUESTERED with Laxton in a back room at The Devil's Staircase. Jax stood guard outside the door, in case West needed him.

"Why haven't you challenged me yet?" Laxton demanded. He puffed out his chest. "Are you a fainthearted coward?"

"You want me to challenge you to a duel."

"If you're a gentleman you would avenge your sister's honor."

"Nothing happened to her. She hit you over the head with her reticule and jumped from the carriage."

"Says she."

"And I believe her."

"I should have finished the deed."

West gripped the edge of the table. "Think carefully about the next words you say."

"Very well. Maybe I'm glad she ran away. Maybe I let her go because she wasn't worth the trouble. She lectured me about lace for most of the journey. Maybe I was relieved when she escaped."

Ha. West could believe that. He leaned backward in his chair. What was Laxton's angle? "It seems to me that you want me to challenge you to a duel with pistols because you know that you're a better shot than I am."

From the guilty look on Laxton's face, he'd hit the mark.

"You may have bested me with your fists in a surprise and ungentlemanly attack, but I'm a champion marksman."

"Did you abduct Belinda because you wanted revenge on me for the thrashing I gave you?"

"Among other things."

"What have I ever done to you before that evening?"

"You really don't remember, do you." Laxton sneered. "That makes it all the worse."

"Enlighten me."

"The masquerade ball at Beecham's house."

"Not ringing any bells, I'm afraid. Wait . . . yes. I remember it, but only hazily. There were various intoxicating substances involved."

"You stole my mistress, you drunken cur! Miss Lucinda Whiting. Stole her with a wink and a leer."

"I'm sorry, still not ringing any bells."

"You bloody well threw her over your shoulder and carried her away before I could even challenge you. After that night she broke things off with me. Said that I no longer gave her what she needed. I loved her, Westbury."

"And you've been seething with fury ever since. Venting your hatred for me on first Blanche, stringing her along for years, then slandering her, and now Belinda."

"They got what you deserved."

"Good heavens, man, I don't even remember that night."

"Is that supposed to make me feel better? Someone has to put you in your place. You can't just run around London stealing mistresses and giving the nobility a bad name."

"I shouldn't have stolen your mistress. I probably didn't even know she was yours. And you're right. I've done too many wicked, thoughtless deeds. But no more. I'm reformed. And I won't be challenging you to a duel tonight."

"Coward!"

"But you might still die."

"Even you wouldn't kill me in cold blood while I'm being held here against my will."

"Oh, wouldn't I?" West caught him by the collar and hauled him to his feet.

"You . . . you wouldn't dare." Laxton tried to break free but West held him immobile.

"This establishment is owned by a dear friend of mine with a very creative mind. I'm sure we could find a way to make it look like an accident." West released him and shoved him back into his chair. "As much as it pains me to say it, you're not going to die tonight, Laxton. Instead, you're going to be engaged."

"Pardon? I won't marry Belinda, if that's what you're insinuating."

"Not Belinda. Miss Phoebe Trowbridge."

Laxton quailed. "How did you . . . ?"

"I have contacts in the underworld. We've been searching for information on you and we finally found it. You've done this before. You abducted

Miss Trowbridge four years ago but that occasion was more successful. She went with you willingly, assuming she would become Lady Laxton. Instead, she was left with a babe on the way and no husband."

"The chit has no proof."

"I have proof. A signed testimony from Miss Trowbridge, witnesses who saw you leave together, and a signed statement from the innkeeper where the vile deed was done. You're going to marry Miss Trowbridge. She has no father, brother, or protector who could have forced you at the time. Now she has me."

"I can't marry her. She's beneath my station."

"You should have thought of that before you ruined the girl and left her bereft and with a babe on the way. A child who looks exactly like you, as I'm told. I'll expose you publicly if you don't marry her. You'll be a good and devoted husband. You'll hear from me and my associates if you aren't."

"This is blackmail."

West shrugged. "I call it justice. You didn't think you were going to get away with it twice, did you?"

"I thought you'd challenge me to a duel. Any true gentleman would have."

"I'm not a true gentleman. I'm Wicked Westbury."

There was a knock at the door. West opened it.

"Leave him here," Jax said. "I'll finish things up. My men will enforce the engagement and the marriage. Miss Trowbridge is waiting at a hotel.

We'll take him out the back way so he can't make a scene. Go home to your family."

Outside the room, West clasped his friend's hand. "Thank you, Jax. Viola will be so pleased that I found a way to teach Laxton his lesson with no bloodshed. I owe you a debt."

"You paid for half of the renovation of this building with your gambling losses, Westbury. You don't owe me anything. How is Viola, by the way? She did look ravishing in that red gown."

"I proposed to her."

"Good for you!"

"She turned me down."

"Ah. Unexpected."

"I made a right mess of the proposal."

"I see. Then go and get it right, my friend. What are you waiting for?"

West hurried home, rehearsing the words he wanted to say. He'd make her see that she was the reason he'd reformed. It had all been for her. He'd find the right words.

I love you, would probably be the best place to start.

He'd mucked everything up. His proposal had been atrocious. He'd have to do much, much better to win the heart and hand of a wicked wallflower.

HE WAS TOO late. The dower house was empty. Their trunks were gone. The music room held the silent echo of Viola's piano playing. He slid his finger over the keys, plunking some melancholy bass notes.

She'd said she was leaving. She'd warned him.

Birdie burst through the door. "Where has Viola gone?"

"I don't know. Oh, yes, I do know. She and her father were delivering his symphonic score to the Philharmonic Society today."

"Why did she leave without saying goodbye? What did you do to her, West?" Birdie frowned at him fiercely.

"I mucked everything up."

"Obviously." His sister crossed her arms over her chest. "Now what are you going to do about it?"

"I'm going to fetch her back, don't worry."

"See that you do. I shall never forgive you if you don't. You really look terrible, though," Birdie observed. "I think you should have a bath and a shave before you speak with her."

West laughed. "I have my orders then." He kissed the top of her head and they walked back to the house together.

Viola had given him orders, too. She'd said to propose in a more romantic manner.

But first he had some letters to read.

This was going to take some time. And he wanted to do everything right . . . from this moment until he died.

Chapter Thirty-One

❧ 🌹 ❧

One week later

THE HOUSE ISOBEL had provided for Viola and her father was a charming cottage on the grounds of Isobel's aunt's house in the city of Watford. One day after they'd arrived, the handsome Erard pianoforte from the dower house had been delivered. But there'd been no note accompanying the extravagant gift, and Viola had heard nothing more from West.

She tried not to think of him, or search the papers for news of his engagement. The cottage was a brisk hour's walk from Westbury Abbey. There was quite a lot of activity on the estate, she'd noticed on her afternoon rambles. It looked as though the roof was being repaired and the tenant cottages rebuilt. Which she took as a sign that West had decided to marry Lady Winifred. Just as she'd told him to.

She'd made a dreadful mistake, her heart informed her daily. But there was no going back now.

She missed West every minute of every day. As she missed his sisters. They would get along

without her. The plan had always been to leave
her employ after the musicale. Her task was completed.

Their debt to Lord Sprague had been settled
with the delivery of her father's symphony. Her
father had agreed not to accept further patronage
from Sprague after Viola informed him of what the
baron had attempted. Not that her father required
the baron's support anymore. His Symphony no.
10 was already the talk of the town. There were
plans for a grand debut with royal patronage, and
offers of more support rolling in.

They weren't wealthy by any means, but they
could live a very comfortable life, and Viola
would supplement their income with earnings of
her own.

She was very nearly finished with the Christmas carol. She'd written the lyrics but the music
was giving her some difficulty. It was supposed
to be celebratory and joyful, but the ending kept
veering into a minor key. And there were tear-
drops on the ivory keys.

This morning she was determined to pull herself together enough to finish the carol. She shaped
the chords with her fingers but her heart wasn't in
it. Her heart was back in London, with West.

She saw his handsome face so clearly, his broad
shoulders stretching across the doorframe, block-
ing out the sunlight.

Wait. She could actually see him. He was standing right here.

"West?" She rose from the piano bench. "That
is, Your Grace."

"Viola." He strode into the room. "Come with me."

Not *good morning* or *I've missed you*. Come with me. Despite mooning over him for the better part of a week, her hackles rose. "I'm working," she said, sitting down again.

He offered her his hand. "It can wait."

He held out his hand as if it would be the easiest thing in the world to simply place her hand in his and follow him wherever he wished to lead her.

If she took his hand she'd burst into tears. She was holding herself together by a very thin thread. She shook her head, numbly. "I can't. I'm busy. I must finish the Christmas carol."

"Viola, look at me."

"It was always going to end like this, wasn't it, West? You hired me for a specific role and my services are no longer required."

He winced. "Very well. I deserved that. My own cold words back to haunt me. But everything's changed now. Stop being stubborn and come with me."

"I understand that you feel obligated to propose because of what happened. Because of the . . . fornication."

"The wild, glorious fornication."

"It doesn't matter what it was."

"It was wild and glorious."

"All right, it was. But it doesn't make you obligated to marry me."

"Don't you want to fornicate again? We're just getting started." He bent to whisper in her ear. "I have so many more things to show you."

She must remain strong. She mustn't give in to her desire.

She loved him. He desired her, but he didn't love her.

"I gather that you haven't offered for Lady Winifred?"

"I haven't."

"Marrying me is only moonbeams and fairy tales, West. A few years from now when your bills are piling up, you'd learn to resent me."

"I have a letter I want to open with you as witness."

"Where is this letter?"

"At Westbury Abbey. In my bedchamber."

"Oh no," Viola said vehemently. "I know exactly what you want to show me in your bedchamber. I can't visit your bedchamber ever again."

"That will be awkward once we're married."

"I can't go into your bedchamber because my flesh is weak. I'll see that bed and I'll want to . . ."

"Fornicate?" he said hopefully.

She nodded, not trusting her voice.

"Excellent. Then what are we waiting for?" He held out his hand again.

His big, strong hand that had touched her with such breathtaking possessiveness.

"I can't."

"Stop ruining this."

"It's already ruined. I heard what you said to Great-Aunt Hermione. That I wasn't a suitable duchess. I was listening outside the door."

"Then you must not have stayed long enough to hear the rest of what I had to say. I told her that

I loved you, Viola. And that I wasn't worthy of you."

"You did?"

"Damn it, Viola. I have a speech all prepared. Come to Westbury Abbey willingly or I'll . . . damn! I promised Birdie that I wouldn't threaten to throw you over my shoulder. She'll be furious with me if she learns I mucked this up again."

Viola smiled. "In that case, I'll do it for Birdie."

She placed her hand in his.

And was lost all over again.

The ride to Westbury Abbey was brief. She expected him to bring her inside the house but instead he led her around the back to a small graveyard.

"This is my mother's grave." There were fresh red roses placed on the marble statue of an angel. West laid his hand over his mother's name, his fingers trembling. "She would have loved you, Viola. She would have recognized a kindred spirit in you."

"I wish I could have met her."

"And this is my father's grave." West's voice trembled this time, not his hand. He pulled a pile of letters banded about with red twine from his pocket. "I read every single one of these letters. Every word. My father berated me and praised Bertram. And between the lines I read a story about a hard, flinty man who could never relinquish his anger. He made my mother's life, and mine, miserable. But as I read the letters something eased in my chest. A knot of tension that had been there since childhood. The tension of waiting for a physical blow yet knowing that his scorn hurt even worse."

Viola smiled. "And did it make you feel lighter?"

"Not at first. I realized that I'd become just like him."

"Never," she said. "You could never be such a tyrant."

"I mean that I'm a man who was unable to let go of a grudge. And I've caused pain to those around me because of it. Each letter I read strengthened my determination to change, to forgive him, leave the past behind, and begin anew."

The faintest tinkle of victory bells began to sound far off in her mind. "That's wonderful, West."

"I didn't reform in order to attract the perfect duchess. I changed my ways because of you. For you. You make everyone around you want to be better. You made my old life feel hollow and joyless."

He led her toward two marble tombstones set next to one another.

"Is this Bertram's grave?" she asked.

"Read the inscription."

Here lies Brandan, Duke of Westbury, she read, *whose life began in truth when he met his beloved wife, Viola.*

The bells grew louder, beginning to ring with real abandon.

"And the other one."

Here lies Viola, Duchess of Westbury, who brought

music, love, and laughter into the world and taught the sun how to shine with her smile.

She turned to him, tears filling her eyes. "Oh, West."

"You told me to propose properly this time. How did I do? Is it memorable enough?"

"It's . . . perfect."

"You told me that I must become acquainted with the woman I court before proposing. I'd like to submit, for the record, that I have. I know you, Viola. I know that your eyes are a new-fern color of green that makes me believe in the possibility of a new life. I know that you like to slather your toast with butter, read Gothic romances, and compose sonatas of a rainy afternoon. I know that you are kind, and giving, and you bring out the best in everyone around you. I know that you look stunning in scarlet velvet, and even more beautiful in nothing but bedsheets."

"What about poor Lady Winifred?" Viola sniffled.

"There's nothing poor about her. She's wealthy, attractive, and much sought-after. I don't think she formed any real attachment to me. She's never given me any indication of being anything other than complacent and obedient to her mother's wishes."

"I hope you're right."

"I never gave her false expectations and I never showed her more attention than any of the other ladies. I was too wrapped up in you. I lived for so long in the darkness, but this new man standing before you believes in love with a capital *V* for Viola. You hold my heart in your hands. If you refuse me my life will be like summer with no sunshine. An orchestra with no conductor. I want to grow old with you. I love you, Viola Beaton. Most desperately. Will you be buried next to me?"

She smiled through a veil of tears. "Yes, West. I'm yours. I have been since the moment I first saw you. But don't be too conceited about that. I'm still thinking of the perfect cutting insult and may deliver it when you least expect it."

"I look forward to it." He gathered her into his arms and brushed away her tears before claiming her mouth in a searing, heart-pounding kiss.

When she could breathe again, she placed her hand along his angular jaw. "I was a woman who put everyone's needs before my own. I didn't know how else to exist. And I was happy, in a way. I was content with my place behind the scenes. But you made me want more."

"Oh, I'll give you more. Come." He took her hand. "I still have something to show you in my bedchamber. And it's *not* the bed. I promise that what I want you to see has nothing to do with fornication."

She'd rather been hoping it might have *everything* to do with fornication.

When they arrived, instead of lifting her into his arms and carrying her to the bed, he brought her to a chair and placed a sealed envelope in her hands.

"The very last letter that my father wrote informed me that there was one final letter to be collected from Westbury Abbey. I never read the previous missives, so I never knew that he'd left me anything here."

"West. You didn't open it?"

"I was waiting for you. You're the reason I read his letters. I would have gone my whole life without opening them."

"You open it," she said, giving him the envelope. "It's yours."

He tore the seal from the letter and began to read.

"What does it say?"

"Viola." His face was stricken by emotion, his voice choked with it. "This was written two nights before he died. I'd always thought his death was unexpected, but he knew his heart was failing, he knew he didn't have long on this earth. And you were right. That knowledge changed him. This isn't a letter, Viola. It's a new will. Witnessed and sealed."

West sank to his knees before her, clasping her hands in his. "It's been sitting here the whole time. A new will naming me as the sole heir to all properties and the entire fortune that was attached to my mother."

"How extraordinary."

"It's not a large fortune at this point, my uncle has spent imprudently, but it's enough to invest wisely, and to complete the most urgent of repairs to the properties."

"Will your uncle fight it, do you think?"

"I don't think so. He doesn't seem to care about Westbury Abbey in the least. I don't even know where he is at the moment. He was last seen in Prague."

"I can't believe this."

"It's all because of you, my love." He kissed her hand, and then he gave her that wolfish, smoldering stare that had been her downfall on that fateful night the first time they kissed. "Now I'm going to show you the bed."

They came together in a new way this time, with open hearts and cloudless minds.

As the wild bells rang, Viola gave herself to him, and demanded everything from him in return.

Much later, as they lay with bodies entwined, breathing heavily and grinning like fools, Viola nuzzled his neck. "I thought you said that what you wanted to show me had nothing to do with beds or fornication," she teased.

"I lied."

"I can't trust you at all."

"Not when it comes to luring you into bed. I'll fornicate with you as often as possible in as many positions and places as possible for the rest of our lives."

"After we're wed we won't be able to call it fornication."

"Ah, but it will still be wild and glorious. This fire between us will never wane. It burns too hot."

WEST KNEW WHAT a gift he'd been given. A chance to begin again. To be worthy of Viola. He'd strive every day to be a better man.

Mellow sunlight. Golden feeling. Lazy, languid. Nowhere to be. Only this bed and this woman. Her smile brighter than the sun.

This sweet, powerful, intelligent, and awe-inspiring woman. He held her tightly, filling his arms with her, holding her close to his heart. "I thought I was so good at losing that I'd lose you, too, Viola. I'd do something bad, something unforgivable, and you'd grow to hate me."

"Oh, West." She kissed him. "I could never hate you. I love you too much."

"I'm the luckiest man on earth."

"I was trying to create the large boisterous family I always wanted by caring for your sisters and being a part of your life. And I fell in love with you in the bargain."

"Come with me," said West, rolling out of bed.

"Where? We're already in bed."

"To the music room. I purchased a new pianoforte for you."

"Overconfident, were you?"

"I had a feeling you might be here to play it for me." He handed her a silk robe and donned one himself.

"Won't the servants see us?" Viola asked. "Shouldn't we wear more clothing in the corridors?"

"Let them," West said. "I may have reformed enough to win your heart, but I'm still scandalous."

Sunshine slanted across the mahogany and ivory and pooled in the contours of the plush red velvet-covered bench. A sturdy bench. Extra wide. He'd ordered it custom made for the task he was about to ask of it.

"WELL THERE YOU are, my beauty," Viola cooed, sliding one finger down the curving lines of the instrument. "I'm going to make you sing."

"First, I'm going to make *you* sing," West said gruffly. He lifted her by the waist and set her against the piano keys. "I've wanted to have you against a piano ever since I saw you play at the musicale."

Her bottom hit the keys in a crash of notes, the music on the stand sliding to the floor as they kissed. He sat down on the bench.

"Lift your robe."

Viola did as he commanded. Under his spell, as she had been since the day she met him.

"Straddle me."

"What? I don't know what you—"

"You know exactly what I mean."

"I don't think the bench will support both of us."

"I had it custom made for this purpose."

"Oh." She bit her lower lip.

"Straddle me. Now."

She lifted her robe higher and climbed aboard, spreading her thighs until they bracketed him. The velvet-cushioned bench was soft and supportive under her knees.

She was still wet from their earlier exertions. And he was hard, long, and ready for her.

He bunched up the silk of her robe with one fist. "I want to watch."

The expression on his face was rapt, hungry . . . it made her brave.

She lowered onto him, moaning as he stretched her wide. He didn't move a muscle, staring down, watching her take him inside her.

She began to move, rolling her hips, steadying herself with her hands on his shoulders. Her bottom hit the piano keys as she arched backward, and then slid forward and down. He watched, his jaw gone slack, eyes glazed with lust.

This was power. To take all that he had to give. And give him everything in return. To be the very center of his attention, performing this ancient dance for his pleasure and her own. It was intoxicating.

And very, very wicked.

His hands gripped her hips and he clasped her to his chest as he took control, thrusting with luscious, slow strokes that made her moan and shudder in his arms as she came and he followed her there.

Sated and still humming with pleasure, she laid her head against his chest, listening to the percussion of his wildly beating heart.

"I love you, West," she whispered.

"The day you rolled up your sheet music and came at me like a general leading a battalion into battle, you said that love makes life worth living." He kissed her. "And you were right. Your love makes life worth living, Viola. I can't wait to live the rest of my life with you."

Epilogue

❧ 🌹 ❧

Hanover Square Rooms
Christmas Eve

THE LARGE AUDIENCE hushed as Viola's father rose from his seat and walked toward the orchestra. Her Christmas carol had been saved for last as a mark of special favor.

The lovely Italian paintings adorning the arched ceiling of the concert hall were done in soothing tones and the reception for the new song had been enthusiastic thus far, but her heart still thumped erratically as she prepared to hear her carol sung for the first time in public.

West squeezed her hand. "The audience won't know that you composed the carol, but I do. And I'm so very proud of you."

Viola smiled, loving the way his fingers wrapped around hers possessively. He made her so very happy.

His sisters were seated around them, staring raptly at the stage. Birdie turned to give Viola a smile.

Her father tapped his conductor's baton on the

music stand and the sound of silence filled the hall, the breathless moment of anticipation before the orchestra began to play, and the choir to sing.

"I'm a little worried about Papa," she whispered to West. "The sound will be loud, intensified by the acoustics of the hall, but he might not be able to hear well enough to conduct in tempo."

Her father raised his baton. But instead of conducting, he turned around, toward the audience.

"What's he doing?" Viola asked.

"This Christmas carol was written by my daughter, Viola, Duchess of Westbury, a composer in her own right," he pronounced in loud, ringing tones.

Viola gasped. A scandalized murmur traveled through the crowd. The king wasn't in attendance tonight, thank goodness. Such a breach of protocol in his presence would have been unforgivable.

"She wrote it while I was composing my masterpiece, my Symphony no. 10, which the world will have the pleasure of hearing very soon."

"Not very humble, your father," West murmured in her ear.

"What's he doing? This wasn't the plan."

"I submit that my daughter should be the one to conduct this orchestra and choir tonight. I myself taught her the art of conducting, though she's never had the opportunity to put it into practice in public. My dear, please come to the stage," he called loudly.

"Oh my God." Viola's stomach dropped into her slippers. "I can't believe this."

"What are you waiting for, my love?" West asked, his eyes worried.

"I . . . can't. There are too many people here," she whispered.

"Don't think about them. Think only of me." He brought her fingers to his lips. "You may picture me naked, if it helps."

The absurdity of it made her smile. Which was exactly the tonic to overcome her nerves. "Thank you, dear. I believe I shall picture you clothed. Until I get you back to bed and I can have the real thing."

She took a deep, steadying breath, and rose to her feet.

There was only scattered applause as she made her way to the stage.

"Papa, how could you?" she mouthed.

He had the temerity to smile. "How could I not?" he mouthed back.

He handed her the conductor's baton. Could she really do this?

Her hands quaked. She could feel West and his sisters sending their love and support. She straightened her spine, nodding at the cello soloist.

She raised her baton. And began to conduct.

The music swelled around her, rich and powerful, anchored by the cellist and embellished with the chiming of the bells.

She brought the choir in precisely on cue. "All color resigned and left. Cold white embraced the land," they sang, "causing the place bereft to beg for a kinder hand. No light, no jewel, to spice our Yule? Do we hear so faint a peal? In darkness comes a chime, wild bells, unseen but real, to color our joyous time. Not sight, but sound, does now abound!"

After the last shimmering notes rang out, the hall fell silent, and then applause broke out, begun by West, of course, who leaped from his seat, cheering loudly.

"Bravo, bravo!"

That wasn't West. She shaded her eyes, looking over the audience. It was Mr. Atwater and Mr. Herrick, her publishers. This would do wonders for sales. She was a bona fide scandal.

Viola curtsied, walking back to her seat on shaky knees.

"That was sublime," Betsy said when Viola joined them. "And I don't usually like carols."

"You were wonderful," Birdie agreed.

"I can't believe you didn't tell us that you had composed the carol," Bernadette said.

"It was supposed to remain a secret."

"There's no keeping your talent a secret, Viola," West said, tucking her hand into the crook of his elbow. "It shines too brightly."

"I agree," said Blanche, giving her a kiss on the cheek.

As they walked through the crowded hall, they were met with greetings, praise, and much outrage. The indignant audience members received a stern and lethal stare from the formerly wicked Duke of Westbury, which silenced them quickly enough.

"I can't believe that just happened," Viola said

when they were safely in their coach, just the two of them.

"It happened. You're going to be famous, my dear. That carol will be on everyone's lips by to-morrow."

"Infamous, more like."

"You were always going to be infamous, hav-ing made the dubious decision to marry the most notorious duke in London . . . for love."

"I did marry you for love. But it had something to do with kissing, as well."

"One kiss from me had you swooning into my arms, begging for more. I'll have you begging to-night, my love, mark my words."

LATER THAT EVENING at Westbury House Viola and West were sitting with his sisters, except for Birdie, who had gone to bed, when there was a knock at the door.

"Who could that be at this late hour?" Viola asked.

"That will be Lord Flanders," said Blanche, blushing. "He's just now returned from his estate, where he was speaking with his father. He'll be wanting to speak with you, West."

"What's this?" West asked.

Blanche's eyes shone. "He's proposed and I ac-cepted. With your blessing, of course."

Bernadette lifted her nose from the novel she was reading. "I heartily approve. He has a good scientific mind."

"Flanders?" West exclaimed. "But I thought you had no affection for him, Blanche."

"I thought the same thing—I've no idea why. It hit me so suddenly, as though storm clouds had cleared from my mind. I've loved him all along. I assume you'll give him your blessing since you tried to force me to marry him at one point."

"And you were dead set against it. You wailed and carried on."

"He's a dear, sweet, honorable man. I just couldn't see it because I was so fixated on Laxton. Who turned out to be horrid and unworthy."

Belinda lowered her eyes. "The most horrid man in London."

"So you actually want to marry Flanders?" West asked.

"As soon as possible. We're very much in love."

"Oh, Blanche. That's wonderful." Viola rose and gave her a hug.

"Lord Flanders to see you, Your Grace," Sebastian announced.

"I'll entertain him in my study." West chuckled. "This is an unexpected development. But I must have foreseen it when I chose him for you. I think I can take most of the credit."

Viola laughed as West left the room. "I'm so glad for you, Blanche. I know you two will be very happy."

"Viola," said Bernadette, "there's something I want to talk to you about. Your friend the Duchess of Ravenwood has invited me to travel to Greece to assist her and her husband with an important archaeological expedition. Please say you'll convince West to allow me to go. Please, please, *please.*"

"It could be dangerous."

"The duchess will protect me. She's promised to teach me how to wield a dagger."

"I want to learn how to fight with a dagger," Betsy said. "Why does Bernadette get to have all the fun?"

"I'll talk to him," Viola promised. "I do think it would be an enriching adventure for you."

"Really and truly?" Bernadette asked.

"Really and truly."

Viola spoke with West about it that very night as they lay in bed together reading. He was reluctant, at first, but she had her methods of persuasion.

"Do you know, West," she said much later, after they were sated and tangled in each other's arms. "I've come to the conclusion that being a duchess is remarkably similar to conducting an orchestra. One must be ever vigilant, able to perform a dozen tasks at once, and be comfortable with hundreds of pairs of eyes watching your every move."

"I knew you'd be the perfect duchess."

"I didn't know it. I was intimidated by the prospect."

"You rise to every challenge. You were superb tonight. You touched everyone's hearts with holiday cheer." He cupped her cheek with his hand. "But you completely stole mine. Merry Christmas, my love."

His kiss was tender and reverent . . . and then it deepened, becoming wild and passionate until she forgot all about her notoriety and existed only for the pleasure of loving West.

And being loved by him in return.

Wild Bells

Viola Beaton

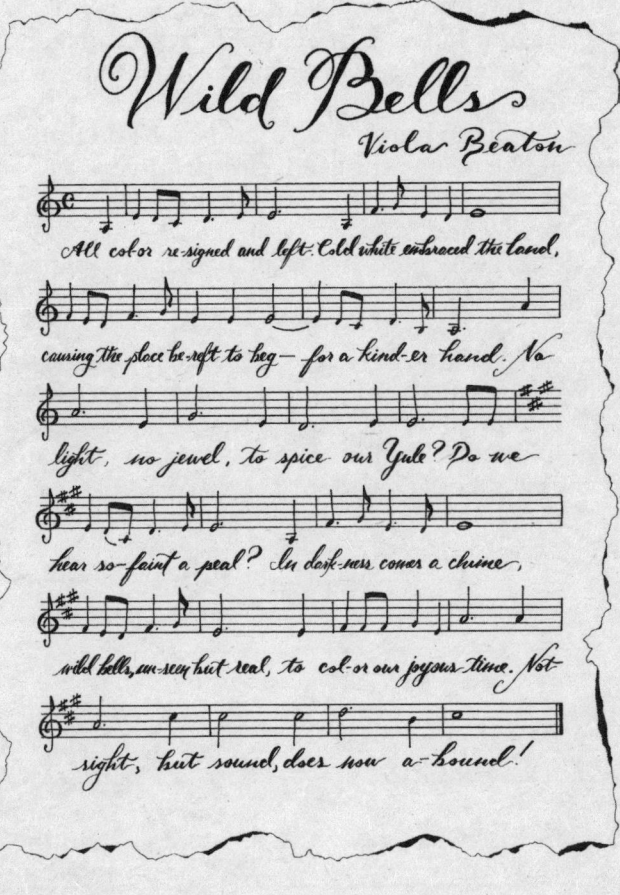

All col-or re-signed and left: Cold white embraced the land,

causing the place be-reft to beg— for a kind-er hand. No

light, no jewel, to spice our Yule? Do we

hear so-faint a peal? In dark-ness comes a chime,

wild bells, un-seen but real, to col-or our joy-ous time. Not

right, but sound, does now a-bound!

Author's Note

My mother, Nancy Nash, composed the lyrics and music for "Wild Bells," the original carol in the book. You can find the full choral arrangement of the carol and a link to a vocal performance on my website. Talented musician and visual artist Maura Lefevre created the hand-calligraphed sheet music. Check out her shop PenandPear on Etsy! The inspiration for the character of Viola Beaton came from my mother, and from numerous women musicians, composers, and conductors whose works have been overlooked, forgotten, or attributed to men: Fanny Mendelssohn, Clara Schumann, Louise Farrenc, Teresa Carreño, and Chiquinha Gonzaga, to name just a few. I'm overjoyed that these brilliant composers are being rediscovered and their works reevaluated.

Acknowledgments

❧ 🌹 ❧

As always, my heartfelt gratitude to my brilliant agent, Alexandra Machinist, and to my editor, the inimitable Carrie Feron. Huge thanks to everyone at Avon Books, especially superstars Asanté Simons, Holly Rice, and Guido Caroti. I wrote this book surrounded by close family in a small town in Alaska. The love and encouragement of my partner, Brian, my parents, and my siblings infused every page. I'm so lucky to collaborate with fantastic beta readers, Rachel and Neile! I'm deeply grateful to the wonderful readers, bloggers, reviewers, librarians, and booksellers who enjoy my books. You're the reason I keep writing. Thank you!